THE
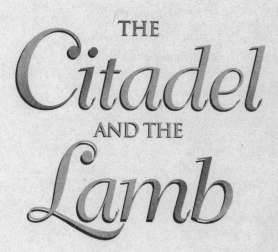
Citadel
AND THE
Lamb

THE SEEKERS

BY ETHEL HERR

The Dove and the Rose
The Maiden's Sword
The Citadel and the Lamb

ETHEL HERR

THE Citadel AND THE Lamb

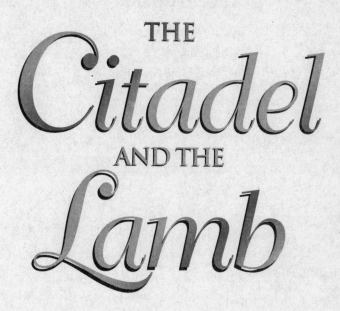

BETHANY HOUSE PUBLISHERS
MINNEAPOLIS, MINNESOTA 55438

Published by Bethany House Publishers
A Ministry of Bethany Fellowship International
11400 Hampshire Avenue South
Minneapolis, Minnesota 55438
www.bethanyhouse.com

Printed in the United States of America by
Bethany Press International, Minneapolis, Minnesota 55438

ISBN 1–55661–748–8

To the PARTS OF SPEECH
Faithful Critique Group
Barbara, for her grammatical and logistical expertise.
Bi, for her theological insights and insistence on tight writing.
Laurie, for knowing what my characters could and
could not do on a horse.
Marjorie, for her company on dozens of trips to Berkeley.
Nancy, for her literary sharpness.
Sherry, for attention to misspellings and misplaced commas.
Wanda, for an artist's view and creative comments and
smiling faces in manuscript margins.
Carolyn, Debbie, Karen, Patsy, Robin,
for help offered in early stages.
To all, for being my cheering section, emergency room nurses,
team of intercessors, excited distributors, friends.
Hartelijk bedankt!

Ethel Herr is a writer/historian, writing instructor, women's speaker, and the founder/director of Literature Ministry Prayer Fellowship. She has eight published books, including *Chosen Women of the Bible* and *An Introduction to Christian Writing*. She and her husband, Walt, live in California.

CONTENTS

LETTER TO THE READER

Years ago, I thought I wanted to become an archaeologist. While I soon discarded the idea as impractical—too much dirt, too much sun, too much science—the fascination never left me.

Then last winter on a Holy Land tour, I stood amidst excavated ruins of an ancient Roman city in Jordan and made a surprising discovery.

"I am an archaeologist!" I said aloud to a fellow member of the tour group. He looked at me as if I were a bit delusional and said nothing. I went on rattling off the new connections my brain had just made.

Archaeology attracted me in the first place because I longed to discover old worlds and give them new life! While I abandoned all dreams of the occupation so named, I have spent my life digging up the past, interpreting it in the light of the present, searching for guidance for the future.

Looking down physically at last on the stones and debris of biblical times I saw an incredible metaphor. *A historical novel is an archeological dig spurred on by the intoxicating joy of discovery!*

My work may give me a backache from too much sitting or twisting around to reach some enticing book on the top shelf in the old library. But my fingernails stay clean, and I have no sunburn.

I don't dig through physical dirt and layers of stones with unpronounceable geologic names. I wander through old buildings, dusty libraries, stuffy museums, in search of the artifacts and companions Pieter-Lucas and Aletta touched, the air they breathed, the thoughts they entertained. At my desk I spend hours devouring history books, armed with markers and red pens and yellow note pads. Sometimes I reread the same chapter or scene a dozen times before its details are fixed in my mind.

Always I am sifting through the stuff, relentless till I've discovered some irresistible gem. It may be a major character to give direction to the story. Often it is a tidbit of description or some obscure anecdote or a morsel of sixteenth-century philosophy that turns a key to a locked door in the story forming in my notebooks and my singularly focused brain.

You are about to go with me on a dig into the sixteenth-century world. Here you will find yourself without most of the conveniences you have come to believe are necessary to sustain life. Even coffee and tea have not yet made their way to the shores we visit. Family names were developing at this time, based on life occupations, geographical location, or some distinguishing characteristic. Many families simply did not yet have one. Language was in flux and rules of spelling almost did not exist; therefore, often names were spelled differently in every resource I consulted. On a few occasions I have opted for one of the archaic spellings to give the story local color.

Microbes had not yet been discovered, nor the theory of circulation of the blood. The local pharmacy was an herb garden, usually in the courtyard of a convent, and at times superstition played as much a role in medicine as the herbs. Security was maintained by armies and stone walls and simple citadels built on imposing hills. Highway robbers were an expected part of traveling. Supernatural creatures were not only credible, but they influenced daily decisions. Baths were not a part of daily hygiene, breakfast was not a common meal, and children were often dressed to look like miniature adults.

Thought processes were not restricted like ours by schedules or scientific or psychological data. Values were drawn in sharp sketches of black-and-white with little allowance for gray zones. Everything theological was in constant turmoil. Holding together the society where you lived was often more important than discovering how true were the rules by which this gluing was accomplished.

Once more you will meet a few characters stepping directly from the history books and archives: Willem van Oranje and his family—Juliana, Jan, Ludwig; King Philip and his infamous Duke of Alva, along with Don Frederic, Romero, Requesens, and Valdez; a few city officials from Leyden; some artists of enduring note—the Van Eyck brothers, Lucas van Leyden, Pieter Brueghel. Interacting with them, you'll find old friends that spring only from The Seekers series: Pieter-Lucas and Aletta with their families and friends—little Lucas and Kaatje, Dirck, Gretta, and Robbin Engelshofen, Hendrick van den Garde, Mieke. A cast of new players has been added: the family of Joris—Hiltje, Christoffel, Clare, and Tryntje; the *glipper* priest of the Pieterskerk; Jakob and Magdalena de Wever, and the

Children of God that meet in their attic; the baker from the sign of The Pretzel; the unruly gang of taunting boys.

Once more I invite you to grab an archeologist's shovel, don a sun hat, and join me on one more journey into discovery—this time in *The Citadel and the Lamb*.

HISTORICAL BACKGROUND

*F*or more centuries than historians can guess, the city of Leyden has stood as a citadel in a watery spot on the Rhine River, rising up out of a low flat expanse of pasturelands. The city is built on at least forty islands. One of these is located between two arms of the Rhine River. Somewhere around the middle of the twelfth century, Count Alwinius Castellanus erected a hill of land on the western end of this island and built himself a fortress tower still referred to as the *Burcht* (Citadel).

The surrounding land was wild and largely unprotected in those days. Because Leyden had a citadel, it soon grew into a settlement, complete with defensive walls and bulwarks and five towered gates with heavy doors that locked. Eventually, the entire region became known as Holland—Hollow Land.

Through the centuries, battles resulted in a continual passing of the lordship of the citadel from one count to another. Warfare was a way of life, and when the citizens needed protection, the door of the citadel was open to them.

By the sixteenth century, Leyden had become part of an emerging state known as the Low Lands.[1] Through a long and complex succession of political intrigues and intermarriages in high places, the whole area had come under control of Hapsburger Charles V, who was also Holy Roman Emperor and King of Spain.

Later, Charles abdicated his throne, leaving the Low Lands to his son Philip, the new Spanish King. Philip, born and raised in Spain, spoke no language but Spanish. His devotion to the Catholic Church was unsur-

---

[1]Low Lands included all the land now encompassed by The Netherlands, Belgium, and Luxembourg.

passed. He sensed a clear mission from God to preserve the pure Catholic religion in all the territories over which he ruled.

His Lowland subjects did not take kindly to his absolutist tactics. Never had they been wholehearted devotees of the Roman dictates of the Church, nor had they willingly submitted to the demands of a foreign sovereign. Revolt had been smoldering in the stewpots of the Low Lands for several decades.

In 1567 it broke out into open resistance under the reluctant leadership of Willem van Oranje, a German prince with Lowland inherited holdings and a mission to preserve the religious freedoms of his adopted peoples. King Philip soon sent his strong man, the Duke of Alva, who boasted that he would promptly squeeze the life out of these Lowlanders like so many pliable butterballs.

Surprisingly to him, the butterballs only re-formed and multiplied until he could not keep ahead of them. His tactics grew ever more bloody, and the rebel patriots' retaliation and dogged determination grew ever more violent.

After seven years of giving King Philip's campaigns against the Low Lands his best in energy and military genius, Alva retired to Spain a beaten man. He left the subduing of Leyden to his successor, Don Luis Requesens.

The battle was not fought in the citadel, or even on the ramparts or streets. Instead, the new governor came with orders to talk smoothly and offer the Leydenaars concessions and overtures of amnesty. As the months wore on (nearly a year of merciless blockade), Leydenaars grew weary and were tempted by dangerous offers of peace. They finally recognized that the price for amnesty was too high. King Philip of Spain insisted that they must promise unswerving allegiance to him as their absolute sovereign and to the Roman Catholic Church as the only religion allowed to be practiced within their walls.

In the long dark hours of near starvation and raging plague, Willem van Oranje urged Leydenaars to hold out for the freedom goals of the entire revolt. He sent them messengers reminding them that "Leyden saved is Holland saved!" It became the watchword of the resistance.

Then he destroyed the city's real citadel of physical protection—the dikes that surrounded them and controlled the raging waters of this unstable land. Willem, Leyden, and all the freedom seekers of the Low Lands prayed and waited until, in the middle of the night of October 2, 1574, the water rose high enough to frighten the Spaniards, who refused to fight in water above their waists.

The city was rescued for the revolt. The battle for the whole nation continued off and on for another seventy-four years,[2] but this was the decisive turning point. Leyden had proven her place as a citadel among cities in the Low Lands, and the province of Holland had been saved.

---

[2] A Twelve-Year Truce was arranged in 1609 by Willem's son, Maurice. Permanent cessation of hostilities and the establishment of an independent United Netherlands came on January 30, 1648, as a part of the Peace of Munster at the end of the Thirty Years' War. The Dutch refer to their long struggle for freedom as the Eighty Years' War.

Leyden

Marcke...

Rynsburgerpoort

Harbo...

Wittepoort

St. Pieterskerk

Beguinage

Koepo...

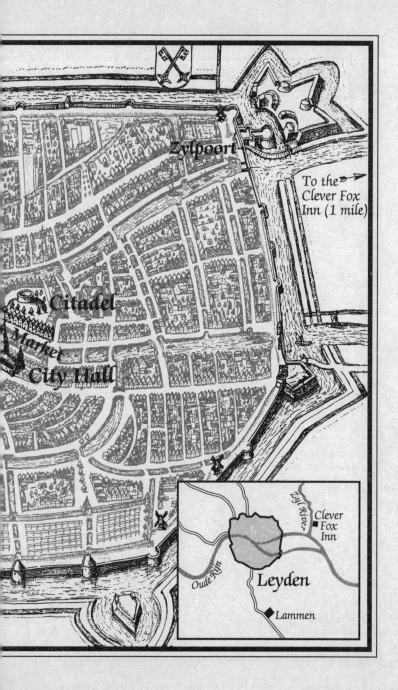

Zylpoort

To the
Clever Fox
Inn (1 mile)

Citadel

Market

City Hall

Zyl River

Clever
Fox
Inn

Oude Rijn

Leyden

Lammen

THE
NETHERLANDS
IN THE 16TH CENTURY

Emden EAST
FRIESLAND

STAD
EN LAND
Groningen
Leeuwarden
FRIESLAND   Assen

Ems R.

DRENTHE
OVERIJSSEL

Alkmaar   Zyder
Zee

North Sea   Haarlem
Amsterdam   IJssel R.

HOLLAND

Leyden   Utrecht   GELRE   Zutphen
Delft   UTRECHT

Briel   Waal R.   Munster

Cleves   Rhine R.

ZEELAND   Breda   UPPER
GELDERLAND   Duisburg

Antwerp   BRABANT   HOLY

Bruges   Maas R.
VLANDEREN   Ghent   Dillenburg
(FLANDERS)   LIEGE

Lys R.   Brussels   Roer R.   Cologne   ROMAN
Aachen

St. Omer   LIMBURG
Lille   Liege
Scheldt R.   Dill R.
ARTOIS   Bergen   Namur
Douai   NAMUR   EMPIRE
Arras
HAINAULT

Cambrai
S. OF LIEGE

DUCHY OF
LUXEMBOURG

Somme R.
Amiens

St. Quentin

Luxembourg   Trier

F   Laon
R
Oise R.   Meuse R.
Aisne R.
A   Rheims   Verdun
N   Metz
C
E

Strasburg

--- Province of Holland
▨ Lands not belonging to
   Lowland Provinces

0   50 miles

Cartography by Philip Schwartzberg, Meridian Mapping

GLOSSARY & DUTCH PRONUNCIATION GUIDE

Ach!:   Dutch for *Alas!*

Anabaptists: Groups of Reformation churches, so called because of their insistence on believer's baptism as opposed to infant baptism. They did not themselves use the term *Anabaptists*, which literally means *rebaptists*, believing their adult baptism as a confession of faith was the only true baptism.

Beggars: Fanatical rebels who wanted to free The Netherlands from the control of Spain's King Philip II. They posed as Calvinists, and indeed many were. Their motives were a mixture of political ambition, personal discontent, and religious zeal.

Beguinage: [Bay-guee-noj] French word for local site of Beguines, or lay order of charitable sisters in late medieval Catholic church. Mostly they lived in the Low Lands and France. They shared their wealth but didn't take religious vows and were free to leave when they liked. They dispensed mercy, medicine, and physical goods to persons in need.

Burgemeesters: City leaders, members of the ruling city council.

Children of God: Name taken by many Anabaptist groups. They never referred to themselves as Anabaptists. Not connected in any way with the current group calling itself by this name.

Ciborium: Covered receptacle for holding wafers of the Eucharist.

Converso:	Spanish word, meaning a *convert*. When applied to Jews who had converted to Christianity, a *converso* was supposedly a genuine Christian who had cut himself off from all Jewish roots, while a *marrano* posed as a Christian but continued to practice Judaism in secret.
Corslet:	Heavy metal breastplate of a Spanish soldier's body armor.
Dopers:	Peasants' disdainful slang word for Anabaptists. Carried the idea of dangerous criminals.
Engeland:	Dutch for *England*.
Freebooters:	Soldiers who chose their own cause, made their own rules, and expected the people they protected to pay their wages.
Ghendt:	City in what is now Belgium. Also spelled *Ghent* or *Gent*.
Glippers:	Spanish sympathizers who tried to turn the patriots and uncommitted citizens against the cause of rebellion against Spain's dominion in the Low Lands.
Goyim:	Common sixteenth-century name for *Gentiles*.
He Has Hid His: Head in a Sock:	Old German expression, meaning, *He's not all there*.
Heatte:	Old English term for *fever*.
Hidden Church:	Any church assembly meeting without approval of existing government, forced to meet in secret, usually in homes, attics, or barns.
Hole peeper:	Literal translation of Dutch word for *spy*.
Holland:	A province in the middle of the Low Lands through which the Rhine River runs. Literally it means *Hollow Land*.
Ja:	[Yah] Dutch for *yes*.
Jongen:	[Yong-un] Dutch for *boy* or *lad*.
Kasteel:	[Kahs-tail] Dutch for *castle*.
Kerk:	Dutch for *church*. Usually added on to the name of a church, as all one word. E.g., Pieterskerk (not Pieters Kerk).
Kusje:	[Kus-yuh] Dutch for *little kiss*.
Low Lands:	Area now encompassed in borders of Belgium, Luxembourg, and The Netherlands (Holland).

Marranos: Derogatory Spanish nickname for Jews who pretended to be Christians but observed their Jewish customs in secret. It literally means *swine*.

Meester: [Mays-ter] Master or teacher.

Moeder: [Mu-der] Dutch for *mother*.

Moeke: [Mu-kuh] Dutch equivalent to *mommy*.

Molen: [Mo-luhn] Dutch for *mill*, usually referring to a windmill.

Nay: Dutch for *no*. Dutch spelling is *neen*.

Oma & Opa: [Oh-ma, Oh-pa] Current Dutch terms for *grandma* and *grandpa*. Belonging to the twentieth century but giving the feeling intended by the sixteenth-century words *grootmoeder* and *grootvader*, which would be too difficult for English-speaking readers to pronounce.

Oom: [Ohm] Dutch for *uncle*.

Oude Man: [Ow-duh mahn] Dutch for *Old Man*.

Popish or Papist: Describing any person or practice that followed Roman Catholic ways.

Poort: Dutch for *gate*. Four gates in Leyden were Koe Poort (*Cow Gate*), Rhine Poort (*Rhine Gate*), Witte Poort (*White Gate*) and Zyl Poort (*Zyl Gate*).

Qué no?: [Kay no?] Spanish phrase meaning, *Is that not right?*

Robustious: Old English word for *robust* (health), used in seventeenth-century herbal book.

Rood Screen: High carved screen that divided the choir and altar from the seating section of a Roman Catholic church.

Speken: [Spay-kuhn] Derogatory name for occupying Spanish soldiers.

Stuiver: Dutch coin comparable to our penny.

"Suja, suja, slaap": [Su-ya . . . slahp] Dutch lullaby in common use in the sixteenth century. Still used today, but each mother makes up her own words to go with it.

Tante: [Tahn-tuh] Dutch for *aunt*.

Torah: First five books of the Hebrew Bible (Old Testament). They contain the Jewish law and are handwritten on scrolls.

Vader: [Fah-der] Dutch for *father*.

Vaderland: [Fah-der-lahnd] Dutch for *fatherland*.

Vrouw: [Frow] Dutch for either *woman* or *wife*.

Wever: [Vay-fer] Dutch word for *weaver*. *De Wever* as a name referred to *The Weaver*.

Willem van Oranje: [Vil-um fahn O-rahn-yuh] *William of Orange*.

Wombe: Old English spelling for *womb*.

PROLOGUE

24th day of Summer Month (June), 1572

With tears running down her cheeks, Aletta van den Garde moved about among her beloved wild roses and healing herbs in the fragrant herb garden on the side of the Dillenburg hill. She snipped at leaves and blossoms and stuffed them into her large gathering basket. She tried not to think about what was happening under the linden tree at the top of the hill, just outside the *kasteel* gates.

Alas! She could bring herself to think of nothing else. Yesterday Prince Willem and his friends had met in that spot and planned a war. Today her husband, Pieter-Lucas, had been called there to receive his orders.

Close behind her billowing skirts, in the herb garden, trailed her three-year-old son, Lucas. He whimpered and waved a small square of canvas with a globby-painted shape in the center.

"*Moeke*," he whimpered, entangling himself in her skirts, grabbing at her leg.

"*Ja, jongen*, what is it?"

"You almost done?" The little voice hung heavy with a tired wistfulness that added to her melancholy.

"One more plant," she promised and hurried to the remaining shrub. She squatted down to snip off a pair of twigs, and Lucas leaned up against her shoulder. From the corner of her eye, she saw a downcast face and curling lip. The blanket of sullen silence that held him tightly enveloped her as well.

He tugged at her arm. "*Moeke*, when's Vader comin'?"

Turning her head slightly to avert his gaze, she said, "When Prince Willem lets him come."

She felt Lucas' warm fingers on the side of her chin, pulling her head around, forcing her to look into his wondering blue eyes. How sad the face framed by golden curls shimmering in the sunlight. If only she could keep her son from seeing the tear she felt sliding down her cheek.

"Oh, *Moeke*," he wailed, smudging the tear with a sticky palm. "Is he goin' far away again?"

She embraced the child and smoothed back his curls with trembling hands. Trying to sound cheerful and reassuring, she said, "Your vader is a messenger for Prince Willem. 'Tis the work of a messenger to go away—and come back."

A shudder ran through her body. For at least five years Pieter-Lucas had been doing this work. Almost she'd grown accustomed to it, especially in recent months when he went mostly to German and French noblemen, trying to raise funds for a war with a noble purpose. Yesterday's meeting under that linden tree had changed everything, though. Now he would have to travel in disguise across enemy-infested roadways to army encampments, alongside swords and guns and trampling horses.

Lucas wriggled free from her grip and held the canvas in her face. "He can't go. We gots to finish my lamb."

Forcing herself to smile, she said, "I'm sure he'll help you before he goes."

Nothing delighted Pieter-Lucas more than helping his son paint. Early this morning he let the boy lead him out to the stables and helped him begin to paint a lamb that Lucas had watched being birthed yesterday. Before the paint was half applied, a servant summoned Pieter-Lucas to go meet with the prince. Lucas followed his moeder around all the rest of the day and never let the half-finished painting out of his hand.

"Come on, let's go get him," Lucas coaxed, pointing to the tree with its fresh greenery just outside the *kasteel* wall. "He's up there."

Aletta let her son tug her to her feet. She patted her skirts into order and said, "*Nay*, son, we can't disturb him. As soon as they finish talking, he will come to us."

"Look, he's coming now!" The little voice grew lively, and the boy charged up the pathway to meet his vader, his arms and legs all moving at once.

Aletta watched her husband hurrying toward them, as always, limping as he came. The wind blew his doublet tails and shoulder-length blond curls around him. In spite of herself she smiled.

For a long moment she stood watching, wishing desperately she could keep him here. She folded her arms tightly around her middle and was reminded of yet another ache, the ache of empty moeder arms. It didn't come as often now as it had two months ago when her second child was born without a single breath of life in her. But when it came, the pain still ran deep. She knew it made letting Pieter-Lucas go away harder than before.

Grabbing up her herbal basket, she hurried toward the spot where Pieter-Lucas was picking up their son, who was shoving the tiny canvas into his face. She soon came close enough to hear him begging, "We gots to finish the lamb."

"I know," Pieter-Lucas said and reached out to gather Aletta into his free arm. Together they began the long walk to the *kasteel* at the top of the hill.

"It needs feet an' ears an' eyes," Lucas was saying, "an' a mouth."

"We'll do it," Pieter-Lucas said.

"And, Vader"—the boy was holding his vader's face close to his own and staring hard into his eyes—"when you go away, you take it with you."

"Ah! Then you'll not have it to look at again."

Lucas pulled back from his vader's embrace and poked his finger in his chest. "It's for you."

"Then I'll carry it with me here," Pieter-Lucas said, pointing to the inner folds of his doublet, "next to my heart and the picture of your *moeke*. It will never leave me, no matter where I go."

"A picture of *Moeke*? Let me see!" Lucas was pulling back the doublet, searching for the surprise treasure.

Pieter-Lucas produced it, and the boy's eyes grew wide with wonder. "Oh!" His little mouth formed into an awed letter *O*, then a smile. He giggled and planted soft moist kisses on both his parents' cheeks.

Aletta and Pieter-Lucas exchanged aching smiles. Aletta hung her head and nestled into her husband's one-armed embrace. Lucas waved his globby lamb and sang and chattered. None but Aletta knew that she wept all the way up the hill.

PART ONE

Smudged Sketches

*To be a Child of God means to live
in constant danger.*

—Jakob de Wever
Fictitious Anabaptist leader of Leyden

*I have come to make my grave
in this land.*

—Willem van Oranje's words as he left
Dillenburg to begin his final assault on the
Duke of Alva and his Spanish troops (1572).

Leyden saved is Holland saved!

—Watchword of the Siege of Leyden

CHAPTER ONE

Leyden

12th day of Hay Month (July), 1573

*B*ending over a pile of steamy manure and straw, twelve-year-old Christoffel, son of Joris, dug in with his short-handled shovel and cleared a pathway out through the stable door. He pushed himself erect, wiped his brow with the back of a wrinkled white sleeve, and muttered, "Why on a day like this?"

A hazy sun glowered at him, filtering through the fresh green leaves of the nearby grove of linden trees. The putrid stifling air vibrated with the familiar buzz of flies, the twitter of sparrows, and an occasional mooing from the neighboring pasture. For a long moment he stood still, sighing, "If only the job were done!"

Then he heard it—the sound his ears seemed always attuned to. From a distance, drawing closer, came the faint sounds of water lapping and voices shouting.

"A ship!"

Dropping the shovel, he grabbed his knapsack off a peg and bounded down the pathway. Past the skittle field, across the courtyard, and around *The Clever Fox Inn*, he sprang toward the gate. Beyond lay the Zyl River with its trekpath that would take him alongside the ship to Leyden. Just as he reached out to unfasten the gate latch, he heard his vader calling from the doorway of the inn, "Hei there, *jongen*! Halt!"

The boy stopped short and spun around. With the toss of his head, he brushed the thatch of dark brown hair back from his face. Already his vader was hurrying toward him, all arms and legs and apron strings flapping.

"Just where do you think you are springing off to?" he demanded.

Christoffel waved toward the ship, which he now saw was only the first in a whole fleet. They were already so close he could hear loud wood-against-wood creaking noises coming from their swaying riggings. "Look!" he shouted. "Five, six, seven of them! All flying the prince's flag! You coming with me?"

His voice felt gravelly and the final word came out on a pitch as high as the sky where the gulls soared above the ships' masts and voluminous billowing sails. Motioning toward his vader, he reached again for the gate latch. But Vader was grabbing him by the arm and speaking with that sharp fretful tone that was a part of what made him Joris.

"You're not going anywhere—not until the stable is cleaned!"

Vader stood with feet spread wide, one hand planted on his hip, and his tummy bulging out beneath his tightly stretched innkeeper's apron. Christoffel searched the familiar thin face with heavy dark beard, sharp nose, and greasy forehead. The close-set eyes sparkled like black diamonds. Today something was missing, that soft border around the edges of those eyes that almost always looked ready to melt into smiles when least expected.

"Can't the stable wait?" Christoffel pleaded.

"Stables don't wait!" Vader retorted. He shook his head in quick agitated movements.

Christoffel stared at his vader, mouth gaping. "But . . . they always have before."

Any time an unusual ship sailed by *The Clever Fox Inn*, one of a kind they didn't see every day, it mattered not what activity was at hand. They'd both leave the work at the inn with the women and go. He couldn't remember a time when he'd been forbidden to go make a sketch.

Truth was, there was nothing in the world his vader would rather do himself than sketch a picture. The two of them made frequent treks into the city together for that purpose. They'd find a spot beside a riverbank, usually in a stand of bushes, and sit on a rock or a clump of grass and draw whatever took their fancy—the pancake lady at the village market or a giant crow atop the sprawling old oak tree down by the Cloister of the White Nuns. Their favorite spot was up against the walls of the ancient circular citadel on a mound in the center of the city. Here they'd look out over the city and draw a church or an expanse of rooftops.

"Inside the citadel there are narrow slits in the wall all the way around," his vader had told him. "Once used to shoot arrows at invading enemies, I know they'd make great frames for paintings of the city."

"Do they ever open the door to the citadel and let us in?" Christoffel had asked.

"Only in times of great danger."

Always Christoffel dreamed of getting inside and seeing the city through the arrow slits. And every time he climbed the hill, he shoved on the door with his shoulder as if begging it to open to him. Always it remained locked, and they had to settle for sitting among the trees outside to draw their sketches. Then they'd rush home and mix colors and paint the scene on a canvas till it hummed and vibrated with life. When Vader had finished one of his paintings, the boy could smell the fresh sea-salty air, hear the insistent calling of the church bells, or feel the squishing of the muddy roads between his toes.

Today, though, Vader raised a warning finger and wagged it in his direction. Hesitating at first, he began, "It is simply not safe to go running through Leyden with charcoal and paper announcing yourself as an artist these days." By the time he'd finished, the words were tumbling over each other.

"What do you mean?" Christoffel jabbed the toe of his clog in the dirt.

Vader raised both hands now, as if to hold him at a distance. "Son . . ." He cleared his throat and started again. "It's just that . . . that . . ."

"That what?"

The now angry innkeeper glared at him. "Those are beggar ships."

"I know! The Beggars fight for Prince Willem. They're not our enemies, you know. They often stay here in our inn."

Joris wagged a finger at him and said, scowling, "And as far as they know, no painters live in this place. Do you understand?"

Christoffel knew that was the rule, but it had never made sense to him. "Why, Vader?" he begged.

"Because they slice paintings to shreds!" Vader's voice was trembling.

"I know. They smash images and glass windows, even make a mockery of sacred chalices and robes stolen from the churches." Something about their wild escapades excited the boy.

"You're not afraid to run after such image smashers with your canvases and charcoals?" Vader was nearly shrieking.

"They only destroy church paintings," Christoffel countered. "What's so dangerous about letting the Beggars see me painting ships that will never hang in a church, and nobody will ever pray to them?"

Vader twisted his apron into a long fat roll over his tummy. "I just don't trust anyone who would slice a painting for whatever reason," he said. "He has no soul for art, and I'll take no chances on being his next victim or letting my son become one."

He looked straight at Christoffel for a long painful moment.

That expression in his eyes! Was it anger? Nay. Sadness? Ja, but there was more. Fear? That must be it. Vader had only looked at Christoffel like this a few times before that he could remember. Mostly it was while they still lived in Brussels. They'd be walking down a street together when he'd just suddenly get that look and hurry Christoffel into a hiding place nearby or off to home. Never would he explain, only demand instant obedience.

He remembered one time when the expression seemed to have a reasonable cause. That was the night Pieter Bruegel, the old artist Vader used to paint with, died. They'd been good friends for as long as Christoffel's memory went back. The boy was only eight years old when it happened, but he knew that if your good friend died, you must feel bad somehow. And that expression of pain or fear or whatever it was seemed perfectly in order on that occasion.

That was four years ago, and he'd grown up since then. He'd learned all about wars and sieges and soldiers. Who could live in Leyden and not know about them? With Haarlem under siege ever since last Winter Month just beyond the lake to their north, and all the comings and goings of the prince and his men and ships, and inn guests that talked long and freely over their wine, he'd have to blindfold his eyes and stop his ears to miss it.

Vader drew himself taller, squared his shoulders, set his jaw, and said, "You are the son, I am the vader, and when I tell you it's not safe to go to the city with your charcoal, you will not ask questions. You'll do what I wish." Then shooing him toward the stable, he ordered, "Now, off to the job I gave you, and no more dallying."

"*Ja*, Vader," Christoffel said.

He watched his vader trudge back across the green grass and buttercups toward the inn, shaking his head and mumbling, "Crazy *jongen!*"

For a long while, Christoffel did not move. What was Vader thinking, anyway? He must be having visits from some troubling spirit. Probably he'd eaten something that didn't agree with him, then heard one more wild story from a drunken inn guest and let it turn him to a fright. He did that sort of thing sometimes.

Christoffel's heart thumped madly. A gigantic tugging was wrenching him, first toward the stable, then toward the city. Back and forth, back and forth . . .

"How can I keep from going against my vader's wishes?" he muttered under his breath. "I've never seen a whole fleet at once! And all those Beggars! *Nay*, but I have to go!"

Always he had dreamed of getting close enough to a Beggar away from *The Clever Fox Inn* that he could paint his portrait in his balloon breeches and ashen gray cape and hat, with a beggar's bowl dangling about his waist and a long chain with a beggar's penny swinging from his neck.

From somewhere out in the pasture behind the buildings, a cow mooed. Slowly, with determined steps, Christoffel headed for the stables.

"I'll do what he demands," he said to the knapsack on his back. "Then later, when he's not looking, I'll slip into Leyden."

Wondering why his heart still pounded, he added, "I don't think he really said I couldn't go once the stable was clean. Besides, I'll draw in the bushes. Nobody will ever see me!"

When he reached the stable, he stood in the doorway and looked after the ships now vanishing in the distance toward Leyden. His eyes scanned the riverbank that led along the trekpath, looking for bushes to obscure his flight. "By the time I get home, he'll be feeling better, and he'll be proud of the picture I've drawn and get out the paints and canvas just like he always does. And the beggar portrait? I can hide it for a while."

———

Pieter-Lucas van den Garde approached the ancient city of Leyden along the trekpath of the sluggish Rhine River shortly before it would trickle off into the long bank of sand dunes and merge with the North Sea. His lame leg ached and his curls blew in the wind while a combination of excitement and dread pounded in his chest. The mass of steeples and spires, windmill blades, and gabled rooftops stood out sharp and weaponlike against a sky turning to watery gold in the glow of the late summer sun.

"Looks invincible!" the young messenger on horseback said into the wind.

He watched a steady stream of farmers and artisans pouring out through ornate gates in the circle of heavy walls that held the city intact. They shoved past him, carrying baskets, pushing wobbly wheeled carts, and, with long willow switches, herding small flocks of sheep, goats, and pigs.

"Peaceful enough, swarming with peasants on market day," he added.

Leyden! City of an artist's dreams long cherished! However, as on every other occasion when he'd come to this place, today he came not in fulfillment of those dreams but rather bearing a message for a never ending war.

Pieter-Lucas smoothed his sparse mustache with long fingers and let a whistle escape through his lips. "Our day will come yet, Blesje, old boy," he said, patting his horse on the mane. "We will come back here with my beloved Aletta and Lucas and the new little one just about to join us. Opa promised. So did Prince Willem—once this cursed war is over! At least the city is on his side now, a part of the new Estates of Holland."

For as many of his twenty-five years as he could remember, he'd dreamed the dreams his grandfather had begun planting in his heart while he was still a child.

"*You, Grandson, are born to be an artist.*" Pieter-Lucas could hear the words as clearly as if Opa stood once more by his side. Always he would add, "*Two things you must do someday. First, after you have turned eighteen, I will send you to Leyden to study with the men who learned from my uncle, the famous artist Lucas van Leyden. There in the Pieterskerk, you will study my uncle's colorful masterpiece, 'The Last Judgment,' that hangs above the main altar. And one day you must go to the city of Ghendt to study the Van Eyck altar painting, 'The Adoration of the Lamb.' Every great painter spends time with that masterpiece!*"

Just before Pieter-Lucas turned eighteen, Opa died of apoplexy. Soon thereafter, image breakers destroyed Opa's painting in the Great Church in Breda. Then Prince Willem van Oranje took Pieter-Lucas, along with his noble family and servants, into exile in Dillenburg, Germany. From there he'd spent most of the last seven years running messages. Always as he ran he prayed that Willem's patriots and foreign mercenary soldiers would soon win back the Low Lands from the control of King Philip of Spain and his ruthless military commander, the Duke of Alva.

In the past year, since Leyden had declared herself on the patriots' side, Pieter-Lucas often found himself here. He was always running to Willem's base in Leyden or Delft or to France, where Willem's brother and military commander, Ludwig, carried on negotiations with the king of France for assistance against Spain, their mutual enemy.

Of course, King Philip did not honor the "legal" declarations of the new constitution of the Estates of Holland. In fact, Alva had spent the whole past year looting and burning and forcing rebel cities to submit to his rule. Mostly small cities they were, not too well fortified, usually caught by surprise.

On this warm and sunny afternoon in what appeared to be a peaceful Leyden, the clear logic of the moment told Pieter-Lucas this city was in no imminent danger. Most of her strongest leaders had firm loyalties to Willem, and she boasted an efficient citizen guard as well.

But the war was not over, and there was still no time for pursuing peace-loving passions, such as searching out a painter or visiting church altars. As Blesje's hooves clattered over the wooden boards that spanned the protective moat at the Zyl Poort, Pieter-Lucas felt his dreams give place to a vague presentiment of disaster.

He sighed. He knew the urgent message he carried had something to do with Haarlem, a neighboring city to the north. For eight months now

Alva's son, Don Frederic, had held Haarlemers prisoners in their own streets. Determined not to surrender, never losing hope that Willem and his forces would relieve them, the citizens had hung on. But eight months was an unthinkably long time to go hungry and to sustain constant assaults from a besieging force.

"Relief must reach Haarlem soon," Willem's brother Jan had moaned when he put the message into Pieter-Lucas' hand in Dillenburg and sent him on this mission.

Nobody needed to tell Pieter-Lucas of the urgency of the plight of Haarlem. Back in the dead of winter, one of his missions had taken him into the city smuggled in a cart of straw and manure. He'd watched the people with hollow cheeks and swollen bellies and felt a wrenching of his gut. If only he'd had a barrow load of bread to put into their grasping hands.

Now, in the middle of summer, Pieter-Lucas urged Blesje over the maze of cobbles and bridges that followed the river into the heart of Leyden. He tried to forget Haarlem and remember his dreams. He watched a smattering of stray chickens, pigs, and dogs roam through the ground cover of market-day refuse in search of an evening meal and tried to imagine himself and his vrouw living here, buying their food and pots and clothes in this very market. But as he guided his horse through the now empty marketplace, the dreams he'd so often dreamed with delight were draped with a heavy blanket of chilling fog.

"Begone!" he yelled out, addressing he knew not what. Demons of fear? Or simply an imagination tormented by the bone-wearying long journey? Whatever, he must be freed from it. A messenger dared not to let despair put the sword to his ribs.

Looking up he saw at the end of the market street, anchored in the waters of the Rhine, a line of tall warships. From every spirelike mast and from each bow, Willem's tricolor flags—orange, white, and blue, with the Nassau lion—rippled in the wind. The ships swarmed with loud shouting men in balloon breeches.

"Beggars! Returned from Haarlem?" Pieter-Lucas gasped. Had the end of the siege come? If the prince's forces had managed to take the city at last, why were they here? They should be in Haarlem, distributing food to the starving survivors.

Visions of hollow cheeks, sunken eyes, twiglike arms, and grasping fingers filled his mind. He shuddered. *Nay*, but Haarlem couldn't have fallen. The patriots' plans for the final rescue were so well laid. Jan had seemed so certain. Nearly blinded by the maddening thoughts his memories inspired, he turned the corner. Just a few more paces to the town hall where he'd find Prince Willem.

Suddenly Blesje's hoof caught on a protruding cobblestone, and the pause in his rhythm caused Pieter-Lucas to look down. There, sitting on a large stone among a stand of shrubby bushes, he saw a boy of about twelve or thirteen. Dark locks of straight hair hung beneath his flat tam, and he leaned over a canvas, busily sketching an outline of the fleet of beggar's ships before him.

Pieter-Lucas brought Blesje to a halt, leaned over, and shouted at the boy, "So Leyden has an artist!"

With a start, the boy grabbed his work, pressing it to his chest. He cast a wary glance over his shoulder toward Pieter-Lucas.

Pieter-Lucas whistled. "What a sketch!" He watched caution melt into a hint of a smile.

"You like it?" the boy ventured.

"Like it? Who wouldn't? You're going to take it home and paint it, aren't you?"

The boy shifted uneasily. "How'd you know that?"

Pieter-Lucas loosened the cord on the little pouch dangling from his belt. Almost trembling with excitement, he pulled out a worn paintbrush and held it up for the boy to see. "I have paint running through my blood too," he offered with a smile, "even as you do."

The boy's dark brown eyes grew suddenly large. From somewhere in their depths, Pieter-Lucas could see and feel the kind of kinship only painters see and feel in each other. "It's a long story," he said. Then leaning over the edge of his horse until his cheek lay alongside the sweaty mane, he said with a confidential air, "If I weren't on my way to the town hall on an urgent errand, I'd sit down and let you teach me what you know about drawing ships. Can you wait till I come back?"

"How long?" the boy asked.

"Not long, I trust."

The boy frowned for a long moment before he said, "Maybe."

Pieter-Lucas straightened and lifted Blesje's reins. "I'll be back as soon as I can."

He prodded Blesje down the street to the town hall, where he tied him to a post. He was just opening the heavy old doors when he heard the furious galloping of horses down the Breestraat. Two horsemen stopped abruptly, tethered their horses, and bolted through the doors, shoving past Pieter-Lucas.

"Haarlem has surrendered!" they shouted. "The bells are tolling, and the people have flung themselves upon the mercy of Don Frederic!" Their voices echoed through the cavernous hall, bouncing off the high ceilings and smooth stone floors.

Pieter-Lucas followed the men into the council chambers, where Willem sat at the head of a long table with a group of city leaders and Beggars. Several men were jumping to their feet, crying out with distressed unbelieving gasps and barraging the newcomers with "why's" and "how's."

Willem held his head in his hands, shaking it from side to side and uttering a low agonizing moan. "I knew it. I knew it. . . . *Ach!* God have mercy! *Ach! Ach! Ach!*"

Pieter-Lucas felt ashamed that he could even think about sketching ships while men's lives were being snatched from them for no good reason. Chastised, he moved quietly to his prince's side. He reached into his doublet and pulled out the thin document he'd brought from Dillenburg. His fingers searched the wax that held the paper closed, tracing Jan's seal. It was a personal ritual he repeated each time he delivered a message, a tangible reminder that for now he must remain a messenger of the House of Nassau. He'd never wanted to become one, could never think of himself as one. He only played the part because during these dark war days, Willem needed him, and it was the one thing he could do for his vaderland.

Without looking up, Willem spoke, and the room grew instantly hushed. "What were the terms?"

"Don Frederic promised that no punishment would be inflicted except upon those who in the judgment of the citizens themselves deserved it. He offered them full and ample forgiveness!"

"And they trusted him?" shouted one Beggar.

Willem spoke again, his calm voice heavy with the sighing of a broken heart. "They had no more choice. The enemy intercepted our messenger pigeons and foiled our last attempt to rescue them." Still shaking his head, he repeated again and again, "May God have mercy! May God have mercy!"

"Have you any idea what has happened since the surrender?" asked Paulus Buys, pensionary for the province of Holland.

"As we left the city, we heard the Spanish officials issuing orders to all inhabitants to surrender their arms in the town hall," said one of the men.

"They were herding the men into the cloister of Zyl and the women into the cathedral," added the second.

Willem leaned back in his chair, stretched his legs out before him and, keeping his head lowered, said, "Preparing for a blood bath. Alva and his son, Frederic, hold strange ideas of the meaning of that word *forgiveness!*"

Pieter-Lucas felt a shudder pass around the room. No one spoke for a long moment. One by one the men seated themselves again and looked to Willem, as if expecting to hear some words of wisdom to the unspoken question that hung heavy in the air: What now?

"Your Excellency," Pieter-Lucas ventured at last, "a word from your brother Jan." Willem glanced up with a start and took the note. As he broke open the seal, sounds of approaching shouts came from the streets. The rest of the men in the room stirred restlessly while Willem ignored the noises, giving Jan's letter his total attention.

By the time he was folding the letter and putting it into his doublet, the voices had reached the street beneath the hall. "Willem van Oranje!" an angry crowd shouted. "Weakling! Coward! Come and face us!"

Pelting stones were assaulting the outside of the building, and Paulus and the city leaders were moving toward the doorway.

"Wait!" Willem called, standing to his feet. "I shall address them."

"Let me handle this," Paulus urged.

"*Nay!* They'll listen to me," Willem insisted, walking steadily out of the room, past the arms outstretched to restrain him. With the leaders at his side and all the others in his wake, he climbed the stairs to the upper level, where he walked out onto the balustrade.

At the sight of him, the crowd burst into a tirade more ferocious than before. "Weak-handed, mealy mouthed Prince!"

"You promise so much."

"Where were you hiding when Alva massacred Naarden?"

"Zutphen?"

"Mons?"

"Haarlem?" The entire crowd took up the final name and chanted it ferociously around the square. The name echoed off the tall step-gabled buildings and sent a chill into Pieter-Lucas' heart. Was Leyden with Willem or against him. . . ?

Through an open doorway, Pieter-Lucas watched the prince raise his hand and heard him offer a clear unflinching defense. "We have done everything according to our means. God is my witness."

"Bah!" shouted the people with contempt. "You fight the iron-fisted duke with mittens. All you ever send to any city's rescue is too little and too late!"

The words echoed around the streets, in a hundred voices of peasants, merchants, soldiers, children.

"Too little and too late!"

"Too little and too late!"

"Is Leyden next?"

Willem spoke again, "I cannot tell what tomorrow will bring. I can only assure you that we go forward in whatever strength and wisdom God provides."

"And will you fight for us or give us over as you did Haarlem?"

"I shall always stand with those who stand," Willem shouted. "Every man must put his trust in God and prepare to wield his own sword. We surrender not until Alva knocks us senseless to our graves."

The crowd rumbled on among themselves like a roll of thunder overhead, no longer addressing the prince. While Willem retreated, Pieter Adriaenszoon van der Werff, Chief Burgemeester of Leyden, lifted his hand and addressed the people with authority. "The sun is about to set beyond the Witte Poort. You must go, each to his own house, remembering the prince's admonitions. Then, before you pillow your heads, gather your families around your hearth and give thanks to God that He has spared us for one more day and pray He shows mercy to our suffering brothers and sisters in Haarlem."

Only a sporadic shout came from the subdued crowd now.

Pieter-Lucas followed Willem into the council chambers. He watched him seat himself again at the long table, pull his writing pen and inkpot from his belt, and begin to write, mumbling as he formed the words.

"My most honorable brother, Count Ludwig,
On this, the twelfth day of Hay Month, the city of Haarlem surrendered to Don Frederic and his emissaries. I had hoped to send you better news; nevertheless, since it has otherwise pleased the good God, we must conform ourselves to His divine will. I take the same God to witness that I have done everything possible, according to my means, to succor the city. Press on, dear brother, and I look with eagerness to the day when you can come here to add your succor as well."

Methodically, ignoring the roomful of men, Willem blotted the ink and folded his paper. Then he touched a ball of sealing wax to the flame of a nearby candle and let a blob form on the letter. Finally, he pressed his signet ring into the wax, stared at it for a moment, then handed it to Pieter-Lucas.

"Carry this as quickly as you can to Ludwig. I shall answer Jan within a day and send word by another. But Ludwig needs to know now—and move accordingly."

Moments later Pieter-Lucas urged Blesje through the streets where people stood in knots on corners and gave themselves to lively conversations. He heard a low rumble of voices and an occasional outburst of distant shouting filling the air. As he rounded the bend by the harbor, he searched the bushes for the young artist and found not a trace. All through the city he kept his eyes on the prowl. Perhaps he'd been frightened by the uproar of the mob.

"Who was he, anyway?" he asked himself. "How will I find him again? And what of the meester that teaches him?"

With a sigh and a heavy reluctance to leave without the thing that had so elusively escaped his grasp, Pieter-Lucas guided Blesje once more through the Zyl Poort and across the bridge. He looked back with an aching yearning. Life always seemed to bring him so near to the passion that drove him that he could feel it in his fingers, taste it on his tongue. Then, just when he'd begun to breathe the air of the coveted promise, something snatched it from under his nose and took away his breath.

"Very well, Blesje, on we go," he said, wishing his horse would talk back, argue with him, persuade him to turn around and go looking for the boy, for the painting in the church, for a place to bring his wife and Lucas, and . . . If Blesje could know anything at all, he would know how important it was for Pieter-Lucas to teach his son, to help him pass on the paint flowing in the blood. But Blesje simply plodded on, headed out across the broad-channeled landscape of soggy pasturelands, flourishing gardens, and groves of trees bearing tiny unripened apples and pears. The sun was nearing the horizon. He must ride hard to reach Delft and the safety of an inn before stick-darkness would make further travel difficult.

When he'd reached the bridge where the Zyl River flowed into the Rhine, he looked north. Not too far distant down the trekpath, he spotted a lone figure walking. "It's a boy, Blesje," he gasped. "Dark hair and a tam, knapsack on his back. Our young artist? I wonder if he goes to the inn just beyond that next grove of trees—*The Clever Fox Inn*, I think it's called. No time to follow."

The messenger and his horse stood still, hiding just behind a drooping willow tree, and watched while the boy walked on, turning into the yard of the inn.

"Leyden does indeed have an artist," Pieter-Lucas said. "We shall find his meester next time."

With a freshly born lilt in his spirit, Pieter-Lucas nudged Blesje into a trot across the steamy amber-colored countryside.

Joris could not sleep. No cooling breezes brought relief from the heat on this most unusual night. As he lay tossing in his straw bed at the back of the inn, he wondered whether there were visiting spirits, as well, hovering in the oppressively warm and humid air about him. And every time an abrupt snore issued from his wife's side of the bed, he started like a man cringing on a battlefield.

"I know that naughty *jongen* of mine ran off to Leyden against my orders today," he mumbled to himself, combing his hair with sweaty fingers. "My vader would have thrashed me with a whole broom of willow switches if I'd defied him so. Why, then, couldn't I do it to Christoffel?"

"Because you've got your moeder's soft heart instead of your vader's soldier one" came the muffled answer from his wife.

"*Hei!* Vrouw Hiltje! One minute you snore, the next you interrupt my conversation with myself," he sputtered. "Don't you think I should have met him in the roadway with a scowl and a broom and scolded the fear of God into him?"

"Probably not!"

"What? You're softer than I am. What will ever become of the *jongen* with such soft parents?"

"He'll become an artist, like his vader, that's what."

"What do you mean?"

"Nothing matters so long as he gets to Leyden to draw the pictures he wants. He learned it from you."

"And you go on feeding him his victuals when he comes straggling home long after the cows have stopped mooing for the night and the inn guests have abandoned their greasy plates for refilled tankards."

"*Ach!* He wasn't that late coming home tonight!" Hiltje snapped.

"Not this time. But I told him not to go, and he did it anyway, and you didn't punish him by sending him to bed supperless. What shall I ever do with the boy, and what will become of him? Oh me! Oh me!"

Both stopped talking, and Joris lay for a long while listening to the chorus of swamp frogs croaking in the drainage ditch behind the barn and the dull rhythmic beating of his heart in his troubled chest. Hiltje resumed her occasional snoring. The sleepless innkeeper got up from his bed and crept out through a series of doors and into the night. To the light of a gigantic flat-sided moon, he stole across the barnyard to the stable.

"Humph! At least he cleaned it before he ran off!" Joris snorted.

He stepped gingerly past the sleeping horses and climbed up into the hayloft. Slowly he crawled to the far corner and pushed open the door meant to let in the hay. Tonight it let in the moonlight. He rummaged in the straw until he'd pulled up a velvet bag. Pulling the cord, he reached inside and drew out a large piece of cloth. He draped it over his head, taking care to frame his face just right. Fingering the long silky fringes around its border, he imagined himself transported into an elegant synagogue, with richly adorned walls and fragrant candles and the large scrolls in their cases, all painted with lilies and grape vines and pome-granates. Resting now on bended knees, he folded his gnarled hands and bowed his head and muttered softly, "Hear, O Israel, *Yahweh* is our God. *Yahweh* is One."

After a pause, he went on. "*Yahweh*, God of our fathers Abraham, Isaac, and Jacob, in times like these, so evil and fraught with demonic intrusions at every corner, I confess to the great and many errors of my ways and most of all to not teaching my son in Thy holy precepts. Nevertheless, may the words of my mouth and the meditations of my heart be acceptable in Thy presence, oh, *Yahweh*. Bless now thine errant servant with sleep and preserve my dear son, who shall remain nameless in my prayers. For robed in this shawl and praying the Sh'ma of my moeder—may she rest in peace—I tremble even to pronounce so Christian a name as the one I myself gave to the boy in my most deeply nighted years. Amen!"

After a long and pleasant moment of quiet contrition, Joris removed his prayer shawl, replaced it in the bag, and buried it beneath the straw. Then he closed the hay door, and as quietly as he'd come, he slipped back into the inn and lay down beside Hiltje. She interrupted the rolling murmur of her snoring to say, "Sleep well, husband."

He put his arm about her, felt her body snuggle into his embrace, and fell fast asleep.

CHAPTER TWO

Dillenburg, Germany

15th day of Hay Month (July), 1573

*I*n her drafty room with the high ceilings and clumsy furniture in one corner of the *kasteel* grounds, Aletta awoke in excruciating pain. Her head was throbbing and her whole body burned with an intense *heatte* such as she'd often treated in her patients but never experienced for herself.

With her eyes still closed, she heard a pounding in her ears and, as if from a far distance, the childish prattle of four-year-old Lucas.

"*Ach!*" she groaned and turned over onto her side, cradling her bulging tummy in both arms. The child beneath her heart thrashed about, stretching the walls of her *wombe* into discernible little fist balls. "Great and gracious God," she cried out, "keep this little one safe!" Gently she rocked the child until it settled into stillness once more.

She'd just begun to wonder what she would do with her son when she felt a soft hand on her cheek and heard a tiny voice. "*Moeke*, wake up!"

Smiling in spite of herself, she pried her eyes open and reached for Lucas' hand. "*Moeke*'s sick, *jongen*," she managed. "Go get Mieke!"

His blue eyes grew large and round, partially obscured by the straw-colored curls that drooped across his forehead. A questioning expression covered the pudgy face, and he thrust it into hers, landing a trembly kiss on the cheek where his hand had lain earlier.

"Go get Mieke," Aletta repeated, nudging him back. "Quickly, son, quickly."

She listened to his feet padding across the floor and realized he could not draw the bolt that held the door. With agonizing effort, she dragged herself from the bed. Nearly overcome with both the pain and a swimming of the head, she crawled on all fours to the door and struggled the bolt and latch free. It was the last thing she knew.

When she came to, she was lying in her bed with a cool compress on her head.

"I sees your eyes a-flutterin' " came a thin pipelike voice from the bedside.

"Mieke! Thank God you're here." Through a hot fuzzy haze, she made out the face of the strange little woman with the sharp nose.

She was pulling back the feather bag and asking, "An' th' baby—is he a-flutterin' too? Let me see."

Aletta grabbed the cover and hugged it tightly around her neck. "*Ja,* Mieke. He moves. Just believe me."

Mieke backed off and wiped her wiry hands against each other. "Very well," she said, "b'cause ye gots to carry him in your belly fer a long time yet."

"Only a week or two, Mieke. That's not so long, you know."

"Anyway," she muttered, "who knows what dreadful things this *heatte* might do to him?"

She propped Aletta's head in the crook of her arm, then reached to the bedside table for a crock of lukewarm liquid and put it to her hot dry lips. Not until she began to sip did Aletta realize how swollen and cracked those lips were.

"Marsh parsley . . . masterwort . . . and wormwood?" she asked between sips.

"Fer that ye'll have to ask Countess Juliana. I doesn't make the stuff, only pours it down the gullet."

Aletta had concocted this very potion many times and always marveled at the way her patients consumed the bitter brew with such relish. This morning she understood. The thirst burning in her throat made her ravenous enough to find any liquid a welcome relief, no matter how bitter.

When she'd drained the crock and begun to drowse again, she heard her nursemaid's piercing voice giving the same kind of instructions she herself had used so many times. "Time now to sleep, Vrouw 'Letta. Lucas is in good care with the servants, an' yer Mieke's goin' to stay right here an' lay on th' fresh compresses, an' one o' th' countesses'll come by in a couple o' eyeblinks an' look ye over good."

Aletta reached for the woman's arm. "The instant my Pieter-Lucas comes home, will you promise to bring him to me?" If only he were here to hold her hand and kiss her forehead and fold her in his arms, surely the *heatte* would scamper quickly away.

Mieke burst into the girlish giggle that marked her presence anywhere she happened to be within earshot. "When yer Pieter-Lucas comes a-gallopin' through that gate on his horse, there ain't a body in this whole *kasteel* what'll ever need to tell him to come a-lookin' fer his vrouw. Ye'll be the first after th' huntin' hounds to know he's home. Now, fergit it all an' let yer body sleep, do ye hears me?"

Aletta tried to nod her answer. But already her eyes were closed and her mind was drifting off into fuzzy-edged oblivion. . . .

18th day of Hay Month (July), 1573

Pieter-Lucas rode through the gate at the foot of the Dillenburg hill, beneath a gray cloudy afternoon sky that promised thundershowers. The hunting hounds announced his arrival, and his heart tumbled about with acrobatic jubilance.

"We're home, Blesje!" he told his horse plodding up the long pathway that led to the old multitowered castle. "To you that means the best oats and stables in the world. To me? Aha! Aletta and my son are both some-where inside those ancient stone walls!"

With undisguisable impatience, he waited in the great hall for Jan van Nassau, lord of the *kasteel*. When the man came, his round stomach strut-ting before him, Pieter-Lucas gave him his message from Ludwig with as much haste as he could.

"May I go now to my apartment?" he asked, with one hand on the door handle. "I trust your next assignment will not be so urgent that I cannot at least spend a night or two with my vrouw."

"Go, young man. Your vrouw is in greater need of you than I."

Pieter-Lucas hurried across the courtyard to his room with the glo-rious visions of an eager husband. But when he opened the door, Mieke greeted him with a worried expression and a finger pressed against her lips. She pointed to the sleeping form of Aletta on her bed with her vader at her side.

"Dirck Engelshofen!" he whispered. "What's he doing here?"

"Your wife's deathly ill," Mieke muttered.

"What?" He stared at the little woman with the sheaf of scarf-bound unkempt curls and shoved past her, ordering, "Out the door!"

Standing and going also for the door, Dirck Engelshofen grasped him by the arm and said, "I'll wait for you outside."

Pieter-Lucas leaned over his vrouw's resting body. Grasping her pale sleeping face with both hands, he cried out, "Aletta, my vrouw!"

Her eyes opened and a smile reached out to take him in. "You're home, Pieter-Lucas, my husband, my love!"

"What is it?" With trembling hands, he smoothed the long tresses of blond hair back from her eyes and kissed her gently.

He felt her weak arms encircling his neck. They held each other in a fragile embrace. Softly her voice spoke into his ear, "At least the *heatte* is gone, and now that you are back, all will be well once more."

He searched her sickly blue eyes for the sparkle that was Aletta until he found it. "And the child?" he asked, almost fearing the sound of his own words. She'd lost one child already last year, and in the anguish that followed, he nearly lost her as well. *Nay,* they could not walk that pathway again.

"The child kicks yet, more vigorously than ever the others did," she said, smiling, guiding his hand to her belly where he felt the mysterious rolling punching motions that always filled his vader heart with wonder.

He looked up, startled. "Lucas! He is well, I hope?" Nothing must ever happen to that boy, the pride of his life, heir of the stream of paint in his blood.

"Perfectly well, may God be praised! Robbin is with him."

"Your brother, Robbin? Did he come with your vader?"

Aletta nodded.

"And when did you take ill?" Pieter-Lucas felt a frenzy building in his mind. Surely she hadn't been ill the whole ten days he'd been away!

"Not many days ago. I slept so much I didn't count them."

"What is it?"

"A simple ague. The herbal potions and compresses should have cured it. Yet it has seemed as though without your smile, your embrace, your words, I could not mend!"

He wrapped her in his arms and buried his face in her silken locks of hair. "I shall give you as large a dose of all three as the time allotted to me will allow."

They held each other in the long silence until he felt her arms slip away and heard her breathing grow deep and slumberous.

He planted a long kiss on her forehead and murmured, "Sleep well, my beloved one—and grow strong." Then taking her hand in his, he sat gazing into the most beautiful face on earth. How she trusted him! And what if his presence did not help her? *Nay,* but she must get well—she must.

If only he'd been here sooner! If Haarlem had not fallen, he might have been already moving her to Leyden. Instead, he was still running back and forth between battle posts and Nassau brothers and burgemeesters' halls. One day soon Jan would go to the Low Lands in person, and then Pieter-Lucas would never have another excuse to return to Dillenburg. Maybe he should take Aletta to Leyden now. *Nay!* Too dangerous! She couldn't move for some time after the baby was born anyway. A lot could happen by then. He sighed.

A faint rubbing, scratching sound from the other side of the door told him that Mieke hovered nearby. He must go talk with Vader Dirck. He stood reluctantly, brushed his vrouw's forehead with one more kiss, and left the room. Each breath went forth like a simple prayer. "Please, God!"

Mieke met him on the other side of the door. "'Bout time ye leaves her so's she can get back to sleep. Poor thing ain't so robustious, ye know. Now, leave her alone till I calls ye, do ye hears me?" She was motioning him away with quick hand gestures and frowning face.

Pieter-Lucas was never sure whether to be amused or irritated at Mieke's blustery audacity. At least he could rest easy in the assurance that she'd never steal a thing from him or his family, and that was more than he could have said a few years back. Besides, she was a big help to Aletta—had even seen to the birthing of little Lucas and the stillborn child they had called Kaatje.

Dirck Engelshofen approached now, grabbing him by a hand and a shoulder. "Greetings, my son," he said.

"You're a long ways from Engeland," Pieter-Lucas said, returning the hearty handshake. "Aletta says you brought Robbin too. And your vrouw, Moeder Gretta?"

"*Ja* and *ja* and *nay.*"

Pieter-Lucas watched his vader-in-law smile. He was the same straight man that he remembered so well, with each piece of his clothing in perfect order. His hair was graying to match the color of his kindly warm eyes.

"Meaning *ja*, Engeland is a long ways away, *ja* you brought Robbin, and *nay*, your vrouw came not along?"

"Right!"

"When did you arrive?"

"Yesterday, just before Aletta's *heatte* left her. When I first saw her, I feared for her life . . . and with an unborn child? God have mercy!" Dirck shook his head, then went on quickly. "You're still running messages for Willem, I see."

"So it goes. I spend most of my days running around the countryside. Guess it's my part in the revolt."

"At least you're not carrying a sword on the battlefield," Dirck reminded him.

"This war's got to end before long. A few more massacres like Alva and his son have been carrying out, and there won't be any Lowlanders left to live in the country, even if Willem managed to wrest it from the Spaniards."

"That's what King Philip ordered, you know. Thought he was going to do it overnight . . . and now, five years later, even Alva grows fearful."

Pieter-Lucas winced and pulled his shoulders up tight. "I still shudder at the thought."

"But we heard that the Beggars had taken Den Brill and that Oudewater and Leyden and all of Holland and Zeeland had declared for the prince. They set up their own rule at a meeting of the Estates—in Dordrecht, was it?"

Pieter-Lucas nodded. "I was there, and that's what they did. But you know as well as I do that Alva is determined to win them back. In fact, before I left Ludwig's camp two days ago, some messenger brought a statement issued by the duke that when he slaughtered twenty-five hundred nearly starved Haarlemers, he was being gracious."

"Gracious?"

"*Ja!* Can't you see? We should be grateful he left a handful of the poor wretches alive—and frightened enough by Alva's power to choose him over Prince Willem."

Dirck shook his head. "Impossible!"

"You never did tell me what brought you so far from home," Pieter-Lucas said.

"Ah, *ja* . . ." Dirck stammered. "First tell me, how safe is Leyden?"

"Leyden? Why do you ask?"

"Remember my friend Barthelemeus?"

"*Ja.*"

"He has friends there, Children of God. He's with them now, delivering some books from Johannes."

"And you're going to meet him there?"

Dirck nodded, then dropped his voice to a whisper. "We have to move our operation from Engeland."

"Surely you don't plan to bring an Anabaptist book business to Leyden now!" Pieter-Lucas frowned.

"We can't stay where we are much longer. The English are getting wary of us. You know, that's the way it is everywhere. No Anabaptist printer can stay long in any one place. We'll always be hunted and chased from one place to another all over this world. Everybody thinks we're so dangerous!"

"Just might defeat them all with your swords, eh?" Pieter-Lucas felt the irony grip his soul. No Child of God would ever carry a sword, and the whole world knew it.

Dirck smiled. "Humph! The only sword we use is the Bible."

"That's what they fear most," Pieter-Lucas suggested.

"Papists fear it, *ja*. But Calvinists and Lutherans? They use the Bible, too, you know. They die for possession of it just like we do."

Pieter-Lucas thought for a moment. "I know that. In this Lutheran household where we live, the Bible is read at every meal and is much revered and mostly lived by. And the now-Calvinist brothers, Willem and Ludwig, trust its power as well. Then there's Dirck Coornhert who'll never join himself to any group but firmly believes every man should use the Bible as an ethical guidebook."

"Then why is it, you think, that Lutherans and Calvinists, as well as Papists, keep us running across the face of the earth?"

Pieter-Lucas cleared his throat. "I tell you, I've asked myself that question a lot of times in the years I've been working for the revolt while still keeping my vows to never carry a sword."

"So? Find any answers?"

He waved a finger in his vader-in-law's face and said, "*Ja!* I've decided it's because nobody uses the Bible in the same way we do. For all the rest, it's *a* sword, next to the swords of the prince and the military commander and the laws of the land. Whichever is strongest at the moment rules. For the Children of God, it's *the* sword, prince and law, all wrapped up in one. We have no other sword."

Dirck Engelshofen nodded his head, slowly at first, then vigorously. Taking Pieter-Lucas by both shoulders, he looked at him with an expression of awed respect. "Well said, brother! Well said!"

From over the hillside just behind them, Pieter-Lucas heard a little voice being wafted on the soft afternoon breezes. "Vader! Vader!"

He turned and gazed down the pathway that led through a rolling sea of rippling grass and little splotches of wild-flower colors across the hillside.

"Hei!" he said, rubbing his hands together with glee. "I see a pair of boys coming toward us up the hill—your son and mine!"

He ran down the pathway, never stopping till he reached his own Lucas chugging with all his strength, pumping fat little arms. He leaned over and swooped the boy up to his chest and hugged and kissed him and held him like he'd never let him go.

"Lucas, my Lucas!" he cried out. The boy's sweaty arms barely reached around his neck, and his kisses got landed in all kinds of places from ears to chin to nose to the cheek end of his mustache.

"Vader, you're home!" he squealed with as much delight as if he hadn't seen him in a year. After all, Pieter-Lucas remembered, when you only have four years behind you, even ten days can feel like a year.

"You've been running all over the fields, haven't you?" Pieter-Lucas asked. "And who's your new friend?"

Lucas pointed to his companion. "Oom Robbin!"

Pieter-Lucas reached out a hand to his wife's little brother. "Welcome to Dillenburg," he said.

"Thank you," Robbin responded, gripping Pieter-Lucas' hand firmly.

Pieter-Lucas hadn't seen the boy in years. He couldn't remember how many. "What are you now, ten years old?"

"Twelve!" Robbin corrected, a shy grin covering his face. "I was seven last time I saw you."

"*Nay!* I can't believe it!" Pieter-Lucas looked at the boy. He'd grown taller, though he was still slender and sharp featured. He had eyes that snapped and toes that never stopped tapping.

Lucas pushed his vader's cheeks with both hands until he'd directed his eyes to look straight at him. "Can you make *Moeke* well?"

"Making her well is God's work, *jongen*."

"Mieke says bein' quiet helps." The boy's eyes grew wide with concern.

Pieter-Lucas smiled. "Mieke's right. *Moeke* needs lots of quiet. And in the morning, maybe we can go down to the garden and draw her a picture."

"*Ja, ja, ja!*" Lucas clapped his hands, then hugged and kissed his vader once more. "Will that help too?"

Pieter-Lucas rumpled the boy's hair, smiled, and said, "Just might."

The little party trudged up the hill with the sky glowing like burnished gold all around them.

19th morning of Hay Month (July), 1573

Only a few drops of dew still clung to the grasses along the roadway when Pieter-Lucas started down the hill into the early morning sun. In one hand he held the tiny hand of his son and shortened his own steps to try to keep pace with the little fellow's vigorous strides. How often when he was away had Pieter-Lucas dreamed of these treasured moments when he and his son would go out in search of something to draw.

"We going to draw a flower in *Moeke*'s garden?" Lucas asked, his voice like a soft clear bell in the expectant hush of the newborn day.

Pieter-Lucas chuckled. To a four-year-old who came to the herb garden almost every day with his moeder, of course it was "*Moeke*'s garden." She let him carry the basket into which she piled leaves and blossoms as she snipped and told him about what each one was good for as they sniffed the aromatic fragrances.

"Whatever you think *Moeke* would like best, *jongen*," Pieter-Lucas said. "You're going to give it to her, you know."

"Will it make her well again?"

Pieter-Lucas sighed. He remembered a time when life had seemed that simple to him too. At this moment, he wished with all his heart for it to be so. There was hope. Already, Aletta looked better than she had when he arrived home. In fact, they'd left her sitting up in a chair, no longer lying in the bed. He rumpled the blond curls atop Lucas' head. "At least it'll make her feel better."

"I know! I know! Let's do her fav'rite flower! C'mon! Faster!" Lucas was tugging hard on his vader's hand now, coaxing him into a run.

They hurried through the break in the hedge, and a chorus of sparrows, blackbirds, and cuckoo birds greeted them. Pieter-Lucas let the boy lead him down the pathway to a thorny bush covered with a profusion of single-petaled wild roses.

Lucas plopped his chubby body on a large stone bordering the pathway and patted the spot beside him. "Sit 'side me, Vader," he instructed.

Pieter-Lucas removed the pouch from his belt and extended the cord as far as it would go. He took his assigned place, then pulled a pair of charcoal pieces gently from the bag and let Lucas turn the bag bottom-side up. A sharpened reed pen, a worn paintbrush, a small square paint-splotched palette, and an assortment of corked containers of ink and paint tumbled onto the hard-packed dirt at their feet.

"So this is her favorite flower in all the garden?" Pieter-Lucas asked, pulling a smallish square of canvas from his doublet.

"They make her smile really big." Lucas was already reaching for the canvas and the charcoal.

"First," Pieter-Lucas said, "show me which one we are drawing."

Lucas rushed to the bush and picked out a clump close to the ground with one fully opened blossom surrounded by a ring of buds in varying stages of flowering.

"This one," he said, then hurried back to his seat.

Pieter-Lucas watched him spread the canvas out on his leg, take a stick of charcoal in his hand, and hold it just above the canvas. Looking up, eyes big with eagerness, the boy begged, "Help me, Vader."

Pieter-Lucas held the warm firm hand in his own and felt a lump in his throat. 'Twas a time long ago when his own grandfather had done the same for him, guiding his unsure fingers across the page. He remembered how always he knew just what he wanted to draw, but in the beginning his fingers seemed to fly off in strange directions. Little by little, as Opa helped him, he felt them grow stronger.

He'd never forget the first day he drew an object all on his own, and it came out the way he wanted it. A sparrow, it was, hopping about on a thin layer of grimy snow left over from winter. He'd painted it with a wash of color, then taken it home to show his moeder.

Gently Pieter-Lucas guided the fingers cupped beneath his hand along the rounded contours of the delicate petals and a long heavy stem.

"Vader! Vader!" Lucas squealed. "We made a rose! Oh! Can we make it pink?"

With growing delight, Pieter-Lucas helped the boy mix the right colors on his palette. Then using the old brush that had once belonged to his own grandfather, he let him cover the blossom with a pearly pink. Next they mixed a tiny splotch of golden color and, using a twig, filled the center of the blossom with bright dots of golden pollen-laden stamens. Finally, dipping his reed pen into the bottle of ink, Pieter-Lucas guided the little hands once more to outline it all with a thin dark line.

Lucas clapped with excitement, transferring blotches of pink and gold from one hand to the other. Looking up at his vader, a smile wreathing his face and a line of black ink smudging his cheek, he said, "It's goin' to make her well, Vader."

Pieter-Lucas gave the boy a squeeze and tried to smile. Someday he must learn that it takes more than a painting to heal a sick moeder, that sometimes nothing can heal her, that God is capricious and takes whomever He wills—and whenever. . . . But . . . not now! Pieter-Lucas couldn't bear to ruin all this childish innocence and implicit faith. Besides, soon enough Aletta was going to mend and there would be no need to talk about the "what-if-not's."

He smiled down into the radiant face. "I'm sure it will," he said.

When all had been put back into its place, vader and son trudged up the hill, the boy waving his masterpiece in the breeze. Halfway there, Lucas stopped and tugged the breeches on Pieter-Lucas' leg.

"Carry me, Vader," he begged in a tired voice.

Pieter-Lucas gathered the boy into his arms and let him lean a tousled head on his shoulder. "Lucas," he whispered into the boy's ear, "I've said it before, and I'll tell you again every day you are alive. You have—"

"I know, Vader," he interrupted, " 'paint running through your blood.' " He paused, then added, "What does that mean?"

Pieter-Lucas chuckled. "It means you will always love to paint pictures more than anything else on earth."

"Oh!" He sighed. "Are we almost home, Vader?"

"Almost."

"That's good, 'cause I think *Moeke* needs her picture pretty quick."

And someday soon, Pieter-Lucas told himself, *I will take this boy to Leyden to learn what I do not know. Opa would not have it any other way.*

Aletta spent most of the morning up and about. She'd just crawled back into bed, weighted with weariness, when she heard voices and feet at the door. Seconds later, the door flew open and Lucas scampered toward her, waving a painting.

"*Moeke*, it's your fav'rite flower. Vader says it'll make you well!"

He shoved the canvas into her hand and stood with a smile of anticipation on his upturned face.

"Ah, but it's beautiful!" she exclaimed. The lines and colors blended together with smudges on the now wrinkled canvas.

Lucas wriggled with delight, then climbed up onto her bed and nuzzled into her arms. "I love you, *Moeke*," he muttered, "and now you can get well, *ja*?"

She took the boy in her arms. "As God wills it," she said while she and her husband exchanged knowing smiles over the curly head.

For the rest of the day, Aletta slept less and talked more. Come nightfall, she crawled into bed rejoicing that her strength was indeed returning.

"Your cheeks glow once more with their lively color," Pieter-Lucas said when he kissed her good-night. "Just the way I want to remember you as I travel about the countryside tomorrow."

"Let's not talk of tomorrow and parting," she mumbled just before slipping into a deep sleep.

She dreamed unsettling dreams. When she awoke several times in the night, she could not remember what she had dreamed but dreaded going back to them. Sometime before daylight she came to with a painful start. Not a head pain this time. Rather, strong invisible fingers constricted her abdomen and seemed to suck the breath from her. She gripped the bed with both hands and stifled a cry.

"*Nay*, God, not the baby now. Not yet!" she whispered.

As suddenly as it had come, the pain subsided. She could not go back to sleep. Her mind whizzed around in dizzying circles of "What if's?" What if the baby came too early? More than once in her herbal healer duties she'd helped deliver an early child. Tiny enough to hold in the palm of her hand, gasping, unable to get enough air. She could never forget the dreadful sight such infants presented or the dagger it sent through her heart to watch them lose the struggle and wither in her hand.

But this child wasn't so terribly early. Nor did he need to be too early to die. Her last one had died before she ever gave it birth. What if this one died while Pieter-Lucas was gone? What if she herself died as Moeder Kaatje had done? She could never forget that awful morning when she sat at the bedside of Pieter-Lucas' moeder, holding her hand, listening to her horrendous tales about vows and dying babies and a vengeful God.

"God will always win!" Those were the woman's final words before she slipped into death's sleep, while in a crib nearby lay her dead child, the last of God-only-knew how many.

Aletta's thoughts were interrupted by yet another grabbing pain. She felt the beads of sweat forming on her brow and heard a little cry escape from her lips. Pieter-Lucas stirred beside her. Before the iron fingers would loosen their hold, her movements had brought him fully awake.

He leaned over her and demanded in an anxious voice, "Is the child coming?"

"*Nay*, not yet," she insisted as the pain vanished, leaving her limp and damp.

"But you're having pains! What do they mean, then? What shall I do?" He was spouting questions, while from the other side of the room, Lucas whimpered in his sleep.

Aletta reached for his arm and patted it as calmly as possible. "Just lie down and wait. Such pains often come long before the child."

"How long before?" He still hovered over her in the dark, his breath warm across her face.

"Who knows?" she said. "Sometimes days or weeks before the time. Like dancers practicing for a festival, so they can do it right when the moment arrives."

He spread the wide fingers of his large hand across her belly. "Does he still kick?"

"*Ja*, Pieter-Lucas. This child is not like Kaatje."

"Should I go get Mieke? Or one of the countesses?"

"Simply lie down and be still before you bring Lucas wide awake and howling for the whole *Kasteel* to hear."

Slowly he lay down beside her and took her hand in his. "Lie down and be still? That I shall do. Sleep? Never. I stay wide awake to get you help when the pains come again."

Aletta smiled and lay her head on Pieter-Lucas' shoulder. "You have a heart most gracious and kind, and I give our God thanks each day for such a devoted husband. But you may sleep soundly, my love. No child will ask to be birthed this night."

She had scarcely finished her sentence when she heard her husband's breathing grow heavy and promptly fell asleep herself. How long the quiet lasted, she never knew. When she awoke once more, she found herself in the fierce grip of a more intense childbirth pain than before. Already she was screaming out.

Pieter-Lucas jumped from the bed with a start. "I go for the countess," he said, his words tumbling from his mouth.

Aletta grabbed the covers around her and held on, yelling for what seemed an endless moment of anguish. When at last it left her quiet, limp, and dripping with sweat, she heard a voice not her husband's and felt a wiry hand on her forehead.

"I knowed it'd be this night."

"Mieke," Aletta murmured. She opened her eyes and saw a lamp burning on the table by the bed.

"I'se been a-sleepin' outside the door, jus' a-waitin' fer this moment. Done sended your man to the kitchen fer some hot water. Th' cook, she knowed it was a-comin' too—I telled her. Now, let me see what goes." And Mieke was throwing back the covers. Not at all the way it was supposed to be done. But she'd learned from Aletta, who had learned from an old lady and from Tante Lysbet's herbal book and from having to do it herself.

One quick look and Mieke let out a shriek. "Th' head's as big as a bowl already. Another pain or two like that one, an' you'se goin' to be a-birthin' a baby, Vrouw 'Letta."

Hardly had she finished her report when the next pain tore at Aletta. Mieke perched herself on the end of the bed and waited, urging her patient to "Push, push, easy now! It's coming!"

When the pain subsided, Aletta felt another hand on her forehead and heard another voice, this one quiet and smooth. "I've a soothin' broth for you when this is over."

"Jus' one more pain, and I can grab 'im by the shoulders," Mieke said with undisguised excitement.

Then the final pain came. Through the haze of mind and pain so searing it made her nearly numb, Aletta felt the child slipping from her body and heard Mieke's shout of triumph, "It's here! A girl!"

The wild choking sobs of an infant followed. A more beautiful and welcome sound Aletta had never heard. No weakling, this one, ready to wither in her hand.

"God be praised!" she mumbled and reached instinctively out to take a measure of the bloody body of the child, now thrashing about on her tummy while the women attending her tied and cut the navel cord that had bound them together for these many months.

The rest of the activity around her blurred into confusion and one enormous struggle to stay awake long enough to see her new little daughter's face, give her suck, and show her to her husband. But when the kindly old lady from the *kasteel* kitchen had put a cup of warm nourishing broth to her lips and she'd swallowed only a few mouthfuls, she drifted in and out of awareness until Mieke nudged her awake.

"Vrouw 'Letta," the sharp voice startled her. "Here she is—th' pertiest little baby girl ye ever goin' to see—an' as hungry as she is beautiful!"

Wrapped securely in a long length of soft warm cloth, only a red howling face showed. Mieke laid the child carefully in her arms. "Now, fer Heaven's sake, give her somethin' to eat b'fore she starves to death!"

"Thank you, Mieke," Aletta said, opening her bodice and guiding the little mouth to a waiting breast. The first drops began to flow, and after a couple of difficult starts, the newborn finally began to suck and swallow it down. Aletta laid a kiss on the forehead and sang softly, her body swaying to the rhythm of the lullaby, *"Suja, suja, slaap."*

The first meal completed, she lay the child down and pulled her snugly up next to her heart. Gently, eagerly, she unwound the swaddled wrappings. "Must be sure nothing's missing," she mumbled. With misting eyes, she stared at the marvelous little body now slumbering beside her and whispered, "As beautiful as any newborn I've ever gazed upon!"

Carefully she wrapped the legs together. As she did, she thought she felt a stiffness in the right foot. With gentle fingers, she massaged it, trying to tell herself it flexed just like the other foot. Surely it was the strangeness of her fancy following the painful ordeal of the birth—for everything else was so perfect! It must be right. *Nay!* Nothing could be wrong—nothing!

She fought off a creeping fear and finished rewrapping the child. Then hugging her tightly to her breast and kissing the cleansed, oiled forehead, she sang once more, *"Suja, suja, slaap . . ."*

Halfway through, she closed her eyes and let tears trickle down her cheeks. "Dear God in the Heaven," she prayed silently, "did you not hear when I asked you to keep her safe?" Lost in quiet anguish, she waited and rocked her baby . . . and listened for an answer that did not come.

When she opened her eyes again, Pieter-Lucas sat beside her, looking down into her face and smiling broadly. "May I see our daughter?" he asked.

Slowly she leaned her own body with the child's as she lowered her to the bed. In the process she wiped her tears on the swaddling cloth and did not look at her husband.

"She's perfect," Pieter-Lucas said, his voice hoarse with wonder.

Shaking off the fearsome thoughts, Aletta forced a smile and said, "It all happened so fast. She couldn't wait! So eager to hear her vader's voice, she was."

"She wasn't too early, then?"

Aletta swallowed down fresh tears threatening to spill out. "Only earlier than I expected," she said. She must not let her husband know of the fear that tormented her. He would be going away again today, and she could not let him carry this burden along. "You see," she said, smiling, "she breathes, she kicks, she suckles. Not like any too early child I ever saw."

"Thank God," he breathed, then grew still. They both stared at the child lying on the bed between them. Her little chest rose and fell in perfect rhythm, and now and again the eyelids fluttered and the mouth twitched. Pieter-Lucas' fingers played absently with the baby's chin.

Aletta felt his hand on hers and heard his voice. "You are tired, my love. Let me put her in her crib and you rest."

She looked up at him and, trying to smile, said, "First she needs a name."

"So she does." A startled little grin played at the corners of his mouth.

"Can we call her Kaatje?" Aletta's heart pounded as she said it. It was the name they'd given to the girl stillborn to her a year ago. Yet she so much wanted a girl to bear Pieter-Lucas' moeder's name.

"I know my moeder would be pleased," Pieter-Lucas said.

"And you?"

They searched each other's eyes for a long and penetrating moment. Then both smiled, and she knew their hearts agreed. Looking again at the child between them, Aletta began and Pieter-Lucas joined her instantly. "Welcome, beloved Kaatje!"

CHAPTER THREE

Leyden

6th day of Harvest Month (August), 1573

Market day was the busiest day of the week at *The Clever Fox Inn*. Hiltje left her bed before the sun slipped up over the horizon. In summer that was earlier than she would even let herself figure out. With something less than eagerness, she dressed and patted her tummy. Then she plaited the long thick hair and bound it up in her stiffly starched white headdress.

"The work of an innkeeper's vrouw is never finished!" she groused, shaking out feather bags and spreading them over the broad windowsill. She checked the glowering sky and continued her conversation with herself. "Rain again! As always—especially on market day. Just for once I'd like to wake up knowing I wouldn't have to brave muddy puddles and splashing horses in order to fill my kitchen larder and my guests' oil lamps."

She moved to the kitchen, where she blew on the reluctant embers in the hearth, coaxing them into life. Her husband's cloddish feet shuffled across the mud tiles behind her.

"He's really done it this time!" Joris muttered, standing over her with his apron brushing against her shoulder.

"Who? Christoffel?" she asked without looking up.

"Who else? That featherheaded *jongen* is going to get himself captured, tortured, killed, who knows what all—and his vader with him!"

"Come, come, my husband!" she sputtered, all the while bustling about the room. Whatever might be bothering him, she still had an inn to put in order and half a houseful of customers to buy provisions for. "Have you any idea how many times we would have buried that son of ours if he had died every time you predicted it as a result of his rash actions?"

Joris crossed his arms across his belly and scowled at her. "One day, when it really happens, you will pay me a mind."

She stood with hands on hips and repressed a laugh. "Well, don't just stand there. Tell me, what's he done this time that you ought to have thrashed him for, but you were too soft? And be quick about it. I've got work to do."

He glared at her without moving a whisker. "I ought to just leave you wondering," he said at last.

"You could." She shrugged and grabbed a broom. She knew he never would, though. Nothing was half so important to him as telling her all about whatever was making him fret.

So she swept the floor and waited, and shortly he grunted, "He's painted a picture of the ragged old Beggar!"

"Oh *ja*? Did he do a good job?"

"Disgustingly good likeness it is. How could he do such a thing?"

"You sound surprised."

"After all I've told him about the scoundrels, why shouldn't I be surprised?" Joris stamped both feet on the floor and messed his hair with the agitated fingers of both hands.

"Bah!" Hiltje said with one hand raised. "Beggars just happen to be your son's heroes these days."

"Heroes?"

"Come, Joris, you remember how it is with boys. They all have heroes, and by the time they're twelve or thirteen, it has to be somebody more exciting than a boy's vader. Tomorrow it may be a gatekeeper, a miller . . . who knows? Today it's a Beggar with his eccentric uniform."

"Uniform?" he exploded. "Baggy breeches, bowls, bags, and pennies in their hats?"

"Who else does he see in uniforms of any kind out here on the banks of the Zyl River? These Beggars are soldiers, Joris, soldiers sailing warships, fighting battles on land and sea, drinking hard, and shouting loud."

Joris wiped his hands on his apron and held his head high. "I've warned the *jongen* so soundly. Beggars slice paintings to shreds." He paused, then jabbed the air with a pointer finger and went on. "Next thing we know, he'll get cozy with that old Beggar. Then while he's feeling his artist pride all puffed and petted, I'll come into our hidden studio one day and find the Beggar in there with him. I hope I don't need to tell you that will be our open doorway to a dungeon or to the point of a sword."

Hiltje sighed. Her dear kindhearted husband could conjure up the wildest stretches of gloomy imagination. "Joris, Joris," she said, shaking her head with exasperation. "That old bear won't let our son get cozy with him. He doesn't pay the *jongen* so much as half a mind."

Joris shuffled uneasily, then muttered, "I don't trust them."

"Joris, the Beggars are only after church paintings, not portraits done by some innkeeper's son to hang on his own walls. They wouldn't even look twice at either Christoffel or his work."

"You are no artist, Vrouw! Can't you see that a man who will destroy the works of an artist's hands is just as likely to take his life as well?"

Hiltje laughed. "When you close your doors to all the Beggars, I'll begin to listen to you."

"You would be the first to complain! They are, after all, good customers."

Hiltje gathered up her market basket and headed for the peg on which her cape hung beside the door. "If you did not take their coins and give them a table and a bed in your inn, Christoffel would have no opportunity to watch and listen to them sitting around laughing, singing, telling their boastful yarns, guzzling down hefty kegs of Delfts beer."

"But we have to eat to live!"

"Which is why I go now to the market," she said, pulling her cape around her shoulders and slipping into her street shoes.

She crossed the threshold out into the rain, looking over her shoulder at Joris. He stood in the middle of the floor, reaching out a hand as if to stop her. With effort she ignored the strong yearning to console him. But he'd get over it, and she had work to do.

———

Hiltje made her way as quickly as possible around the stalls of the old market, filling her basket with freshly caught halibut, oil for the lamps, a pot to replace one broken by her younger daughter, Clare. She had not intended to stop at the weaver's stall today. She had no needs there, and though the rain had let up, it drizzled yet, and she needed to get home.

But she did have to pass that way, and as she did, an unusual rich brown shawl with bright darts of sun yellow caught her eye. Fabrics always turned her head—especially the kind she could wrap herself up in. She could spend all day here, looking at the way they were constructed, feeling their softness or roughness, imagining how well they would protect from the cold, the rain, the snow.

She moved toward the weaver's stall, her eyes drawing her to the beautiful piece. Captivated by its exquisite beauty, she reached out and stroked it, then crumpled and released it again and again. Soft and finely woven, its scattered shafts of light lifted her spirits, and the fat thick fringe that finished all the edges felt like warm silky kitten fur on her rough hands.

"Just what I need for a chilly day when my spirits are sagging," she mumbled to herself.

Only half looking up, she asked, "How much, Magdalena?"

Not until the weaver's wife failed to answer did Hiltje realize she had other customers. Strangers they were. Two men and a young boy of about her Christoffel's age. Magdalena was spreading out several pieces of cloth for them to examine. As they looked they spoke little and soon thanked her for her time and walked away.

"How much, Magdalena?" Hiltje repeated.

The short woman with graying hair showing around the edges of her cap lifted her eyebrows and went on folding up the items the strangers had looked at. "More than you can pay me, Hiltje."

"What do you mean?" she asked, trying to sound indignant.

"That one is very expensive. My husband made it of some of the finest woolen yarns he has ever found. I told him when he did it that Hiltje would be stopping by for a gaze. Here, put it round your shoulders, friend," she went on, a wide smile lighting up her face.

"*Nay*," Hiltje countered. "Not over my wet clothes. My mind tells me just how it would feel and how it would look and . . ." She sighed. "How long can you keep it for me while I collect enough coins to make it my own?"

Magdalena lifted her eyebrows, pursed her lips, and said, "For you, Hiltje?"

"*Ja*, for me!"

Magdalena stood staring at the fabric for a long moment. Then she lifted her head and met Hiltje's gaze with an inspired sparkle in her faded blue eyes.

"Those three men that just left us," she began with a touch of excitement quivering her voice, "did you notice them?"

"You mean the two men and a boy?"

"*Ja*, they are the ones."

"Well, what about them?"

"A suggestion is forming in my head. They've come to Leyden on business of their own—something my husband will help them with. As usual, he expects me to give them lodging under my roof. Two of them, that is. The third is on some other kind of mission and says he must move on before the day is half spent. But I already have several guests, and to be plain about it, the house is full to the rafters."

"So," Hiltje felt a thrill of excitement running through her body. "How many nights' lodging at *The Clever Fox Inn* will it take to pay for the shawl?" She fingered the fabric with a feeling approaching ownership.

"Probably two or three, with meals and Delfts beer. That is, if your Joris will allow it."

"Has he ever before turned away one of your guests?" Over the years that they'd been here in Leyden, it did seem as though Magdalena and her husband entertained a lot of strangers. Just what their business was Hiltje neither knew nor cared to know. It was enough that Magdalena's overflow was always good for Hiltje's business.

"*Nay*, he never has," Magdalena agreed. "But always before we have paid him in coins."

Hiltje looked first at the shawl, then into her friend's face and said knowingly, "Remember, my Joris is a lover of beautiful things, especially when they drape around his vrouw." She nodded her head and chuckled. "In spite of all his grumbling, he has the kindest, softest heart you ever dreamed of. Of course he will allow it. It's not as if we have a long line of folks waiting at our gates these days. War keeps people at home, unless they're soldiers—Beggars and such."

Already Magdalena was folding the shawl, helping her friend stash it under her cape, where she held it firmly beneath the wing of her arm. Hiltje felt her heart soar!

"I shall love to see you wearing it," Magdalena said, a huge smile covering her narrow face with its sharp chin and nose. "When the men have finished their business for this day, I send them on to you."

"Not before time for the evening meal is all I ask. And for your kindness, I give you gratitude."

Hiltje hurried home across a soggy landscape pierced now and again with a shaft of sunlight. "Just like the shawl next to my heart," she breathed and quickened her steps.

———

With two messages from Willem's brother Jan in Dillenburg tucked away in his doublet—one for Paulus Buys and another for Willem—Pieter-Lucas accompanied his vader-in-law and Robbin to Leyden. Here he helped them find Barthelemeus and their Anabaptist weaver friends. Then he bade them farewell, delivered Paulus' message in exchange for another for Willem, and slipped back out into the rain-slickened streets.

Dirck Engelshofen's words followed him with each step: "*When we've moved our printery to this place, you must bring Aletta and the children. We will yet find a way to put this family back together.*"

Pieter-Lucas had smiled, slapped the older man on the shoulder, and hurried off. He had no need for his vader-in-law to coax him to bring his family to Leyden. He'd planned that far longer than Dirck Engelshofen could guess. The thought of finally living in the shadow of his famous Lucas van Leyden ancestor made the paint course madly through his blood. Instinctively he grabbed for his brushes and sighed. If only he could go straight back to Dillenburg and get them!

Ach! But Opa's promises and Vader Dirck's dreams were still only dreams. Aletta had just given birth and would not be ready to travel for weeks. Besides, the only artist Pieter-Lucas had found in Leyden was a boy with enthusiasm and promise. Most ominous of all, Haarlem had just fallen to Spain, and there were rumors about Leyden being next, and . . .

It was enough. Now was no time for dreams. Pieter-Lucas still had messages to carry to Willem in Delft. He'd hardly turned his mind into the channels where it belonged when he realized he was passing by the large plain door of the Pieterskerk. Unbidden, his heart quickened with a vision of what lay just beyond his reach. Inside those doors Lucas van Leyden's great work, "The Last Judgment," hung above the altar and begged him to come sneak just a peek. How often Opa had reminded him of his obligation to look at it, to learn something of the nature of his own inheritance. 'Twould only take an eyeblink of time. No need to study it now, but he was so close. He had to see it before he could move on.

Trembling, he looked back over his shoulder as if he expected someone to be watching there to pounce on him. He grasped the huge iron handle, heaving at the heavy door and shuddering when it squeaked. Leaving his shoes at the door, he glided over the cold grave-slab tiles. He shivered in the cool dampness and stared about him in the dim light of the cavernous old building with its endless aisles and vaulted ceilings.

Led by the scent of burning candles and incense, he hastened toward the high altar flanked by ornately carved pulpits. It was set off by a broad, intricately carved rood screen of the kind he'd once watched the image breakers topple to the floor with malicious glee back in Breda. Eagerly his eyes scanned the wall up behind the altar just beneath a delicate pattern of colored-glass windows, which let in jeweled blotches of light— pale yellow, deep rose, forest green, and blue the shade of Aletta's wondering eyes.

"It's gone!" he whispered and stared harder, unwilling to believe it. "*Nay!* It has to be here!"

He crawled up into the forbidden altar area and brushed past the rows of choir stalls till he stood with hands grasping the edge of the white-clothed altar. The wall gaped with nothingness, and a handful of lightning-shaped gashes marred the plaster.

"Image breakers!" he gasped. Inside, his stomach churned like the never ceasing roll of a threatening thunder in an ominous gray afternoon sky. Memories of Opa's painting, "The Anointing," being yanked from the wall and shredded into a hundred slivers before him on the floor at his feet haunted him. Each remembered thrust of Vader Hendrick's parade knife pierced like a bolt of lightning in the storm intensifying in his gut.

What was this? A family curse of some sort? *Nay!* "The Last Judgment" had to be here somewhere, and he'd find it if it was the last thing he did. Blinded by his inner tumult, spurred by desperation, he dashed from the altar up and down the aisles of the hollow old church, searching every side altar. The little moans that escaped from his throat echoed around the walls and pillars. His search revealed nothing but more blank scarred walls.

Vader Hendrick used to tell him that the sacred altars in the papist churches were inhabited by demons. So back in the Great Church of Breda, Vader Hendrick wrenched the paintings and other sacred trappings from their places and ground them to shards into the floor. This morning Pieter-Lucas stood at the last of the altars with hands hanging at his side and heart racing topsy-turvy in his doublet. He felt as if all the demons of hell had been loosed to chase him through one more desecrated place of cold stones and suffocating incense.

He rushed out into the drizzling street and did not look back at the church. Nor did he look carefully ahead of him as he rounded a corner and headed down the street where Blesje waited in the stables. In his rush he bumped soundly into an oncoming traveler. Reaching only to his ear lobes in height, the person he collided with let out a loud "Ugh!" then sputtered, "What's your hurry?"

"Sorry, *jongen*," Pieter-Lucas stammered, grasping the boy by both arms to steady him. One look at his tam cap now knocked ajar and his knapsack hanging from one shoulder, and he gasped, "*Jongen!* It's you again—Leyden's painter!"

The boy stared at him with perplexed eyes. Before he could speak, Pieter-Lucas was demanding, "Tell me, have you ever seen 'The Last Judgment' that once hung above the altar in the Pieterskerk?"

The boy pulled himself free from Pieter-Lucas' grip, wriggled into order, and answered, "Why do you want to know?"

"From the time I was just a little fellow, my opa used to tell me about that great painting. His uncle Lucas van Leyden painted it. Opa promised to bring me here someday and teach me some secrets of the painter's art from it. He died before he could keep his promise, and I've been trying ever since to get here and see it. Today I get into the church and find it's been wrenched from the wall by some image breaker!" He couldn't believe he trembled so at the thought of it.

The boy laughed. "Didn't belong there anyway!"

"Why not?"

"Paintings aren't meant to be prayed to."

Pieter-Lucas looked at the face upturned before him. Some sort of Calvinist was he? Surely not an Anabaptist! "You don't talk like a painter!"

The boy shrugged. "That's what my vader tells me, even though our studio is filled with my paintings."

"Your studio? Is your vader your meester?" Pieter-Lucas caught his breath. He watched the boy still grinning, studying his expressions, clearly enjoying holding him in his grip as if dangling him over a precipice.

"My vader has strange ideas," he drawled and pursed his lips. "Gets upset when I paint things he doesn't like."

"Did he like the ship you were drawing down at the harbor?" Pieter-Lucas watched carefully each expression, eager to understand this precocious artist.

"Ships are approved. We've painted a whole fleet of them. It's the Beggars that make him furious. I did one of my favorite Beggar and he found it. You should see how he flew into a rage over it."

Pieter-Lucas nodded and stared harder than ever at the boy. "I understand that kind of rage."

The boy's face clouded. "You do? Aren't you a servant of Prince Willem?"

Pieter-Lucas stirred quietly for a moment. "I am, but that doesn't make me a lover of Beggars." Then pointing to the long arched scar below his left eye, he added, "I found myself at the piercing end of a beggar's knife once. Mark my word. A painter can't be too cautious of those wild creatures."

The boy shrugged and threw him a cocky self-assured look. "Just don't get between a Beggar and a church painting. That's all you have to watch for."

Pieter-Lucas gulped, then laid a hand on the boy's shoulder and looked squarely into his mischievous eyes. "'Tisn't so simple, *jongen*. I can't take time now to tell you my story. But if you're smart, you'll heed my warning: Beggars are never the friends of artists—never! Don't trust them, *jongen*!"

The boy laughed. "Don't worry about me. I don't paint church pictures!"

"Like I said, don't trust them, or you will get hurt! Speaking of church pictures, do you know what happened to 'The Last Judgment'?"

"*Ja*, I know right where it is."

"It's not destroyed, then?"

"*Nay!*"

"Can you tell me where I can find it?"

"*Ja*, it's at the St. Jan's Hospital."

"Can you take me there some other time?"

He grinned. "I could, but it won't help you any."

"What do you mean?"

"They wouldn't let you see the painting anyway."

"Why not?"

"You might slice it with your knife." With a disinterested air and a shrug, the boy walked away, whistling as he went.

Pieter-Lucas stared after him. "Arrogant *jongen!*" he mumbled. Then he rushed to the stables and was soon across the Koe Poort bridge and halfway to Delft, musing as he went, "I hope he pays a mind to what I told him—or he could pay for it with his life!"

A large red sun slipped near to the horizon on the edge of the pasture beyond the Zyl River and cast long shafts of golden light in through the murky glass windows of *The Clever Fox Inn.* One shaft caught Christoffel squarely in the eye where he sat on his three-legged stool in the corner of the raucous dining room.

The tables stood at random angles, each crowded to capacity with an assortment of tipsy seamen. All wore ragged gray doublets and balloon britches and sported tricolor flags and shiny beggar's pennies in their caps. Around their necks hung wooden bowls and from their waists, dark brown bags, crude wine cruses, and long curved swords in plain leather sheaths.

Christoffel eyed the whole bunch, grinning. One day yet he would draw their picture just as they sat here tonight with tankards in hand, shouting, singing,

> Beat the drum gaily, rub a dow, rub a dub;
> Beat the drum gaily, rub a dub, rub a dow;
> Beat the drum gaily, rub a dow, rub a dub;
> Long live the Beggars! Is the watchword now.

An uproarious round of shouts and foot stompings ensued, and Christoffel joined in, clapping, jumping to his feet, cheering them on.

"Tell us the story of Den Brill!" shouted Christoffel. He'd heard this story from these same men more times than he'd counted. But he could never hear it one time too many!

"Den Brill! Den Brill!" he joined in the chant with the men, stamping out its rhythm with cloddish feet in the rushes that covered the old clay tiles.

> On the first of Ap-ril
> Alva lost his Brill!

Christoffel joined, too, in the loud cheers that followed. He knew the rhyme well—a play on words it was. Den Brill (The Eyeglasses) was the name of a small sea town on the North Sea that Alva had under his power until the sea Beggars sailed in and captured it on the first of April 1572.

The men tipped up their tankards and guzzled down boorish draughts of Delfts beer—the best Vader Joris could buy. Then they swiped at dripping beards with the back of tattered sleeves and grinned broad gleeful grins.

"Tell us the story, Oude Man," they shouted, all shoving one older man to his feet.

"Ja, Oude Man," Christoffel echoed. Nobody told stories like he did. He made them brave and adventurous enough to stir any boy's blood.

The man scowled at his audience, stood to his feet, and took one enormous puff on his long-stemmed pipe. Something in his fierce countenance made Christoffel think of the words of the stranger he'd met today in Leyden. *Never trust a Beggar.*

Christoffel lifted his head and laughed. That stranger didn't know this Beggar!

"Looks just like my opa," he mumbled. "Dark, fierce, and strong, he has a voice big enough to make a whole building tremble."

The man was squinting out at them all with small eyes and patting a paunchy stomach, holding a tankard in one hand and pipe in the other. He cleared his throat and began. "It happened on a gloriously lucky day! The Queen o' Engeland had chased us from her ports, and we was a-driftin' homeward, a-fumin' and a-wonderin'."

The men moaned in unison and repeated after him, "a-fumin' and a-wonderin'!"

He puffed once more on his pipe, and while the smoke swirled round his head, he went on with his story. "Then the winds o' Providence reached down and blew us wildly, straight for the port o' Den Brill. Nobody was expectin' us—'specially not Alva. Didn't have a single Spaniard waitin' for us in the town!"

A shout of "Long live the Beggars!" rose from the tables all around, and tankards clinked, and loud sounds of guzzling and foot stomping once more filled the air.

They all paused and waited till the old man began again. "We gave the town exactly two hours to surrender. And did the abominable papists ever scurry to try to escape! But we got 'em all."

From the far end of the room, a younger voice piped, "We raided their idol-hole churches!" Shouts followed from all over the room.

"Smashed their images!"

"Sliced up their fancy altar paintings!"

"Turned the windows into slivers."

Christoffel watched his vader frown directly at him, then slink off into the shadows. This part of the story brought Christoffel more pleasure than all the rest. While it was an awful thing to think about paintings being destroyed, deep down inside he knew that paintings and statues were not supposed to be worshiped. He'd learned it from his old oma. Before she died, she'd told him a hundred times that God had given Ten Commandments and the second one said you should not pray to anything you could make with your own hands. Surely what the Beggars did in the churches was right. Why couldn't Vader see it? Had Oma never told him?

The old man was in control once more. "It was just like going back to 1566 and the image-breaking fever. So long we'd been badgered about, we was like men nearly starved into a frenzy—ready for any little crumbs of victory what might fall from the duke's fancy tables. The sacking of this place was more like the king's own spread. It fed our lean blood with a strength what had to be divine!"

With one voice, the crowd burst again into song, the same tune as the first stanza:

> The Spanish Inquisition, without intermission—
> The Spanish Inquisition has drunk our blood;
> The Spanish Inquisition, may God's malediction
> Blast the Spanish Inquisition and all her brood.

Vader Joris was pacing the floor now, hands clasped behind his back, a frown knitting his brow. It was almost more than the man could do to keep from stopping his ears with greasy fingers and shouting orders to his guests to cease their uncouth rowdiness. Christoffel knew his mood well. Christoffel had heard him and Moeder discuss it more than once. Moeder always won. *It's the business, my man, the business!*

The men were all on their feet dancing around the room now. The old man had stationed himself on the table and went on with a wild abandon. "We loaded our choice loot, gleaned from the churches and abbeys and cellars, onto our beautiful beggar ships and sailed down the Hollandse delta in rare style. In marvelous madness we shed our ragged beggar's uniforms and replaced them with rich holy robes, glittering vestments, cowls, and mitres. We swarmed over our ships like a flock of crazed priests, bowing and scraping to one another, calling our beggar brothers, 'Your Holiness.' "

They burst into the final stanza of the war song that came so easily from their lips:

> Long live the Beggars! Wilt thou Christ's word cherish—
> Long live the Beggars! Be bold of heart and hand;
> Long live the Beggars! God will not see thee perish;
> Long live the Beggars! Oh, noble Christian band.

The old man lifted his tankard high and laughed a deep foghorn laugh. But before he had brought the vessel to his lips, he stared open-mouthed at the doorway, a look of shocked terror freezing him into momentary inaction. Then suddenly he shrunk downward and slid off the table, burying himself between his now silent companions.

Christoffel looked toward the door where two strangers had just entered the room. One, a tall straight man, solemnly surveyed the situation. Beside him a boy of about his own age stood gripping a large black bag in his right hand.

Vader Joris moved officiously across the room. With a wave in the direction of his rowdy guests, he announced, "The feast is over! Now off to your rooms, and remember, we run a respectable resting haven here." Then he wiped his hand on his apron and reached out to welcome his latest guests.

Christoffel sat in stunned silence and watched as the Beggars tumbled clumsily, grousing and jostling one another, from the room. Normally Vader left the rowdy bunch till half of them had collapsed on or under the tables before insisting that they cart one another off to their rooms upstairs. In the confusion Christoffel searched for the old man who'd been filled with such unquestioning bravado one moment and had turned so fearful the next. But he'd managed to obscure himself completely. What was he running from?

Christoffel glared at the newcomers with pinched eyes. "What have they done to him?" he mumbled. Then, before his vader could arrest him and insist on his offering the boy any sort of hospitality, Christoffel slipped out into the hall and hurried to his cupboard bed on the back wall of the family room. Tomorrow would be soon enough to face this one.

CHAPTER FOUR

Leyden

6th evening of Harvest Month (August), 1573

C hristoffel had barely peeled off his doublet and crawled only halfway into his bed cupboard when he heard the excited barking of the dogs that guarded the inn. Hurriedly backing out, he landed with stockinged feet on the floor and rushed to peer out the window. The innyard lay in undisturbed array, bathed in the eerie wash of a sparkling moon peering between heaped-up clouds.

"Did Oude Man run away?" he mused. First time he'd ever seen the man so agitated. Something about those strangers at the door did it. They didn't look dangerous. Not Spanish soldiers or government officials. What was it? Holy men of some sort? They weren't dressed like clerics or monks, and one was just a boy. Looked like an ordinary traveling merchant with his son.

It shouldn't matter a clog to Christoffel what the old man did or why. Unless, of course, the newcomers were more dangerous than they looked. Vader Joris didn't seem worried. In fact, he almost looked as if he expected them, was glad to see them come and bring a halt to the drinking and storytelling. He probably was. Vader Joris didn't like the Beggars' wild celebrations.

Christoffel didn't want Oude Man to go away and never come back. The way he told all those stories about the brave and dangerous life he and the others had was so exciting! It made him want to be a Beggar himself, almost worse than anything—as long as they'd let him carry his charcoals along.

So it did matter what had happened to the old man. Without pausing to put on his doublet, he padded in stocking feet past the cupboard bed where his two sisters slept, grabbed a stool, placed it below the window, and climbed up onto it. Lifting the frame with its precious glass, he pushed the window away and let himself out through the hole. He landed as lightly as possible, then scampered around the house, steering well clear of the kitchen door where he knew his moeder was preparing dinner for the late-arriving guests. With care he darted from one clump of trees to the next until he'd let himself out of the gate. Leaning hard against the giant oak tree that held up *The Clever Fox Inn* sign, he looked both directions along the trekpath.

He could see the lone figure of a man hurrying away, halfway to the junction with the road that ran to Leyden. Staying close to the trees and shrubs lest he be detected, Christoffel followed. The moon moved in and out behind the clouds, sometimes leaving the way so dark he could scarcely see the figure he pursued. Always the wind blew the river in little swishing slaps against the bank beside him, and now and again a mournful owl swooped into a tree above his head and startled him with its sudden screeching.

From deep inside a voice began prodding, *What did you come out here for, jongen?* But he shoved it down.

"Got to find my favorite Beggar what's been chased out of my house. Can't stop for shivery breezes, eerie shadows, and hooting owls."

The fleeing man slowed his pace once he joined the Rhine trekpath. He had almost reached the Zyl Poort Bridge before Christoffel came within easy reach of him. Now as the moon shown full on the man's pointed beard, Christoffel stared hard from behind a clump of bushes. "It's him all right," he told himself. Then wiping his hands on his breeches and smoothing down the pell-mell racing of his heart, he sprinted forward. Just before he reached the man, he stepped into a huge mud puddle. The stillness of the evening was shattered with the splash.

Instantly the man wheeled about and faced him.

"Who dares to chase after me?" he demanded in an angry tone and pointed a knife directly at the boy.

Christoffel gasped, covering his mouth with his hand, springing back, stumbling once more into the water. He'd never seen the man like this before! In the back of his mind, he heard the words *"Never trust a Beggar"* echoing and reechoing!

"*Jongen!*" the Beggar shouted without pulling back the knife. "What are you doing out here?"

Christoffel opened his mouth, but no words came out.

"You got Dirck Engelshofen's *jongen* with you?" he asked, his dark eyes glinting menacingly in the moonlight.

"Wh-who?" Christoffel stammered.

"What do you mean, 'Wh-who?'"

"I . . . I don't know either Dirck whatever or his son, sir. I swear to God and all the holy angels." Confusion rolled through his chest like a thunderstorm that never stops. He must be calm.

"Humph!" the Beggar grunted. "Then what you doin' out here in the middle of the night?"

If only he'd put the knife away! Christoffel swallowed hard, wiped his hands on his breeches once more, then looked up and said as calmly as he could, "I couldn't bear to see you run out of our house by strangers."

Slowly a hint of a smirk crept over the man's face. As he stared at the boy, he began to chuckle and twirl the knife in his hand. "What makes you think any strangers ran me out of your vader's inn?"

Christoffel stood speechless for a long moment. "Why, I watched the look on your face when you saw the man and boy in our doorway. You slid down off the table awful fast!"

Still chuckling, still twirling the knife, the old man said, "You got a lot to learn, *jongen.*" Then stuffing the knife into its sheath, he said evenly, "You'd best run home to your vader and your idolatrous painting—and let me take care o' myself."

Trembling, Christoffel pleaded, "Promise me you'll come back and tell us some more of your stories!"

The man pointed to his own chest and asked in an incredulous voice, "My stories?"

"Nobody tells them like you do. Tonight when you told us about Den Brill again, I was ready to put on a beggar's suit and walk out of there with you and never go back."

The man stood quietly, staring a hole through the boy. Then he reached out and placed a finger under Christoffel's quivering chin. The boy recoiled at the touch. "Stories are for drinkin' over and shoutin' and singin' 'Long live the Beggars!' But beggarin' is about swingin' a sword and squeezin' the life out of a papist priest and smashin' shiny colored glass windows—and slicin' altar paintings."

Christoffel gulped. "I . . . is that what you do?" He felt rivulets of sweat running down the back of his neck and legs and refused to let his mind paint pictures for him of what his beggar hero had just described.

The man laughed that same foghorn laugh Christoffel remembered from the end of his great performance on the inn table. He wagged his finger under the boy's nose and roared, "*Ja,* that's what we do. Like I say, beggarin' ain't for *jongens*—or for painters! Now, be off to your vader and your paintbrushes. And if I catch you doggin' my steps again, be it day or night, you'll not find me half so kind as I am this night. Do you hear me?"

"*Ja!*" Christoffel nodded and backed up a few steps. Then with one final look at the angry man who was already crossing the Zyl Poort Bridge, he turned and ran for home.

7th day of Harvest Month (August), 1573

With the first appearance of daylight, Christoffel jumped from his bed, pulled on his breeches and doublet, and dashed out into the fresh morning. At the entrance to the stable, his vader met him with a look of perplexed firmness.

"Early, aren't you?" Vader Joris asked.

Without stopping, the boy tried to squeeze past him through the doorway. "*Ja*, well, it's a sunny morning," he said nervously.

Vader Joris grabbed him by one shoulder and spun him around to face him head on. "Wait a minute here, son. Any time you're this eager to get to work, you have a plan. You will tell me about it."

Christoffel squirmed. "Please just let me go. I have some drawing to do today."

Vader Joris pursed his lips and nodded, obviously in no hurry to bring this conversation to a quick conclusion. "Something I can help you with?"

Stifling a sigh and forcing a smile, he answered, "*Nay*, that's all right. I just heard one of the Beggars last night say they'd be moving their last ship out of the harbor soon, and I need one more good sketch." Surely he couldn't object to that.

"You've already done a hundred paintings since they began sailing in and out of Leyden at the end of Haarlem's siege. I need you to stay close to home today, maybe make friends with the boy who came in with his vader last night."

"Vader," he whined, "I don't know him, and he probably wouldn't even like me, and besides, they didn't come here to visit the innkeeper's family. Probably traveling through and anxious to be on their way."

"The truth of the matter is, they'll be with us for two or three more nights—here on some business with a friend of your moeder's in the city."

"Then let me get my work done now and go. Sooner I go, the sooner I'll be back. I just got to get this view to make my collection complete. Besides, this might be the day they sail away. Don't you understand?"

Vader screwed up his nose, scratched the back of his head, and sighed. "You could take the boy with you."

"What? You know a painter doesn't take a stranger along on a drawing spree! Let me go now and I'll be back!" The last person in the world he wanted to meet was the boy whose vader had frightened his favorite Beggar away.

Vader Joris raised both hands, shrugged, and looked painfully resigned. "All right. All right! But get your work done first, do you hear me?"

"*Ja*, Vader, that shall I do!" With a sprint, he was off into the stables.

Never had he applied himself with such diligence or speed to the task of brushing the horses and feeding all the animals about the inn. He did not dally to play with the new brood of kittens, nor kick stray pebbles across the skittle field, nor sit in the morning sun and whittle at a stick. He stayed as far as possible from the house and people who could slow him down.

He'd just curried the last horse and was feeding the chickens when he heard the Beggars shouting from the inn.

"*Ach!*" he mumbled. "Got to go now!"

He grabbed his knapsack from its peg inside the stable, then made his way around the edges of the innyard, over the stone fence, and onto the trekpath.

"I'll get there before they do yet," he told himself, feeling proud and smug and terribly wise. "I'll not have to talk to the stranger boy, and the Beggars will never see me where I sit to draw!"

In as short a time as he'd ever made the trip, Christoffel was creeping into his safe drawing place at the base of the ancient citadel overlooking the harbor. Mysterious tales of soldiers raining down flaming arrows on their enemies below sounded in his mind like some stories his beggar friends might tell. Only, Oude Man would have scars on his arms or legs or forehead to prove he'd been there and hadn't always stayed protected inside the citadel.

Christoffel walked carefully around the section of the wall that overlooked the harbor, searching for just the right view of the tattered old ship. If only he could go inside the citadel and view it through one of the arrow slits! He finally chose a spot that highlighted the ship's proud bulkhead, intricately carved with lions and sea monsters and twining plants. Once, long ago, it had been gilded with gold and painted with bright greens, reds, blues, and yellows.

Since its last encounter with a paintbrush, it had plowed through many a fierce battle with Alva's Spanish galleons in the river estuaries and city moats of the Low Lands and with the winds and waves on the high seas between here and Engeland.

So eager for his morning's venture that his fingers trembled, Christoffel perched on the rock ledge beside the citadel wall and removed the canvas and charcoal from his knapsack. Sturdy willow charcoal sticks they were, well baked in Vader Joris' oven, perfect for drawing with clear firm lines and for making enough subtle shadings to remind him how it should be painted. Quickly he outlined the prow nudging up against the bridge, the sail-wrapped masts and tricolor flags, the clean-swept decks where a flock of Beggars now swarmed about. He could hear their voices wafting on the breeze, smell the fishy musty harbor smells, watch the gulls soar and dive around it.

When he'd filled in the roof lines and trees and shrubs in the foreground, he held his work at arm's length and smiled. "Aha! Just the view I always wanted!" he murmured and heard himself singing the martial melody he'd heard so often, "Long live the Beggars! Oh, noble Christian band!"

From behind him, he heard an unexpected echo, "Long live the painter! So keen of eye and hand!"

He turned to see the boy who'd come to the inn last night. Standing several paces behind him, the boy was clapping his hands and laughing vigorously. Dressed in a plain rust brown suit of clothes, a profusion of straw-colored curls protruded out from under his feathered cap with the narrow brim. A mischievous light danced in his gray-blue eyes.

"Who are you?" Christoffel demanded.

"Robbin is my name," he said with a smug smile, "and you're Christoffel."

Christoffel held his painting behind him and swiveled fully around to face his uninvited guest. "Are you the stranger who came to my door last night and frightened away Oude Man?"

Robbin pointed at himself. "Me? Frighten anybody?" He laughed again, his voice like a brook running over stones, sometimes flying off in a high key skyward.

"You knew the old Beggar who was standing on the table telling his story, didn't you?" Christoffel looked at the boy with narrowing eyes. "You and your vader came to our inn with the intent of chasing him away. What did he ever do to you?"

Robbin raised both hands and protested. "*Hei!* Halt! I don't know anybody in this place. Never been here before. Your moeder's friend didn't have room to sleep us, so she sent us to *The Clever Fox Inn.* Believe me, that's the whole truth!"

"Humph! Just shows how much you know. Your vader knows the old Beggar, all right. Maybe not from Leyden, but from somewhere he knows him!"

Robbin shrugged. "He didn't say anything to me, and it's for sure I don't know him. Look, I didn't come here to make a quarrel. It's just that I think we're getting ready to go get my moeder and come live here, and I was hoping maybe you and I could be friends."

"Where you moving from?" Christoffel asked, bracing himself against the unknown danger that he felt creeping upon him from this too friendly boy.

Leaning close, half looking over his shoulders and lowering his voice,

Robbin answered, "We've been in Engeland for a long time. But my parents don't like it there. They say it's not home, and besides, my sister lives in Germany."

Christoffel looked the boy over. Skinny legs and arms, sharp nose and small chin. Probably not too good at heaving manure but could be a good runner. Warily, he muttered, "You really want to live here?"

Robbin shrugged. "I don't know yet. We've lived so many places I don't know where home is, except with my parents."

Christoffel sighed and wondered if they had anything in common to be friends about. "Can you paint a picture?" he asked at last.

Robbin laughed. "Nay, not too good at that. My sister's husband is, though—paints and draws and carves the most perfect little animals you ever imagined from a block of wood. I write poems to go with the paintings." He reached out toward Christoffel's canvas. "Let's see, what can I do with your picture? Maybe something like,

> Decks all scrubbed, flags a-fluttering in the breeze,
> The stout and mighty ship strains its anchor as it heaves—

"Nay," Christoffel protested, raising a hand. "Not now." Then quickly, eager to change the subject, "Can you ride a horse?"

"When I get a chance," Robbin answered.

"How's your skittles game?"

"Always wanted to learn. Would you teach me?"

"Maybe," Christoffel grunted. Then he watched his strange visitor reach into his pocket and pull out a scuffed wooden top and an eelskin whip. With nimble fingers, he wound the thong of the whip tightly around the top. Then with a flared twist of the wrist, he threw it to the ground and sent it on a gliding spin across the hard-packed dirt of the pathway that ran around the citadel. With a skill Christoffel didn't want to recognize, he whipped it into a long spin. When at last it stopped, Robin held up the whip. "Here, you do it," he challenged, a triumphant smile lighting up his thin face.

Christoffel took the whip with sweaty fingers, and picking up the now silent top, he wound it tight. Top spinning wasn't the thing he did best. At least he'd done it enough so he could send it spinning toward his challenger—wobbling just a little, but moving.

"Here, let me try it again," Christoffel begged.

The next one went better—more fun than he'd expected. Before he knew it, he and the new boy were laughing together over the top and its lively gyrations up and down the pathway.

Then just when Christoffel managed to send it on a perfectly smooth spin, Robbin nudged him with his elbow and begged, "Can I watch you paint your picture?"

Christoffel ignored him, cheering on the top. "Look, it's not wobbling a bit!"

Robbin was not looking. "I can always do the best poems while I watch the painter."

"You missed it, dumbhead!"

"*Nay*, I saw it. Really good, but I was just thinking about the poem to go with your picture. Can I watch you paint it? Please!"

Christoffel stood glaring at the boy. "*Nay!*"

"Why not?"

If only the boy would go away! Everything was fine as long as they spun the top. But to take him into the studio? That was too much! Besides, Vader Joris had one rule he never, never broke or even bent the tiniest bit—nobody was ever allowed into his studio.

"My meester won't let you in his studio 'cause you're not a painter," he said.

"Oh!" Robbin backed away.

Christoffel began stuffing his things into his knapsack. Aware that Robbin was chattering on about finding somewhere else to paint, he tried not to listen. Then his ears picked up the loud shouting of the Beggars, and he looked down to see the sails on the ship loosening and the ship slowly turning around.

"They're leaving!" he muttered. "Toward the Rhinesburger Poort."

"Who's leaving?" came Robbin's voice from behind him.

"The Beggars!"

Grabbing his knapsack, Christoffel bounded to his feet and skittered down the hill and into the street. In no time he ran up alongside the old creaking ship on the trekpath. The Beggars were waving at him and he shouted back, "Long live the Beggars!"

He followed through the street until the Rhinesburger Bridge was drawn. Robbin trotted along at his side, chattering all the way. Christoffel ignored him. At last the ship began moving through the harbor on the final stretch of its journey beyond the city. As he gave the ship one last wave and shout, he saw Oude Man standing on the aft deck shaking a fist at him and shouting. The wind blew the man's voice back into his face, and Christoffel could not make out a word.

He stood watching till the ship had slipped over the horizon and the harbor buzzed with its normal daily sounds. Then jabbing his unshakable companion in the ribs with an elbow, he snarled, "It's all your fault!"

"What's all my fault?"

"The old Beggar knows your vader—Dirck somebody, right?"

"*Ja!*"

"Well, they're enemies for some reason. So when the Beggar saw you with me and recognized you from last night, he thought I'd brought you down here to spy on him. He'll never come back to the inn, and I'll never again hear him tell his wonderful stories."

"Sorry," Robbin muttered. "Like I said, I never saw him before. Looks like he might be a kind of dangerous man to have around."

Christoffel worried a pebble with the toe of his shoe, kicking it ahead of him as he walked. "Look, why don't you just leave me alone?" he groused.

"I guess you don't want to be my friend, then?"

Christoffel didn't look up but thought hard for a long minute. "*Nay!*" he mumbled. "I never invited you to come trailing after me in the first place."

"Very well!" Robbin said with a saucy tilt of the head. "I'll go find one somewhere else."

Without another word or glance in Christoffel's direction, the boy with the wild blond curls scurried off toward the market.

"Good!" Christoffel shouted at the figure already disappearing around the corner. "And don't bother to come back!"

With a huge sigh and a smug laugh, Christoffel clapped his hands and took off running toward home. "Got to get out of here quick before he changes his mind."

———

Delft

It was late at night when Pieter-Lucas arrived in Delft and found Willem headquartered in the picturesque old building that had until recently housed the nuns of the St. Agatha cloister. Shut up in a small room in the far corner of the upper story, Willem sat alone, bent intently over a pile of papers on a large wooden table. A single oil lamp burned before him and cast elongated shadows on the plain white plastered walls.

"Greetings, Your Excellency," Pieter-Lucas said.

"Ah, you've brought me a message." Willem looked up, and the lamplight turned the deep wrinkles on the tired face into almost eerie shadows.

"Two of them," Pieter-Lucas said, putting the sealed documents into his prince's outstretched hand. "One from your brother Jan and another from Paulus Buys."

"Not more news of disaster, I hope." Willem quickly devoured his notes, looked up, and said simply, "Go to your rest for the night. I shall call you in the morning when I have new notes ready."

Pieter-Lucas slipped quietly out into the damp silence of the old "holy place" down the long hall and stairway to the kitchen, where he found a cook to give him a cup of soup and a crust of bread. Shortly he was sleeping soundly between soldiers, armed guards, and servants in the large sleeping room a few paces down the hall from the prince's room. All night long he dreamed that he was bringing Aletta and the children to Leyden. They were waylaid, first by robbers, then floods, and finally by a crowd of angry Beggars swarming off the ship in the Leyden harbor.

He awoke suddenly to the sound of excited voices. "Wake up! The prince needs every armed man in this room."

The room was dark yet, but one look out the single high window told him the sky was already turning pink in the east. He raised up on his elbows to see men scrambling to their feet, pulling on breeches and doublets, grabbing swords and spears, and stumbling out the door.

What danger could it be? He pulled on his breeches and padded across the room. Opening the door a slight crack, he peered out into the hallway. A crowd of soldiers and guards swarmed the way between their sleeping room and Willem's. Pieter-Lucas could make out two or three men in the middle, dressed in the dark capes and wide-brimmed hats of Baltic merchantmen.

"Merchantmen visiting the prince in his bed at dawn?" he muttered to himself.

"Smells like a rotten eel, if you ask me" came a voice from behind him. He turned to see one of the kitchen servants sitting up on his sleeping mat, hair sticking up in all directions.

"What happened?" Pieter-Lucas asked, running fingers through his own curls and putting on his cap.

"Don't know," the servant said, yawning and lying back down. "Heard somebody say something about supplies for Ludwig's troops."

"At this hour?" Pieter-Lucas shook his head.

"Ah, they comes and they goes at all the hours of the night in this place," the servant drawled. "Might as well go back to sleep."

Pieter-Lucas could not think about sleep. Whatever the business of the strangers newly arrived, they would give Willem something to write to his brothers about—or the burgemeesters of who-knew-which city, and Pieter-Lucas' services would soon be required. Besides, if the eel was rotten, how could he sleep while his prince was in any sort of danger?

He slipped out the door into the low-ceilinged hallway, still crowded with soldiers and guards shifting on restless legs. They broke the silence with a periodic grumbling between themselves, mostly about interrupted sleep, and punctuated it with an occasional jostling of spears against each other.

The wait grew long, until Pieter-Lucas' lame leg began to hurt, and he entertained a few grumbling thoughts of his own. When at last the prince's door opened and the merchants marched back through the lines of now attentive soldiers, he managed one more glimpse of them passing by.

Baltic merchants? he asked himself. *With those dark faces and mustachios, I would guess they were Spaniards with shifty eyes and some mischievous mission having nothing to do with the sale of army supplies or any other sort of goods.*

His heart beat wildly. As soon as the procession of visitors and their attendant guards had passed, he rushed to the door of the prince's room. The guards that met him there would not let him enter.

"The prince is not ready for you yet," one guard said, and the spears the men held high made their word believable.

Shortly, though, the door swung open from the inside, and another guard stepped through. He turned toward the sleeping room and nearly ran into Pieter-Lucas.

"*Ah!*" he cried out in surprise, "just the man I search for. Prince Willem asks for you."

He ushered him quickly into the prince's room, where candles were burning from every corner. The prince sat at his table, his nightcap still covering his head, scribbling on a paper before him.

"Excellency, you called for me," Pieter-Lucas said with a short bow.

"Ah, *jongen*," he mumbled without looking up.

Willem had known Pieter-Lucas for so many years that even yet now at times he called him *jongen*. Always it stirred something deep and warm in Pieter-Lucas, made him feel as if he had a vader looking after him.

"I need you to take these messages to my brothers for me."

"I am at your service—and the service of your armies."

Willem went on writing, mumbling as he scratched his pen across the paper, "Baltic merchants, indeed! Spanish soldiers! I knew it before I saw the whites of their eyes." After a long pause, he wailed, "Forty thousand guilders to buy a city! *Ach*, me!"

Pieter-Lucas snatched each disconnected line. For what seemed forever, he waited and watched and tried to make sense of it. He was only a messenger, and it was not always his privilege to know the nature of the messages that he bore. Sometimes it was not even good for him to know. This time he already knew too much to let it lie easily.

With a heavy sigh Willem laid down his pen, folded the letters, and sealed them.

"Is it a trap?" Pieter-Lucas ventured hesitantly.

Willem eyed him, frowning. "I think not. The men were Alva's unpaid troops—mutinying soldiers from Haarlem. Such things happen all the time. All the same, my soldiers will not quickly leave the impostors without a hole-peeping presence."

"Strange!" Pieter-Lucas muttered. "Ludwig's men mutiny before a battle. They refuse to fight till they have coins jingling in their pockets. Do Spaniards always mutiny after a battle?"

Willem nodded. "Always! Something in their blood is eager for the victory, they rush forward pell-mell and win the battle, then mutiny and render their general's victory fruitless. I still can't believe they offered me Haarlem—for only forty thousand guilders of unpaid wages for the soldiers Alva left to guard it." He shook his head.

"Then you will do it?" Pieter-Lucas felt his heart leap with hope.

"It might as well have been a million!" the prince moaned. "Even if we managed to raise the money, nothing would come of it!"

"You think they could make good on their offer?"

"If enough of the soldiers occupying the city are in agreement with the idea, and Alva doesn't learn of it soon enough to stop them."

"Would they?"

Willem grunted. "What I expect is that Alva will scrape the money from some helpless victim's barrel, quell his mutiny, and not only keep Haarlem locked up but proceed to put the siege in order against Alkmaar as well."

He picked up the messages and handed them to Pieter-Lucas. "One to Ludwig in France, the other to Jan in Dillenburg. They need to know this latest reason for watchfulness." He smiled briefly. "Carry them as quickly as possible. And in Dillenburg, take a moment with your vrouw. I pray God every day that this war will soon end so you and all our men can return to your families."

"Before the children are grown?" Pieter-Lucas heard the words escape from his heart.

"Before the children are grown." Willem nodded with a half smile.

Pieter-Lucas bowed, then hurried out into the newborn day.

CHAPTER FIVE

Dillenburg

10th day of Harvest Month (August), 1573

*B*athed in a late afternoon sun, the herb garden on the side of the Dillenburg hill buzzed with pollen-gathering bees and sent out a mixture of scents that set Aletta's nostrils to vibrating. No place on earth tugged more powerfully at her heart. Soft and quiet like the subdued profusion of blossom colors that gave it its gentle tapestry texture, it inspired peace and beckoned her to its warm comforting bosom.

Holding her swaddled baby to her breast, she stepped lightly on the gravelly pathway and let her long skirts brush deliciously against the wide-spreading bushes of lavender, rosemary, borage, and sage. When she'd reached the wide stone bench she called her Pondering Bench, she lay the baby in her lap and removed the herb-collecting basket from her elbow. For a long while she simply watched with delight as the tiny rosebud mouth of the sleeping infant pushed and pulled itself into an unceasing variety of shapes.

"Kaatje, Kaatje, what a treasure from Heaven!" Aletta leaned over and kissed her on the forehead. "If only God would show me how to heal your foot!"

She gazed into the infant face through a growing veil of moisture and shook her head as she blinked back the tears. From far back in her memory, she recalled the painting of "The Healing" done by Pieter-Lucas' opa. It hung above the altar in the Beguinage in Breda, and she had gone often to look at it when she still lived nearby.

The kindness on the face of Jesus as He touched the lame leg of a young girl seemed so real she felt almost certain He must be just down the garden path, waiting for her to bring Him her own crippled child. But when she looked, He was not there.

So reaching into the folds of her bodice, she drew out a tattered leather-bound book and began to leaf through its pages. "Tante Lysbet's herbal book! I've already searched every page," she mumbled, "and I've tried everything it has to offer—red lily roots roasted in embers and stamped with honey, juice of primrose leaves, ashes of grapevine wood mixed with oil of rue, oil of chamomile, cyclamen root roasted with oil . . ."

If Tante Lysbet, who gave her the book, were here, she'd know just what to do without even consulting it. Old Oma Roza would know as well. She'd learned much from both teachers, as well as from the two Countesses Juliana here in Dillenburg.

Wiping back the tears that flowed freely now, she argued with herself, "I cannot bring myself to tell the countesses. Pieter-Lucas does not know, nor has Mieke discovered it yet. Only God and I know. Dear God in the Heaven, I cannot talk about it lest someone tell me she has a demon causing the difficulty. That I could not bear to hear. Please show me what to do!"

She lay the book on the bench and set to unwrapping the sleeping child from her swaddling bands. On such a rare day of sunshine, perhaps it would help to warm the foot in its rays. Bit by bit she uncovered the arms, the belly, the legs, baptizing them with her tears as she went. Then wrapping the infant loosely lest she grow frightened, she took the foot in her hand, lifted it to her mouth, and kissed it. From a tiny vial of oil of ripe olives, she poured out a few drops, mixed them with her tears and a crushed chamomile blossom, and began to massage ever so gently. According to the herbal, some famous doctor named Dioscordes was convinced this would affect a cure.

In the beginning Aletta could not even admit that the stiffness in this ankle joint was a problem. Today, holding it up for the sun to kiss it, she knew she was seeing what her moeder love had not before allowed her to see. "Ach! Great and merciful God, 'tis more than stiff. 'Tis twisted! Until these constraining sinews are released, the heel can never touch the ground. She must always walk on her toes and be the brunt of endless cruel taunts and accusations from the pious souls who see some demon behind every twisted limb! Nay, God, nay! It cannot be. It cannot be!"

Grabbing up the child in both arms, she hugged the body to her and wept as if her heart had been pierced through with a quiver full of arrows. The swaddling bands falling around her arms in ribbons felt like blood dripping from her heart.

"Suja, suja, slaap!"

With sobbing voice, she sang the familiar old cradlesong, needing its consolation for her own bleeding soul. The child slept on, blissfully unaware of the tragic state into which she had been born, totally trusting the arms that held her in their tight embrace. A slight breeze began to blow the dampness from Aletta's cheeks, and from somewhere down the course of the Dill River, she could hear the faint roll of thunder. It sounded in her soul and stirred up a dark fury of unsettledness, anguish, and dread.

When she was so completely overwhelmed by her grief that she no longer knew where she was, she heard a gentle voice.

"Dear child, what has reduced you to such anguish?"

Startled, she clutched at the baby and looked back over her shoulder. Juliana von Stolberg stood there. Straight, tall, gray, the Lady of the *Kasteel* and moeder of Prince Willem, radiated compassion. If there was anyone on earth who could help her, this was the person. Yet something inside the grieving moeder would not let her say the simple words, "My baby has a twisted foot." So she continued to hold her Kaatje close to her heart and sob, almost as if she had no visitor.

The countess came closer now, resting her hand on Aletta's shoulder. "You are lonely again, is it not so? Your Pieter-Lucas has been away ever since this little one was born."

Without looking up, Aletta mumbled between sobs, "True, I am lonely for him, as always . . . but that is not the reason for my distress."

"What, then?" came the quick reply. The woman sat beside her on the bench and added, "Is there something wrong with the child?"

Aletta squeezed Kaatje as if both of their lives depended on it. The countess sat in silence, waiting. Her strong presence both threatened and consoled. The answer was simple enough, but did she dare to divulge it? Her mind raced with all the reasons why—or why not.

Always Countess Juliana played the part of protective, efficient moeder to every member of her large household. And her warm devotion to God and practical piety showed at every turn. Yet she was a Lutheran. Not a papist who refused to allow the reading of the Bible. In fact, under Juliana's direction, all who came to the dining hall for meals must listen to the reading from the Holy Book both before and after each of the six meals they were required to attend every day.

But Aletta was not a Lutheran in her heart, no matter how often she attended the Lutheran chapel on the side of the hill. Her vader and moeder were baptized by those who called themselves the Children of God, known by outsiders as Anabaptists. She and Pieter-Lucas would follow their lead and submit to believer's baptism themselves once the war was over and he was freed from his messenger duties. For now, they must live in the *kasteel* in Dillenburg and were expected to live like Lutherans.

Aletta knew well this included having Kaatje christened. But a Lu-theran christening involved baptism and was a public declaration that the child was Lutheran. The Children of God would not let their children be christened in another church. Neither did they practice infant baptism themselves. In their eyes, the rite was reserved for adults as an intelligent, personal witness to the world that they had identified themselves with Jesus Christ in His death and resurrection and were ready to live by His power and His precepts.

Yet nothing had been said about christening Kaatje, and perhaps nothing would be said. However, if Aletta talked about this physical problem, she laid herself open to a Lutheran suggestion that she could not expect God to help if she did not follow church tradition and have the child christened. On the other hand, if Aletta did not reveal her secret, there was nothing even Juliana could do to help, and Kaatje must suffer for it for the rest of her life.

Confused, torn, she looked at the woman beside her and sensed a strong desire, almost like an ache in the motherly heart to help. Little by little, she prodded herself to let go of the anxiety that gripped her.

Finally, kissing the child as if she were bidding her farewell, she lay her gently back in her lap and ever so slowly pulled back the wrappings. With trembling fingers, she lifted the foot and let the sunlight fall directly on it. "I tried for days to tell myself it was not misshapen," she began hesitantly. "I have massaged it continually and applied all the remedies in Tante Lysbet's herbal. But it grows no better. Oh, please, Countess Juliana, tell me not that she is hopelessly cursed!"

Juliana gasped, then laid a hand across Aletta's shoulders . "*Nay, nay*, a thousand times *nay!* That I shall never tell you, dear, suffering little moe-der."

"What more can I do? There has to be a way. I simply cannot let her face a life of ridicule and cruel suspicion, all on account of a twisted foot that makes her limp." The words poured out now. "I have read of cures that come from faraway places—wild citrull and laserwort and the fruit of the chaste tree. But how am I ever to come by such exotic herbs?"

The countess smoothed Aletta's hair with her hand and sat quietly while she rattled on. Then softly she spoke. "We shall search day and night until we find the last word of advice that has been written on this subject. My daughter, Juliana, has probably all the herbal books that exist in every language. We shall exhaust every possibility known to herbal healers." Looking directly into Aletta's eyes, she added, "But when all is studied and applied, as you know, we must place her into the hands of our Almighty Heavenly Vader."

"I know He will care for her as He sees fit," Aletta answered, trembling.

"And you will be christening her soon, when your husband comes home for a day or two?"

Aletta felt the stare of the gray eyes upon her. She stiffened and tried to cough down the rapid beating of her heart. "I . . . you must know, my beloved countess, that it is not the way of our people to christen infants," she stammered.

"*Ja*, I do know," the countess said, her voice heavy with disappointment. "But I thought it would be different while you live in Dillenburg where it is the way."

"A Child of God is a Child of God," she said, not looking up, startled at her boldness. "What we believe does not alter just because God opens a door for us to live with a kindly and God-fearing Lutheran family."

Juliana laid a hand on her shoulder. Aletta started. Was this the moment when the woman who had befriended her would turn her out of her household?

"I am sorry, Aletta," she said with feeling. "I did not realize how deeply you were committed to your family's religion. May God always grant you the courage to stand for that which you perceive to be right. In the meantime, may He have mercy on the child."

Kaatje stirred in her moeder's lap and, curling her bottom lip, began to cry. Aletta unlaced her bodice, then lifted the child to her breast and let her suckle. She laid a pinkie in one tiny hand and watched with delight as the new little fingers grasped it. "Her hand is straight and strong," she muttered. "She breathes deeply, her eyes move as an infant's eyes are created to move. Her vader thinks she is absolutely perfect. God help us on the day when he must know 'tis not so."

"Continue to massage the foot as you have," the countess said calmly. "Who knows whether the massaging and the relaxing herbs, oils, and juices may yet persuade the sinews to let go?"

Aletta looked up at her kind visitor. "I give you thanks for coming to our aid," she murmured.

Long after the countess had returned up the hill, Aletta sat nursing Kaatje and singing, "*Suja, suja, slaap,*" and massaging the twisted foot with oiled and tender fingers. When the breezes grew chilly and the distant clouds and thunder came closer, she swaddled the little body once more and started for home.

Halfway up the hill, a fine patter of raindrops began to fall, spattering her nose and creating little mud balls in the warm earth on the path beneath her feet. She covered Kaatje with her shawl and looked away to the hills that ran along the riverbank. There, a perfectly arched rainbow joined two hills. Each band of color radiated like a jewel.

Aletta nuzzled her nose into the bundle under her shawl and whispered, "Without the rain, there could be no rainbow, and without our pain, no healing. Someday soon your eyes will see the rainbow, and your foot will know the healing!"

———————

12th day of Harvest Month (August), 1573

The trekpath that ran along the banks of the Dill River called to Pieter-Lucas and Aletta in the long summer twilight hours after their evening meal. Both baby Kaatje and little Lucas had been tucked into their beds for the night and slept peacefully under the watchful eyes of Mieke.

"I'll hear the slightest peep an' run to their beck an' call," the little housemaid had promised. Shooing the young parents away with exaggerated movements, she scolded, "Ye hasn't had a minute to look into each other's perty eyes an' say sweet things since ye done birthed this here little girl. Now, git to goin', do ye hears me? I don't want to see ye, either one, again till th' late sun's done gone to snoring behind them hills."

Pieter-Lucas had exchanged chuckles with his wife all the way across the courtyard and down the hill. In the glow of a light rendered golden by the slow setting sun, he walked arm in arm with her, and neither of them spoke for a long while. The silence of the night and the warmth of her body next to his filled him with a fresh vigor such as he hadn't felt in a long while.

"Are you strong enough for such a meander?" he asked at last, looking down into the wondrous depths of his lifelong sweetheart's adoring blue eyes.

"One step at a time," she said, smiling. "With you by my side, I feel as if I could walk the whole world around on this magical summer night."

"Bearing children and suffering through the ague hasn't stolen a bit of your glowing beauty," he said, squeezing her tightly around the waist.

"Nor have your many travels taken aught from your great comeliness," she responded, reaching up to smooth her soft hand across his stubbly cheek.

He pulled her off the pathway under the umbrella of a trailing willow tree. Enveloping her in his arms, he gave her a lingering kiss while a gentle breeze blew their curls against each other's cheeks, and in his heart, the day grew suddenly young and bright and new. They stood rooted for a long while, exchanging gazes of admiration and basking in the wonder of togetherness that had been denied them so much for the past weeks and months.

Once more moving along the trekpath hand in hand, he heard her speak at last. "What did Vader and Robbin find in Leyden?"

"Ah, *ja*!" he answered. "They found the weaver's wife in the market-place, a jolly woman with beautiful wares. She sent us to her home, where the weaver was busy already making plans with Barthelemeus for moving the printery."

"Are they Children of God?"

"That they are."

"With a meeting place?"

"I think they have a hidden church somewhere, either in their house or the house of one of their friends nearby. The house was full of people. I never knew just what brought them all there, but evidently many Anabaptist travelers use the place as an inn."

"Have you found an artist in Leyden yet?" He felt her questioning gaze heavy upon him.

"*Ja*, and *nay*, and perhaps."

"Oh?"

He laughed, then told her about the boy who drew ships in the harbor and talked in riddles and told him where "The Last Judgment" was. "I think his vader is his teacher, perhaps, though he did not actually say so in those words. I believe the man is an innkeeper, and innkeepers are not artists."

"You sound so certain. Have you met the man?"

"*Nay*! It just doesn't seem to fit. Innkeepers are such uncouth creatures."

"Was the boy uncouth as well?"

"Hmm!" He'd never given that a thought. "He's young . . . about Robbin's age, I'd say, a bit cocky, maybe with a streak of rebelliousness. But uncouth?" He shrugged. "Not exactly, not the way I'd expect to see an innkeeper."

Aletta had stopped and pulled him down to sit beside her on a log. "What if I were to ask that boy about you?" she asked. "Maybe you don't quite fit his idea of an artist either. After all, life has not allowed you to live like one, so you're more likely to look like a messenger. Who knows how many things his innkeeper vader may be hiding, things even the boy does not know about."

Pieter-Lucas looked at her with wondering eyes. Such deep, wise thoughts came from that beautiful head. He nodded and smiled. "*Ja*, my clever vrouw. *Ja, ja*!"

She grabbed his arm in both hands and began excitedly, "Wouldn't it be great fun to rummage through the inn where they live and see what all its deep secrets might be?"

"The boy did mention a studio, but I don't know whether it's at the inn. Actually, I don't know for sure he lives at the inn. I just saw him going that way and surmised it. For all I know, he may live with his vader like a hermit in some old deserted farmhouse."

"Or his vader could be a famous painter whose name you'd know instantly if you heard it," she suggested.

"*Ja*, out in one of the surrounding villages beyond *The Clever Fox Inn*. You have stirred my imagination, Vrouw."

"And now," she said soberly, once more laying a hand on his arm, "I must stir something more."

"Whatever now?" he asked, not sure whether to laugh or brace himself for a sword.

"Two days ago the Countess Juliana asked me when we planned to christen our Kaatje."

He straightened. "*Ach!* And what did you tell her?"

"That it was not the way of our people."

"You said that to the Lutheran countess who gives us lodging?"

He removed his cap and ran fingers through his curls, waiting for her to go on.

"I was frightened, Pieter-Lucas. I knew not what else to say."

"As long as we are living in a Lutheran household, it is the law of the land that we should live like Lutherans. So the countess had every reason to put the question to you. What more did she say?"

"She said she thought I was courageous to stand for what I perceived to be right."

"She did not scold you or try to change your mind?"

"*Nay*. She only concluded with 'May God have mercy on the child.' "

Pieter-Lucas sighed. "*Ach!* I had been so occupied with my travels and the urgencies of the war that I had not even given this a thought. You're certain she was not angry with you?"

"Not that she showed. She is a gracious woman. I know not what she might say another day when her son Jan and the others have suggested otherwise. You yourself said it—it is the law of the land. Oh, Pieter-Lucas, is this the time to flee to Leyden?"

He saw a pleading look on her face and felt her fingers pressing his arm. Never before had he been so eager to swoop her up and carry her off without another day's delay. Mentally he was already arranging the carting of their few necessary belongings and the children—and Mieke, of course. With effort, he stopped himself.

"*Nay!* Not now! You're less than a month out of childbed, and rumors are still swarming about that Alva's men will soon put Leyden under siege. *Nay!* It would be foolhardy." He embraced her in silence and listened to her breathing grow audible and rapid.

Inside his breast he fought a monstrous battle. The dream of a lifetime—to go to Leyden—lay within his grasp, and his vrouw was begging him to take her. If she was right, there likely was a good painter there to give him the instruction his opa had once promised. Yet everything about it seemed so dangerous, so ill timed.

"Give me another week or two, and I shall be ready," Aletta begged. "We need not travel with great haste. We could perhaps stop in Duisburg along the way. And by then, my moeder may be in Leyden, either helping or needing my help. I am just so fearful of what will happen when someone besides Juliana remembers that there has not yet been a christening."

"I know. I know." He held her as tightly as if he feared she would get away and be forever lost to him.

Reaching up to stroke his cheek, Aletta said softly, "Remember how when we talked about Lucas' baptism, I said I would pray to God to find a way for us to do what He asked?"

He nodded. "And I laughed it off. 'Impossible,' I insisted. Yet He did answer, and we never even had to face the question with the child. So will you pray it once more?"

"I already have, Pieter-Lucas. I am beginning to believe God especially enjoys answering impossible requests."

He pressed her against his chest, stroking her hair and mumbling, "My dear, dear woman of so great faith! What ever did I do to deserve you for a vrouw?"

Then straightening, taking her by the hand, he coaxed, "Come, let us go home. Enough for one night, which is already growing dark."

He helped wrap her securely in her shawl, and they walked back along the trekpath and up the hill, talking about pleasant things—Lucas' latest sayings, Kaatje's winning ways, and their new life in Leyden.

By the time they had reached their apartment, the night was nearly stick-dark. Mieke jumped up from her sitting position outside the apartment door and ran to greet them.

"Vrouw 'Letta," she gasped and grabbed Aletta by the hand. "Your baby has a dreadful awful twisted foot! I seed it t'night when I changed her diapers an' put on clean swaddling bands. I swear I didn't let any demons sneak into the room while they slept. I swear it an' ye gots to b'lieve me!" Her voice was nearly hysterical.

Pieter-Lucas felt a sword pierce him through. His daughter with a twisted limb? *Nay!* Aletta had not mentioned it. This was Mieke talking— flighty confused Mieke.

In the gentle manner so typical of his vrouw, she was laying a hand on Mieke's trembling shoulder. Stunned, he heard her say calmly, "I know all about it, Mieke. 'Twas not the work of a demon, nor did you do anything wrong. The countesses and I are searching out all the possible cures, and God will touch her with His healing hand."

In the flickering light of the lamp she held, Mieke's eyes glinted with fear, and her cheeks sparkled with tears. "Was it th' *heatte* from yer ague what done it?"

"Only God can ever know that, and as I said, He will show us what to do to heal it yet. Now please go on to bed and sleep without a worry in your mind, Mieke."

The distressed nursemaid edged toward Pieter-Lucas and looked up at him with a pleading expression in the eerie light. "Do ye b'lieves me too? I swear to God, I didn't let no demons into th' room."

"Of course I believe you, Mieke. Now go on and get your rest."

Without another word, the elfin little woman scampered off into the night. Pieter-Lucas and Aletta stood quietly listening to the patter of her feet, then entered their apartment.

Pieter-Lucas held his wife by both shoulders and demanded, "Why did you not tell me?"

"I hoped it would be healed before you would discover anything amiss. You carry the weight of a warring world already, my husband. I never thought of Mieke saying anything. All this time she had not seen it herself."

He let her go and walked to the cradle. Kneeling in the rushes beside it, he gazed in the faint lamplight. So peacefully the child slept. Her breathing came smooth and clear. How could she be anything but perfect?

"Maybe the sinews just need to be loosened." It had to be so.

"For days I told myself that same thing. I searched Tante Lysbet's herbal book and tried all she suggested. I've spent day and night, ever since, massaging the tiny limb with oil of ripe olives and a gardenful of herbs, each of which some doctor has sworn to be a sure cure. At last, just two days ago, I admitted it was more than a stiff joint. It is truly twisted."

Rising from his knees, he sat beside her on the bed and slipped an arm around her. "You talked to Mieke as if you knew God was going to help you find a cure."

"I had to reassure her. And it is one more impossible thing I've asked Him for."

"Does asking help to dry your tears?"

"Sometimes," she said.

For a long while they sat shoulder to shoulder. Neither of them spoke, and the only sounds in the little apartment came from the rhythmic breathing of their two sleeping children. He folded and unfolded his hands between his legs while his mind folded and unfolded the conflicting messages it carried. How could he take his family away from the watchful care of the Julianas at this crucial moment? Yet how could he suggest otherwise to his vrouw, already so distraught over the child's deformity? Her faith was big—bigger than anything he'd ever seen before. But that big?

Finally, without looking up, he said as gently as he knew how, "My love, it sounds to me as if we dare not take Kaatje away from this place just now—not even two weeks from now. She needs the Julianas."

In a flash Aletta came back, "And if we do not submit to the baptism, what is to assure that they will not cease to be helpful after all?"

Pieter-Lucas sighed. "Is the wholeness of our child worth a baptism?"

Aletta drew back and turned to face him. "The God who asks us to withhold the baptism is the same God who will lead us to a cure. I cannot believe He disagrees with himself. Who knows what herbal healers He has waiting for us in Leyden?"

Pieter-Lucas looked up. Aletta had removed her cap and was pulling her hair free. It fell in golden cascades around her shoulders and framed her beautiful face. In the flickering candlelight, he saw there a powerful combination of sadness, conviction, and hope. Trembling before her, he stammered, "If you will pray me Godspeed, I will go back to Leyden . . . and find a plan!"

"God will show you the way," she corrected, and he could not argue it away.

CHAPTER SIX

Leyden

18th day of Harvest Month (August), 1573

*T*he cobbled streets of Leyden ran with rainwater, and Pieter-Lucas arrived at the house of Jakob de Wever drenched and weary. In no time the weaver's vrouw, Magdalena, had dried him off and found him a seat beside a roaring fire. An assortment of children played in the corners of the big room, and the long table in the center held several adults engaged in spirited conversations.

"You should have come yesterday when the sun was shining," the jolly woman said, placing a cup of steaming broth in his big chilled hands.

Pieter-Lucas blew ripples across the broth and sipped at it. "I would have been here several days ago, except that Prince Willem and his brother Jan have kept me running around with their messages."

Jakob had come from his loom to stand beside his latest guest. Balding in the front, his graying hair stuck out in unruly little tufts beneath a tight-fitting cap. The slight-framed man laid a hand on Pieter-Lucas' shoulder and asked, "And what is the cause for such urgency?"

He sighed and questioned for the hundredth time just how he ought to begin. Whatever else he'd done since he left Dillenburg four days ago, it seemed as if his mind had done nothing but rehearse this moment. Swallowing down a soothing draught of broth, he blurted out the question, "How soon do you look for Dirck and the others to move their printery here from Engeland?"

Jakob winced and pulled up a three-legged stool beside him. "*Ja!* I wish I could have talked them into waiting till all the troubles were resolved here. They assured me I had no idea how bad things were getting in Engeland and said they were coming directly. But"—he threw his hands heavenward and shrugged—"no one can know how long that will be. 'Directly' means one thing from here to Delft, or even to Dillenburg, and quite another from Engeland, especially in these times."

"There is a place awaiting them when they come?" Pieter-Lucas went on.

"*Ja!* A family in our flock owns a small warehouse with an upper story. It's just around the corner from here, and they've agreed to make it available."

"For living as well as setting up the printery?"

Jakob nodded. "For both." He paused and shook his head. "It's not very large, but may God himself be praised! If this is His doing, we must consider it marvelous in our eyes and give thanks for small provisions."

"I see," Pieter-Lucas answered simply and went back to sipping his broth.

"Dirck Engelshofen is your vader-in-law—is that not it?"

Pieter-Lucas smiled and nodded. "To tell the truth, my concern goes beyond him to his daughter, my vrouw, and our children."

Jakob started! "Oh *ja?*"

Pieter-Lucas turned the warm cup around in his hands and tapped the rim with his right index finger. "The story is long."

"All stories are long," Jakob interrupted. Then, thumping Pieter-Lucas on the chest, he added, "As you know, among the Children of God everyone has a story ten leagues long, and we close the door to them and go on. I ask no questions about your past, you ask none about mine."

"So I am learning."

"That way, when our enemies arrest us and put us on the rack to wring information from us about our brethren, we have less to give. 'Tis impossible to squeeze blood from a turnip, you know."

Pieter-Lucas shuddered. All through this war, he'd met people who suffered for what they knew and would not tell, and once they got away, they spent their days running for their lives. "Let me just say this much," he concluded pensively. "The time has come that I must remove my vrouw from the prince's *kasteel* in Dillenburg. She has a newborn, and we will not have the child baptized as a Lutheran."

"You and your vrouw are both Children of God, then?" He stared at Pieter-Lucas with penetrating eyes.

Pieter-Lucas gasped inwardly and struggled with his answer. Thanks to the war and Prince Willem's demands, neither of them had yet been baptized. He could not tell the man his long story. He could simply say, *"Ja!"* But was it true? When did a man truly become a Child of God—at the moment he accepted their creeds and trusted their Christ, or must he first be baptized?

Carefully he worded his answer. "We have been a part of the fellowship of the Children of God for several years now, and *ja*, we hold to the doctrines, the Christ—and the baptism." It had been a long time since anyone had asked him for such a statement of his faith. Every part of his body trembled and felt warmed all at once.

Jakob shook his head and wagged a finger. "You need say no more. How soon can you bring her here?"

Pieter-Lucas gulped, nearly choking on the broth in his mouth. In spite of all he'd said about finding a way, somehow the whole idea had remained only a dream. He and Aletta owned the dream and held it tightly. Jakob did not question the wisdom of the move but only asked, "How soon?" Could it really become more than a dream?

"I . . . I don't know just how long it will take," Pieter-Lucas stammered. "In fact, I still question how safe it is. Alva's men are threatening Alkmaar. Surely Leyden will be next. . . ." His head was spinning and his heart beating madly.

Jakob scooted his stool toward Pieter-Lucas, leaned close to him, and said urgently, barely above a whisper, "To be a Child of God means to live in constant danger. We may find refuge from it for a time, but never for long. We learn to trust in God with all our hearts and help each other along the thorny, muddy, robber-infested ways that we cannot avoid."

Pieter-Lucas watched the man sit erect, straighten his clothes, and look heavenward with eyes closed as if praying for wisdom. Then suddenly he looked directly at him and said, "Young man, bring her here as quickly as you can!"

"But your house is always filled, and the warehouse is small even for Dirck and his family."

"That means nothing. Our flock exists to help one another. We have many corners in this house and friends who help us with the overflow."

"Most gracious of you!" So much he offered! And so speedily!

" 'Tis just your wife and the newborn?"

Pieter-Lucas' head still swam and he heard himself as from a distance answering, "We also have a boy, four years old, and a refugee nursemaid who has attached herself to us."

Jakob was counting fingers and muttering to himself. At last he looked up and announced, "Very well. The sooner you bring them here the better for all involved."

Pieter-Lucas lifted a hand. "One more thing, Heer de Wever. My vrouw is a skillful herbal healer. Is there such a woman in the flock here with a garden of herbs? Or perhaps a place where my Aletta might plant such a garden?"

The man beckoned to his wife from the other side of the room where she looked after the children and called out, "Vrouw, come here! This man has a question which only you can answer."

Her long skirts rustled through the floor rushes, and she stood soon before them. Pieter-Lucas repeated his question. Her eyes grew vibrant. "Praise be to God in the Heaven! We have a couple of women in our group who have dabbled in the herbal arts and will be overjoyed to be joined by a kindred spirit who has had experience—and has learned from the famed Julianas, you say?" She clasped her hands excitedly.

"There is no garden, then?" Pieter-Lucas asked, his heart sinking a bit.

"There are several. In the Beguinage, of course, and with the other orders of nuns about the city. The best garden of all is outside the city, beyond the Zyl Poort."

"Near to *The Clever Fox Inn*?" Pieter-Lucas asked, his heart skipping a beat.

"Just this side of it, on the west side of the Zyl," she said, nodding. "Two solitary nuns—some call them hermits—have a shrine out in the fields. I've heard it said that they know everything there is to know about herbs and healing. Of course, they are papists. . . ."

"Herbal healing is a gift from God," Pieter-Lucas said.

"*Ja!*" Magdalena stared at him briefly, then wiped her hands on her apron. "Now, can I give you another cup of broth?"

"*Nay*, thank you!" Pieter-Lucas offered her the empty cup. "I must be on my way as quickly as possible to Alkmaar with more messages. I fear disaster awaits us there soon. I shall be so glad when this awful revolt is ended, and I can stop chasing after men who live by their swords."

Jakob stroked his trim beard. "I would ask how you fell into your position, but that's a part of your long story, right?" He grinned.

Pieter-Lucas laughed. "Indeed! I will say this much, though. If I ever had doubts about my vows of nonviolence before I was dragged into this messenger duty, they lie forever buried in the blood-soaked soils and waterways of these Low Lands."

Jakob leaned his hands on his thighs and looked at Pieter-Lucas with question marks in his eyes. "Tell me, when Prince Willem has won the land back from Spain, think you that it will be worth all the bloodshed?"

"On the day when we meet in our own building and call our people to worship with our own bells—ask me that question again!" Pieter-Lucas shook his head as he stood, pulled on his heavy cape, and stepped out again into the rain.

21st night of Harvest Month (August), 1573

Joris shuffled through the rushes of an empty dining hall between neatly ordered tables and benches. He pulled the towel from his waist, wiping away crumbs that didn't exist and straightening baskets and pitchers and salt cellars that already stood in readiness for guests.

"Too quiet!" he sputtered.

"At least you didn't have to drag a bunch of drunken Beggars out from under the tables tonight," Hiltje said from the doorway, "or clean up the foul vomit they left behind."

He dropped onto the end of a bench. "And how many of these quiet nights think you our purse is ready to endure?"

"Only one at a time," she said. "It's all life gives us." She laughed a rich warm laugh.

Startled, he turned and looked up. It was the same laugh he'd heard the first time he ever saw her. In this very room it was. In the undulating candlelight, with an amused smile on her face, she looked a lot the same tonight too. He chuckled in spite of himself.

"Remember the first time you laughed at me from that doorway?" he asked.

Coming toward him, she answered, "*Ja*, you were sitting in the middle of that bench right there." She pointed at a spot beside the next table. "You told a joke and it was so funny I had to laugh."

As she sat beside him, he patted her leg and mused, "You were a shy little innkeeper's daughter then."

"I thought you were the best-looking traveling merchant I'd ever seen. But when you looked at me, I was so frightened I ran back into the kitchen."

"Oh *ja*?" Joris laughed. "I only recall how you always managed to be in a corner somewhere whenever I was around. Anyway, if you hadn't, I would have rooted around till I found you."

She shook her head and laughed again. "You really hooked my heart, Joris. Guess that's why I can still put up with all your sputtering when you've got too much business and your grousing when you don't have enough."

"*Ach*, Vrouw! You always make it worse than it is," he protested. Then eager to change the subject, he asked, "Where's Christoffel?"

"In the studio."

Joris nodded. "Good place for him. I don't understand what's happening to that boy—always hanging around those Beggars, running off whenever he feels like it, painting a hundred pictures of the same beggar ship. And do you know, the whole time Dirck, the weaver's friend, and his son were here, I never could persuade him to say one decent word to either of them? Where'd he learn that kind of rudeness?"

Hiltje clasped her fingers together and stretched her arms out before her. "So long as that sour old Beggar, Oude Man, is his hero, you shouldn't need to ask."

"*Ja, ja,* I know." He shivered at the thought of the dark pointed beard and the glint of vengeance always shining in the man's eyes.

Hiltje sighed, raised her hands and eyebrows, and added, "Anybody could learn rudeness from him without half trying."

Joris drew little circles in the rushes with his toe. He knew she was right. Maybe she was also right when she'd said he shouldn't let those unsavory image breakers stay here anymore. But . . . he looked around at the empty tables and benches and scratched his head. *What's a man to do?*

"At least," Hiltje said, jostling his shoulder, "he's not a priest—nor likely to become one."

Joris grunted. That was one subject he wouldn't discuss with her. While they'd still lived in Brussels, Christoffel had a friend whose parents dedicated him to the priesthood. When the boys were six years old, Christoffel announced that he, too, was going to become a priest. That was too much!

True, they were Christians in this household. At least, that's the way it had to be. Which was why he'd insisted on naming the boy Christoffel, "Christ bearer." For his own part, Joris had grown up learning that being a Christian was the only way to keep his Jewish head attached to his shoulders. His parents both came from Spain, where to let anyone suspect you of being a hated Jew was an act of instant suicide. In fact, he knew there were people in Brussels who would have taken his head gladly had they known that he was in fact a Jew. He suspected the same was true here in Leyden as well. Only reason you didn't hear about it was that very likely he, Joris, was the only Jew living anywhere near. Only he knew it— even Hiltje hadn't a clue—and he intended to keep it that way!

Ja, it was smart to want Christoffel to act like a devout Christian. But to become a priest? He couldn't let him carry it that far. Surely his ancestors would rise up out of their graves and do something unthinkable to them all. So, in a hurry, he had begun taking the boy to Meester Pieter Bruegel's studio with him, and it worked. Got him distracted by the painting, and he never did talk about the priesthood again. At least so far the Beggar hadn't inspired him to give up his charcoals and paints. Amazing, given the way Beggars hated paintings and bragged about slicing them to shreds—in front of Christoffel, no less!

Hiltje looked sidewise at him, nudged him with her shoulder, and added, "Besides, your son's a painter!" Without warning, she hugged him around the neck and planted a quick but vigorous kiss on his cheek.

"Hiltje, stop laughing at our God-given talent," he said, gently prying her arms off him. "Our son gives promise of big things and—"

"I know, I know," she interrupted with exasperation. "One day he'll make us very proud! You've told me enough times, I probably keep you awake mumbling it in my sleep."

With an excited wag of the finger, Joris went on. "But the whole world doesn't know it yet, and if he doesn't get an artist for a hero pretty fast, they never will!"

"Then maybe it's time you find him another Bruegel."

"Like there's another Bruegel this side of Heaven!" He threw up his arms. It did no good to try to talk with this woman about important things—no good at all!

Joris stared at the floor for a moment. Then clapping his hands on his thighs, he pushed himself up off the bench and announced, "I think I'll go out and join the boy."

"So you're his Bruegel, eh?" she said, laughing again.

Joris waved a hand above his nodding head and started for the kitchen. He was halfway there when a loud knocking came on the outside door. Joris straightened his towel and apron and hurried across the room. With a candle Hiltje followed close behind, sputtering, "What decent traveler would come at this hour?"

"A tired one," he mumbled back.

When Joris opened the upper half of the split door, he found a young clean-shaven man, with horse in tow. His curly hair was askew and a worried expression furrowed his face. "Can you give me a cup of soup and a room for a couple of hours?"

Joris chuckled. "When I give a man a bed, I let him keep it for a whole night."

"I don't have all night. Just can't go any farther without food or sleep."

"You'll need a stable for your horse," Joris said, opening the bottom door and stepping out into the night. "Here, I'll take him around. My vrouw in there will give you some victuals, and I'll show you to your room."

The young man disappeared into the inn, and Joris led his horse to the stables. "Pretty hot and sweaty," he mumbled to the horse. "You've been riding hard. I'll send my son out to give you straw and a blanket."

He called Christoffel from the studio and hurried back into the dining hall where the guest sat hunched over his bowl, slurping up the hot soup and devouring chunks of black bread. Joris hovered near him, fussing over the table appointments.

"Haven't eaten all day, have you?" he asked.

The young man gulped down a mouthful of bread and answered, "No time. It's war out there, you know."

Joris stiffened and cleared his throat officiously. "What's the latest?"

"Don Frederic—Alva's son, you know . . ."

Joris nodded. "What did he do now?"

"He invested the city of Alkmaar with the siege they've been threatening."

"Haarlem all over again?"

The man nodded. "'Tis!"

Joris sighed. "*Ach!* Alkmaar's the last city between us and the North Sea! Alva's got all the rest. Is Leyden next?"

"Probably," the man said while Hiltje refilled his bowl and tankard. "When Leyden's magistrates heard the news, they hurried out and began spreading the word to all the residents outside the city to prepare to destroy their buildings now!"

"What?" Joris exploded.

"Can't be!" Hiltje added, resting both hands on a pitcher of beer.

Weeks ago, back before Haarlem fell, rumors swirled about every street corner that Willem was ordering that very thing. Evidently at that time the magistrates thought it was as ridiculous as the residents did, because they hadn't insisted, and nothing had been done.

"It's the only sensible way," the guest explained. "Any building around the city is an open invitation to Spanish soldiers to hide out. Gradually they'll take one after another until they've strangled the city."

"What of all the farmers and their crops?" Joris asked.

"What's ready will surely be harvested and stored in the city," the young man offered. "Who knows about the rest?"

"Without food, how'll the city survive?" Hiltje wailed.

The visitor had just put the last of his soup and bread in his mouth. He looked up, startled, and almost choked. With a faraway look in his eyes, he ventured, "That's what the Spaniards are counting on."

Then drinking down the last of his beer, the young man wiped his mouth on his sleeve and stared hard toward the innkeeper, his gaze still detached. "How far away toward the city is the nun's shrine and herb garden?"

Joris and his vrouw glanced sidewise at each other and frowned.

"Why do you ask?" Joris demanded.

"Just wondered if they'd be affected too."

Joris breathed deeply and answered, "They are about halfway to the Rhine and back off the trekpath a piece. Probably not the first to go—nor the last."

"And *The Clever Fox Inn*?"

"They won't come for us—not this far out."

"I also understand there's an artist lives out here somewhere with his son. The boy draws the most marvelous beggar ships I've ever seen. Will they be affected as well?"

Joris felt his legs grow weak. Who was this man and what did he know about Christoffel's drawings? What sort of trap was he setting for him? He gave his vrouw a questioning look, then shrugged and shook his head.

"Whoever pointed you in this direction was probably trying to mislead you. You know how people are, especially in these crazy times!" Joris managed a chuckle. Then promptly, before the young man could come up with more questions, Joris stood up and said, "I think you told us you were in a hurry for a bed."

"Indeed I am," the young man said. He pushed back from the table and rose to his feet. "With that fine warm soup in my belly, I am more than ready."

Joris led him up the stairs and to his room, the whole time muttering, "Thank God we live so far out! At least we'll be safe. But the rest? *Ach! Ach!* God have mercy!" Mustn't give this guest a chance to ask more questions. What did he really want? Was he indeed a messenger for the revolt? Or a hole-peeper? If so, for which side?

Dillenburg

22nd day of Harvest Month (August), 1573

At the end of the ten o'clock meal in the *kasteel* eating hall, Aletta gathered up her two children and headed for the door. The baby was crying for food, and little Lucas, distracted by a group of noble schoolboys, had to be held by the hand and forcefully urged along. Outside, a gusty wind swirled leaves and layers of skirt around her feet while one phrase from Count Jan's Bible reading swirled through her mind. *"God is our refuge and strength, greatly available to help in tight places . . . a strong tower is the God of Jacob!"*

If only she had her vader's Bible so she could reread the whole psalm! As Count Jan had read, she felt it pouring over her wounded soul like the oil of olives mixed with soothing powdered chamomile that she continually massaged into Kaatje's foot.

Little Lucas tugged at her hand and pointed toward the twin towers that loomed at the far edge of the cluster of *kasteel* buildings. *"Moeke,"* he asked in plaintive voice, "which one of the towers is God?"

Aletta started. "God is not a tower built of stones, *jongen*."

"The man said so."

Aletta smiled. How could she explain it to a four-year-old? Letting go of the boy and rearranging the baby in her arms, she answered, "We don't know what God looks like because nobody has ever seen Him with their eyes."

Lucas stared up at the towers, his nose screwed up and his eyes squinting in the bright light of the sky. "Then why did he call Him a tower?"

"A tower is strong, Lucas," Aletta began, "a good place to hide when somebody is chasing after you with arrows and spears." She knew he'd seen such weapons carried by the men who guarded the place and soldiers who arrived occasionally. More than once they'd had a conversation about what weapons were for.

"Oh!" He nodded, then looked up at her. "Is God that strong?"

"Even stronger, *jongen*!"

Lucas stopped and stared in wonder at the towers beyond him.

Grabbing him by the hand once more, Aletta prodded, "Now, come on, let's hurry home. Kaatje needs her meal too." She pulled him along, while he insisted on looking back at the towers and dragging his feet across the cobblestones. Deep in her heart, she cried out, "God, just how strong are you? I need a tower right now."

She had nearly reached the door to her apartment when she heard a voice calling her name and looked up to see the younger Countess Juliana following. "When you have fed the child, can you bring her to me in the apothecary? I must show you what my inquiries have produced."

Aletta's heart thumped wildly. Giving Kaatje an impulsive squeeze, she answered, "Ah, Countess Juliana! *Ja*, we come shortly."

Moments later Aletta sat nursing her baby, all the while rubbing the foot with herbed oil. Had the countess found a hidden cure in the pages of her big books with the leaves and vines and flowers engraved into their heavy dark leather covers? Lucas hovered nearby, leaning on her knee.

"*Moeke*," he asked at last, "why do you rub Kaatje's foot so much?"

Great God, must he know what is going on? So young he is, and with such a tender heart. How often before the child was born Aletta had taken him with her to visit the sick of the village of Dillenburg. Always he watched her carefully as she applied salves, bound up wounds, and gave elixirs. At times she watched his little face grow cloudy when one of her patients was in pain. Over and over he would ask, "*Will God make them well?*"

Now while she hesitated, he jostled her arm and added, "Is it a sick foot and you're trying to make it well?"

Aletta smiled gently down on her son and whispered, "*Ja, jongen*, I fear it is."

"What's wrong with it?" His eyes were big and round and filled with a mixture of wonder and fear.

"It doesn't move up and down like yours does."

She watched through a thin veil of mist as the boy promptly sat on the floor. Taking one foot in his hand, he moved it back and forth and all around. He repeated the process with the other foot, then looked up with a questioning frown on his brow, and asked, "How will she walk?"

Choking back a flood of tears, Aletta said, "On her toes, I expect, at least with the foot that is not well."

Jumping up, grabbing her arm with both hands and leaning hard against her leg, Lucas looked straight into her eyes and asked, "If God's so strong, can't He make Kaatje's foot well?"

She took the baby from her breast and laid her on her shoulder. As she patted Kaatje's back, she nodded toward her son and said simply, "*Ja, jongen*, God is strong enough to do anything He decides. That's why He gives us herbs that grow in the garden and people like the countesses who know which herbs to use to heal which sicknesses."

"Then the countess will give you something for her?"

"She will try. For now, you go play while *Moeke* changes the baby's diapers." So easy to dismiss the child and so quickly his mood changed as he stacked his blocks of wood and shouted victor's shouts when they tumbled. But what when he would ask her again about Kaatje's foot? How could she tell him that there was more to this than God being strong enough?

Worse yet, what could she tell her own fragile heart? Why were some children born with defects that even God did not cure?

She stared hard into the peaceful face of her infant daughter, now drifting off into a satisfied, worry-free slumber. "Be not so doleful, young moeder," she chided herself.

"Surely you shall not need to answer such questions again," she muttered under her breath. "Not ever again!"

Next to the herb garden at the foot of the hill, no place held more delights for Aletta than the apothecary of the Julianas. Larger by a lot than Oma Roza's herbal closet in her one-room house on the harbor in Emden, its wonders were of the same sort. Rows of shelves, drawers, and bins lined the walls, laden with boxes, bottles, jars, and baskets with every imaginable sort of powders, ointments, elixirs, crushed leaves, and blossoms. Fragrances mingled in the air, teasing the nostrils and sending the herbal healer into a frenzy of passion to linger here sniffing, mixing, packing. From the rafters hung huge bunches of drying herbs that rustled in the breeze every time the door was opened or one of the herbalists swept through the room.

Aletta crept over the threshold and found the countess seated at a table amidst piles of books. A young noblewoman, barely older than Aletta, with plump cheeks and upturned mouth, greeted her herbal assistant with what Aletta perceived as a bit more reserve than she was accustomed to. She indicated a seat at the table. Aletta sat quietly and clung to the child now sleeping in her arms.

"Have the sinews in that foot withdrawn any since last I examined it?" the countess asked.

"Not that I can perceive."

"You have continued to massage it daily, using all the various balms and ointments we have suggested?"

"Indeed! Some days it seems I do nothing else, and my apartment is redolent with their strong aromas."

"Can we disturb the sleeping lambkin that I might look once more at the foot?" Juliana stood and leaned over the child. She smiled with that special delight of the sort reserved for the admiration of infants. Aletta laid her on the table and unwrapped her foot.

"Truly a beautiful child!" Countess Juliana exclaimed with awe.

She lifted the foot with long fingers, then turned it and flexed it and carefully examined the heel joint. She compared it with the other foot, felt along the muscles of the entire leg, then wrapped it again with the blanket.

"My moeder and I have searched the books through and through," Juliana said. "We have found ideas and supposed cures."

"Anything we have not yet tried?" Aletta tried to mask her eagerness.

"Only the recipe for laserwort root, pounded with a little pepper and myrrh."

"Where shall we ever find laserwort? It grows not in these cold northern climes."

"I know. Quite honestly I must say, though, that I have my strong doubts about its efficaciousness. I did find one more item, small and tucked away in a book from Engeland—another idea from Dioscordes. He makes great claims for the drinking of the seeds of the ladies thistle as a 'remedie for infants that have the sinews drawne together.'"

"Oh?" Aletta felt a leaping of hope within.

"Again, I have not too much confidence therein. We might attempt it.

Ladies thistle seeds we do have in supply, and more will be forthcoming in a few months." She pulled a walnut-sized pewter box from behind a pile of books and handed it to Aletta.

Aletta clasped it in her hand. "Thank you, gentle countess. Tell me, have you and your moeder observed many children with similar maladies?"

"A handful, perhaps. My moeder has seen more in her many years at this art."

"Tell me truly," Aletta pressed her, not because she wanted an answer, but because she had to know, "how many have you known to experience a cure?"

Countess Juliana sat erect and breathed deeply. At first she looked away, then back. Aletta saw in the noble face a soft compassionate look and a painful hesitancy. Quickly, before the woman could force herself to answer, Aletta spoke again.

"You have never seen such a foot cured, have you?"

Both women sat in silence for a long while. The wind whistled around the corner and rattled the single window just behind the table. It sent a cold draft along the floor over Aletta's feet and up into her heart.

At last the countess stretched out a hand and laid it tentatively on Aletta's arm. "In herbal healing, we never say it cannot be done. Never! Did I not hear my brother read at mealtime this day that 'God is our refuge and strength . . . a strong tower!'?"

"You did. It appears I must cast all my confidence on Him in this distress. That I shall do."

Quickly she gathered up the baby and hurried out into the windy afternoon.

When the last meal of the day had been served and the children were both tucked into their beds for the night, Aletta sat on the edge of her lonely bed, not wanting to climb in. She heard a rapid tapping on her door.

Mieke! What could she want this time?

"Vrouw 'Letta, I gots to talk with ye. I jus done heared somethin' dreadful!" Mieke entered the room chattering. Her face was wreathed with lines of anxiety in the flickering light of the lamp Aletta shone on her.

"Speak softly," Aletta whispered.

"I isn't goin' to waken th' little ones, but ye gots to hear this."

Aletta put a hand on the trembling shoulder and felt the bones. "Has it anything to do with our well-being, Mieke? You're sure I need to hear it?"

"'Tis all 'bout ye an' yer family, I swears to God in th' Heaven 'tis!"

Aletta sighed. "Then I listen."

"In th' kitchen t'night, th' chief cook an' th' others what helps her was a-askin' me when ye an' yer man is a-plannin' to have th' christenin' fer yer Kaatje."

Aletta's heart quickened its pace. "What did you tell them?"

"I told 'em they'd have to be a-askin' ye b'cause I didn't know anythin' 'bout yer plan fer such a thing. Then they started in to complainin' 'cause ye hadn't done it when Pieter-Lucas was here last time."

"How would we have done such a thing then, even if we wanted to? He wasn't here long enough to plan, and I never know when he's coming."

"I told 'em that much, but they said they's been a-plannin' it already, jus' a-waitin' for ye to say th' word. So one o' th' cook's helpers started whisperin' that he was sure th' reason ye hadn't done it yet was b'cause ye was *dopers*. An' ye knows how Lutherans hates dopers!"

Dopers! It was a common peasant word for the Children of God. Unlike the word *Anabaptists*, it implied outright scorn. Her fears expressed to Pieter-Lucas had not been without good reason.

"You didn't tell them we were dopers, I hope!" Alletta's mind whirled with dizzying pictures of angry fists and shouts and scowls.

Indignant, Mieke made an outraged face. "Only Mieke th' street thief would o' done that! That ye knows right well. I'se not 'bout to say a word, not even if they gits me down on th' ground an' pummels th' life out o' me!"

"I know, I know, Mieke."

Mieke grabbed her by the arm. "Ye gots to git ye out o' this place now b'fore they starts their tongues a-waggin' all over th' *kasteel*!"

A look of sheer terror and earnest pleading glinted in Mieke's eyes. What could Aletta do? What could she say? Suddenly the words of the count's Bible reading came calling through the confusion and clashing of swords in her mind.

"Mieke," she said in as calming a manner as she could conjure up. "Listen to me and be still. 'God is a refuge and strength, ready to help in tight places. . . .'"

"Tight places? We'se sure 'nough in one o' them."

"The only place we can go from here before Pieter-Lucas comes back is right down on our knees."

Without another word Mieke dropped to her knees, pulling Aletta with her. She laid her face in the rushes and began to mumble, "Dear

Vader God in the Heaven, ye done told us that ye's ready to help us—here an' now—b'cause we'se in a dreadful tight place. I hasn't got any idea how ye can do anythin' 'bout it, but my vrouw 'Letta done reminded me that we kin pray. So here we is on our faces like they done teached us how to do in Duisburg. I guess th' rest is up to ye, God!"

Then nudging Aletta in the shoulder, she added, "It's yer turn now, Vrouw 'Letta."

How could she pray with Mieke listening in? The idea was strange and uncomfortable. For the most part in the assembly of the Children of God, except for the leaders, all prayed in silence. Yet Mieke waited, and God was surely with them, so she began, simply expressing the pain in her heart.

"Dear Vader in the Heaven, our refuge and strength and strong tower, we beg of Thee for deliverance from all our enemies and that not a hair of the children's heads will be plucked or damaged. And if it might please Thee, bring Pieter-Lucas home to us soon. In the name of Jesus, Amen."

Suddenly Mieke was helping her to her feet, brushing the rushes off her skirt, and directing her toward her bed. "Well, Vrouw 'Letta, I'se goin' to my bed an' ye best get into yers. We jus' might be a-seein' yer Pieter-Lucas come mornin' light."

Aletta smiled. "One of these mornings soon—soon enough!"

CHAPTER SEVEN

Leyden

23rd morning of Harvest Month (August), 1573

When the bells of Leyden's many churches began to call for worshipers, their insistent plea wafted out across the pastureland, garden plots, and waterways of the surrounding area. Almost instantly, the pathways came alive with pilgrims. Under a canopy of gentle mist, the people pulled cloak hoods over their heads and flooded through city gates.

Crossing the Zyl Poort Bridge, Hiltje moved a bit closer to her husband. As on every other Sunday, the feel of the city walls and cobblestones resonating with the sound sent a shiver up and down the length of her body. But this morning the bells seemed to be sounding a death knell. The burgemeesters' orders to demolish buildings had spread over the whole countryside. Fear loomed, huge and somber, an ominous bank of storm clouds—coming from Alkmaar and the North Sea.

Like a moeder hen, Hiltje reached out to make sure her brood followed as they mingled among the crowds of city dwellers and country folk making their way through the ancient streets. A disquieting spirit pressed against her from all sides, and she heard it in the low mumble of anxious voices.

Time was, when Hiltje was a child, that Leydenaars all went to the same kind of church and cared about the same things. But ever since the outburst of the new faiths—Calvinism and Anabaptism—the citizens began to divide up into groups. And since the revolt had begun, divisions were growing sharper.

Patriots lined themselves up on the side of Prince Willem and his campaign to bring freedom from Spanish rule. Loyalists supported King Philip's authority. Once the burgemeesters threw their official support behind Willem, a new name appeared. *Glippers* were the strong loyalists committed to doing all they could to keep Leyden both Spanish and papist. Most Leydenaars lay somewhere in between. They'd like to be free from Spain and generally thought it was all right for Calvinists to be Calvinists. They wanted to believe in Willem but weren't too sure, especially about his ragtag army of unruly Beggars.

When it came to orders to raze their buildings, all but the staunchest patriots in Leyden balked. That was a bad idea!

On this hazy Harvest-month Sunday morning, when the last bell had stilled its clapper, Hiltje sat with her family in the folding chairs they'd brought with them for the purpose. Even this hallowed spot seemed filled with apprehension.

The priest conducted the service as he did on every other Sunday. His obeisant flock proceeded to stand or kneel as the liturgy dictated. Hiltje's seasoned memory carried her through the rituals, while her mind drifted off in pursuit of things that really mattered. She always did this. Even when she joined her husband at the altar and let the priest slip a wafer onto her tongue and put her lips to the cool silver chalice of red wine, she was usually counting how many guests had to be fed back at the inn or making a mental list of things she would need to purchase at the market.

This morning, though, she found herself watching all the other worshipers, wondering how many of them, too, had wandering minds. Their beloved Leyden was in danger—a fear none but the gray heads among them had ever experienced before. Not since the days when her own moeder was a young woman had an enemy come near with arms and violent intentions. Even then, so Moeder had told the story, when their warlike enemies from the neighboring province of Gelre had swept through the surrounding countryside plundering and destroying homes, they never entered the city.

And now? The burgemeesters were ordering all who lived in those same surrounding areas to dismantle their buildings—with their own hands! What if Prince Willem won Alkmaar and turned Alva back so he never reached Leyden's environs? Who was willing to destroy their homes when they knew it might be for nothing? She felt the pressure of Joris' arm and shoulder, rigid and immovable against hers.

He, for one, will never remove a plank of wood or a spadeful of dirt from The Clever Fox Inn, she told herself. *In matters such as these, my Joris will take his chances.*

While the congregation knelt to the droning of the choir's chants, Hiltje stole a glance at her husband. Hands tightly folded, head bowed, lips softly moving as if in response, as always he was the picture of a devout worshiper.

Joris never talked about religion. But she watched him worship, listened to his exhortations to the children to *"make sure the whole world can tell by the way you speak and live that we are Christians of the most avid sort in this household."*

Often, too, he went out alone in the night, and while he never told her where he went or why, she knew he had a secret shrine out there somewhere—a spot he called his own and used it for some sort of evening prayers. She'd heard him mumble about it when he returned, thinking she was asleep.

There were times, however, when she felt an air about him that made her question something she couldn't quite identify. But then, what did she know about such things? In her family, religion was a matter for the men to ponder and decide.

"Women tend the fires and children and the purse, and just go with their husbands to church," her mother always taught her, *"unless they are called to give their lives to the church."* That had never happened in her family—not that anybody could recall.

She looked at her daughters, Clare and Tryntje. Going through each ritual with obvious eagerness, they were as devout for their seven and nine years respectively as she could imagine. Even she had been that way herself at their age, and she wouldn't want to deprive them of the benefits of such childish piety. Somehow it seemed to help make girls into strong women. She didn't worry that they would always be this way, though. Life had a way of balancing things out. Already she was teaching them to run an inn, and in time that would become their primary occupation of mind. They were her daughters, after all.

By the time the priest began his sermon for the morning, Hiltje already felt as if she'd been in this cold damp sanctuary for half a day. As on every other Sunday, the robed man was cajoling his parishioners to remain loyal to both Church and the absentee foreign King Philip. Hiltje bristled. Absolutely, she did not trust the King of Spain, nor did she trust the *glipper* priest who defended him with such passion.

"Must a priest of God preach to us about kings and swords and revolts?" Hiltje had questioned Joris more than once.

Joris never looked her in the eyes when he answered this question. "I guess the fate of the church—and the priest's livelihood and head—may be determined by this revolt," he had suggested.

"That doesn't make it right," she had countered.

"To a *glipper*, I don't think right and wrong make any difference," he answered with a strange tone akin to anger in his voice.

Hiltje wondered what kept him going back to church. Probably the same thing that prompted her to return week after week.

"Something a woman's got to do," she told herself, "unless she wants to be called a heathen and face the executioner's sword!"

This morning the priest grew eloquent, impassioned, then agitated as he harangued his flock from the old pulpit. "Your ears these days are being filled with subtle evil words from our burgemeesters. Dangerous admonitions they give you—to raze your buildings outside the walls, prepare to resist the forces of Alva when they come, to rally round the tricolor flag of the prince with its usurped lion pretending an authority never given by God or His Church!

"I command you to turn a deaf ear to it all, whether you hear it from the lips of a swaggering Beggar in the harbor or from Van der Werff, the chief burgemeester! For if you let it filter in and ruminate over it, you will be tempted to collaborate with Heaven's enemies. To all who yield to such traitorous ideas, I can only cry out in warning, May God have mercy on you!"

Hiltje looked at her son sitting on the other side of his vader. He tapped his foot nervously on the grave-slab floor, hands clenched into a frustrated double fist. He clamped his teeth and jaws and stared with fire in his eyes. Nothing could anger that boy faster than when someone made his beggar heroes out to be villains.

She stared hard at him until at last she caught his eye and smiled guardedly. "Hold on to yourself just a few more minutes. It can't last much longer," she tried to tell him with her eyes. He looked instantly away, and the priest went on with his seemingly endless tirade against the men whom he perceived as enemies of peace and tranquility.

When at last the service ended, the family picked up their chairs and hurried out the door. No one spoke a word all the way home.

They'd barely stepped inside the inn when Christoffel grabbed his vader by the arm and pleaded, "Vader, you can't let them take our studio!"

Joris replied in his most patriarchal manner, "Nobody is going to raze any buildings at *The Clever Fox Inn!*"

Hiltje chuckled and mumbled, "Just as I said—not a plank or a spadeful!" Then ordering her daughters to "Follow along now, girls," she headed for the kitchen.

24th morning of Harvest Month (August), 1573

The sun had scarcely risen when Joris found two men on his doorstoop. One wore the official dress of a burgemeester—dark breeches and many buttoned doublet, long black cape and wide-brimmed hat with a fluffy ostrich feather. The other's ashen gray clothes and bowl dangling from his waist identified him as a Beggar leader.

"Pieter Adriaanszoon van der Werff, Chief Burgemeester of Leyden," the first introduced himself.

Joris had never met the man but knew about him. A Leydenaar from birth, exiled for a time by Alva as a religious rebel, just last year he was not only returned but placed in his high office through Prince Willem's influence.

"Montigny de Noyelles, Military Governor of the city," said the other.

Joris choked down a gasp. This man's reputation did nothing to commend his cause. Profligate, overly fond of the bottle, sacrilegious—undoubtedly he was not the kind of Beggar Joris wanted Christoffel to fix his eyes on.

"*Ja?*" Joris muttered, staring through the open upper door, regarding his visitors with anxious reserve. What had brought them to his inn this morning? Surely they were not going to order him to raze his property! Not way out here! Not that he would do it, of course. But saying "*nay*" to the men at the head of the city in whose shadow he rested for protection—that was not so simple! These men could wipe him and his home off the land and into the Zyl River.

"May we come in?" asked the burgemeester. "We have a matter of importance to discuss with you."

Joris cleared his throat and asked, "What sort of matter?"

"A matter that affects your livelihood," the Beggar said quickly.

"If you must," Joris grunted and opened the door, taking care not to disguise his displeasure.

With pounding heart, he watched the swaggering bearing of the Beggar and the eagerness with which both men searched the room with their eyes before they seated themselves at one of the tables.

"You have a more commodious tavern here than it appears from the outside," said the burgemeester. "How many people will the rooms hold?"

Joris hesitated. Then gesturing toward the tables, he answered, "As many as we can feed at the tables—fifteen, twenty, twenty-five if we pack them tightly."

"You are aware of the prince's orders to raze all the buildings outside the city?" the Beggar asked, his voice forceful if a bit icy.

"Surely not all the way out here!" Joris fought to keep his voice from rising. His toes tapped the floor, and he could feel the muscles of his face twitching.

The burgemeester drew a circle on the table with his finger. "I wish I could agree with you. I know well what a service you have already rendered to many of the men coming and going on business with the revolt."

Impatiently the Beggar interrupted. "Of course you will be happy to comply and go to work immediately." He smiled too broadly and ended on a hollow-sounding note of triumph that rankled Joris clear to the core.

Determined to keep his voice as low as possible lest he rouse Hiltje—or worse yet, Christoffel—Joris placed both hands on the end of the table where the men sat. Leaning toward them, he said, "You must be aware that the longer my building stands, the longer I can serve your messengers and fellow Beggars."

He saw a fire smoldering in De Noyelles' leathery face. However, the man had scarcely opened his mouth, when Van der Werff was drawing himself up, putting his shoulder forward, and speaking.

"You realize it is a game of chance, Joris. I know full well that in the razing, you and your family stand to lose much, although we ask you not to destroy, only to dismantle it all. We shall offer you a place to store the planks and windows and furnishings inside the city. Once the threat of a siege is past, you can reassemble it as new."

Joris paced the floor beside them, his arms swinging in rhythm to his accelerating steps. "And where shall we lodge? How do we continue to gain a livelihood?"

The Beggar jumped in. "This is war! At such times we all live wherever a door opens to us with a place to lay our heads and eat whatever crumbs fall onto our host's table and pray for a speedy end to the troubles!"

"The other choice," said the burgemeester smoothly, "is no more pleasant. If the Spaniards decide they can use your inn to their advantage, they will simply put you and your family to the sword and occupy all this you have built with your hands. If not, they may still put you to the sword and torch the buildings. At best they would force you at sword point to operate it for their benefit and on their oppressive terms."

Joris pounded his fist on the corner of the table and faced both men with fire in his eyes. "When the last of my neighbors between here and the Zyl Poort have flattened their houses, I shall do the same. Until then, remember, I do nothing in haste."

"Either way, you strike a bargain for haste," Van der Werff protested. "How so?"

"If you wait from this end, you may have very little time to work at the other."

"Uncomfortably little time!" Noyelles added, a look of exasperation flowing out of his eyes and setting his feet and hands to stirring.

The burgemeester sighed. "When the day comes that the deed must be done at the farthest extremity, I fear we may have no choice then but to put it to the torch."

"And you'll have no time to retrieve any of your priceless possessions!" Noyelles finished.

"In the meantime," Joris spoke with growing agitation, "when our far neighbors in Alkmaar prove themselves better than Don Frederic and bring him to his knees in defeat, I will not have dismantled my life for no good cause."

"Do not fasten your hopes on so slender a slip of good fortune," the Beggar warned, his voice heavy with mockery.

"Indeed!" The other man nodded heartily.

Joris planted his hands on his hips and spread his feet wide. Assuming the air of the innkeeper and owner in charge of his property being be-deviled by men with official appointments, he said, "I repeat. When my neighbors have all complied, and when the noble houses Steenevelt and Zylhoff have been razed, you may come back here and find me busy with the hammer and spade. Until then, I remain in this place, committed to serving the revolt with rooms and victuals and the best Delfts beer in Holland."

The two men stirred uneasily on the bench. Joris watched them nudge each other and exchange unspoken messages with their eyes and fur-rowed brows. Finally they pushed themselves from the table and stood to leave.

Van der Werff sighed. "Very well, Joris. We have laid the choice before you. When time slips by and you do not hear from us, think not that we have forgotten. We expect you to be a man of your word."

"That I have always been, and I see no reason now to alter my ways," Joris said flatly.

"Just remember this," De Noyelle added, "we allow nothing to hinder the revolt—especially not the stubborn will of a paunchy innkeeper."

They turned and left. Joris shut the door behind them and instantly felt Hiltje's arm around his middle. He stood once more with hands on hips and feet spread wide in the rushes and said, "We shall never remove one plank nor one spadeful of dirt from *The Clever Fox Inn*!"

Hiltje squeezed him hard, and he thundered, "Never!"

Dillenburg

24th night of Harvest Month (August), 1573

Sweating and more bone weary than he'd been for a long, long while, Pieter-Lucas pushed open the door into his apartment. A flicker of anticipation quickened his steps across the floor to the bed where his vrouw lay sleeping. Peeling off his doublet and trousers, he climbed in beside her, enfolded her in his arms, and kissed her awake.

"Pieter-Lucas, my love, God brought you home," she said drowsily.

"Are you well?" he whispered.

"Perfectly well, and the children too. Oh, Lucas will be so happy to see you! You cannot imagine how much he misses his vader."

"Nor can you imagine how much I miss his moeder."

"Ah, but I do, I do, I do," she said and laughed lightly.

"You must tell me all that happened while I was away."

"In the morning," she said with a tone of motherly authority that always brought a smile to his heart, "when you've had a good night's sleep."

He needed nothing worse than sleep. With that he could not disagree. But with morning light he must leave again.

"There are some questions I must have answered," he mumbled, "and I may leave again early tomorrow."

"*Nay*, not so soon," she protested.

"Alva has invested Alkmaar—three days ago—and I know not what urgent messages Jan will need me to run to Ludwig and Willem. Tell me, how is Kaatje's foot?"

He heard his vrouw's silence and answered his own question. "No better, is she?"

"*Nay!* The Julianas have tried all they know. Only God knows the remedy, or whether there is one."

He held her close and nuzzled his nose and lips down into her hair. Did God know indeed? Pieter-Lucas' mind told him it had to be so, but in his heart he questioned.

"At least you are safe here for now," he whispered.

"I fear even that is not true," she protested.

"Just a little longer, my love." He stroked her arm gently.

"*Nay*, it is as I thought it might be, Pieter-Lucas. Mieke hears the cooks and the servants grumbling because we have not yet let them do a feast for Kaatje's baptism."

"What? I haven't been at home enough to do such a thing."

"Mieke says they already have all the plans for the feast made and are angry because we have not made a date for it to happen. Further . . ." She paused and he felt her warm moist hands gripping his. "Worst of all, they are saying that the reason we have not baptized the child is that we are '*dopers*'!"

"*Dopers?*" Stunned, he lay immobile and remembered the words of Jakob de Wever, "*Bring her here as quickly as you can!*" What was that he said about how the Children of God would always be in danger no matter where they chose to live? Was it worth it? If only Aletta were not so insistent, Pieter-Lucas would be willing to go through with the baptism, to keep the peace, until this war was over.

But he knew she would not budge. One time, before Lucas was born, they'd argued almost to the point of irresolvable anger over it. If anything, over the past four years, she had grown more firm in her convictions. So little time they had together. He could not let disagreement and anger consume their precious moments.

"Oh, Pieter-Lucas," she pleaded, "we must leave this place now before the Julianas have turned completely against us and put us outside their gate."

"Surely it will not come to that!"

"You said it yourself, Pieter-Lucas. They have the right to demand that we live like Lutherans in their Lutheran household. It is the law of this land, you know. We shall never be safe until we live with our own people."

"I cannot take time to move you there now."

"Did you find the group in Leyden? Are my vader and moeder on their way there yet?"

He sighed, reluctant to tell her what Jakob de Wever had urged him to do. She needed nothing to encourage the venture at this moment when he simply had to run quickly from place to place and could not be dragging a family along with him. "Your vader and moeder are supposedly coming soon," he admitted cautiously.

"Then we can stay with them!"

"I think their place will not be large enough. . . ." He let his voice trail off lest he'd end up telling her the whole story. Not tonight!

"Pieter-Lucas, if there's a group of the Children of God in Leyden, they will make a spot for us somewhere. They never turn out a refugee! You know that well, and you know that I know it well."

"I know, it's just that . . . You must wait a little longer. I will take you as soon as I can, I promise."

In the silence of the dark, they clung to each other and neither spoke another word. At last her arms released him, and he heard her breathing rise and fall to a different rhythm from that of the children across the room. Pieter-Lucas spent the rest of the night prying away at the gigantic perplexity. It loomed like an immovable boulder in the pathway before him, bordered on either side with a deep snake-infested swamp.

PART TWO

Flawed Portraits

We may find refuge for a time but
never for long.

—Jakob de Wever
Fictitious Anabaptist leader of Leyden

An eel caught by the tail is only
half caught.

—Flemish Proverb

One who forces people into the church is
like a man who, to augment the wine,
fills the barrel with water. He has
more—but what is it like?

—Sebastian Castellio
Counseil a la France Desolee,
1562

CHAPTER EIGHT

Leyden

30th day of Harvest Month (August), 1573

*A*ll the way home from church, Joris fumed with rage. He charged forward down the road and never spoke a word to anyone, leaving his family trailing far behind.

The storm had been brewing in him for months, ever since the Lowland revolt had turned Leyden's priest into a haranguing politician. Often on his way home from services, Joris had told himself that if he heard that *glipper* urge his congregation to come to the aid of Alva's bloodthirsty forces one more time, he'd be tempted to muzzle him. Then he'd walk off his anger, and by the next Sunday he'd be calmed down enough almost to forget how bad it had been.

Today, though, the priest pushed it too far. He had leaned over the edge of the pulpit, pointed his finger straight at Joris, and shrieked, "All you supporters of Willem and his unruly rebels are nothing but a horde of heathen *marranos*!"

No other word could create so much anger thundering in Joris' heart and mind! It was an ugly Spanish gutter word for swine. But it had an even uglier history.

Long ago, when the Spaniards wrested control of their country from the Mohammedan infidels, they decided to purge the land, as well, of the "filthy defilement of Christ killers," as they called the Jews. Many Jews, like Joris' grandparents, had converted to Christianity at sword point.

Not that it brought an end to their griefs. The Spaniards continued to suspect these *conversos* of practicing Judaism in secret. They taunted them with the despicable title of *marranos* and sent a whole army of relentless inquisitors to find evidence to prove that they were not genuine Christians. Eventually these "pure" Spanish Christians slaughtered or hounded Joris' people out of their confiscated homes by the thousands.

Never, never, never will I go back to that church, he promised himself. *If the priest must make a sacrilegious mockery of my people, he'll not pour it into these ears again!* At *The Clever Fox Inn*, Joris stood on the doorstoop smoldering till Hiltje and the children arrived. Then he shouted, "I'm going to my studio for the rest of the day, and I will not be disturbed by anyone, for any reason!"

"Joris . . ." He heard Hiltje pleading but shook his head, waved a restraining gesture, and marched straight through the hallway. Inside the long narrow room with windows stretching the whole length of the eastern wall, he bolted the door securely and moved toward a plain dark wooden chest in the far corner. He lifted the lid and stared at the assortment of canvases and sheets propping each other up on their ends.

"Got to pull them all out to get to the one I want," he grumbled, removing canvases, blank sheets, drawings, half-finished and abandoned sketches, piling them in fall-as-they-may fashion on the nearby table. "Exercises in futility, every one. And to think I let that priest put a Eucharist wafer on my tongue this very morning." He wiped his tongue on his sleeve and wailed, "What a traitor I've been."

When he'd removed the last of the papers and canvases, he yanked up the boards that formed a false floor beneath them. There it was! Gently he lifted out the package, wrapped in plain paper of the kind you might affix over a broken window but you'd never draw on, and laid it out on the table. He hadn't opened this treasure up since the day he'd moved here from Brussels four years ago and hidden it away out of the range of prying eyes and fingers.

His fingers stiff and sticky with trembling, he peeled back the wrapping, which cracked at the folds it had held so long. There, looking up at him as if with a silent nostalgic rebuke, lay the one piece of unfinished artwork he most loved and most dreaded, all at once.

"More nearly complete than I remembered," he gasped, removing it from the last restraints of its wrapper.

He held it up close to the window's light and ran his fingers lightly over the surface and let the awe seep into his heart and out through misting eyes. The cloud-threatened landscape was finished. A desolate windswept mountain loomed up out of a wide expanse of fields. To one side, a single tree with sparse foliage leaned precariously near to the precipice edge of the peak. Hugging its trunk, a bramble bush held the beginnings of an animal caught in its thorns. In the foreground, a crude altar of piled-up stones was also perfectly drawn, along with its covering of carefully arranged twigs.

The figures were sketched in outline form. Atop the altar, the body of a young man knelt with arms tied behind his back. There was also an outline of an old man standing in his patriarchal robes, hand raised. Above them both hovered the barely discernible form of a heavenly being.

Joris tried to look away, but the work drew him, and his mind began filling in the missing details. He saw the *jongen's* waistcloth fluttering in the wind, his eyes blindfolded, head bowed. The vader's beard and tear-stained cheeks seemed already to be fleshed out—and the angel's robe and wings and restraining hand and voice. But the object in the man's hand—*nay!* He could not, would not see it!

Feeling weak and trembly all over, Joris sat on the short bench beside the table and gazed, unseeing, out the window. The eyes of his memory carried him far away to the day he'd begun the picture.

In the Brussels studio of his once meester, Pieter Bruegel, a giant easel sat beside the slightly opened lead-paned window. It was the meester's favorite painting spot. A large painting was in place, set among rolling hills on the fringe of an unnamed Flemish city. For weeks Joris had been watching this massive picture grow, with its hundreds of Flemish peasants, nobles, and a few Spanish soldiers, all thronging up a hill toward a circle of execution. In the very center of the picture, a small space had remained empty. In this spot, Bruegel was working on the figure of an emaciated man in smudged green robe, falling under His cross on the muddy ground.

Jesus! "Procession to Calvary!" Joris had gasped in unwanted recognition.

Joris felt again, as he recalled the moment, that awful choking sensation that had grabbed him. "Meester," he'd begun without thinking it through, "only a handful of men pay Him the slightest attention. The rest ignore him, and if it weren't for the long clean lines of the cross He bears, no one would spot Him in the crowd."

Bruegel had not looked up but slightly nodded his head with the high squarish forehead and long dark beard.

With frustration building, Joris had continued. "I see children playing their games, a peasant man chasing his hat! Others squabble with each other or stroll and chat as if on some pleasant outing. All seem intent only on reaching the appointed spot where they will enjoy the entertaining spectacle. Does no one know—or care—that a man is to be executed at the end of their gala procession?"

Still not looking up, Bruegel had muttered, "Only his moeder and her friends care. I will paint them last."

He'd stood watching for a long while, then heard himself blurting out, "Who killed him? Lowland peasants? Surely not! Yet you have no Roman soldiers—or Jewish rabbis!" His heart was pounding hard and his mouth was dry.

Bruegel had put the finishing touches on Jesus' fingers curled around the cross above His head, then said, "We all killed Him."

"What?"

Bruegel had turned slightly and looked at him out of deep-set, thoughtful eyes. "There's a little bit of Roman soldier and Jewish rabbi in us all, Joris."

"Nay!" Joris had shot back. Too fast, he knew, but he could not stop it.

"It was my sin," the artist had explained, "and yours—the sins of every man who climbs the hill but never cares a whit!"

Something akin to anger had welled up within Joris. He should have been glad the man hadn't painted the scene filled with hateful, spiteful Jews, the way the Church seemed so fond of remembering the story. But he, Joris, was not a Christ killer!

In all the years he'd posed as a Christian, he'd tried with all his heart not only to convince the world so he could keep his head, but he truly wanted to be one deep down inside where no one but he and God could see and know who and what he really was. Otherwise, he never would have married a Christian woman. One thing always pushed him back.

That he was a sinner before a holy God, he readily admitted. That his sin had caused the death of an innocent man? Try as he might, he could not believe God demanded the life of a man. He'd provided animal sacrifices to make atonement until the Temple was destroyed. But a man? Never!

Although his parents had raised him to be Christian, and his vader never spoke of their Jewish roots, his moeder took him and his older brother, Frans, almost daily into a secret room and taught them fascinating things from the Torah. One story never left him—about Abraham, Vader of all Jews. God had asked him to take his only son, the son of promise, to Mount Moriah and offer him as a sacrifice. When he'd tied the boy to the altar and raised the knife to plunge it into his heart, an angel stopped him and pointed him to a ram caught in the brambles nearby, waiting to be sacrificed in the young man's place.

"This story was given," his moeder told him over and over, with an emphasis he could never forget, *"to teach us that human sacrifice is always wrong! No matter what you have to do in the church to keep your head, never forget the lesson of Abraham and Isaac!"*

After watching Bruegel paint Jesus into the procession, Joris had gone home and taken out his own canvas and charcoals and begun to draw his own "Lesson On Moriah." He worked on it nightly for as long as it took Bruegel to finish his piece. It was the only way he knew to cleanse himself of the traitorous feeling it gave him to spend his days mixing paints for the creation of the "Procession to Calvary."

Once Bruegel's painting was done, Joris could never bring himself to finish his own work. For no matter how he felt or what he thought deep down inside where he seemed powerless to undo being Jewish, he must protect Hiltje and their children. So he'd put the work away and gone on pretending to be head of a "most Christian household."

Today, though, feeling once more the need to make atonement for his treachery, he knew he had to finish the picture. With a mixture of excitement and remorse, he breathed in the familiar aroma of paints and roasting charcoal and gathered his materials together.

Once he'd touched charcoal to canvas, the figures took shape with amazing ease. He had soon turned the young man on the altar from a ghostly shadow into a living, breathing, sacrificial offering, with the face of Christoffel. The angel came next, with fuzzy indistinct lines and hints of facial features. The restraining arm had lines that bespoke strength, and in his mind he heard the clear forceful voice echoing from cloud to cloud around the outline of Abraham's head, *"Abraham! Abraham! Stretch not out your hand against the* jongen. . . ."

Then he went to the bramble bush and sketched in a young ram, its thick wool coat snared by the thorns, its mouth open, bleating plaintively. He drew a few stray tufts of wool affixed to other branches and found himself hovering over the animal, reluctant to leave him.

Where could he ever find a ram to make atonement for the awfulness of all his years of ignoring the demands of the Torah, pretending to be something he was not?

Repeatedly he tried to go on to sketch the face of the old man, the heroic vader—his own ancestral Vader Abraham. But nothing worked, and the ram kept calling him back.

"I need a model," he mused at last, then burst out laughing. "A model for Abraham? Where would a man find such a thing in this land of *Goyim*—non-Jews?"

Somewhere in that pile of sketches on the table was one of himself. Christoffel had done it. *Nay*, that would never do. "I am no Abraham! Nor could I ever obey a voice—not even God's—if it told me to sacrifice my son. But I must use a Jew, and I don't know another one this side of Ghendt. . . ."

His older brother, Frans, lived in Ghendt. Genuine Christian though he may be, Frans was the perfect living model of a patriarch!

Joris started. "Ghendt? How many days away is that? *Nay*, I cannot leave *The Clever Fox Inn*, especially right now. . . ."

With effort he fixed his mind on a memoried picture of Frans and tried to draw. But as soon as the charcoal neared the canvas, the image vanished, and he had no idea how to go. Maybe he had done enough for the day and should just put it all away.

For a long while he stood studying the picture. Again and again his eyes went back to the ram. "I shall give it a new name," he announced, " 'Vader Abraham and the Ram!' *Ja*, that is it!"

He slapped his thigh and chuckled. Then with gentle fingers and almost reverent movements, he wrapped the aging unfinished masterpiece in its fragile paper and replaced both the package and its false floor covering. He stood before the disheveled piles of papers and canvases strewn about the table, resting his hands on his hips. He sighed. "Dear me, what a mess I made in my haste!"

Reluctantly he began to reassemble the pieces and return them to their chest. About halfway through, a completed drawing of the Zyl Poort caught his attention. "First thing Christoffel drew in Leyden! How did it get into this pile?"

He carried it close to the window and examined it carefully. "Not bad, not bad! It ought to be hanging." Then glancing up at the walls already covered with paintings and drawings of all kinds and sizes, he added, "Instead of that abominable Beggar over there!"

Half grumbling, half chuckling, he carried the long-buried masterpiece across the room where next to the lineup of ships, the Oude Man Beggar stared down at him, so like the man to make him shiver. With an eagerness born of haste to finish the deed before his son might come pounding on the door, he held up the drawing and pierced a hole in its border, slipping it over the peg that held the Beggar.

He stepped back, rested folded arms across his belly, and laughed. Going back to replacing the contents of the chest, he said with decisiveness, "I must find a way to go to Ghendt. And until then?" He shrugged and put away his drawing tools.

Wiping charcoal-dusted hands on his dark-colored breeches, he stepped out into the hallway, drew the bolt with which he'd shut himself away, and sputtered, "Whatever else I do, I'll not go back to that *glipper*'s church! *Nay*, never!"

Midst the buzzing of a swarm of late summer flies, Christoffel jabbed his pitchfork into a pile of hay and dragged it into the horses' feeding boxes in the stables.

"Ought to be enough to keep your innards from growling at you till morning," he said, distributing the feed evenly.

Then piercing the ground with the fork, he leaned against the doorpost and looked toward the row of windows at the far end of the house. "Whatever is Vader doing locked up all alone in that studio?" he questioned aloud. "He's never done this before. He was so angry."

Christoffel picked up a stick and swung it around in little circles. Even in the service this morning, he could tell his vader was not happy. Of course, Vader was never happy in a church service. "Not sure why he goes to church at all," Christoffel said aloud. But Christoffel had never seen anger like this in his vader. Something the priest said about the people who supported Prince Willem seemed to sting like a bee in his breeches. He'd dashed off for home as if he couldn't get away fast enough!

All afternoon, the family had gone about their affairs without him. Everything felt strange—too quiet, like something was missing. Christoffel kept a watch on the studio door. Once, he lay his ear against it, listening. He heard nothing but a sound like the rustling of papers and a grunt or two. His moeder found him there and dragged him away. She sent him to the stable with orders to "Move like a greased pig and victual those horses!"

Now the horses were victualed and watered. "Surely he's got to be out by now!" Impatiently Christoffel threw down the stick and sprinted across the yard. Crouching beneath the windows, he raised himself slowly till his eyes reached the level of the hazy glass. He stared hard, making out the familiar forms of tables, chairs, easels, and chests—and the charcoal-burning oven in the far corner. No sight of the plump man who'd retreated there earlier.

Eager to go inside, as if somehow he might find a telltale trace of his vader's mysterious afternoon activity, the boy hurried in through the kitchen door. He heard his vader's voice booming from the hall where guests gathered to eat and talk. Elated, Christoffel scampered through the inn and let himself into his painter's paradise.

Everything sat silent and in perfect order. Brushes, charcoals, paint-pots, and palettes, all had been stowed away. Both painters' smocks—Vader's and Christoffel's—hung side by side on their pegs, with their flat tams over them. A sketch rested on the man's easel—a broad view of Ley-den from between the poplars that lined the banks of the Zyl in front of the inn. It had no paint yet except for a blue sky with billowing clouds of white and silver gray, just the way it had looked for days—maybe weeks. He moved closer and touched the clouds.

"Dry!" he said and wiped his finger on his doublet. "Nay, he didn't do a thing with this today."

Turning to his own easel, he stared at the beggar ship in the harbor. "Nor has he been meddling with my work! What, then? I heard him shuffling papers. Which ones?"

He wheeled around, his eyes searching the room—behind the tables and cabinets, along the walls where Vader hung his completed works. "Nothing I haven't seen a hundred times!" he spouted, gesturing his frustration.

"Ah, but I haven't looked in the chest! Why, of course! Where else would he find papers to make so much noise?"

He went to it, his heart aflutter with excitement and a twinge of uneasiness. Just as he reached out and grasped the lid, he noticed a piece of paper sticking out from behind the heavy old chest. He grabbed it up and gasped. "It's that sketch Vader did of me while I was working on my ship the other day! Aha! So that's it! He's started a new picture and used me for a model."

With renewed eagerness Christoffel opened the chest and began digging through the pile of sketches, drawings, and paintings. Not that Vader usually stored the pieces he was working on in here. It was the place they both went when they wanted to search out some face or animal or tree or building they needed to put into a scene. Yet today was different— whatever Vader had done, he obviously didn't want anyone to find it. So why not bury it here?

A thin voice from deep inside called to him like a warning bell, *If Vader wants you not to see it, then you are stealing his secrets.*

"Nay!" Christoffel protested aloud. "He never keeps his work from me."

Then why has he hidden it and not left it on the easel?

"To keep out the men who want to raze the building." *Ja,* that must be it. He nodded, impressed with his great wisdom.

But as he searched, he found only things he'd seen before—full-sized sheets with completed paintings, scraps with hasty sketches, some of his own early drawings with misshapen animals and crooked buildings, portraits of every member of the family—some with too-big noses, others with cheeks that didn't curve in the right places or eyes too close together. Nothing new! No new scenes using his portrait for a model!

The boy leaned both hands on the edge of the chest and grunted, "Where did he hide it?" He reached down to shove the stack of papers back into place so he could close the lid. But as he began, he thought he saw a curled corner of paper protruding from the floor of the chest along the line where it joined its back wall.

"*Hei!*" he whistled and pulled back the papers for a closer look. "It is a piece of paper, it is!" He tugged at it until he could feel it easily between his thumb and forefinger. "There's more of it under the floor. And the floor moves!"

Mad with curiosity, Christoffel began dumping the contents of the chest out onto the big table. Then, his whole being quivering with excitement, he pressed the floorboard at one end and watched it lift at the other. When he'd removed it, he discovered, just as he'd suspected, a large piece of the strange brownish paper wrapping something. It was old and brittle, filled with cracks along the folds. Carefully he leaned over the big chest and folded back the wrappings.

What greeted him inside the mysterious package was a frightening sketch in charcoal and ink. He stared aghast at a faceless old man holding a sharp knife over a boy tied to an altar. The boy had Christoffel's face! It was copied from the model he'd found on the floor. In the sky above them, an angel seemed to be holding back the attacking hand. Christoffel felt his legs wobble and his mouth go dry.

"Why, Vader?" he asked the silence. "What is the meaning of this . . . this awful picture?"

Hardly had he spoken the words into the cavernous chest when he felt a warm hand on his shoulder and heard his vader's booming voice, "Why yourself? If I'd wanted you to see this picture, I'd have left it on my easel!"

Christoffel hung his head and tried to fight off the terror beating in his chest. Holding up his own portrait in sketch, he said, "I found this on the floor and just had to know what you had used it for."

Vader took the boy by both shoulders. "Look at me, *jongen*," he ordered.

Slowly he obeyed, and the look he saw in Vader's eyes was like none he'd ever seen before. Pain and pity mixed with fear and something else he could not begin to define.

"Now, listen to me." The man's words were firm but earnest, almost pleading. "Some things an artist must do for himself. He hides them away because they are for no other eyes to see."

Christoffel felt an enormous guilt wash over him. He opened his mouth to say he was sorry, but instead he heard himself asking, "Will the man without a face kill me, Vader?"

Vader looked first angry, then confused. He shook his head. "*Nay, nay!* Abraham will never kill his son! This story is not about killing, but about rescuing. There is a ram in the thicket."

"I see, but for what?"

"For a sacrifice—don't you understand? The Lamb of God that takes away the sins of the world . . ." His voice trailed off, and he shoved his way in front of Christoffel and began wrapping up the sketch. As he replaced the false floor over the package, he added in a dreamy faraway voice, "I must find a face for Abraham. When I go away, that is why."

"Go away?" Christoffel stared at his vader as if he were some stranger he'd never met before. He felt his brow furrow into a mass of tightly crimped lines and muttered, "What do you mean?"

Vader closed the lid of the chest, then laid a hand on Christoffel's head and said simply, "One day soon I am going away in search of new faces."

"New faces, Vader?"

"New faces—for Abraham and Isaac. But I'll be back—you'll see!"

Scowling, he took Christoffel by the arm and marched him out of the room. They left the contents of the chest scattered over the table.

"New guests just arrived," Vader said in a flat tone. "A couple of horses in the stable need to be fed. And the sky grows toward darkness."

"*Ja*, Vader," Christoffel replied. He knew his job and went to perform it.

But his mind lingered in the studio. "Where will he go to find new faces?" he mumbled to himself as he went about his new duties, "and what must I do while he is gone?"

4th night of Peat Month (September), 1573

Sleep did not visit Christoffel all night long. During the evening hours, Vader Joris had scurried around the inn, lamp in hand, settling in the guests and attending to a hundred little matters, the likes of which he normally did only in daylight. Before the family had crawled into their beds, he'd given each of them a long list of instructions for things he wanted them to care for in the week ahead. Christoffel watched him with curious apprehension.

"This is the night he goes away," he told himself, and every time he said it, he felt a fresh terror in his soul. How would they manage without Vader? How long would he be gone? Where was he going? What did he mean about getting new faces?

Once he'd climbed up into his cupboard bed and begun pretending to sleep, the questions swirled around with dizzying speed in his mind. He felt every part of his body tighten into one massive knot. He heard

Vader coming and going all through the night.

Finally abandoning any intentions of sleep, he stationed himself beside the window at the foot of his bed and watched the man trudge out across the yard and into the stable.

"He's leaving!" he whispered and watched for him to emerge with his horse. Instead, after what seemed half a night's wait, he came out without a horse and returned to the house. Christoffel climbed back into his bed and went on waiting. For what little remained of the night, he heard the soft mumble of voices coming from his parents' cupboard bed in the opposite corner of the room.

Then, just when he thought he could not bear the muscle-cramping agony of this sleepless exercise another moment, he heard a rustle of feet outside his bed. Through the parted curtains, he heard a hoarse whisper, "I go, son, and leave you to do the man's work until I return."

"Vader!" he started, reaching out to him.

"I go," Vader repeated. "Do not try to stop me, son."

Christoffel sprang from his bed, but by the time he had reached the floor, Vader was gone. He hurried once more to the window. In the pale pearly grayness of a birthing day, he watched Vader Joris, with a knapsack on his shoulder, lead the horse from the stable across the yard and out of sight.

Christoffel crept as soundlessly as possible into the studio. He pushed open the door gently. The silence of this ghostly hour was heavier and more oppressive than he had imagined. In the growing light of dawn, he looked at the table. Every piece of paper and canvas had been removed. One quick lift of the chest lid revealed what he suspected. Vader had replaced everything the way it was before. Had he replaced the secret sketch in its fragile package? Or had he taken it with him? In either case, Christoffel could not bring himself to look at it again.

He looked around the walls. All the paintings were in place. The pancake lady on her three-legged stool at the market, the citadel on its hillock, the unfinished landscape on Vader's easel—each inflicted a sharp barbed memory on his mind. Even his own row of ships reminded him of his vader's presence, his vader's laugh, his vader's scolding. Only, in this row, something was amiss. Where was the Beggar?

Christoffel walked closer. Right there in the middle . . . in its place hung another painting. Squinting up close, he made it out. "The Zyl Poort!"

He yanked it from the peg and began to crumple the painting in both hands. Vader never would understand! Not only did he run off and leave Christoffel to do his work, he expected him to forget the Beggar as well!

His mind seething with a mixture of fear and anger and deep sorrow, he stood in silence before the Beggar. He detected an unexpected fire burning in the man's wild eyes staring down at him in the dim light. Slowly fear overpowered the anger. Loosening his grip on the crumpled painting, he looked down at it.

"Vader taught me how to do it," he mumbled. He opened up the wounded canvas, talking to himself as he smoothed it out. "It was on the first trip we made to Leyden to sketch. We brought it home and together we mixed the paints and spread them on. He taught me how to get the shadings just right and make the sharp outlines around the beams on the drawbridge and . . ."

A tear was trickling over his cheek. He rushed to the chest on the other side of the room and stuffed the painting somewhere in the middle of the pile. This was no time for remembering Vader and fighting back tears! *Nay*, he would board up the studio and go do the man's chores on his list. Why, he didn't know, but for some reason too deep to question or dislodge, he just knew he couldn't go on painting now. . . .

"Not until Vader returns—with new faces!" he mumbled to himself. He rushed through the door without a backward glance and locked it with the big key he carried always in his doublet.

CHAPTER NINE

Ghendt

8th evening of Peat Month (September), 1573

Joris crept through the streets of Ghendt on the fringe of dusk, feeling infinitely small in the shadow of the huge buildings that loomed over him from every side.

"City of giants!" he muttered.

In no other city had he ever seen so many massive towering buildings. There were too many spired churches to count, the largest fortified castle imaginable, and an ornate bell tower with a huge copper dragon on its peak. Joris stopped on the first step beneath the tower and gazed upward till the grand old spire melted into the clouds above. At that moment its historic bell began to ring out over the city filled with bustling citizens headed for home. He counted nineteen sonorous peals. Each one set his whole body to trembling from the inside out.

Footsore and eager to end his journey, he hurried on. Then just as a shaft of sunlight broke through the clouds near the horizon, he passed a line of paint-scarred cargo boats anchored in the harbor. Irresistibly, he paused on the St. Michels Bridge to watch the row of intricately carved workers' guild houses reflecting in the placid waters. This was the spot he remembered most in all of Ghendt. On his several visits to the ancient city said to be built by Julius Ceasar, he spent more time here watching the reflections and the boats than anywhere else. Yet he'd never drawn a sketch or painted a picture of it.

"Too grand to confine to a canvas what it makes me feel," he told himself again.

In a flash the sun was gone, and he felt the threat of imminent darkness. Turning his back on the harbor, he rushed through the remaining streets until he reached the tall narrow building that housed the linen shop of his brother, Frans, with the family's apartment in its upper rooms.

He stood before the door and tugged his doublet tails into place. From inside, in the rooms above the shop, he could hear the sound of laughing voices. Would he be welcome? Especially when Frans learned why he'd come? How would he feel about sitting as a model for Abraham?

Frans was as genuine a *converso* to Christianity as one could hope to find anywhere. Married to a woman from a long line of *conversos*, holding a position of prosperity among the world-renowned linen merchants of Ghendt, he lived a life of impeccable Christianity.

Joris kept remembering, though, that the two brothers had sat together at their moeder's knee and learned all the stories from the Torah. Always she warned them never to talk about her words—not even to each other. She spoke with sufficient severity to put the fear of Hades in their minds, and they'd never discussed even one of the stories, not so much as one time!

Six years had passed now since they had even seen each other. Only Frans could know what Frans really thought about it all. Joris nodded and felt an inaudible chuckle rumble in his chest. "Nor does anyone but Joris know what Joris thinks about it either! Like, what does Joris know himself? That's the real reason I've come here. I don't know what to believe, and as long as I stay with my *Goyim* vrouw in *The Clever Fox Inn*, I'm never going to find out."

Once more he adjusted his doublet, tugging down the tails that so loved to creep up over his paunchy belly. Then he held his breath for a long moment and knocked vigorously on the door. The sounds of merriment continued, and no footsteps approached down the stairs.

He knocked again, this time harder and longer. Above the increased beating of his own heart, he heard the laughter cease, followed by the scurrying of feet. He waited. Was something going on in there that they wanted to hide? Once more he knocked, now pounding firmly, persistently.

This time, after another swishing round of movements and a short space of silence, he heard ponderous footsteps. The upper half of the door opened, and in the fluctuating glow of lamplight, the bearded face Joris had come in search of filled up the crack.

"Brother Frans!" Joris exclaimed.

Frans pulled back the door far enough to let more light escape and squinted in his direction. "Who?" he asked. "Joris? *Nay!* How can that be now?"

Joris let himself laugh, a genuine joviality bubbling up in him, eager to be heard. "*Ja*, indeed, 'tis your little brother, Joris, standing on your doorstoop begging entrance."

Frans heaved open the door and gathered him in with a warm embrace. "Don't stand out in the cold and the dark. Come in, come in, and let my vrouw bring you something to eat."

The two men held each other by the arms and stared into faces once so familiar, now so long separated. Frans led him up a flight of short cramped stairs to the warmth of his living quarters. His vrouw greeted Joris with a quiet smile.

"Welcome to our home," she said. "I must bring you an evening meal." She hurried out of the room, and Frans indicated a seat at the table.

"You've not grown a day older since I left for Leyden," Joris said, marveling at the leanness of his brother's figure, the smoothness of his skin around the dark eyes.

Frans smiled a troubled smile. "I've no time, it seems, to think about the passage of days and years—and youth. You are looking well. Still keeping the inn, are you?"

"There's nobody else to do it, you know. And with a vrouw like Hiltje, what grew up there and knows the innkeeping business better than another on earth . . . ja, it goes well, brother—as well as possible with a war raging around all the corners!"

"Still painting landscapes?" Frans gestured toward a picture of the bell tower that Joris had done for him so long ago he'd nearly forgotten about it.

Feeling a bit of a flutter inside, Joris answered, "Always! Got it in my blood, I think—and Christoffel too. Does right fine work, that boy!"

Frans' vrouw placed a bowl of soup before him.

"What brings you all the way to Ghendt?" Frans asked. "You traveled alone?"

Joris grinned and nodded while he bit off a hunk of bread, dipping his spoon into the steaming soup and wondering how to answer. For the last four days he'd asked himself continuously what he was going to say, and he still didn't know. So he went on chewing. At last he answered, lamely dodging the real question, "Nobody would want to come all this way with me. Guess it's not too safe these days anyway, what with armies of different sorts roaming the countrysides, a-hunting each other down, looking for unsuspecting travelers with bags of gold a-hanging from their waists."

"Then you must have had a pretty strong reason!" Frans stared at him with a look that made Joris uncomfortable.

Joris dipped his bread in the soup and shrugged as he lifted it to his mouth. "You know," he mumbled, mouthing the soppy bread as he talked, "there comes a time when a man has a passion to get something. Nay, but you wouldn't know. You're no artist! Just don't you laugh at me, do you hear?"

Frans cocked his head to one side and a look of bewilderment spread across his long bearded face. "Very well. What is it this artist brother of mine must have so badly that he's braved four days of weather and war-mongers to get it?"

Joris swallowed down the bite of bread in his mouth, looked up, and said softly, "I have to have a face for Abraham."

"You're painting Abraham's portrait?" Frans didn't close his mouth when he'd finished the question.

"Not exactly his portrait . . . he is one figure in a scene. . . ." He wanted to go on and tell him what the scene was, but not now. The man was, after all, a Christian head of a Christian household, as he himself must always pretend to be.

"You couldn't find a model in Leyden?"

Joris leaned forward and spoke barely above a whisper. "Not a Jewish face!"

Frans stiffened. "Ah, but of course, of course. . . ."

Ja, he is indeed as Christian as I remembered, Joris told himself. *I only hope we can talk about it while I am here. But . . . not . . . tonight.* He sighed.

After a long cool pause, Frans began again. "You must tell me about your children. Mine have all just retired to their beds, and you will meet them tomorrow."

For the rest of the evening, they talked about children and the linen business and the state of the war. Then Frans showed him to a tiny cubicle of a room up in the attic, hugging the fireplace chimney. Joris pulled off his trousers and doublet and sat on the edge of the bed, wishing for the warmth and chatter of Hiltje. He reached over to blow out the candle on the table beside him, and something caught his attention. On a plate next to the candle lay half a sliced apple and beside it a miniature crock of honey.

Joris gasped! "Rosh Hashanah! Jewish New Year!" he whispered. "In a Christian household?"

With fingers trembling he reached for a slice of the fruit, dipped it in the honey, and slipped it into his mouth. Every year on this day, in the secret spot where his moeder told them all the stories, she gave both brothers apples to dip in honey.

He dipped a second slice and had it halfway to his mouth when he remembered. Before they were permitted to eat the sweet treat, Moeder repeated the words of some great Hebrew scholar whose long unpro-nounceable name he had never learned. He heard those words now as clearly as if Moeder sat next to him on the bed. " *'Awake, you sleepers, awake from your sleep! Search your deeds and turn in teshuva.'* "

"*Teshuva,*" Joris mumbled. "Meaning, recognize your sins committed since last we celebrated this holy day, feel sincere remorse, undo the damage, and resolve never to do it again. . . ."

He stared at the apple slice in his fingers. Then he shook his head and returned it to the plate, blew out the candle, and crawled into the bed. He spent a miserable night moaning over a host of sins he could neither atone for nor promise never to do again—all sins of acting like the Christian he now knew he could never be—nor could Frans!

Leyden

17th day of Peat Month (September), 1573

Hiltje prepared to go to market. She made sure her headdress was stiffly starched and neatly ironed. Then she hung her basket over her arm and gave her clothes an extra smoothing down as she walked out through the door. Since Joris had gone off on his mysterious journey to visit his brother in Ghendt, she especially sought out the opportunity to meet other adults who weren't gardeners, cooks, or inn guests.

This morning something didn't feel right, though, as she made her way through the street that ran along the Rhine River. The women she considered her friends clustered in tight little knots and whispered and gasped and turned their shoulders away from her as she walked past. Even the people who sold her their produce and lamp oil, people who usually asked about *The Clever Fox Inn* and the children, remained sober and distant.

What did I do? she wondered. True, she had not gone back to the Pieterskerk on Sundays as those who knew her had expected her to do. Joris had forbidden it before he left. No explanation, just a clear decisive order. "You are never to take the children and go back to that church again! Never!"

Even though they'hadn't discussed his reasons, she'd rejoiced at the new freedom this gave her—a freedom she'd long yearned for. So with no hesitation or apprehensions, she dragged the family to the Marekerk near the Rhinesburger Poort. For more than a year now, the Calvinists had been permitted by the burgemeesters to hold their services there. Hiltje was more than a little curious to know what they did in a sanctuary without images, paintings, chalices, or hosts.

Last Sunday she got her answers. They sang together—all the people, not just the choir—from words posted on a board. Psalms, she learned they were, passages from the Bible put into a rhyming form that made them fit the music! The priest—they called him a preacher—didn't lead the audience through the same kind of liturgy she was used to. Instead, he read to them from a big Bible the size of the preaching desk.

Unthinkable! This would never happen in the Pieterskerk! She thought she probably should be fearful because she'd always been told that reading the Bible was a heretical activity.

"Opens doors for demons to come in," she'd heard since she was a child.

Strangely enough, when the preacher read to them and then talked about faith instead of fear, she felt a kind of peace washing over her. Never once did he mention kings or swords or revolts.

The only thing she missed was her friends. She saw few familiar faces and practically no friendly ones—just cold stares. Now from her friends in the market, she received only hostile looks. Was going to a different church some sort of unallowed offense?

She drew her shawl around herself in the brisk autumn breeze and hurried through the market aisles between stalls of pots and breads and butchered hogs. With a scant shower of yellowing leaves dancing around her, she hurried to gather up the items on her list. Then cautiously, head held high, she approached Magdalena's stall of woven goods.

Not that she was prepared to buy anything there today. She plied her fingers in the luxurious softness of the shawl with the dashes of light that she'd so recently purchased from Magdalena with her lodging services. It would last her for a long time. *Nay*, it was not goods that drew her to the weaver's stall. It was Magdalena, her last chance to find a friend.

The weaver's vrouw greeted her with the same smile as always. "Hiltje, I see you are wrapped in my shawl," she said with warmth.

"Just the thing for such a blustery day," Hiltje said, hesitantly letting the tightness slip from her arms and neck.

Magdalena reached out a hand and laid it on her arm. "I'm sure you remember the man and his son whom you lodged for me in payment."

"Indeed! Fine guests—as are all those you have sent my way."

"He has returned."

"Oh?" Hiltje watched her friend closely. Was she going to ask for a room again?

Magdalena went on. "This time he brought his wife as well—a quiet somber little woman and an eager worker. They are soon to move into a place belonging to some of our friends. But it's an old warehouse that's stood empty for years and needs some cleaning and repair before they can occupy it. I thought maybe the man with his wife and son might be a help to you out there in your inn, what with your husband gone these days." A look akin to pity creased Magdalena's brow.

Hiltje didn't answer for a moment. "Most kind of you, Magdalena. Truth is, we are doing quite well. I am amazed at how big a help Christoffel has been—and the girls." She sighed. "Yet there are things that only a grown man can do, and the gardener is just that—the gardener, not an innkeeper."

"How much longer will Joris be away?" Magdalena asked.

"I wish I knew." All the bravado that had held her together since he left—was it really only twelve days?—seemed to crumple in a heap at the pit of her stomach. Out of her despair an impulse rose, and without a thought she heard herself begging, "Oh, Magdalena, last Sunday I followed my husband's orders and took the children to services at the Marekerk. I thought I might find you there."

The woman started, clapping her hand over an open mouth.

"Forgive me, friend," Hiltje said, recovering from her bold outbreak. "I should not have said that."

Magdalena swallowed, then leaned across the table of colorful woven cloths. "You did no harm. Tell me, did you hear words of life in the Marekerk?"

"Words of life? I know not what they might be." She leaned closer and dropped her voice to a whisper. "But the preacher read from the big Bible!"

"Not quite what you are accustomed to, is it?"

"I'd never even seen a Bible before. Strange, but when he read from it, I felt a peace roll over me like I never felt in any church service I've ever attended."

"Will you go back there?"

Hiltje sighed, raising eyebrows and hands. "The children may object. Christoffel said it was no church without candles and censors, and the girls missed the chants and prayers. Besides, it appears that I have lost all my friends by going there. Not a one of them would speak to me this morning as I passed them in the street."

Magdalena eyed her with a curious expression. "These are troublesome times, Hiltje. People don't know what to think when everything around them is changing. And . . . sometimes strange tales get blown about by the winds of their imagination when you change your ways, and they know not why."

"Joris made it terribly plain before he left that I must never go back to the Pieterskerk. Where—" She stopped. Something in Magdalena's reticent manner told her she did not dare to ask where she went to church and what it was like. "Where else shall I go?" she finished lamely.

"Where else did Joris tell you to go?"

"He didn't. I know there are other churches in Leyden, but they're all papist, and . . ." She could not go on. Magdalena may be a friend, but not close enough to spill her heart to. Best to change the subject. She clasped her hands together in front of her and cleared her throat. "If your latest guests need a bed, I shall take care of them until their warehouse is ready. Living in a warehouse? I hope that will be only for a time."

Magdalena grabbed her with both hands and, smiling enormously, said, "Ah, Hiltje! God will smile upon you for your generosity!"

"You may send them to me this afternoon. One man with his wife and son, right?"

Magdalena nodded, still smiling. Hiltje smiled back and hurried home, paying only scant heed to the onetime friends still clustered about the streets.

———

18th evening of Peat Month (September), 1573

In the fast-deepening darkness of late evening, Pieter-Lucas cantered Blesje northward along the Zyl trekpath and reined him up at the doorway to *The Clever Fox Inn*. He knocked on the door and wiped the sweat from his brow. Must he always come here at night? And in haste? At least he should find familiar faces this time.

After a considerable wait and the sound of voices, he watched the upper door gape, sending a yellow patch of lamplight shining directly into his eyes. The innkeeper's vrouw greeted him with a worrisome expression.

"*Ja*, and what will you have?" she asked in a voice neither soft nor discomforting.

"Good evening, Vrouw Innkeeper. Last time I came in search of a bowl of soup and a bed for two hours."

"I remember, and you nearly frightened my husband to death with your battle tales. We wish not to hear any more such messages tonight."

Pieter-Lucas chuckled. "*Nay*, but I come in search of a family of your guests—a man named Dirck, with his wife and son."

She eyed him uncertainly. "Who sent you here?"

"Jakob and Magdalena de Wever from the weaver's shop told me I would find them with you."

"And who might you be?" Her expression bore the intense scrutiny of an inquisitor.

"Dirck is vader to my vrouw, and he expects my arrival." Where was this woman's husband, and why did he not greet him at the door? He would have let him in instantly.

"Tonight? He has not told me to look for you."

Growing irritated, Pieter-Lucas raised his voice. "Dirck always looks for me, though he can never say when or where. I told you, he is vader to my vrouw."

"Welcome, son" came Dirck's voice from behind the woman. She lowered the lamp and moved slightly to one side.

"Fear not, Vrouw Innkeeper. You need not protect me from this man."

The lines in her face softened, and she turned, calling into the room, "Christoffel, come tend to this man's horse! Clare, bring out a plate of victuals!"

A lanky boy with darkish hair came toward him. It was the artist from down at the harbor! As he approached, Pieter-Lucas saw a flicker of recognition in the boy's eyes, then watched him cover it up and reach for Blesje's reins.

So he was right. The boy did live here. But the innkeeper he'd met on his last short visit—was he the *meester*? How much truth had he heard from these young lips? Or from the innkeeper's? Clearly the boy had no intention of letting on that they had met before. But this time Pieter-Lucas had come for an urgent mission. No time to be concerned about the painter or his son.

He motioned Dirck toward a table in the corner, saying, "I haven't much time and must have your help now!"

When they'd seated themselves and a young girl with pretty face and long dark curls brought him a plate of soup with a hunk of bread, he said to his vader-in-law, "I'm on my way to Dillenburg, with a stop in Delft to deliver my message first to Prince Willem before carrying it on to Count Jan. Things go not well for Alva's son in Alkmaar." He shook his head and chewed off a big bite of bread. "I still cannot believe the stories I heard. Alva has stuck his foot in a mad hornets' nest up there. You've never seen ordinary burgers, children, and housevrouws fight so hard and frighten so many Spaniards. Well-skilled they are . . . at dumping boiling oil, tossing burning rings, and pelting stones from the city walls onto the enemy."

Dirck smiled. "Then perhaps the tide is turning."

"Let's hope. Outside the walls the patriots have flooded the fields, and the Spaniards are growing daily more uneasy. Today Don Frederic could not entice so much as one soldier close enough to the city walls to launch a formidable attack. But that's not what I came to you for."

"What, then? How is my daughter?"

"That's what I need to talk about. This is neither the time nor place to tell you the reasons. You'll simply have to trust me when I say I must bring Aletta and the children back with me."

"I know. Jakob told me about it. Are you sure now is the time? We cannot move into our warehouse for a time yet, until it is cleaned and repaired. They've brought us to this place. Where will we put three more people?"

"Four more. Mieke comes too. Jakob and I have talked it over and it's all set. I must return to Delft first thing in the morning, and I need you to go along."

"I am needed here! The innkeeper, it appears, has run off to somewhere else for nobody knows how long, and I have been helping with things here as payment for our lodging."

Pieter-Lucas stopped eating and looked up at his vader-in-law. "This is a matter of life and death. Jakob will send one of the other brothers out to help if that's needed. It's just that Aletta cannot travel as fast with the children as she used to, and I haven't time to travel at her speed. You must go along and stay with her all the way."

Dirck scratched the back of his head and threw Pieter-Lucas a mystified look. "Robbin can take care of his moeder, if he and the boy that lives here can get along better than they did the first time we were here. Besides, I think Gretta and the innkeeper's wife are going to be friends."

"I leave here before the sun rises," Pieter-Lucas said. "Have you a horse?"

"That I have."

"Then we go. We have no choice!"

"I suppose!" Dirck shook his head forlornly and added, "Will life never be quiet again?"

Pieter-Lucas wiped the last of his supper from his face onto the back of his sleeve. He leaned as far across the table as he could reach and whispered, "That Christoffel—does he paint pictures?"

Dirck shrugged. "Haven't seen him do it."

"What about his vader, I wonder?"

"Who knows? Doesn't seem a likely occupation for an innkeeper. But I've heard stranger things."

Dillenburg

23rd day of Peat Month (September), 1573

Early on Aletta's last morning in Dillenburg, she watched the elder Countess Juliana descend the hill toward the herb garden. Then she pulled her shawl tightly around her arms against the blustery autumn chill and followed at a distance. At each step, she took in all the golden-hued sights and aromatic fragrances with especial attentiveness.

"This may be the last time I will look on this sight," she mused and brushed a tear from her eye. "For how many weeks now have I urged Pieter-Lucas to take me away from here? Yet now that the time has come, I begin to suspect how much I love it here. If only I could be content to become a Lutheran!"

She raised her head to the wind and let it caress her face and play with the pair of curls she'd allowed to hang free of her headdress. With her eyes she surveyed the broad expanse of green hills and fields and the twisted Dill River running through those unforgettable mountains rising up beyond. Her vaderland had nothing but church spires and clumps of trees to break the flat monotony of fields and nearly obscured waterways. A lump rose in her throat now as she thought of never again seeing these hills.

And the herb garden? There was no spot on earth like it. She set her sights on the neat enclosure and headed toward it with bounding heart. How many hours she'd spent in this treasured spot since Pieter-Lucas brought her here fresh from their wedding! Not a day went by that she did not come here to harvest herbs, to learn from the Julianas, to play with Lucas, to sit on her Pondering Bench and laugh or cry or simply ponder some weighty matter and cry out to God for help.

By the time she walked through the hedge of herbs and yellowing trees, she felt in her heart an incredible jumble of confused feelings. Gliding as soundlessly as possible over the hard-packed path, she walked to the spot where Juliana was snipping whole stems of goldenrod in full powdery golden bloom. The woman looked up, putting a stalk of the flower in her basket as she straightened.

"Will you miss this place?" she asked in her straightforward manner that never hedged the question of the moment.

Fighting back the flood of sadness washing over her, Aletta strove to be calm. "Very much, Your Excellency," she answered, her voice feeling all a-tremble.

"You shall be missed as well." The countess stood quietly for a long moment, not quite looking at her. Then she wiped her hands on her billowing white apron and said with studied cheerfulness, "You should have brought your basket to collect one more supply of herbs for the days ahead."

"I think you have already loaded me down with a sufficient store to hold us until we have found another garden in Leyden," Aletta stammered. Ever since her vader and Pieter-Lucas had arrived and told her to prepare to travel, she'd been filling her basket several times each day at the urging of both Julianas.

"This is the day of your departure, is it not?" The countess' eyes shimmered with a combination of a moeder's tenderness and pain.

Aletta nodded. "I've come to thank you for all the kindness you have extended to my husband and me, and our growing family—and to Mieke as well. I wish we need not move on, but . . ."

They both stood silent, staring at each other for a long moment, hearing nothing but the call of the meadowlarks and cuckoo birds in the trees around them and the distant surging of the Dill.

Then Juliana spoke in meticulously measured phrases. "When I kneel to pray in the *kasteel* chapel, your face shall always come to mind, and I shall remind Almighty God that you and your family are in need of His protection. Nor shall I fail to ask His mercy in touching the little one's twisted foot."

Almost unable to control herself now, Aletta struggled to offer the noblewoman her final words. "I pray that I shall grow to be the gentle and God-fearing sort of woman in my household that Your Excellency is in Dillenburg. And I look always to the day when your prayers for Kaatje will be answered."

She bowed herself in a deep curtsy. When she'd straightened, she gazed with an aching longing into the countess' warm blue eyes. Then she turned her back on the spot and hurried up the steep hill, with tears smarting her eyes, washing her cheeks and blinding her last sight of the long familiar way.

She must make haste. Pieter-Lucas would be waiting by now—with Lucas and Kaatje, Vader Dirck and Mieke. Leyden was a long trek away!

CHAPTER TEN

Leyden

29th day of Peat Month (September), 1573

On a gloomy afternoon Christoffel and Robbin started off for Leyden in a thick layer of mist that rolled up off the Zyl River and held them tightly in its cocoonlike embrace. It dampened their noses and lips and entered their throats with every breath.

"I love to walk in mist," Robbin announced, reaching out his hands to feel the moisture and his tongue to lap it up.

Christoffel looked at him askance. "Well, I don't like it," he said, wiping at his nose. "So why don't you run this errand, and I'll go home?"

"*Nay!*" he protested. "Your moeder sent you, and I just came along because walking is more fun with a friend."

Robbin thought they were friends? Christoffel had to admit that they came closer to it than they had on his first visit here. Maybe it was because Christoffel had given up painting and didn't have to listen to Robbin try to compose rambling poems to go with the pictures. He hated those poems.

Once or twice in the beginning, Robbin had asked Christoffel about his paintings, but he just told him he wasn't doing that anymore since his vader left. Anyway, they were both busy taking care of the animals and running errands for Moeder. She could find more things for them to do.

"Nothing more than your vader does when he's home," she reminded them every time they complained.

Christoffel wondered how there could be so much work when they had so few guests stopping at the inn these days. Even the Beggars had not been back to *The Clever Fox Inn*. They were fighting Alva's men, and Alva wasn't in Leyden. For the past week Robbin and his moeder were their only guests. Though he wasn't sure, Christoffel thought that was probably the reason he'd heard his own moeder crying in her bed a few times recently—that and the fact that Vader had been gone so long. He shook his head vigorously. Mustn't let his mind wander off in that direction.

"Race you to the Rhine," he challenged his companion, "if you dare!"

Instantly Robbin began to run, and Christoffel regretted having suggested it. In his impetuousness he'd forgotten how good a runner the boy was—and about the mist. The way was both slippery and hard to see. But he couldn't back down now. Fortunately the corner came quickly, and he reached there only a step or two behind Robbin.

From here the outline of the city began to loom up through the shadowy mists that grew abruptly thinner. By the time they'd reached the bridge, only a few wisps wrapped themselves around their feet, and the sun was actually shining. They rattled across the wooden planks into the city and headed for the first corner that would lead them up and down short little streets to the shop where they'd buy the loaves of fresh bread from the baker at the sign of The Pretzel.

At the corner a group of boys a year or two older than Christoffel and Robbin were milling about under a spreading oak tree with crimson leaves. The moment they spotted them, they spread out to block their way. Pointing at Christoffel, they began to laugh.

"*Marrano*," they shouted. "There goes the *marrano* with his *doper* friend!"

"I am not a *marrano*!" Christoffel protested. "And he's no *doper*!"

Christoffel had no idea what either word meant. He'd heard the first one only once in church on that Sunday when the priest scolded the people because they were supporting Prince Willem and the revolt. He meant to ask his vader later what it meant, but that was the day that Vader was too angry to talk to anybody. When he asked his moeder, she had gasped and grabbed him by both shoulders.

"*Never utter that word again!*" she had ordered him with daggers in her eyes.

As for *doper*, he'd only heard the name used in scandalous whispers, and again, his moeder simply told him it was a word no decent boy would ever mouth.

The boys that stood before them now, using such bad language, were not decent boys. That he already knew. He'd heard many stories about their rowdy ways and how they'd beaten up on younger, smaller boys. In fact, he'd often seen them roaming the streets of Leyden, but they'd never paid him so much as an eyeblink of a mind before.

Robbin spoke up now. "We have an errand to run down that street."

The whole parcel of boys broke out into uproarious mocking laughter.

"You think we'll let you go down our streets? Ha! Ha!" they snarled and puffed. "We are sent here to guard our beautiful city from all such lepers as you two—both of you as filthy as a herd of *marranos*!"

From the mob came a loud cry that echoed up and down the street. "Joris the Innkeeper ran away because he is a *marrano*, a Christ killer. And you'd best run, too, or we'll tie you to a stake and turn you into a raging torch!"

"Just like we'll do to Joris if he ever comes back!" shouted another, echoed by more laughter.

Intending to disregard them and skirt the mob of hecklers, Christoffel stepped forward. But they stood immovable, a solid mass of bodies rooted to the cobblestones. "Go back to your *Clever Fox Inn*!" taunted the tallest of them. He had a long nose, bushy eyebrows, and hands so large they frightened Christoffel.

"Stinky, mucky, squealing pigsty!" came another shout.

"*Marranos! Dopers!*" shouted the others in cacophonous confusion.

Then as one long body with interlocking arms and many legs and monstrous heads, they advanced, pushing Robbin and Christoffel back the way they'd come.

Steadily they pushed on, moving to the rhythm of their bloodcurdling shouts. "Go home, *marranos*, go home! Go home to your pigsty, go home!"

Irresistibly they forced them onto the bridge. Christoffel and Robbin had no choice but to retreat.

"Isn't there another gate into the city?" Robbin asked.

"*Ja*, there's a bunch of them, but what good will that do? There's no secret passage to any of them, and by the time we get to one, the rowdies will be there waiting for us."

"Your moeder needs the bread."

"It'll just have to wait!" Christoffel said with all the finality he could command.

By the time they had returned to the trekpath, the mist had lifted, though it still veiled the sun, turning it a watery pale yellow.

"Tell me," Robbin asked, "why did they call your vader a *marrano*?"

Christoffel shrugged. "Who knows? Just needed something to do, I guess."

"It's not true, is it?"

"Of course not!" Christoffel said impatiently and hoped the boy would never ask him what the word meant.

The rest of the way home he engaged Robbin in a perpetual conversation about anything that happened to pop into his mind. At times he didn't even know whether what he had to say made sense. All that mattered was that the dreaded subject of his vader and the *marranos* never came up again.

At home Christoffel sought out his moeder immediately and tugged her into the family's sleeping room. She followed, protesting all the way, "I have no time for this, *jongen!*"

When he'd shut the door and stood facing her, she questioned, "Now, what is the meaning of this?"

"Moeder, what is a *marrano*?" he asked, his heart beating with frantic desperation in his doublet.

"Where did you hear that word?" she demanded.

"You know Cornelis and his mob of naughty boys?"

"You don't listen to their language, son. I've told you that a hundred times."

"Moeder, listen! They blocked our way and would not let us pass into the city streets. They chased us back across the bridge, and all the time they jeered at us, calling us *marranos*. They said my vader is a *marrano* and that's why he ran away, and if I ever go back to the city, they'll tie me to a stake and turn me into a torch!"

"*Nay!*" Moeder clapped a hand over her mouth and gasped. For a long while she stood in silence, and Christoffel watched her chest rise and fall with heavy breathing.

"Tell me what the awful word means," Christoffel persisted.

"You only need to know that it is a bad, bad word, and that what the boys said about your vader is a big, big lie."

"They also said *The Clever Fox Inn* was a stinky pigsty and that Robbin is a *doper!*"

"More lies!" she said.

He saw a look of terror on her face. After a long pause she spoke, her manner detached, her eyes not looking at him. "I shall go for the bread myself."

Christoffel grabbed her by the arm and pleaded, "Don't go, Moeder. They'll call you by that awful name, too, maybe even beat you!"

Calmly she extended her hand toward him and spoke with an urgency Christoffel could not ignore. "Now, give me the coins. I go!"

He reached into his pocket and pulled out the battered pieces of silver he'd carried to Leyden and back. Hesitantly, feeling guilty for not somehow stopping her from going, he laid them in her hand and listened to the ominous sound of their clinking together. Without a word, she took them and fled through the door.

Hiltje walked fast all the way to Leyden. It helped to relieve the trembling she felt in every limb. Not that she, a grown woman, matron of a wayside inn, was afraid of a bunch of naughty boys. Mean-spirited little tyrants! What they needed were moeders who weren't afraid to use long willow switches on them.

Why did they taunt her son? Of course, their accusations were lies, but where did they get names like those? In Brussels, where Joris had taken her to live when they were first married, there was a whole community of Jews, and it was not that uncommon to hear the ghastly word bantered around the streets. But Leyden had no Jews! And certainly not her husband!

Why did he run off so suddenly? To visit his brother, indeed! He had so steadfastly refused to give her a reason. But that was Joris—always keeping things to himself. If she'd had any idea what his running off would lead to, she would have tied him to his bed and never let him go.

She pushed her way on into the city, doing all she could to give off confident airs. With her nose slightly lifted, her arm snugly hugging the shopping basket to her side, she headed straight for the bakery at the sign of The Pretzel, situated at the foot of the citadel hillock. From the corner of her eyes, she kept a wary lookout for the boys who had chased her son home.

She passed a few people on the way—not friends, just familiar faces rushing to and fro on their day's business. No one spoke to her, and she spoke to no one.

When she opened the door into the bakery, fragrances of warm fresh bread greeted her and made her feel almost welcome. But the baker rushed up to fill the doorway, blocking her entry into the room.

"I've no more bread," he said shortly, his manner cold, rude—not at all his way.

"No more?"

"Just sold the last loaf before you came," he added, shoving her back out the door. "On my way to locking up for the day."

Hiltje turned awkwardly and stumbled back out into the late afternoon street. *He lies*, her heart told her. Why else would he be so anxious to keep her from seeing his shelves? The aroma her nostrils had picked up just approaching the threshold told her they were filled with bread.

Yet why would this man lie to her? She'd been buying bread in this bakery since she was a young girl. The man's vader was living back then, but she'd been buying from the son ever since she and Joris returned from Brussels. Never had he been rude to her.

She heard the door close behind her and the drawing of the bolt. What made her so dangerous that even the baker must lock her out of his shop? And what was she to do for bread to feed her family and guests? She had enough to last through the day, if they ate it sparingly and no new guests arrived. She could make waffles. But they weren't bread!

Perhaps tomorrow he would sell her some. Why could she not quite believe it? For some reason that made no sense at all, she doubted that the baker would ever sell her bread again. At least not until she found out what was at the bottom of this scandalous matter and managed to straighten it out.

Blindly she started off down the street toward home. She was just turning the corner when she heard loud jeering laughter coming from beyond the bakery. Then above it all rang out a clear young voice. "The *marrano*'s vrouw!" followed by a volley of angry shouts. "Go home, Vrouw *Marrano*, go home!"

Hiltje looked back over her shoulder. The mob of naughty boys was facing her, punching the air above their heads with their fists. Her knees grew limp, and her heart pounded in her ears. *Nay!* It could not be! The whole city must know this lying rumor by now. Why else would the baker close his shop on her? But who would send such a vicious accusation flitting about the streets?

And what was there for her to do now? If she ran away, her actions would lend credence to the awful words. If she stayed and fought them, they would not believe her, and she had to admit that she had no intention of tangling with that nasty bunch of boys. She may be bigger and stronger than any one of them, but taken all together? And what if the baker and other merchants on the street joined in? Just once, in Brussels, she'd seen a mob beat up on a lone Jew. Merciless they were to him and left him bloody on the cobblestones. In spite of the best his family could do to restore him, before the sun had set on that day, he died.

She must simply walk on, pretending not to have heard, or having heard, not to have had the slightest suspicion that they spoke of her. So drawing herself up tightly once more, lifting her nose toward the heavens, she walked on, outwardly quiet while inside she trembled like the oak leaves being blown from their branches. The voices followed, always just the same distance behind as they had begun. When she clattered across the Zyl Poort Bridge, she could hear they were standing at the gate, still yelling at her, "Go home, Vrouw *Marrano*, go home!"

Safely out on the trekpath, she talked softly to herself. "I must find a new way to provide bread. There's an old oven out behind the inn. Moeder used it on holidays. She loved to bake special breads for Sinterklaas feast and New Year's, sometimes even hot cross rolls for Easter. Nobody's touched it for years. Probably grown up with weeds and filled with spiders! And where can I find yeast and meal enough for such a venture? Besides, how to do it? I've never baked bread in an oven. Maybe Gretta will know."

Hiltje walked on, listening to the water rushing by, the meadowlarks calling to her from the poplars that lined the bank of the Zyl. Here and there a butterfly flitted past, its wings glittering in the afternoon sunlight. She looked up and watched a flock of gulls circling above the thatch of the inn not far beyond. In her mind's eyes she envisioned her husband standing on the doorstoop, his apron stretched tightly across his paunch, one hand on his hip, the other holding tightly to a broom, calling out to her as she walked.

A great sadness, tinged with a kind of fear she was not familiar with, welled up inside of her. "Joris, my strange runaway husband with so many secrets locked up in your head," she mumbled, "when will you return and put the sword to these mad rumors?"

———

Ghendt

29th evening of Peat Month (September), 1573

Joris planned to stay in Ghendt only long enough to make a sketch or two and then return home. Frans had obliged him, and within a few days he had new faces for both Abraham and Isaac. Frans' son was a boy about three years Christoffel's senior and the ideal model for Isaac. While he was at it, he sketched Frans' vrouw and daughters as well. Not that he had a picture in mind for them, but the process brought him more pleasure than he had expected. And his chest full of models back home needed some fresh portraits—Jewish faces for more Torah subjects? Indeed!

Three weeks later, he was still here. He missed Hiltje and the children, but he was enjoying being back in a big city, working with his brother in a shop not terribly unlike the one he used to work in when he lived in Brussels.

He had a deeper reason, though, for staying on. On that first night when he'd discovered it was Rosh Hashanah, he felt as if he belonged here in some special way. He knew the Jewish New Year was only the first of a whole season of Jewish holy days. So every night when the evening meal was over and he and Frans had visited about everything but religion and he had climbed the stairs to his attic room, he'd lay his ear on the floor and listen for the muffled sounds of celebration.

Sometimes he could make out chanting, sometimes laughing, occasionally even singing. As he listened, he kept track of the passage of days and decided they were attached to the ongoing celebrations of Yom Kippur, the Day of Atonement, and the eight days of Sukkot—"Feast of Booths," Moeder used to call it.

Though Joris dared not to take part in any of it without an invitation, yet deep down inside it felt good just being with Jews on their holy days. Tonight was the eve of the last day in the season—Simchat Torah, a day to celebrate the books of the Law from which their moeder had garnered all those fantastic stories she told them as boys. After this day he must go home. He longed to see his family again, and in some strange way, he even missed *The Clever Fox Inn*, if not the parade of Beggar troops that tramped through its shabby old rooms. And there were rumors of war and threats to tear down the buildings. *Ja*, he really must go home—tomorrow!

Joris savored the evening meal with its family orderliness—something the busyness of the inn never allowed for at home. On every other evening this was the signal for him and Frans to converse about their businesses over a mug of beer brewed by a friend two streets over and another street down from the linen shop. With no more exciting things to say to each other, they would slip off to bed.

Joris would climb the stairs and lie awake yearning to ask Frans how he'd managed to give up being the devout Christian he'd always known him to be. Tonight, though, he would not go to bed without some answers.

He stood slowly to his feet, lifting his beer mug as he arose. "Tomorrow I go to home," he said.

"Why?" Frans laid a restraining hand on his forearm.

"Follow me, brother," Joris begged and led the way up the two flights of winding stairs to his attic room with a still warm chimney and a murky little window looking out on the city.

They each pulled up a three-legged stool and sat at a table that matched the cramped size of the little room.

"Why must you go now?" Frans asked, his brow wrinkled and his eyes registering earnestness.

"Why not?" Joris questioned, searching his brother's face for some evidence that he was ready to talk for once about things that mattered.

"It's just that . . ." he began, looking down, "that I've begun to grow accustomed to our evening conversations."

"Humph!" Joris puffed. "Conversations that go nowhere—bolts of linen, inn guests—we amble over the same tedious circuits every night.

Nay! I've been away far too long already. 'Twas on the one hand selfish of me to come in the first place. With Leyden facing a siege and the burgemeester threatening to tear down *The Clever Fox Inn* . . . *Ach!*" Joris held his head in his hands, pressing fingers into his temples. "My poor dear vrouw and children!" he moaned.

Frans breathed deep and stared at the fingers of both hands intertwining each other on the table before him. Finally he looked up and asked, "Why did you come, little brother? I mean the deep reason, not what you told me about sketching Vader Abraham. Something else drew you here."

For how many nights had Joris climbed into his bed in this room disappointed that he had not yet been asked this question? Yet now that he heard it, his heart beat a rhythm that would not be ignored, and his mouth felt sticky. He looked in Frans' direction and saw earnestness in the dark eyes.

"I came with a longing once more to talk with our own people, to touch Jewish flesh and mind and heart."

"A Jewish heart? What made you think to find such a one in this *converso*?"

" 'Twas a chance I had to take," Joris mumbled. "In the beginning I wondered. Then almost immediately I began to see what you have become—a public Christian on Sundays and a secret Jew on all the other days!"

Frans cringed. "You saw that in me?"

Joris laughed. "That I did, because the real water deep within your wells is Jewish, not Christian at all. What has caused my pain these days is the awful way you have refused to tell me from your lips, nor ask me about my heart." He paused, questioning whether to go on. Then taking Frans by the arm and looking intently into his eyes, he pleaded, "Tell me, why did you refuse to respond when I urged you into conversation?"

"I . . . I feared you were lying in wait for me," Frans stammered.

"Lying in wait for my own brother?"

"Forgive me, Joris, but I've seen so much betrayal, and neither had I good reason to believe for an instant that you were anything but true to your Christian profession—married to a *Goyim*, naming your son Christoffel. Besides, we have never talked about the religious beating of our hearts together—never!"

"*Ah, ja!* Moeder wouldn't allow it." Joris felt the fear go out of him like an expiring breath. "I guess you could not know any more about me than I about you."

Frans hesitated. His eyes somber, almost wary, he began. "I have watched you and listened to you since you came. Each night when we gathered our children around us to celebrate, first Yom Kippur, then Sukkot, my vrouw urged me to call you in to celebrate with us. She has been convinced, almost from the beginning, that you were one of us. 'A true Jew,' she calls you." He paused, swallowed hard, then added, "I feared too much to believe her. After all, I am the protector of this household."

"That I understand." Joris nodded and went on. "When your vrouw put the apple and honey by my bed that first night, I knew she at least could be trusted. I wondered about you."

Frans' face relaxed almost to a hint of a smile from behind the heavy beard. "When did you know you were not a Christian?"

"Truth is," Joris said, nodding, "for all my life, I have tried with every sinew in my body to be Christian."

Frans nodded. "I too. Vader insisted."

"And Moeder could not say him *nay*."

"But she taught us how to be Jews, Joris."

"Think you that she knew the day would come when we could no longer lie to ourselves?"

"Not only did she know it," Frans said with animation, "she prayed for it. In spite of all that Vader said and did to deny his Jewishness, every humor in her body remained Jewish. Some inner compulsion drove her."

"But did she begin to know the pain her efforts would inflict on us?"

Frans pursed his lips for a long moment, then nodded. "She had to be no stranger to the pain, Joris. Think what she suffered."

"Then why, Frans, did she not let us go on in the way Vader laid out for us? She could have saved us the agony of one day being forced to choose."

Frans cupped his chin in both hands and pondered a moment before he answered. "She lived by Deuteronomy six, 'You shall impress [*Yahweh's* precepts] upon your sons . . . bind them as a sign on your hand . . . write them on the doorposts of your house and on your gates.' "

"I could never obey those words in my home." Joris stared at his brother, not seeing his expression, only pleading for companionship in his agony.

"I thought I couldn't, either, until the anguish in my soul grew too unbearably great. Then one day the local priest began circulating rumors that some of my friends were *marranos*. He sent inquisitors into their homes."

"Were they actually practicing our religion in secret?"

"Some were, some weren't. In either case, I know the church meant their threats to warn us to give up all such deceitful ways. With me it worked just the opposite."

"Made you sympathize with our people and want to live like we were taught, right?"

Frans nodded and raised his hands with enthusiasm. "How did you know?"

"That's what it did to me when our priest told us that all who insisted on supporting Prince Willem were *marranos*!"

Frans smiled. "Then you'll understand when I say I began to swell with a great indignity. Christianity talks about love and kindness, but in the priest's witch-hunting actions, I saw only cruelty. From that point on, I knew I was no Christian at heart."

"Think you that Jesus intended Christianity to be so harsh?" Joris felt a trembling in his heart as he posed the question.

Frans frowned and stared at his intertwining fingers for a time before he shook his head and said, "*Nay*. That much I can't quite believe. Whatever else we have to say about Him, He was a good man."

"Was He the Christ? The Messiah? The Lamb of God?"

Joris listened to the silence and probed his own soul for an answer. It did not come. Finally Frans spoke. "Must we answer those questions, Joris?"

"I think our vader has made it forever impossible to do so."

"I fear I must struggle with those questions till my dying breath."

"Is that why you still take your family to the St. Bavo's Kerk?"

"Maybe. I only know for sure it's the one thing Vader taught us about religion that I will continue to do. I must protect the family *Yahweh* has given to me. Deep down inside, though, I shall never again take a part with them. Nor shall I cease to lead my family at home in the ways our moeder taught us."

"*Ach! Ach! Ach!*" Joris pounded on the table with his fist and felt the sweat beads oozing from the pores in his forehead. "Frans, think what would happen if I tried that under my thatch. My vrouw has not even the faintest glimmer of a reason to suspect that I am other than she. Never could I change her beliefs. Nor would *Yahweh* ask it of me!"

Frans sighed. "That is a great perplexity, Joris. But what of your children? They have as much Jewish blood running in their veins as they have Hiltje's *Goyim* blood."

Joris stirred uneasily, rearranging his rotund body on the wobbly little stool. "In the nights when I slip out and climb up into the loft and drape the prayer shawl over my head and recite my Sh'ma, I always ask *Yahweh* to forgive me. What more can I do?"

Frans shook his head and tapped a forefinger gently on the table between them. "I don't know . . . unless . . . perhaps you can paint more of the stories Moeder told us from the Torah and teach your Christoffel to do the same."

Joris felt a leap of hope. "You think so?"

"Why not? Even the Christians have our stories in their Bible, you know."

"But the priests don't let them read it. In fact, to own a copy of the Christian Bible is as great a sin in the eyes of a priest as to celebrate the Sabbath."

Frans frowned and tugged at his long beard. "The Calvinists approve of Bible reading. Have they a church now in Leyden where you could go?"

Joris shuddered. "Indeed they do have use now of our Marekerk. But they offer no good answer, Frans. They will string up a man in an instant if he paints an image. They uphold the second commandment with more rigor than we."

"I thought their objection was only to paintings in the churches."

Joris shook his head. "So they say, but . . . *nay*, I cannot go in their direction. Perhaps the day will come when we shall no longer be allowed to make our way through the gates into Leyden anyway. Then no one can hold us to account that we go not to church at all." He sighed, stood, and walked to the window. Looking out at the round fuzzy blob that was the moon, he said, "When I go to home tomorrow, I shall let my son watch me paint the new faces for Abraham and Isaac. What more, *Yahweh* only knows."

Frans joined him at the window. "You shall talk of our ways 'when you walk in the way'—or paint in the studio," he said. "And I trust *Yahweh* will show you that way."

The brothers embraced. "You have restored my shriveling soul, my brother," Joris muttered into Frans' broad shoulder.

"Now you must come with me to the cellar," Frans said in a bright tone, laying a hand on Joris' arm. "For all the other nights of the season of holy days, we have celebrated with our family alone in our living rooms. On this last night, several Jewish families from this part of the city will join together in the celebration of Simchat Torah. Remember what Moeder taught us about it—Rejoicing in the Torah?"

Joris gulped. "I do remember it well. Dancing around the room with the Torah, kissing it, reading the last verses of Deuteronomy to close out the old year and the first verses of Genesis to begin the new. But . . ."

"But what?"

"None of your friends know me. Will they not fear my presence?"

Frans laughed. "When I tell them you are a true Jew and my brother, they will not question."

Already he was on his way down the stairs. Joris followed, his heart beating a rapid warning signal. What was he about to do? In his bosom he knew that to participate in a Simchat Torah was to admit to being a true Jew.

By the time they had finished their descent into the bowels of this tall deep building and passed through a series of locked rooms, his head was spinning almost out of control. They stopped in a squarish windowless room with a table in the center and crude benches all around the stone walls. The table held a candlestick with seven candles, and from the benches reflecting the undulating light, Joris could see many pairs of eyes fixed on them. Frans' family was among them.

Frans bowed, then spoke softly, "Shalom." With a gesture in Joris' direction, he added, "My brother, Joris, a true Jew."

Joris felt his heart jump. A true Jew? Was he really that? Looking out at the little community prepared to accept him on his brother's words, he mumbled, "Shalom."

He felt clumsy, but the swimming of his head was subsiding.

A soft murmured response came from around the room, "Shalom."

They took seats, and a warm vibrant sensation welled up inside of Joris. Was it a synagogue of sorts? He felt his eyes grow large with wonder. He'd heard whispers of how Anabaptists were forced to meet in hidden churches. Was this a hidden synagogue? Why not?

An older man with snowy white beard rose from his place. Must be a rabbi. Joris blinked and stared hard. He'd never seen one before. Together with Frans the old man went to a far corner of the room. Carefully they removed several stones until they pulled from a hole in the wall a large heavy object, looking much like a bolt of linen. They carried it to the table, where they peeled off its outer shell, and the rabbi lifted out a scroll.

A real Torah! Joris stared in wonder. Never had he thought his eyes would rest on such a treasure!

The services began with the rabbi invoking the favor of Yahweh upon their assembly. Joris sat as in a trance, listening to the prayers and chants and the reading of the assigned Scriptures for the day. Before he knew it, they were all on their feet, dancing and chanting, "Hosanna! Hosanna!"

In the midst of the jubilation, the rabbi began to circle the room, carrying the Torah scroll.

"Is he doing what Moeder used to call the *hakafot*?" Joris asked Frans.

"You remembered? Ah, Joris, 'tis in your heart indeed!"

As the rabbi passed the congregants, they leaned over and kissed the sacred book. When he'd completed his encirclement, he handed the scroll to another who carried it around. This was followed by another *hakafot* and yet another. Some carried it in pairs, some alone. On the seventh *hakafot*, the scroll was handed to Frans. He nudged Joris and said, "Help me, brother."

No longer allowed to play the safe observer, Joris was torn between a strong impulse to carry the Torah and an equally strong impulse to run from the place. From some buried spot inside, a voice seemed to remind him that to carry the Torah was to shout to the whole world, "I am a Jew!"

Nay, he argued, he must always keep his Jewishness hidden away— his prayer shawl in the stable loft, Vader Abraham in the bottom of his painter's chest. The whole world must never see him for who he really was.

In the deepest part of his being, where he knew what was true and what was not, he knew that if he carried the Torah, God would always hold him to his declaration. He could never again play Christian in the same way he had done all his life. Once back home, he must go to his stable every night without fail and wear the prayer shawl and recite the Sh'ma. And he must take Christoffel with him. Could he do it?

One end of the scroll was already in his hands, his feet were stumbling around the dirt floor next to Frans, and his lips were joining in the continuing cries of "Hosanna!"

They returned the Torah to its place on the table and joined in the dancing and singing, "Let us rejoice on Simchat Torah and honor the Torah!"

For the rest of a long and exciting evening, Joris celebrated and shuddered, both at the same time. 'Twas one thing to do the rituals here where his Jewishness was no secret. But back at home with Christoffel? And Hiltje? Yet he must do it, for to carry a scroll on a *hakafot* was a promise to be a Jew for all days and in all places.

Frans' vrouw served drinks to the merrymakers, then took the children up to their beds. The celebration went on far into the night. Little by little members of the group slipped out. When the last had gone, Joris and Frans stood in the dim light, still clouded with dust from the trampled floor. They embraced once more.

"Can you imagine what Simchat Torah must be like in an open synagogue, where voices need not be muffled by layers of walls, and singing can be wholehearted?" Frans suggested.

"It could never be more glorious than it was tonight," Joris said softly.

Together they made their way up out of the cellar, climbing the flights of narrow winding stairs. When they'd reached the floor where Frans would sleep, he took Joris by the arm and said just above a whisper, "Next year you must come back to celebrate all the feasts with us—and bring your Christoffel along. In the middle of Wine Month next year."

"That shall I mostly gladly do!" Joris knew he'd found in his brother a rare comrade of the soul.

CHAPTER ELEVEN

Leyden

2nd day of Wine Month (October), 1573

On a cool blustery morning with only a thin veil of clouds scudding across the heavens, Hiltje knew she had to bake some bread. She stood in her kitchen and tried to decide where to begin. Three days ago, when the baker first refused to sell her bread, she had begun growing her own yeast culture. As much as she could remember, she did it the way her moeder had done it years ago in a pot. She mixed meal and water with a spoonful of honey and some already fermenting hops from the shed behind the barn where Joris brewed beer for the family. She set it in the back of the fireplace to keep it warm and had watched it bubble ever since.

"Looks plenty bubbly enough to me," she said, holding the yeast pot for Gretta to examine. "What think you?"

The older woman shrugged. "Just remember, I've never made bread before, never even watched my moeder do it." Then peeking into the yeasty pot, she agreed. "It does bubble . . . and begins to send off a bread-like aroma."

The time for decision had come, and Hiltje must sound more sure than she felt, or they would all go hungry. She smoothed her apron down with nervous hands and said, "First, I think we call the children to clean the oven, then build a fire."

"Sounds wise," Gretta said and helped her gather their four children in the innyard.

Together they all converged on the long deserted bread oven. They cleaned out at least a six years' accumulation of weeds, leaves, and storm-blown sand from the oven above, its firebox beneath, and the ground all around it.

Hiltje sent her daughters, Clare and Tryntje, climbing up to the top of the old structure with a long-handled broom wrapped in rags. They shoved it down through the chimney to remove any bird nests, spider webs, and debris that lodged there.

"Bring the washtub and all the buckets you can find," Hiltje told the boys. "Fill them with water and place them near the oven. And don't forget to bring the ladders out where you can grab them in a flash if you need them," Hiltje sputtered as the boys ran off to do her bidding.

Gretta shook her head. "I've never even been this close to such an oven. Only the bakers had them in the cities. Too dangerous for the rest of us, we were told."

"More than one city fire has been started by an oven flame leaping out of its bounds," Hiltje said.

Gretta shivered. "Can we get the fire hot enough to bake the bread and still not burn down the inn?" she asked, her dark eyes flashing with a kind of wariness that seemed to match the sharpness of her nose and chin.

"This oven sits too far from the inn to do any damage," Hiltje countered.

"And if a spark gets away? Old thatch goes quickly up in flames. I've seen it."

Hiltje fought down a growing uneasiness and tried to reassure her fearful "city" guest. "This is not the city. My moeder has fired this oven many times, and her moeder before her even more times. I've never heard any stories of fires in this inn. Besides, the boys have the buckets and washtub ready in the event of a mishap."

By the time she'd assembled kindling twigs and wood, all stood in readiness. The children gathered around for the lighting of the fire.

"Let me do it, Moeder," Christoffel begged, extending his hand.

Something inside Hiltje felt like a quickly twisting knife. Joris should be here to do this. Nay, rather, if he were here, they'd still be going to the sign of The Pretzel for their bread and not have to worry about resurrecting crumbling ovens and trying to draw recipes from a brain where they did not exist.

Without saying anything, she handed the tinderbox to her son and watched as he struck the flint, created a spark, and soon had the wood afire.

Shortly Hiltje noticed Gretta holding her arms at the elbows and moving about uneasily. Her eyes grew wide, staring at the growing fire, mumbling something unintelligible beneath her breath.

"Now into the house we go to make the dough," Hiltje said, taking Gretta by the arm and trying to sound as if she were in charge. "And you, *jongens*, keep the fire going and watch for sailing sparks. Clare, Tryntje, go to hanging out the feather bags to air."

Once inside the kitchen, Hiltje and Gretta conferred and mixed and kneaded until the lump of dough they produced was smooth and spongy. Hiltje punched it with her finger and watched the hole fill up to make a solid round ball.

"Is it ready?" Gretta asked eagerly.

"*Nay*," Hiltje said. "I seem to remember that my moeder let it sit by the fire and grow until it had reached twice its size."

No sooner had they set the bowlful of bread in the corner of the hearth than a dreadful shriek came from the barnyard.

"Fire! Moeder, come!"

Hiltje dashed into the yard in time to see a tiny flame with a long smoke tail curling from the thatch on the stable roof. Christoffel was putting a ladder in place, then clambering up, dragging a wet rag with which he tried to smother the flame. By the time he reached it, it had grown too big for the rag to cover and was spreading quickly across the thatch.

"Save the horses!" Christoffel screamed.

The girls scurried into the stable. Hiltje, Robbin, and Gretta were passing buckets of water along to Christoffel, who dashed them onto the now hungry flames.

"Back off!" Hiltje shouted at her son. "Go to the inn with a wet mop. Sit on the rooftop and beat off any burning sparks that may sail there."

Leaving Robbin and Gretta to keep pouring water on the barn, Hiltje went to help her girls tether the horses to a tree in the front of the inn. They all returned to draw water from the well and pass along buckets to keep the water on the fire. In no time the entire stable was wrapped in flames. Still they doused it, hoping it would not spread. When the roof collapsed, pulling the walls with it, it sent an enormous shower of sparks heavenward.

"Throw water on the inn!" Christoffel screamed from his perch above the studio.

Hiltje turned to do that and discovered the figure of a man on the ridge of the roof at the kitchen end of the inn. He, too, had a stick in his hand with a wet rag and was waving it at the dangerous flying sparks. Like a flash, two new flames sprang to life along the ridge of the inn roof between the men. Frantically they swung at them with their rags. Hiltje scrambled up the ladder with a bucket, while the newly arrived man met her halfway and took it from her hand, transforming both flames into a cloud of hissing steam.

It was Dirck, Gretta's husband! She turned to go for another bucket and found Robbin at her feet handing one up. The bucket line continued passing empty buckets down, full ones from the well, up the ladder, along the rooftop.

"Have to soak this roof," Dirck shouted down at Hiltje. "Sleeping sparks roar to new life when we do not watch."

"If only the heavens would open and shower down upon us," she yelled back. Her mind began now to fret and fume. Day after day when she did not want it, the rain always fell. Why not today? What if the tall linden trees bordering the pasture behind them, with their autumn-dried leaves, should burst into glowing candles and spread more sparks?

What would Joris say when he came home, if he ever did? *Joris, Joris, Joris!* The name crescendoed in her brain like the thundering of an approaching horse. Where was he? Why did he not come? If he'd stayed home in the first place, she never would have had to build a fire in the oven, and this would not have happened.

Maybe . . . an unthinkable thought began to form in the farthest back reaches of her weary mind. *Nay!* She shoved it back down and grabbed for another bucket. The thought would not go away. *What if Joris is a Jew, and he'll not come home again ever, and all this happened as a curse of some kind?* Hiltje didn't know much about curses, only that they happened and could wreak dreadful ruin on their victims. She'd heard a lot of stories in her years of living in the inn. Stories both about curses and Jews. Amazing the things people talked about when they were warmed and filled with Delfts beer!

She passed another bucket to Dirck and tried to block out the thought that had just left her feeling dead inside—dead and deserted and hopeless! From out beyond the Zyl she heard a roll of thunder and saw a bright glow from a distant flash of lightning. Minutes later the first drops of rain began to fall like a refreshing promise.

From her hard seat in the coach that had bumped and jostled along the roadways all the way from Dillenburg, Aletta sat waiting. She looked out on the typical countryside inn through a veil of shivering autumn leaves and dripping sheets of water from the rain shower finally slowing to a stop.

"*The Clever Fox Inn.*" For the hundredth time she read the words on the large sign that hung just beyond the coach doorway and sighed. She hugged Kaatje to her breast and watched plumes of smoke diminish and disappear from behind the old wooden building with its low-hanging, shaggy roof.

Somewhere, probably inside the building now that the rain had taken over the fire-fighting job, were her moeder and brother, Robbin. How she'd yearned to see them again! Could Pieter-Lucas be here to meet them? Reluctantly, she stifled the burst of eagerness that threatened to overtake her.

Lucas pranced about the coach, his little legs a never ceasing rhythm of motion. Even as he leaned against his moeder's knee and raised a pleading face toward her, his feet didn't stop moving. "Can we go in that house, *Moeke*?" he begged.

"When Opa comes for us, *jongen*," she said, trying to soothe him, all the time wishing desperately that it would be soon. Her back and shoulders and head ached from so long sitting and so much little-boy wiggling, not to mention Mieke's perpetual prattling.

"Can't be long now," Mieke spouted. "Haven't seen a whisker o' smoke since th' rains started a-comin', and surely ain't no fire a-smolderin' anymore." She paused to poke her head out. "*Ja*, here comes yer vader now."

Before she'd finished her last statement, Mieke was already lifting Lucas up and out and setting him on the ground, where he ran to meet his grandfather.

"Now, c'mon, Vrouw 'Letta," she coaxed, taking the baby and helping Aletta to her feet.

Vader met her at the doorway and helped her to the ground.

"Is Pieter-Lucas here?" she muttered.

"Not yet, but within a day or two—as quickly as he can," Vader said, looking at her with that special protective look he'd always reserved for his daughter.

"I know," she mumbled.

She looked beyond Vader to see Moeder Gretta already stooping down to greet her grandson and Robbin hurrying forward to scoop up the boy in gangly arms. Aletta reached out and embraced her moeder. Almost she'd forgotten how small and bony her body was.

"O Moeder, my moeder, how long it has been!" she said as they squeezed each other.

"How very, very long indeed!" Moeder answered.

Then shoving back and holding each other at arm's length, moeder and daughter looked with excited admiration at each other.

"What a fine and beautiful young moeder my daughter has become!" Gretta said.

"And you, Moeder, look far more lovely than I had remembered in my happiest dreams."

"Where is that baby?" Gretta asked.

Mieke shoved her way in between them and placed the child into the eager grandmother's arms. "Ain't she a beautiful one?"

"*Ah!* Just like the little one I birthed so many years ago," Gretta said, her sharp-featured face turning into one huge smile.

They made a triumphant procession entering *The Clever Fox Inn*, Lucas waving from his grandfather's shoulders, Robbin close beside, Gretta holding her prize out for the whole world to see, Aletta and Mieke following behind all aglow.

When they'd come through the doorway, Vader Dirck said with jovial grandeur, "My family, if you please!"

One by one the innkeeper's family, ash-smudged and sweaty and reserved, stepped forward and greeted their new guests. When Aletta greeted Hiltje, she thought she'd never seen so sad a face in all her life. Her wide eyes were underlined with deeply sagging bags and looked ready to rain tears. Without a smile, the woman spoke while wiping sooty hands on her apron. "Welcome to *The Clever Fox Inn.* It gives me pain that you must find me so covered with ashes and mud and not even a crust of bread in the house. Your moeder and I tried our best, but it seems it was in the stars to heap disaster upon us."

A hint of an attempted smile softened her face ever so slightly, and she laid a gentle hand on Kaatje's head, murmuring, "What a pretty little one." With a wary half glance at Aletta, she added, "So tiny she is . . . for such long traveling. Here, you need a bed." She showed Aletta a worn wooden cradle with a low stool beside it.

"My thanks to you," Aletta said.

Assuming an air that went with being mistress of the house, Hiltje began giving orders all around the room, and Aletta knew the celebration was over.

"Clare and Tryntje, revive the fire in the hearth and get the soup going. *Jongens,* do what you can to care for all the horses." Clapping a hand over her mouth, she asked, "*Ach!* Did the fire leave us any straw for fodder?"

"We'll find some, Moeder," Christoffel said.

"Where?" she demanded. "The harvest was all in the loft of the barn."

"Not quite all," Christoffel insisted and both boys started for the door.

Once they'd left, taking along little Lucas who refused to be parted from his Oom Robbin, Vader Dirck said, "I shall pack my family all into the coach and take them into the city to Jakob de Wever's."

"*Nay!*" Hiltje retorted.

"My family, with children and one more horse—so many mouths needing sustenance—will only add to your worries these days," he insisted.

"You forget," she said, "that I run an inn here, and I have ample experience in watching over the needs of far more than this little handful!"

"I am sure of that, and I know you do it right well. But . . . with your barn burned to ashes and . . ."

She grabbed him by the arm and pleaded, "Leave me not alone here with my children and this inn with its ashes—and ghosts of a husband run off and—*Ach!* Promise me you'll stay at least until my Joris returns!"

Vader looked toward Moeder, then around the room, as if taking each one into account before he could give an answer to this most unusual request.

"You've still no idea how long he will be gone?" he asked at last.

Hiltje swallowed hard and bit at her lip. She shook her head. "Worst of all, somebody's started ugly rumors about Joris in the city, and the baker refuses to sell me bread. So we were trying to bake some ourselves when the fire got away and burned down the barn." Her tale spent, along with her strength, she stood with head bowed.

"I'll get ye some bread," Mieke offered.

Hiltje looked at her, then back at Vader Dirck.

"If anybody can get the bread, Mieke is the one," he said quickly, reassuring.

"Ye gots coins?" Mieke asked, her hand extended.

Once more Hiltje hesitated, until this time Gretta spoke up. "It's all right, Hiltje. You can trust her."

"Here," she said, pulling a pair of coins from her bag and putting them in the outstretched hand. Then, with wildness in her eyes, she added, "Tell not a soul you come from *The Clever Fox Inn*! Do you hear me? Not a soul!"

"Vrouw, ye'll learn it soon enough that when Mieke's out to git somethin', she doesn't tell a soul nothin' what he oughtn't to be a-hearin'." She paused and smoothed down her ragged-hemmed dress, then snatched a large basket sitting by the door. "I'se on my way," she said and disappeared out into the afternoon.

"I hope the baker gives it to her," Hiltje moaned. "*Hei!* But she doesn't even know where to find him!"

Aletta smiled in spite of herself. "You don't know Mieke. There's nothing she can't find, nothing she can't get when she sets her mind to it."

"You're sure she can be trusted? Looks like a street thief to me. Only she's not got shifty eyes."

"She's been living with us now since before little Lucas, over there, was born. She was my midwife with both children. I'd trust her with my life in any circumstance."

"Where did you get her, anyway?"

"That's a long story. Ask her. She loves to tell it to anybody who will take the time to listen."

Vader was standing near Hiltje now. "I can take our horse and coach into the city and leave them with Jakob de Wever. If he has room I'll come back and get your horses to board there as well." He sighed. "If only the war weren't threatening, but maybe it won't reach us here."

Hiltje looked at him darkly. "What makes you think that?"

"The Spaniards are losing Alkmaar—or so I've heard. May not come to Leyden after all."

Hiltje shook her head and gave off a mocking laugh. "I don't believe it. When the Duke of Alva sets his eyeballs on a city, he goes after it, and Leyden's been in his eyes for a long, long time. He's still got a lot of *glippers* here yet, too—priests, people in high places."

Aletta gulped. Pieter-Lucas had warned her there would be dangers here. But nobody had told her that *The Clever Fox Inn* would be their new home. Who was this woman, Hiltje, anyway? Not a Child of God, surely. Didn't talk like one, didn't look like one. And why had her husband run off, with war almost at the city gates? Vader Dirck had only told her that they were staying in an inn for a short time while the Children of God family cleaned and repaired the building where they were all to live and open the printery.

Vader started for the door. "I go and come quickly back."

Hiltje stared at him for a long moment, one hand on her hip, the other cradling her chin. "While you're there," she said slowly, "can you find out who started the rumors about my husband and why?"

"What rumors?"

"Ask anybody you meet. The whole city knows them."

"Are you sure you want to know?"

"Very sure!"

"Rumors are easy to hear but not so simple to track." Vader was gone.

When he had closed the door, Kaatje was beginning to cry for her next meal. "Gretta, take your daughter to her quarters," Hiltje said. Then without warning, she threw up her hands, let out a shriek, and started for the kitchen. "Must be bread dough all over the kitchen! Gretta, come back when you've shown Aletta her room and tell me what to do with runaway bread dough when you got no oven to bake it in. Dear me, dear me!"

The room Hiltje had chosen for Aletta and her family was located above the kitchen, warmed by the chimney coming through.

"She wanted you to have her warmest room for the baby," Moeder Gretta explained.

"I think she is a kind woman," Aletta said, opening her bodice and feeding Kaatje. "Now go on, Moeder, to help her with the bread."

Gretta shrugged. "I've no ideas what to tell her. Can she cook it in rolls on a griddle?"

Aletta laughed. "You're asking me? Wait! *Ja*, I think I saw a cook do that once in Duisburg."

Moeder hurried off to the kitchen, and Aletta snuggled her Kaatje close, listening to the delightful suckling sounds her child made. Gently she began to unwind the swaddling bands until the fingers were free to wrap themselves around her own fingers as she nursed.

"Dear Vader in the Heaven," she prayed, "thank you that this child is beautiful and whole and has not some ailment that would keep her from eating well. We have come now to this place where you brought us. Show me where to find the help we need for her twisted foot. If there is anyone on earth who can bring her healing, let them be here in Leyden."

She closed her eyes and put her lips to the warm head in her arms. The deep feeling that welled up inside was a contentment that only the arrival of her Pieter-Lucas could intensify. May it be soon!

———

The journey from Diedrick Sonoy's headquarters near Alkmaar in the far northern hook of the country to Willem's headquarters in the old St. Agatha Convent in Delft was wild and cold—and long! Every time Pieter-Lucas traveled it, he hoped and prayed it would be the last. North of Leyden, the road was infested with Spanish troops, and its villages held hostage by the terror those soldiers inspired.

So he usually left Blesje somewhere near to Leyden—never the same place twice—and went on by foot or boat or coach. He had hidden in wagonloads of hay or disguised himself and joined groups of pilgrims, even Spanish soldiers. Beyond Haarlem, the road ran along the line of desolate sand dunes that held back the North Sea on the west and kept him frightened all the way.

Always when he passed through Leyden, his heart tugged at him to turn in for an hour or two of rest. But the messages he carried in his shoe or his doublet or sometimes his hat were too urgent for that—unless he happened through there late at night. Even then, rest times must be short.

"When we have won the war, we will have earned our rest," he'd grown accustomed to telling himself.

Once Aletta had arrived in Leyden . . . *Ah!* that would be different. Then he must face a new set of perplexing decisions every time he passed this way.

On this cool windy evening in the beginning of Wine month, Pieter-Lucas retrieved Blesje from a wayside inn just north of Leyden. As they started out and he was trying to fit his body to the saddle on the horse's back, he spotted the familiar church steeples of Leyden on the horizon, glowing faintly in the light of a setting sun. The tug grew stronger with each clop of Blesje's hooves.

"I think she's here by now, Blesje," he said. "We left Dillenburg over a week ago, you know. Besides, the news we bear from Alkmaar is hopeful, and there's nothing in my message that Willem can take care of before morning. We can stop now and still be in Delft by then."

With his heart tripping over itself for joy, he hastened through the Rhinesburger Poort and soon stood face-to-face with Jakob de Wever on the man's doorstoop.

"Has my vrouw arrived yet?" he asked, his eyes eagerly searching into the room beyond.

"That she has indeed, but not here. You'll find her out at *The Clever Fox Inn*."

Jakob motioned him into the room, but Pieter-Lucas refused. "I have so little time, must be in Delft early in the morning. Just have to see my vrouw and try to snatch a little shuteye with her in my arms."

Jakob took him by the arm and pulled him into the room, shutting the door quickly behind him.

"What is it?" Pieter-Lucas asked, struggling to go free.

"I'll only take a short minute. You need to know one thing before you go there."

"*Ja?*" Pieter-Lucas grew impatient as the man paused to clear his throat and look for words.

"Your vrouw is well. The children are well. But the innkeeper is in difficulty."

"He's home, then?"

"*Nay*, he's not been back, and no one has heard from him since he left. But there are rumors all over Leyden that he fled because he is a secret Jew—*marrano* is the word being passed around from house to house and shop to shop."

"Is it true?" Pieter-Lucas gasped.

"Who knows but Joris?"

"Do the Leydenaars believe it?"

Jakob nodded. "The whole city has been treating the poor man's vrouw and her children like a pack of lepers. Nobody will even sell them so much as a loaf of bread."

"So why have you let my vrouw stay there?" Pieter-Lucas was already reaching for the door latch.

"They just came today. Dirck was here late in the afternoon asking questions about the source of the rumors, which I have no idea of. He said the innkeeper's vrouw was frightened of being left alone, desperate to have them stay with her."

"*Ach!* If the news from Alkmaar is good, then must the news from Leyden cause a man's heart to fail. Good night."

Magdalena met him at the door and thrust a bulging bag into his hands. "Here, young man, take this to Hiltje—some bread and a few vegetables from our garden. Dear soul needs all we can do for her."

Pieter-Lucas hurried out into the darkening streets, mounted his horse, and hurried toward the Zyl River. All the while, he mumbled, "Always something, always something. Great God, is there no safe place on earth? Oh, to be free to care for the woman who holds my heart and the little ones she's birthed to me! *Ach*, how can I go to Delft tomorrow? Yet how can I not? Willem counts on me, and at least Aletta has her vader and moeder with her. . . ." One after another, the troubling thoughts rolled through his confused mind like clouds tumbling over one another across the windblown skies above him.

At *The Clever Fox Inn*, his knock was answered by the harried-looking woman in charge.

"From your friend Magdalena," he said, handing her the bag.

Hiltje stared at him. "What is it?"

"Bread . . . I don't know what more. She wanted to help you."

Hiltje shook her head and led him to an upstairs sleeping room. Pieter-Lucas knocked gently, opening the door as he did.

"Pieter-Lucas!" In a flash, Aletta leapt at him from across the room and let him lock her in his arms. Nothing else mattered now, and he would not allow a single worrisome concern to distract him from this pleasure for the few hours he had left.

———

3rd day of Wine Month (October), 1573

It was still dark when Pieter-Lucas came wide awake. Never had the temptation weighed so heavily on him to turn over in the bed made warm by his vrouw's body and ignore the call of loyal duty. He kissed his wife on a bare shoulder, then forced himself up and into his clothes. He tiptoed to the cradle and cot where his children slept. The light of a full moon shone through the single window and splashed a golden path across their angelic faces. He stooped over and placed a kiss on each little cheek and let his nose savor the delights of the warmth of soft rose-petal skins.

Halfway across the room, Aletta stood shivering in his way.

"So soon?" she whispered. "The night is not even over."

Holding her gently against his chest, he stroked her long golden hair and murmured, "Nor is the war, so I must go. Now that you are so close and Alkmaar is nearly won, I shall see more of you—much more!"

Then he kissed her and went for the stairs.

In the dining room below, he found Dirck Engelshofen seated at one end of a table, his face golden and distorted in the light of a lone lamp.

"What do you up so early, ahead of the sun?" Pieter-Lucas asked, his voice almost a whisper.

"I had to talk with you before you leave. How long will you be away this time?"

Pieter-Lucas shrugged. "I really believe the end of the siege of Alkmaar approaches. The fields for miles around it are now flooded, and the people of the city have so brutally treated their would-be captors that the Spanish soldiers, to a man, have refused to fight them again. They are convinced the city is inhabited by demons with supernatural powers."

"So what will it mean when the Spaniards let down the blockade of Alkmaar?"

Pieter-Lucas sighed. "I wish I knew. Only that I shall not so often run there. Beyond that, I dare not to think. How long must you stay here in this unprotected wayside inn with these people accused of the great 'sin' of being the family of a Jew?"

"You must have talked to Jakob before you came last night."

"I did."

Dirck made circles on the table with his finger. "I hardly know what to think—or do. Hiltje has been ever so kind to us all, and she and my vrouw have become fast friends. Even Robbin and Christoffel are warming to each other. And Mieke has found a way to persuade the baker to sell her bread."

Pieter-Lucas smiled in spite of himself. He'd all but forgotten that she was here too. Nothing remained impossible with her on their side. "But . . . what happens when the Leydenaars discover you are guests here and decide to put you under whatever curse they've imposed on the inn-keeper?"

Dirck looked hard into Pieter-Lucas' eyes and said, "I must ask you simply to trust me, son. I know not what I may have to do before this is over. Just remember, your vrouw was first my daughter, and those children are my grandchildren. I shall do what is best for them all—if God will just show me what that is. As you say, you will be back soon. Perhaps you can stay longer next time."

"*Ja!*" Pieter-Lucas said. He clapped his vader-in-law on the shoulder, then slipped out of the inn just as the horizon began to lighten.

CHAPTER TWELVE

Leyden

4th day of Wine Month (October), 1573

*M*orning broke to the howl of a raw and powerful wind. Hiltje heard it and slunk down deep into her bed, pulling the feather bag over her head. She drew her knees up into her belly and wrapped her cold feet tightly in her night shirt, rubbing them with equally cold fingers.

"There's nothing so cold as an inn's back bed without a husband," she groused.

The thought of Joris wiped from her brain the last cobwebs that drowsiness might ensnare. Where was that man, anyway? And who was he? After all these years of being his vrouw, fussing with him over a hundred things, birthing him five children and losing two, teaching him to run an inn, and trying to understand what drove him so often into that strange room he called his studio, she thought she knew him pretty well.

Now this sudden flight to Ghendt—was that where he really went?— and these awful swirling rumors . . . and silence from Joris himself. *Ach!* She rubbed her toes till they seemed to squeal for a reprieve.

It was Sunday once more, the day when all good Christians must go to church. Where must she go today? Every Sunday since Joris had left, she'd honored his word and never gone back to the Pieterskerk. Instead, she continued going to the new Calvinist church in the Marekerk. It never felt like church, but those words from the big Bible held a fascination for her that she could neither understand nor ignore.

What about this morning? She trembled at the thought of taking her children through the gates of Leyden. None of them had been back since the day the boys chased Christoffel home and the baker refused to sell her bread. That strange little woman who came with Gretta's daughter might find a way to buy bread and whatever else they needed. But even Mieke couldn't bring them a church.

Hiltje sighed and smiled in spite of herself. For once she didn't have to go to church! She could stay home all day and fancy that this was a Monday or a Friday and just think about being the innkeeper's vrouw—*nay*, the innkeeper! She swallowed down a lump. Lumps in the throat always came when she had to remember that Joris was gone.

"No matter what day it is," she mumbled to herself under the covers, "it's time to be up and getting the fire going and the children moving." Not that they had as much work to do these days, since the fire had burned down the barn, along with a year's crop of hay. Gretta's husband had taken their horses into town, and Magdalena's husband was giving them shelter and food. She didn't know what to think about the weaver and his family and friends. Surely they knew the rumors as well as anybody else. Why, then, were they not afraid to give her aid?

Her toes felt warmer at last. In a flash, she threw back the covers and sat on the edge of the bed. She pulled on her hose, then dressed quickly and hurried toward the kitchen. When she'd shoved open the door, she blinked back her surprise. There by a glowing fire sat Mieke, holding Aletta's baby, rocking her back and forth with quick, almost jerky motions. Now and again the baby burst into distressing infant cries.

"Is she hungry?" Hiltje asked.

"*Nay*, her moeder done fed her a hundred times all th' night through, an' she jus' keeps on a-cryin' like as if somebody was a-pinchin' her an' never a-lettin' up. Vrouw 'Letta's all a-wearied from it, so I bringed her here an' bellowed th' fire back to life. I'se a-hopin' when I gets her warmed up she might fall asleep."

Hiltje sighed. "Babies are like that sometimes. Mine did it, too, especially the *jongen*. I think the devil gets into their tummies, just because he loves to torment them—and their moeders."

Mieke lifted her sharp chin and looked at Hiltje with a frown. "I don't know nothin' about the devil," she said.

Hiltje caught herself throwing a darting glance in the woman's direction. If she'd met this ragged person on the street of Leyden, she would have expected her to be able to tell her all there was to know about the devil.

Mieke went on. "Vrouw 'Letta's done gived her all th' herbs what she bringed from Dillenburg fer settlin' a grouchy tummy, an' this night the child jus' goes on a-frettin'. Calmin' down now, though, an' I'se a-hopin' her moeder's a-gettin' some sleep." She paused and scooted her chair to the side of the hearth. "Here, come an' get yerself warm too," she urged.

Hiltje stood on the hearthstones with her back to the fire, tilting her skirts so as to soak up the heat. The baby had fallen asleep at last, but Mieke went on rocking her.

"Tell me, Mieke," Hiltje began, "how did you come to attach yourself to this family?"

Mieke chuckled. "Ye truly wants to know?"

"I wouldn't have asked you if I didn't want to know. My mind is no searcher after prattle. So just give it to me the way it was."

"If that's th' way ye wants it, that's th' way ye gets it. Fer most o' my life, I was a ragged street thief in Breda. I stealed from ever'body what I could an' spended half my life in th' tower."

Hiltje drew away from the creature beside her. "Whatever happened to change you?" she asked.

"It's a long story—lots longer'n ye'll want to hear. But ye gots to know that th' last time I was in th' tower, there was two others in there with me. Both imprisoned fer no good reason 'tall. They was th' kindest, most lovin' people I ever done seed or heared. But th' thing what changed me to th' core was th' words one o' those women used to read from pages she'd done teared out o' her meester's big book. Th' Book o' God, she called it."

Hiltje felt her heart race. "A Bible?" she gasped.

"Jus' what it was, fer sure," Mieke said, nodding her head and smiling from one rim of her bony face to the other. "That's what done changed me, an' I'se watched it change a lot o' others since then too."

"How did your friend in the cell have a Bible? I've heard it said if a person that's not a priest or preacher of some sort is caught with such a book in his possession, he can die the death of burning at the stake or beheading or . . ." The thought was too awful to pursue any further.

"That's jus' what happened to one o' those women—Tante Lysbet was her name. She wasn't th' one what read th' Book, but she listened an' got some changed herself."

"And the woman with the Book?"

"They was preparin' to burn her when she up an' died o' th' consumption, so they burned Lysbet instead. At th' same time, they banished a schoolmeester and his vrouw to Germany, an' I followed along. Later, when Vrouw 'Letta comed to th' same place with herbs and healin' fer th' flocks o' people what was a-fleein' there from the sword o' Alva, I helped her birth little Lucas, an' I'se been with 'em ever since."

Hiltje stared hard at the woman. In her experience, a thief was always a thief and nothing ever changed her. This story sounded far too strange to be true. Yet Aletta had told her to ask Mieke about it. Surely she thought the woman would tell it right. Besides, there was a look of purity, honesty, and peace in her eyes that didn't belong either to a thief or a liar. And what about these people she lived with? Did they have a Bible of their own? Did her own friend, Magdalena, have one? What sort of people were they? Not Calvinists, or she would have seen them at the Marekerk. What else was there? Surely not Anabaptists—wild lawbreakers with many wives—or so she'd always heard.

"Mieke," she said at last, a trembling in her heart and voice, "does Gretta's family have a Bible with them?"

Mieke didn't look up when she finally answered. "I think ye'll have to ask her husban'," she said as if she maybe knew the truth but didn't want to tell it.

" 'Tis just that on this Sunday morning, I want to hear somebody read from God's Book." Hiltje was amazed at the strange longing inside her. She'd never felt it so strongly before on any Sunday morning! "When you take this baby back to her moeder," she finished, "will you ask her if her vader has a Bible and if he'd be willing to read it to me?"

Slowly cradling the infant in her arms, Mieke rose from the stool until she stood in front of Hiltje and looked up into her face. Just above a whisper, she said, "I tells her fer ye."

Hiltje watched her go from the room and felt her own heart beating with the rapidity of anticipation. What would Joris say if he came home and found an inn guest reading a Bible to her and the children?

"Hiltje!" she cajoled herself. "What difference does it make? He's not here, not about to come today, and besides, who knows whether Dirck will do it, even if he has the Book among his belongings brought from Engeland?"

She went to the well. Her day must begin.

———

Aletta feigned sleep while little Lucas climbed over her in her bed and played with his menagerie of wooden animals his vader had carved for him. In her half-dozing stupor, she heard his voice cooing like a dove, barking like a dog, roaring like a lion, talking like a four-year-old. Though she desperately craved sleep, there was something in that voice like no other on earth that soothed her moeder heart.

Because the day had dawned, she dared not sleep more anyway. It would soon be time to feed Kaatje again. Dear, dear Kaatje! A child to suckle at her breast, delight her with her smile, and torment her with a nightlong tummy ache.

Reaching her arms out from beneath the feather bag, she stretched them toward her son and invited him to "Come to *Moeke* for your morning *kusje!*"

He bounded instantly across the bed and into her arms. She kissed his head and prayed aloud, using the same words she used every morning, "Dear Vader in the Heaven, I offer Thee thanks for giving to me the two most beautiful children to be created by Thy powerful hands. Please bring this war quickly to an end that our Pieter-Lucas may be able to paint and teach Lucas to do the same. Watch over my beloved in the byways and battlefields and official halls of great men whose lives stand constantly in danger. And cause my feet to come into the pathway of the herbalist in this place who can instruct me how to treat and heal our Kaatje's foot. Amen."

Lucas squirmed out of her arms and begged, "Can we get up now, *Moeke?*"

"That you may," she said, feeling less than rested but charmed by the *jongen*'s open face and winsome smile.

She let him tug her erect and was just watching him bound to the floor when the door opened and Mieke entered, carrying a sleeping infant. Aletta grabbed the boy by an arm and motioned for him to be still, then began dressing him for the day. Setting him on the floor, she gave him quiet instructions to "Move about without noise, *jongen*."

Mieke had put Kaatje in her cradle and padded softly across the room to Aletta. "Has yer vader a Bible in his baggage?" she asked.

"I'm sure he does," Aletta answered. "Why do you ask?"

"B'cause it's Sunday mornin' an' th' vrouw what runs this place is a-wantin' to know if yer vader has a Bible he'd be willin' to read to her an' her family." She stood with feet apart, hands on hips, and waited for Aletta's answer.

"What did you tell her to make her even think he might have one?" Aletta asked. "'Tis not a common thing for an inn guest to carry around a Bible, not even when he's moving from one place to another. And even if he has one, he keeps it hidden. More than one man has been beheaded for possession of God's holy Book, you know."

"I know. I know." Mieke gestured irritation. "Hiltje done asked me how I came to be a-livin' in yer family an' I told her about Betteke an' her pages from th' Book an' about th' folks in Duisburg."

"I hope you didn't tell her it was Duisburg or that our friends were Children of God refugees?"

Mieke shook her head with its stringy hair protruding in matted fashion from beneath a halfway clean cap. "O' course I didn't tell her no such thing. I'se not all th' way addled in th' brain, ye knows. I jus' had to tell her 'twas th' Book o' God what done changed me from a rotten thief into yer trusty midwife an' nursemaid."

"And she asked for my vader to read from the Bible to her? For what reason, do you know?"

"Says she's a-wantin' to hear it." She shrugged and spread her open palms toward Aletta, adding, "More'n that I can no way say."

"If you stay here with the children, I'll go talk with Vader."

Aletta slipped on her clothes, combed her hair, and fastened it in place under her headdress, then padded down the stairs to her parents' room. They let her in and she gave them Hiltje's request in Mieke's words.

Hands behind his back, Vader stared at the floor for a long while. "It sounds believable enough."

"You do have the Bible in your baggage, don't you, Vader?" Aletta asked, not at all sure she was ready to trust the woman who gave them lodging either.

"Of course I have it. I thought I would gather my family together to read from it later on. Not wise to traipse into Leyden to the Wever's hidden church, so long as we stay here with a woman under suspicion. But what if . . ." He stopped.

"What if she proves to be a hole-peeper?" Aletta suggested.

Moeder Gretta moved in closer, speaking in low tones to match the rest. "In all the weeks I've been in this place, I've seen nothing to cause me to fear. Truth is, while you were gone to Dillenburg, I went to the Calvinist church with her."

"She's Calvinist, then?" Vader asked.

"I'm not sure all about it," Moeder answered, "only that she said her husband forbade her to go back to the papists, and so she tried this, and she doesn't altogether like it, but she loves the reading of the Bible."

"You believe what she says, Gretta?" Vader frowned as he asked the question.

Moeder laid a hand on his arm and said with deep conviction, "I believe, Dirck, that this woman is looking out to find the God she never found in the church. Who knows but that He has put us here to help her find Him?"

"And what of her children?"

"They go where she goes."

"Will they run off behind our backs and report us to the burgemeesters? Eager as some of them may be to protect the rights of the Calvinists, nobody wants Anabaptists lurking about. Else De Wevers would not have to hold a hidden church. And who knows about this woman's husband?"

Moeder shook her head, lay a hand on his arm, and spoke in a reprimanding tone. "My husband, we both know that to be a Child of God will always carry its risks, but when God puts an inquiring soul in our way, we have no choice but to obey."

Vader nodded, slowly at first, then faster and deeper. "Then will you go to her, Gretta, and bid her bring her children and come to our room to hear the reading of God's words?"

"I go to tell her," Moeder Gretta said easily, her face filled with a light that bespoke excitement.

————

Christoffel had no desire to go to the church in the city. He was angry with the *glipper* priest at the Pieterskerk, and the Marekerk was no better.

The singing was strange—no choir with white starched smocks. Instead, all the people tried to sing as they huddled together for warmth in their backless wooden chairs. The dissonant noise they made was not music to his ears. And the songs were nothing he'd ever heard before—Psalms, they called them, supposedly from the big book the priest read from. They didn't call him a priest, and he didn't say the mass or wave a censor filled with fragrant smoke. Worst of all, as the blank spaces on walls and ceiling stared down at him, they seemed to show angry scowls. He missed the bright colors, the decorated altar cloths, silver chalices, and the ciborium that held the host.

He and his sisters had talked about it every week since Vader left, and Moeder insisted they could not go back to the Pieterskerk.

"It's not church without the chanted prayers," Clare said.

"Or the organ," Tryntje added.

"It's cold and empty, without a smile," Christoffel concluded.

On this chilly morning he was rejoicing with the thought that, because of the rumors, Moeder wouldn't cart them off to that unchurchy church again. Inside, something was urging him toward the studio. He hadn't been back there once since Vader left, though at least once every day his whole body itched to go back and hold the charcoals and the brushes, to smell the paints and mix the colors. For no reason he could identify, on Sundays the urge always grew stronger than on any other day.

Today when he'd finished the last of his duties, he found his feet carrying him almost irresistibly toward the studio. His moeder's voice arrested him halfway there.

"Christoffel, come with me," she called out.

He spun around and faced her. She thrust his folding chair into his hand. Clare and Tryntje stood behind her, holding their chairs and looking not a bit pleased.

"We're not going to go into the city, are we?" he asked.

"*Nay*, not the city."

"Where, then?"

"Just follow me," she urged with a tone that told him she would say no more and he had no choice.

He fell in line with his sisters behind her. "Where's she taking us?" he asked the girls.

They both shrugged. "She won't say," Clare whispered.

By now they were standing before the door of the room where Robbin and his parents stayed, and Moeder was knocking. Robbin's vader opened to let them in. His whole family was seated around the room—his vader and moeder and sister, with Lucas and the baby and the strange little woman they called Mieke.

Christoffel set up his seat next to Robbin's place and whispered, "What is this?"

"Vader's going to read from God's book and pray over it."

"But it's no church!" Christoffel looked about him at all the members of Robbin's family sitting quietly, attentively, as if it were.

Robbin raised his eyebrows. "Then just watch and listen."

Uneasily he sat on his chair and watched Dirck pull a large book with decorative leather cover from a chest beside his bed. The book looked very much like the Bible the Calvinist preacher read from. Probably every bit as somber and dull to listen to, Christoffel decided. Dirck carried it to his own chair and opened it to a spot so near the beginning that he had to raise his right foot to the toes to hold it from falling off his leg.

"This morning our Old Testament reading is about the story of Abraham and Isaac," he began.

Abraham and Isaac? Those were the names from Vader Joris' drawing. Christoffel had no idea their story came from the Bible. How did Vader learn about them? He didn't even own a Bible, and the priest never read to them from one. He clasped both hands together and slid them between his legs, sat forward in his chair, and listened. Maybe it wasn't the same story.

"We read as follows," Dirck said. " 'After this it happened that God put Abraham to the test. He said to him, "Abraham," and he said, "Here I am." And He said, "Take now your son, your only son whom you love, Isaac, and go to the land of Moria, and offer him there as a burnt offering upon the mountain I will show you."

" 'Then Abraham arose early in the morning, saddled his donkey, took two servants with him, along with his son, Isaac. He bundled up wood for the sacrifice and started his journey to the place where God had called him.' "

Christoffel saw in his mind once more the faceless old man in Vader's picture hovering over him with the knife in his raised hand. He felt little shivers run down his backbone. What kind of a vader would do a thing like that? What kind of a God would ask it? And what kind of a man would want to read such a story?

He looked at his sisters, but they were staring into their laps at hands primly folded. His moeder was looking hard at Dirck, without an expression on her face. Robbin sat watching as if this were one of his favorite stories and he wasn't going to miss a word.

Christoffel swallowed hard, then gave his full attention to the unbelievable story.

" 'When Abraham, on the third day, looked up, he saw the place in the distance. He said to his servants, "Wait here with the donkey while the boy and I go over there; when we have worshiped, we will return to you." ' "

Did he really expect to bring Isaac back alive? Then he was not planning to do what God had asked of him. Christoffel felt some of the fear slip away. But if this was the same story, he had to slay the boy. Yet Vader said Abraham never killed his son. He must hear it through.

" 'Then Abraham took the wood for the sacrifice, laid it on his son Isaac, and took fire and a knife, and the two of them went on together. Then spoke Isaac to his vader, "My vader, here is fire and wood, but where is the lamb for a sacrifice?" And Abraham said, "God will provide a lamb, my son." So they went on together.

" 'When they came to the place God had called them to, Abraham built an altar, laid out the wood, bound his son Isaac, and laid him on the altar on top of the wood. Thereupon Abraham stretched out his hand and took the knife to slay his son.' "

Did Vader Joris know the story right? Did Abraham really kill Isaac or not? Christoffel clasped his hands together tightly and squeezed them with his legs. He had to know, yet the story had to come out right, or . . . he wasn't sure just what, but something would happen if it didn't.

" 'But the Angel of the Lord called out to him from the heaven, "Abraham, Abraham! Do not stretch out your hand against the boy, and do him no harm, for now I know that you are God-fearing, for you have not held back your only son from me." ' "

Christoffel raised his hands to his mouth and gasped. He looked at Robbin next to him and smiled. Robbin smiled back, but with a look that seemed to say, "Didn't you know it would turn out right?"

Dirck was still reading. " 'Then Abraham lifted up his eyes and looked, and there he saw a ram with his horns entangled in the brushwood.' "

The ram! *Ja!* It was in the picture too. What did Vader say? It was for a sacrifice. Something about the Lamb of God and sins.

" 'And Abraham offered the ram as a sacrifice in place of his son. Then the Angel of the Lord called to him a second time and said, "I swear by the word of the Lord that because you have not withheld your only son, I shall richly bless you. And through your descendants shall all the peoples of the earth be blessed, because you have obeyed my voice."

" 'Then Abraham turned back to his servants and they all went together on the road to Beersheba where he lived.'

"And in the New Testament," Vader Dirck said, turning to another place in the Bible, almost as far to the back as the first had been to the front. He read, " 'By the faith, Abraham, when he was tested, brought Isaac for a sacrifice . . . he of whom God had said, "Through Isaac shall your descendants speak of you. He considered that God by His power was able to raise him from out the dead . . ." ' And finally, these words." He turned over several more pages and read with a sort of excitement Christoffel couldn't quite understand, " 'Abraham believed God and it was reckoned to him for righteousness, and he was called a friend of God.' "

Righteousness? Christoffel wondered whatever that might mean. Nor could he imagine how God would ever call a man His friend. One thing did seem clear enough. God must have thought that Abraham did the right thing. Christoffel only hoped his vader would never get the idea that he had to do such a thing. As long as he went on painting such pictures, who knew what he might do?

Dirck had stopped reading. He closed the Bible, cleared his throat, and said, "Now we pray." Then he knelt down on the floor and lay his cheek against the floor rushes. His vrouw and daughter, even Robbin and little Lucas, did the same.

Christoffel looked quickly up to his moeder, who sat still and stiffly in her chair. From his undignified position, Dirck was talking to God. Christoffel didn't understand half of what the man said. When he'd finished, he and his family all rose to their feet and embraced one another.

Moeder Hiltje motioned her children to her side, then nodded toward Dirck and his vrouw. Christoffel moved toward her, not sure what to think of these most unusual inn guests and their strange goings-on. Following his moeder's lead, he slipped out into the hall. In silence, they all went to their own room in the back of the inn.

"Moeder," Christoffel began when he could keep still no longer, "does Vader have a book like Dirck's big Bible?"

A look of painful shock crossed her face. "What makes you ask such a question as that?"

"How else would he know the story about Abraham and Isaac?"

She took him by both shoulders and her eyes seemed to bore holes clear through him. "What makes you think he knows it?"

Beginning to tremble, Christoffel stammered, "Why . . . why . . ."

"Why, what?" she demanded, squeezing him with her fingers.

Maybe Vader never intended him to tell anyone about the painting. Else Moeder would know. He had tried to hide it even from him. *Ach!* What could he say now? He shrugged, trying to pass it off as a foolish error. "I guess I was mistaken," he said as offhandedly as he could manage.

"Where did you get the idea?" Moeder was insistent.

"Just something I saw among his pictures one day. The story Dirck read made me think of it, that's all."

"Did you tell anyone else what you just said to me?" Her voice sounded fearful.

"*Nay!* Why should I?"

Staring him hard in the eyes, Moeder said in her sternest voice, "You are never, never, never to say one word of this to anyone! Not anyone, do you understand? Never!"

Christoffel squirmed to get free from her grasp, which was becoming more and more painful. "I won't tell anybody. There's nothing to tell. Vader draws a lot of things, Moeder. Only he knows what they're all about, and nobody else cares anyway."

Before she'd let him go, she gave him one more uncomfortable warning. "These are family secrets, do you hear? Don't ever take even Robbin or his vader into that studio with you. They must never know about your vader's pictures."

"*Ja*, Moeder. Now can I go?"

Slowly she released him. He rubbed his sore arms and headed for the studio. He had to go take one more look just for himself to see if Dirck's Bible got the story straight.

CHAPTER THIRTEEN

Leyden

5th day of Wine Month (October), 1573

*T*he afternoon sun was already halfway to the line where pasturelands met leaden skies when Pieter-Lucas finally saw the first blurry outline of the towers and rooftops of Leyden. He nudged Blesje's flank and urged him forward.

"Make haste, old boy, for Aletta and the children lie almost within reach. The sooner we get there, the more hours we can steal with them."

He pulled his cape tightly around his body, shielding it from the penetration of a windblown shower of misty rain, and mumbled, more to himself than to the horse, "If we are lucky, this could be our last trip to Alkmaar. Don Frederic can't hold the city much longer. Spanish soldiers are terrified of rising water! Landlubbers of the most frenzied sort!"

He laughed at the Spaniards' fear. To every Lowlander it was nothing but unthinkable cowardice. Then he remembered the slaughter of Jemmingen and the Spaniard he had pushed into the swirling waters, and his laughter turned to a shudder. The point here was not fear of water, but fear of war. No matter how you looked at it, war was ugly, never laughable.

He rode on in gloomy silence, hearing only the occasional call of a pair of gulls soaring overhead and Blesje's hoofbeats on the damp trekpath beneath him. Shortly they entered a small dense stand of oak trees. The moisture hung heavier here, and he heard it dripping all around him on the carpet of orange and brown leaves, like the weeping of the eaves of a thickly thatched roof. He'd only passed a handful of trees, however, when he heard another sound, not a part of the wood, yet coming from it.

"Do you hear that, Blesje?" he asked and his heart picked up its tempo. "It's the moan of a man."

Everything he'd learned in this business of running messages for a prince told him to rush on past or go back and find another way around

the wood. He'd no idea what dangers might be lurking in a planned am-
bush nearby. His life was important to the whole land and to his prince.
He only had to remember the tragic loss of Yaap up in Friesland. If Yaap
had lived, Pieter-Lucas would not have to be doing his job these days.

He also remembered how he'd found Yaap dying in the peat bog beside a road. Pieter-Lucas had been on an urgent mission that morning,
too, when he heard the man's moans and, not knowing who he was, struggled sorely over what to do. But Hans, his Anabaptist weaver-preacher,
had taught him that a part of nonresistance was offering help to all who
suffered. So he'd stopped. He couldn't save Yaap's life, but he did carry
his message, which probably saved Ludwig's army.

Quickly now, he searched the wood all around him. He found not a
sign of life moving anywhere. The moaning came from a spot directly
beside him on the left of the pathway. He brought Blesje to a halt and,
squinting into the dimming light, discovered a crumpled human form
that had been shoved facedown into a thicket of bramble bushes.

"Robbers!" Pieter-Lucas gasped.

Wary, yet no longer questioning what he must do, he lept from the
horse. The man lay heaped in a large bloody ball. His clothes were ripped,
and there was not a sign of knapsack or staff.

"*Ach!* My head" came the weak moan.

Pieter-Lucas knelt beside him in the damp sandy soil and tried to roll
him over.

"Oh!" the man cried out, resisting all efforts to move him from his
prone position.

"I must give you a drink, then put you on my horse and take you to
a healer lady," Pieter-Lucas explained. Lifting him would not be the easiest
thing he'd done. The man was solid and rotund and obviously suffering
from some injuries that would probably be made worse by being moved.
Yet move him he must if he was not to die by the wayside. Surely this
was no place to bring Aletta so she could attend to him.

Ignoring the man's painful protests, Pieter-Lucas managed at last to
turn him over enough to give him a drink of beer from his skin bag. As
he did, the man stared at him through puffy dark eyes. A gash across his
forehead was streaked with blood like a hundred battle wounds Pieter-
Lucas had seen before. Something in the face caught his attention. Dark
eyes and hair and mustache, sharp nose. Where had he seen it before?

Ah, but of course! He started.

"You are the keeper of *The Clever Fox Inn*! Joris the innkeeper!"

The man stared on at him, not uttering a word.

"Your family is grieving that you have taken so long in returning," he went on. Then Pieter-Lucas wrapped Joris' limp arm around his neck, put his shoulder into the man's chest, and struggled to raise him to a sitting position.

"Can you stand and walk with my help?" he asked.

"I'll try" came the grunted reply.

With great effort and several false starts, Pieter-Lucas got him at last to his feet and pulled him to his horse. Here he helped him into the stirrup, then shoved him up and onto Blesje's back. Holding the man's doublet firmly, Pieter-Lucas swung himself into the saddle behind him and wrapped him securely, first in his cloak, then in his arms. He gave Blesje instructions to "ride gently, old boy," and they started off.

"My vrouw and her whole family are at your inn," Pieter-Lucas told Joris. "You are in the best of good fortune, in spite of your misfortune, for my vrouw is an excellent healer lady. She will know what to do to make you as whole as new."

The thought of carrying a suspected *marrano* through the streets of Leyden sent a chill down Pieter-Lucas' back. After the warnings both Jakob and Dirck had given him, he would have gone any other way just to avoid it—if he knew any other roads. On his own, he might simply take off over pasturelands. But they often had boggy spots, and more than once while pursuing such a course, he'd ended up in a corner between ditches of fast-flowing water. Alone and on foot he could pole jump most any ditch, but he was neither alone nor on foot, and clearly Joris was not fit for pole-jumping.

By now Joris was leaning heavily against Blesje's neck, breathing noisily. So Pieter-Lucas pulled the cape up over his head to cover it completely. Keeping utterly silent, as if somehow that would hide them from those they had reason to fear, they slipped across the bridge and through the Koe Poort into Leyden. Then they skirted the city just inside the walls.

"Great God," Pieter-Lucas breathed a prayer each time he saw people coming his direction, "protect us from this man's enemies and help me to keep him from falling off the horse."

No one spoke to them. No one stopped them. They reached the Zyl Poort on the other side of the city without incident and hurried toward the man's home.

About halfway down the trekpath along the Zyl river, Joris began to stir and mumble a string of barely audible words. Gradually they grew louder until he uttered a desperate cry, "*Yahweh!* Where is the ram? *Yahweh!* Where is the ram?"

He was out of his head! And wasn't that word, *Yahweh*, the Jewish name for God? Then the rumors could be true after all. Pieter-Lucas trembled.

He didn't know that he'd ever met a practicing Jew before. Most of the little he knew about Jews he'd learned from Hans when he gave him lessons on becoming a member of the Children of God.

"Many people hate the Jews passionately." He remembered how Hans' statement had shocked him.

"Wasn't Jesus a Jew?" Pieter-Lucas had asked.

"He was," Hans had answered. *"His disciples were too. So were the men who carried Him off to Pilate and had Him crucified. To this day, many Christians still call Jews Christ killers. Sad to say, those who believe in defending their church with a sword will not hesitate to cut off a man's head and steal his property just because he refuses to convert from Judaism to Christianity."*

That had never seemed quite right to Pieter-Lucas. Nor was it right that these same people burned other Christians too. As far as Pieter-Lucas knew, the preachers of those who called themselves Children of God were the only ones who taught their people to break their swords and live only by the Bible. Hans had assured him that, while he would always pray and work for the conversion of every Jew he ever met, he would also treat them with as much compassion as any other man, whether they converted or not.

"If we don't show them God's love in the name of Jesus, how will they ever believe that Jesus loves them too?" That was another of Hans' unforgettable lines.

Pieter-Lucas felt the man in his weary arms and pondered how he could show him kindness. "The way the Children of God handle things like war and Jews is the right way," he mumbled to himself.

The Clever Fox Inn lay just ahead. Inside, the man's vrouw was grieving over his strange journey and the cruelty of her neighbors who had somehow learned the truth, which she still thought was a vicious lie. How could Pieter-Lucas tell her the truth? How could he be certain it was the truth? A man's mad ravings could hardly be final evidence against him. Or could they?

Pieter-Lucas rode Blesje up to the inn and kicked on the door. Hiltje opened and stared at him with consternation.

"What's this?" she demanded. "I don't run a house for sick people."

"That I know," Pieter-Lucas said calmly, "but I thought you would want me to bring your husband home to you."

"Joris?" Her hands flew to her mouth, and she charged out the door and pulled back the cape. *"Ach! Ach! Ach!"* she moaned. "Where did you find him?"

"Along the roadside, just the other side of Leyden. Now call my vader-in-law to help me, then show us where to put him."

Dirck burst through the doorway and without a word helped Pieter-Lucas lift the unconscious man off the horse. They followed Hiltje's bustling lead into the family room, where they eased him into his cupboard bed. The distraught vrouw almost shoved them away in her eagerness to get to him.

"My vrouw will tell us what to do to restore him," Pieter-Lucas offered. Hiltje ignored him and was already patting her husband's face, calling out to him, trying to rouse him.

Pieter-Lucas turned to Dirck. "Where is Aletta?"

Dirck beckoned him to follow, but before they'd reached the doorway, she was coming toward them, her apothecary chest in hand.

"What happened?" she asked, her eyes full of concern.

"I found Joris alongside the road. Robbers attacked him, I think. He has a lump on his head and blood coming from his head and arm."

"Was he awake when you found him?"

"Halfway. Before we'd reached the inn, he was rambling with madness and has since fallen into a noisy sleep. Look! His vrouw cannot seem to rouse him."

"Has he a *heatte*?"

"I think not. Shall I go for water to clean out the wounds?"

"If you please," Aletta responded, approaching the bed. "Don't let the children come in. And you, Vader, stay by me. I may need your help here."

Pieter-Lucas grabbed a pitcher from the table beside the bed and hurried toward the kitchen. His mind whirred with memories of that long summer night up in Friesland when he and his newly wedded vrouw had spent half a night attending the wounded on a battlefield. How he had admired his angel of mercy! Compassion and tireless energy hovered over her like a halo over some saint in a cathedral painting and lent grace and beauty to each move she made.

He would go to the end of the earth to fetch an herb for her if she but said the word. And once he stepped out into the innyard to go to the well for water, he thought for an instant that that was where he'd gone. Half the yard lay in a heap of black soggy ashes. Christoffel and Robbin were sifting through the rubble of what had no doubt been a building of some sort. The dull acrid smell of wet ashes stung his nostrils and throat.

"What's happened here?" he said under his breath.

He dashed toward the well and began lowering the bucket into the water far below. What would Joris say when he discovered it?

A darting thought made him stop short with the bucket perched on the rim of the well. He'd never seen this innyard in daylight. Once or twice he'd led Blesje from the stable, but always before sunup. How big the shed was or how many other buildings may have stood with it, he had no idea.

"That wasn't your vader's painting studio, I hope," he shouted to Christoffel.

The boy looked up at him, face smudged with ashes, eyes wide and wistful. With a faraway kind of voice, he said, "*Nay*, just the stable."

Pieter-Lucas stood where he was for a moment and took in the whole scene while confused questions ran through his brain. Did the innkeeper really have a studio in the inn? Or was the whole story he'd heard from the boy's mouth nothing more than a wild tale designed to deceive him? He still couldn't believe this disappearing innkeeper was a painter. But if he didn't get to him soon with the water, the wounded man would no longer even be a living man of any kind.

Pieter-Lucas emptied the water into the pitcher, then dashed through the door and back to the room. Here in the light of a freshly lit lamp he found Aletta still hovering over her patient. Hiltje was sitting on the edge of the bed, cradling his silent head in her arm. With her other hand, she waved a sprig of lavender under his nose and whimpered, "Joris, my Joris, come back, come back!"

Pieter-Lucas poured water into a basin on a table by the bed, then submerged a cloth and handed it to Hiltje to hold to the lump on Joris' head. Then he and Aletta set to work cleaning out the wounds on the arm and spreading them with a healing Paré salve. As they did so, the man began to groan. He let out an enormous shriek of pain, then opened his eyes and stared about him.

"Joris!" Hiltje shouted. "You're alive and awake!"

"Where am I?" he muttered.

"In your bed," Hiltje answered eagerly.

He frowned. "How? *Ach!* My aching head!"

He put his hand to his temples, then closed his eyes once more and sighed so heavily he nearly shook the frame of the old cupboard bed.

With frantic movements, Hiltje began again waving the lavender beneath his nose. "*Nay, nay!* Faint not away," she pleaded.

Joris grunted something unintelligible, then moved his leg and began to moan, "Ow, that hurts. What happened?"

"Looks like some highway robbers clubbed you, stole your coins and whatever else you carried, then left you by the roadside," Hiltje said.

He stared at her, agitation brimming from his eyes and wrinkling his forehead into a massive frown. "*Ja? Ja!* I was almost home. . . ."

Pieter-Lucas caught the man's stare directed at him and watched his face writhe into a grimace.

"Who are you?" Joris demanded, his voice still weak but heavy with bewilderment.

"Pieter-Lucas, husband to the daughter of Dirck," he said gently, pausing to watch the dull stare.

"This man found you by the roadside and brought you home to us," Hiltje said, almost impatiently. "He's a good man."

"Oh," he said, his voice flattening out to nothing, his eyes closing once more.

"Move aside, Hiltje," Aletta coaxed, "so we can cleanse and dress the gash in his head."

"*Nay!*" She surrounded him with both arms and offered Aletta a look that combined defiance with fear.

"Then you may help me," Aletta conceded, taking the cloth from her hand, washing it out and offering it back to her.

Hiltje held it limply. "Me? I'm no healer."

"A vrouw is always a man's best healer," Aletta said with a smile.

Pieter-Lucas stood watching. Admiration flooded him clear to his toes. With a gentleness like he'd never seen in any woman—not even the Julianas from Dillenburg—she showed Hiltje how to spread on the salve and cover the wounds with a length of cloth. Each time the innkeeper groaned or turned his head, she reassured him in ways and words that only Aletta could ever think of.

Pieter-Lucas turned away and walked across the room to his vader-in-law, sitting on a three-legged stool, staring out the window at the charred ground beyond. "She's got a touch like no other," Pieter-Lucas said.

Dirck smiled up at him and nodded. Then his face grew sober, his voice hushed. "Got to keep the man down until he's completely healed."

Pieter-Lucas shrugged. "Think that'll be difficult?"

"Could be. When he sees his barn is reduced to ashes and . . ."

"And what?" Pieter-Lucas asked. "And learns about the rumors?"

Dirck didn't answer right away. Instead, he leaned the heels of his hands on the edge of his seat and sighed, nodding his head firmly, slowly.

"*Ja?*" Pieter-Lucas asked. "What then?"

"Don't know, son, don't know. After all, I don't know these people much. They're not even Children of God, and here I go sitting in this man's room watching my daughter spread healing salves on his mortal wounds and worrying about him as if he were a brother."

Pieter-Lucas thought for a long moment. In his mind he heard echoes of all sorts of lessons about Anabaptism from Hans and words from the Holy Book and a dozen preachers, and before he could sort it all out, he heard himself saying, "Not only does our belief in nonresistance refuse to wield a sword. It always searches out ways to make a man our brother and do him good." Then leaning over and whispering into Dirck's ear, he added, "Even if he is a Jew!"

Dirck started and jumped up to face him. "Shh! Don't say it aloud," he whispered. "You don't believe it . . . do you?"

Pieter-Lucas nodded. "I fear I do. I've heard Jewish words proceed from his mouth."

"Ah!" Dirck breathed out long and quietly, then searched the room in every direction. With his mouth almost in Pieter-Lucas' ear, he concluded, still whispering, "Then we have to do him good—especially if he is a Jew! That's the way of the Book!"

A rustling in the rushes came from the other side of the room. Pieter-Lucas looked up to see his vrouw coming toward them, her cheeks rosy and glowing warm in the lamplight. He went to her, circled her waist with his arm, and led her out of the room.

"Thanks be to you, my love," he said, still whispering, "for caring for the man."

" 'Tis God will touch and heal," she reminded him. "And He will. I know it."

"When I return from Alkmaar next time, perhaps he will be well and we can move into the city." He kissed her on the forehead.

"You're not leaving soon, I hope." She grabbed at his arm and looked at him with eyes full of pain.

"Hinder me not, my love," he said with a deep sigh. "I only stopped here to see you briefly on my way, and I've already been detained longer than was prudent."

"It's night outside," she reminded him. "Surely you will not start out now."

He enfolded her in a lingering embrace.

"*Nay*," he whispered into her golden curls that escaped around the edges of her cap. "I shall not leave before I've slept, but before the light of day bursts forth, I must go."

Arm in arm they walked toward the kitchen, where aromas from the evening meal hung heavy in the air. Perhaps these frequent visits were worse than the more infrequent ones while the family stayed in Dillenburg. At least then he had fewer partings to rip his heart in pieces.

13th day of Wine Month (October), 1573

Eight days later Pieter-Lucas returned to *The Clever Fox Inn*. He sailed through the door in the rays of afternoon sun, shouting out good news for all to hear.

"Alkmaar is relieved! Without another fight! Don Frederic could not move even one of his soldiers toward the city. He had to admit defeat and lift the siege."

"Where did they go?" Vader Dirck asked.

"To Amsterdam, the only city in the North still loyal to Spain," Pieter-Lucas said. Aletta hurried to him, Kaatje in her arms and little Lucas running ahead of her. He swept them all into strong arms and went on. "Then yesterday the sea Beggars defeated the Spanish fleet on the Zuyder Zee. And there is a rumor that Alva will soon be recalled to Spain!"

Christoffel clapped his hands and called out, "Long live the Beggars!"

Little Lucas did the same, in mimic. Aletta watched his chubby hands meeting awkwardly and wished he might never have to know what it all meant.

"Does this mean the war is over?" she asked, her heart leaping at the prospect.

"I wish it did," Pieter-Lucas responded. "At least it means the Low-landers are proving that we will not sit down and let Alva run over us any longer."

"Then Leyden is safe at last!" Christoffel said in a triumphant tone.

Pieter-Lucas turned toward him. "Don't count on it. Alva is a man of revenge! I've seen it before. It'll take more than a battle defeat or two to stop his plans. Whoever Philip sends to take his place most likely has something even worse in mind for Leyden."

Christoffel came toward Pieter-Lucas, raising a fist at the end of a strong arm. "The Beggars are strong and fierce—and they'll win!" He concluded with a firm punch of his fist and a screwed-up nose. Robbin joined with him and the two boys began an arm-wrestling match, with little Lucas struggling to get between them and join in their game.

Aletta opened her mouth to speak once more to her husband when Tryntje tapped her on the arm and said with urgent voice, "Come, my moeder needs you."

"What is it?" Aletta asked, her mind suddenly filled with thoughts that did not cause rejoicing. She handed Kaatje to Pieter-Lucas and hurried after the girl.

"She cries," Tryntje said.

Aletta put an arm around a trembling shoulder and tried to console the girl. "She's sad, Tryntje. Your vader has been sick for many days, and she never leaves his bedside."

"I know," the girl said. Then shaking her head, she added, her own voice quavering on the brink of tears, "But Moeder never cries. I think she grows sick too."

Ever since Pieter-Lucas brought the innkeeper home, Joris had not left his bed. Sometimes he awoke and actually talked with his vrouw. But mostly he slept, often tossing restlessly, grimacing and crying out in pain. With the help of the older children, Vader Dirck and Moeder Gretta managed the inn, though they had few guests. Mieke did the marketing and helped with the little ones while Aletta attended to the needs of Hiltje and the ailing patient and tried to teach Clare and Tryntje something about herbal cures.

They had all grown weary of the long wait through the anxious days, but Aletta worried over the man. He'd obviously taken a blow to the head, and she'd known of more than one person to die of that sort of injury.

She worried over Hiltje as well. No one could persuade her to leave her husband for anything, nor would she laugh or cry or talk with anyone except about his condition and the herbs Aletta dispensed. Her daughters faithfully took her food to eat, but often it lay untouched.

Aletta walked behind Tryntje into the dingy room, which now reeked with the heavy odors of chamber pots, herbal potions, and sickness. It echoed from corner to corner with loud wailing sobs. Hiltje sat on a stool with her head resting facedown on both arms spread out on the bed. Clare stood with a hand on her moeder's shoulder and continually begged, "Stop, Moeder, stop!"

The girl looked up at Aletta, tears streaking her own cheeks, and her face suddenly wrinkled far beyond her nine years.

"What is it?" Aletta asked.

"I don't understand. When I came into the room, Vader was mumbling in that strange voice he uses when he's not awake. Then he sat straight up in bed, looked at Moeder, and said very sadly, 'Don't tell Hiltje, but I'm really a Jew.' Then he lay back down and fell asleep.

"Moeder screamed at him, 'How could you? Nay! Nay!' He didn't answer and she's done nothing but cry and shout, '*Nay!*' ever since."

Aletta gasped. "Do you know what he meant?"

"*Nay*. It must be something pretty terrible, though, to make Moeder so sad." The girl latched on to Aletta's arm now and pleaded, "Oh, please, Tante 'Letta, can you do something?"

"It sounds like she suffers from a broken heart, and we have not so many herbs for that sort of cure, but I shall try."

Aletta lay her hands on Hiltje's heaving shoulders, rubbing them gently. "My dear woman," she said, her own heart overwhelmed with vicarious pain, "calm, calm now. Whatever your husband says to you, just remember his brain is not working the same as it did before his injury."

"*Nay!* But I fear he speaks the truth," she cried out and went on sobbing.

"Still, Hiltje, still. When he is well, he will put your mind at rest."

She did not answer. Aletta prayed silently, *Great God in the Heaven, you are the only healer that can touch this woman's heart—or her husband's body and brain. Show me what to do next, show me what to do.*

Almost without thinking, she reached into her bodice and pulled out Tante Lysbet's tattered old herbal book. How many things she had been through with this treasure! It had helped her deliver a baby when no one had shown her how. She'd used it for creating salves for all wounds that Paré salve would not help, potions for coughs that refused to go away, little roots hung about the neck to chase away stubborn evil humors. Now she must search its pages for a cure for a broken heart.

She found nothing but borage. Everyone knew about borage and everyone used it when they could find it. It didn't always work, and Aletta continually searched for something better. She hadn't tried it with Hiltje yet because there was none growing in the inn garden. She'd brought many herbs with her from Dillenburg, but borage must be fresh.

Turning to Clare and Tryntje who hovered nearby, she asked, "Do you know what borage is?"

"Borage? I've heard of it," said Clare.

"Is there an herb garden anywhere nearby? Anything this side of the city?"

"There is the cloister of the hermit sisters," Tryntje said and Clare nodded.

"Where is it?" Aletta asked.

"Just down the river a few paces and off to the east at the end of its own tiny path," Clare explained.

"They have a whole big garden full of herbs." Tryntje spread her arms wide.

"Moeder always said there isn't a thing they can't heal with one of their herbs," Clare added.

Aletta felt a quickening in her heart. "Can you take me there, Tryntje?"

"Me?" The seven-year-old pointed to her chest and her eyes lit up. "*Ja,* if you will let me go. We both go there whenever Moeder needs anything."

"And what shall I do with Moeder while you're gone?" Clare asked.

"I'll send my own moeder in to help you," Aletta said. Then rubbing Hiltje's back once more, she promised, "I go to fetch an herb for your sorrow, and we come directly back."

————

The cloister hardly fit any description Aletta knew for a religious house. Nothing more than a thatched hut, it was set, as Tryntje had said, back from the trekpath at the end of a weed-grown pathway. All the way around the ramshackle old hut, Aletta saw rows of familiar plants—dried stalks that had three months ago been bright with red hollyhocks, and purple foxgloves, and low shrubs of old greenery that had bloomed with calendulas. In neat little rows and blocks, there were hundreds of the herbs Aletta had grown to know and use. Her heart swelled up as if it would burst at the sight of so much healing power—and all so close to *The Clever Fox Inn*! Could it be that there might be something here she had not seen elsewhere, something that could help her own Kaatje? *Nay,* not now. Joris and Hiltje were in mortal danger at this moment. Kaatje could wait.

The sister who opened the top half of the dilapidated old door at their knock greeted them with a wary smile. Her sharp-featured face was nearly swallowed up in her voluminous nun's habit.

"Good afternoon, and what can I do to serve you?" she asked pleasantly.

They called her a hermit, yet Aletta felt a warmth in this shriveled-up woman that both frightened and attracted her. "We've come in search of a stalk of borage," Aletta answered, "to bring cheer to a man and his vrouw in much distress."

"Come you from far away?"

"*Nay*, only down the Zyl trekpath a short ways . . ." Aletta hesitated to go on.

Tryntje spoke up, "From *The Clever Fox Inn*!"

The woman leaned over the doorsill and stared at the child. A smile spread across her face. "Ah, *ja*, you are the child that comes for herbs. And your vader and moeder are ill?"

"Vader was attacked by robbers, and Moeder is sad to watch him lie so ill in bed."

The sister opened the whole door now and welcomed them in. "What is this about?" she directed her question to Aletta.

Aletta nodded. "The man was indeed attacked by robbers, and I have given him every herb in my stock. I came here from Countess Juliana of Dillenburg, Moeder of Prince Willem, and she sent me with a full supply.

Nothing I've tried seems to touch him, and his vrouw does not leave him day or night. She eats so little and sleeps so little that she, too, has grown thin and sorrowful. She has not so much as a plant of borage on the place, and I thought you might have some we could take back and root in the garden of the inn."

As she talked she was aware that the sister had been joined by another, a taller woman with round cheeks. Both sisters seemed to be eyeing her up and down, as if trying to decide whether to believe and trust her.

"Have you tried rosemarie," asked the first sister. "It dries the brains and quickens the senses and memory."

"And balm that opens the stopping of the brain?" asked the second. "It also drives away sorrow and care of the mind, as does saffron when used in moderation."

Aletta nodded. "All these I have tried, along with marjoreome in his nostrils and a chewing of the combination of pellitorie and luyscruit roots. Nothing seems to work."

"Also sneezewoort?"

"It is powerful, as is white hellebor, to mightily bring forth slimy phlegm from the brain."

Both women stood in silence and sighed. "What more?" the first asked of the second.

"Primrose roots, fennell juice, galingale root, sage?"

Aletta shook her head and fought down a huge feeling of hopelessness rising in her breast. "I've tried them all. Joris sleeps on and on, waking only now and again to talk to his vrouw. And now that she is so low, I begin to fear for her. Surely the borage will help her if nothing more. With her husband, we must wait and pray. Such illnesses can take much time to begin to heal."

The women looked at each other, nodded, and started toward the door. "Then borage you shall have."

"This is not the good time of the year to dig it up and replant it. But we've aplenty. Take what you need and come again for more as often as you need it." The smaller sister was cutting an entire stalk from the large shrub of a plant that grew in a sheltered spot up against the south side of the house.

Aletta took the precious leaves in her arms, thanked the sisters, and hurried home with Tryntje running to keep up with her. These women were going to be her friends. She could feel it. No matter that they lived alone in this desolate place, they had a compassion for bodies and spirits in need. If Hiltje spoke the truth about them, people came here from far around in search of herbal potions, salves, roots, powders, and remedies of a hundred sorts.

Someday, when Joris was well and Hiltje's household restored to order, Aletta would come back—with Kaatje. There must be a cure for that stiff foot somewhere. Why not here? Hadn't she asked her Heavenly Vader to show her the way—in this place?

CHAPTER FOURTEEN

Leyden

20th day of Wine Month (October), 1573

J oris awoke with a start and sat straight up in bed. Where was he? A loud familiar snoring came from the other side of the bed.

Am I home? Surely no one snores like my Hiltje. But how and when did I come here? He scratched his head and felt a dull pain. A procession of fuzzy thoughts marched through his brain—memories of excruciating pain, flashes of faces coming at him through a foggy and desolate darkness, sounds of voices—weeping, calling, whispering.

He pulled back the curtains of the bed cupboard and stared. A pale light filled the room and silence held it lightly. From somewhere out beyond, a rooster crowed. Carefully, so as not to disturb his sleeping vrouw, he moved toward the edge of the cupboard and attempted to sit up and let himself down to the floor. But his head swam, his legs wobbled like unwieldy stilts, and he had to grab on to the bed to keep from falling.

"Joris!" came Hiltje's voice and instantly she was tugging at him. "You can't get out of bed."

"Why not?" he asked, dumbfounded first by his weakness, then by her highly unusual advice. Couldn't a man even leave his own bed without being browbeaten by his vrouw?

She shoved him solidly back down under the covers, and he found no strength to resist her. "For weeks now you've been lying as still as death," she said, "like a man with his head in a sock. . . ."

"What do you mean?" He shook his head and tried to clear the fog that kept him from understanding what had happened.

"Joris, Joris," she cried out, tucking the feather bag under his chin and patting his shoulders as if to anchor him to the bed. "Have you no memory of the long days and nights we've spent in this spot?"

He frowned at her and did not answer. What was she talking about?

"Nor do you remember anything you said in your sleep—or out of it?" she prodded.

He shook his head and shuddered. What kinds of secrets had he divulged? He listened to her sigh the sort of deep gut-wrenching sigh she always used when she couldn't get rid of an impossible inn guest or when she insisted he ought to be more firm with Christoffel for misbehaving.

"You ran away from us all, forever ago," she began in the haranguing manner that made her Hiltje. "You said you were going to visit your brother in Ghendt. We waited and waited for your return. Then one day Dirck's son brought you home on his horse. All bloodied and groaning with pain, you were, not a *stuiver* in your pocket, no knapsack on your back, a lump on your head. You've lain in this bed ever since. That was weeks ago. We're halfway through Wine month already."

Straining to remember, Joris shook his head and mumbled, "Then it's time I get up." With great effort he pushed himself up again on wobbly arms and attempted to swing his feet over the edge of the bed.

She grabbed and held him fast.

"Not until you have had something to eat to give you strength," Hiltje insisted, then called out, "Oh, Clare! Come quickly, Clare!"

Feeling suddenly faint, he leaned against the wall of the cupboard, moaning, "What is wrong with me?"

"On your way home from Ghendt, you were nearly killed by some robbers," Hiltje said, "and the herbal healer daughter of Dirck and Gretta has spent days giving you first one herbal cure, then another, watching and waiting for you to come to your senses. She called on the hermit sisters down the lane several times, and they gave her everything they had, from borage to distilled wine. Look at you, Joris, you've lost your paunch, and the skin hangs like a monk's robe on your arms and chin."

He looked at his arms. They were sagging. Then into her eyes, and she was looking into his. He saw compassion and concern there, of her deepest kind. She was always a worrisome woman—that he'd known for years. This time, though, he fancied that she worried for him, not at him.

Clare and Tryntje were both padding across the room now, rubbing their eyes and crying out, "Vader! You're awake!" Shortly Christoffel stood behind them.

"Now go, girls," Hiltje ordered, "and fix your vader a cup of broth with an egg and a handful of borage sprinkled on top. Add it at the last, remember, so it turns not the whole thing bitter."

The girls scurried off to do their moeder's bidding, and Christoffel came close and stood beside his vader. He laid a hand on his arm and just stared, saying nothing, his face a portrait of uncertainty—like the old portrait of Isaac on the altar. The portrait he must change now that he had new faces. Wait! What was that Hiltje had said about his knapsack?

"Vrouw," he said, "where did you say my knapsack is?"

She threw up her hands and looked as if she might burst into a flood of tears. Not that he'd ever seen her cry, but that was the way the children looked when they were about to do so. "Ask the robbers who attacked you in the road! The way you looked, you were fortunate to come home with your life. Who could worry about a knapsack?"

Joris's mouth went dry. He felt Christoffel's eyes boring into him and heard his voice, soft but urgent, "Were the new faces in your knapsack?"

He looked up at Christoffel, shook his head, and said with genuine pain, "I'll find more, I promise."

"What are you talking about?" Hiltje asked.

"Just painter's talk," he said and stared at his son, wanting to say more.

Hiltje jumped from the bed and waved at the boy with shooing motions. "Now, off with you, *jongen*, so I can dress and be about the day's business. And you go do the same."

Christoffel turned, saying nothing, then hurried across the room toward his own cupboard bed.

30th day of Wine Month (October), 1573

Near the end of a long day of hard riding, Pieter-Lucas entered through the Koe Poort and headed for the town hall at the center of Leyden. How he wished he could skirt the inside of the wall and go straight for Aletta by the way he had carried Joris home in a heap of bloody senselessness. But today he must first deliver an urgent warning from Prince Willem to the burgemeesters.

Just as he'd expected all along, Alva was going for his revenge for his defeats at Alkmaar and on the Zuyder Zee. It would be a parting legacy to leave behind on his own soon departure from the Low Lands. Already Don Francisco Valdez, his most able of military captains, was preparing for a siege of Leyden. Hole-peepers had reported to Willem that they planned not to bombard Leyden as they had done with such prolonged expense to Spanish life and treasury in both Haarlem and Alkmaar.

Rather, they would blockade Leyden, imprisoning the citizens in their own city, that they might perish by starvation. Then "some wintry night, when the canals and ditches are frozen hard, I may succeed in surprising and overwhelming them," the retiring Alva had boasted.

Pieter-Lucas delivered the message and started from the building.

Before he could reach the doors, a trio of burgemeesters stopped and led him quietly into a side room where they tethered the door and encircled him tightly. In rapid succession the men fired questions at him, waiting only shortly for his answers.

"You and your family are staying at *The Clever Fox Inn* these days, is that not so?"

"That we are," Pieter-Lucas answered. "What difference should that make?"

"You may or may not have heard the rumors about Joris, the innkeeper."

Pieter-Lucas felt six eyes staring at him. "I have heard some rumors." That much he was willing to concede.

"What you may not have heard is that they were started as a part of a plot by the *glippers* in our midst to entrap the man."

"*Glippers*? What have they to gain by such a scheme?" Pieter-Lucas asked.

"If they can intimidate the innkeeper, they might persuade him to give over his inn for the boarding of their soldiers."

"So long as they have a live rumor to hang over his head, they believe he has not much choice in the matter."

"We foresaw this weeks ago and tried to persuade him to dismantle the inn and move into the city. But he flatly refused—like so many others have done."

"Then just before the priest began to circulate the rumor, old Joris fled—on some secretive mission."

"Making him look all the more guilty of the accusations."

Pieter-Lucas shivered. "So the *glippers* were the men who robbed him on his way home, intending, no doubt, to kill him so they could take over *The Clever Fox Inn*?"

"Indeed. In fact, they thought they had accomplished it. But news has been circulating of late that he lives yet."

"And what can I do to save the man, his inn, and my family all at once?" Pieter-Lucas asked.

"You must warn him immediately of his danger. Tell him under no circumstances is he to yield to their pleadings."

"Under no circumstances, is that clear?"

Pieter-Lucas stared at the three men surrounding him, his heart beating wildly. "What, then, is he to do when they continue to hassle him?"

"Stand firm. He must refuse to give lodging to the Spanish army."

"Or any other army, for that matter. These men may pose as patriots and suggest the men they're bringing him are Beggars or some such."

"He must not listen to them!"

"Not for a minute! Remember, it is a traitorous plot."

"You must convince him of this, keep him from giving in!" The man who spoke the final words was pointing directly at him.

"What if they try to force him with swords?" Wild thoughts spun around in Pieter-Lucas' brain. "What will happen to my family?"

"We will be watching and rescue you all. Just be prepared, when we say the word, to flee into the city."

"All of you!"

"But not until we say the word!"

"And when we say to leave, you must see to it that no one dallies. We will raze the buildings at once. Do you hear? At once!"

"I hear," Pieter-Lucas said. "Will I see your faces when it happens so I know the orders came from you and not from the enemy?"

The men hesitated, looking at one another. Then one spoke for them all. "At least one of our faces."

"And you will do as you are told. That is agreed, eh?"

"I shall," Pieter-Lucas stammered, though the spinning of his head went on. What had he agreed to? So far as he knew, these men were unfeigned patriots. But these days, in Leyden, you never knew for sure who had changed allegiances since last you saw him.

"Now, be on your way and waste no time about it!" The man with the largest voice said the last word, all the while pressing his finger into Pieter-Lucas' chest. Then the circle opened to let him through. Dazed, he moved out into the late afternoon on trembling legs, shaking his head all the way.

He slapped Blesje on the flank and prepared to mount. "What next will this war bring to my family, old boy? What next?" Today, riding out of the city and toward the trekpath, Pieter-Lucas felt like an old man with a heavy black bag strapped to his shoulders.

———

In a rare moment when Hiltje was not watching over his every move, Joris took to his still-wobbly legs and made for the kitchen door. He'd been growing steadily stronger ever since he awoke several days ago. And he'd become eager to go out to the stable and stroke the horses. He longed to climb up into the loft and don his prayer shawl and intone the Sh'ma in the moonlight. How or when he'd ever get away at night, he couldn't imagine. Not the way his vrouw hovered over him. He couldn't even turn over in bed without her grabbing at him.

"What's she so afraid of, anyway?" he'd asked himself at least ten times a day. True, he'd evidently come home badly beaten, though he couldn't recall how it happened. All he remembered was walking along the road not far from Leyden, thinking about the promises he'd made to God in Ghendt and wondering how he was going to make good on them. The rest was gone!

This late afternoon, looking out into a world made golden by the sun slipping to the horizon at pasture's edge, he still had no answers. With amazingly difficult effort, he stepped up over the doorsill. Leaning against the doorframe, he looked up, as if intending to count how many halting steps it would take to reach his destination.

He gasped! The stable was gone! And the old oven was tumbled into a heap of charred bricks. The leaf-bare branches of the lindens beyond were blackened and the ground a mass of fresh green sprouts of grass on a background of more black. Ashes? A fire? He took his head in both hands and groaned, "*Nay*, it cannot be."

Numbly, he wandered out into the yard until he stood where once the stable had been and stooped to pick up what was left of the ashes. "My prayer shawl!" he whispered, sifting the ashes through his fingers. "Hear, O Israel, *Yahweh* is One *Yahweh*!" he went on. "How will I ever be able to teach my children in His ways? Am I too late?"

For a long while, he allowed his fingers to roam over and through the ashes, while in his heart there smoldered a faint spark of hope that somehow he might yet uncover even a tiny piece of the shawl.

"Ashes! Nothing but ashes!" he began to mutter, a wild and dizzy feeling growing in his mind. Surely this was not real. He must still be lying in his bed dreaming. He looked up from the grimy graveyard of his best intentions. There, standing nearly on top of him, he saw four legs. He hurried to his feet, automatically wiping smudgy hands on his breeches, and faced two strangers.

"Are you Joris, keeper of *The Clever Fox Inn*?" asked one of the men.

Joris swallowed and spread his hands out behind him in a struggle to gain his balance after standing so quickly up. "That I am," he answered. "And you?"

"Representatives from the army of Prince Willem," said the other.

Joris stared at them askance, his brow wrinkled, his eyes squinting. "Beggars?"

The men laughed nervously. "Not all Willem's men are Beggars," said one.

Joris sensed a hollowness in the men's words. They didn't even wear uniforms. Dressed like ordinary burgers, they were. Merchantmen from

Leyden. While he didn't know them, he'd seen them before—he was al-most sure of it.

"So what is your business for Willem?" Joris asked, wishing for a door or a post or a stable wall to lean against. He began to walk back and forth, his clogs scooping up ashes. It was easier than standing unsupported.

The men cleared their throats. "Since Alva's humiliating defeats in Alk-maar and on the Zuyder Zee, he's begun his revenge. His men are about to raise a massive siege to strangle Leyden. And Willem needs *The Clever Fox Inn* to house a regiment of his men to fight off the blockade."

Joris frowned. "I was told that Willem wanted us all to dismantle our buildings to keep the Spaniards at bay. Now you say he wants to board his men here. What shall I believe?"

His visitors exchanged uneasy glances, then shrugged and smiled too eagerly for Joris' comfort.

"Aha, but that was weeks ago," said one.

"The war has changed everything," added the other.

Joris stared at them, saying nothing, wishing they'd go away and let him find his way back to bed.

"So we have come to alert you that tomorrow we shall bring Willem's men here to lodge them in your quarters."

Joris bristled. A fresh flow of strength possessed him and he spoke up quickly. "You cannot do that."

"What is to stop us?"

"My inn is occupied by permanent guests, and I am too ill to care for so many soldiers just now." His palms grew stickier with each word. His mind brought back pictures of the dining room swarming with noisy, swaggering Beggars. It was the last thing he wanted.

One man drew closer to him and laid a hand on Joris' shoulder. Lean-ing his head forward, he spoke with an entreating tone. "I know those Beggars are rowdy creatures. If I owned a decent inn like this one, I would not want to let them in either. If you refuse them, though, most likely before the week is over, the Spaniards will come and force their way in. You will have to accept them at sword point."

"Spanish soldiers can be really ugly," added the other man. The grin that spread across his face made Joris more uncomfortable than the thought of either Beggars or Spaniards in all his rooms.

The first man reached for the black money bag tied around his waist. Shaking it till its coins jingled, he said in a honeyed tone, "Besides, as Willem's men, of course, we are prepared to pay you enough coins to make up for all the loss in business this nasty war has already occasioned."

Joris stared at the men who were both grinning like naughty boys.

Beggars with coins to jingle? *Nay!* Something didn't hold together here. He had to stop them.

Feeling weak and trembly all over, he raised a hand and said, "Come back tomorrow, if you must have an answer."

The men straightened in response, their smiles vanished, and they assumed a rigid military pose. "We will be back tomorrow, not for your answer but for your rooms. We did not ask your permission, we simply gave you warning."

One man thrust his face up close to Joris', poked a finger in his chest, and said, "You know, if you do not cooperate, you could find yourself locked up in the tower dungeon in a cell reserved for *marranos* like you!"

Both men laughed loud devilish laughs, then turned on their heels, mounted their horses, and took to the trekpath. Dazed, Joris stumbled toward the house.

"Did they call me by that most despicable of all names? Surely not! No one in Leyden knows my secrets." He shook his head and felt it ache. Every part of him wished for a bed where he could put both body and mind to sleep till this awful war was past. *Ach,* but what would tomorrow bring? Inquisition? In Leyden? *Nay!*

Just as he reached the house, a young man walked around the studio end of the inn and hurried to him. Bewildered, Joris stared at him in the fading light. He'd been here before. . . . Ah, *ja,* that messenger who always came at night.

"Sit, Joris. I have urgent news, and you are not well." His visitor was guiding him to a bench near the door and sitting with him.

"Pieter-Lucas is my name," he began, "and my wife has been your herbal healer for these days."

"Humph!" Joris grunted. "What do you want with me?" If he also asked him to take in a bunch of Beggars, he'd throw out the whole family.

"Those men that just talked with you," Pieter-Lucas said quickly, "I knew they were coming."

"Because you're one of them, *ja?* Well, I've already decided, the answer is *nay, nay, nay!*" Joris waved a finger in his face with all the strength he could muster.

Pieter-Lucas raised a hand in protest. "*Nay,* I'm not one of them. They're not from the prince at all. I was sent to warn you not to be fooled by them."

"But they said—"

"I know what they said. I heard it all. Lies, they were all lies."

"Who are they, then?" Joris sighed.

"*Glippers!*"

"Glippers?" A menacing picture of the priest from the Pieterskerk filled his fuzzy brain.

"One thing they said is true. They will be back."

"I won't let them in. I'm still the innkeeper here!" Why did he not feel as strong as he sounded?

"You can't stop them, do you hear me? They'll bring with them a whole army of Spaniards!"

"So what do we do—desert the place and let them take over? Just what they wanted all along!" Joris raised a fist. *"Nay!* That I shall never do!"

"Joris, hear me." Pieter-Lucas looked hard at him, his eyes filled with a soberness that almost frightened him. "The burgemeesters are coming tonight—to raze the inn to the ground."

"Nay!" he protested. "They'll have to kill me first!"

"You're ready to sacrifice your family?"

"Nay, not my family!" He felt a sudden tightness in his chest and leaned against the younger man's shoulder.

"Don't you see, Joris? It's the only way to keep the Spaniards out. We must begin this moment to collect all the things you need to take with you. When they come with their torches, it'll be too late."

The whole world was spinning at a dizzying speed in Joris' head now. "Where will we go?" he gasped. He felt himself slump to the ground and everything went dark once more.

When he came to again, he was ensconced in his bed. Flickering candlelight pranced about Hiltje as she hovered over him, and the strong odors of herbs nearly gagged him. Something tickled his nose and he reached up to scratch it. But the feather bag held him so tightly around the throat he could not move.

"Joris, Joris, thank God you live!" Hiltje cried out. "Go, Tryntje, fetch the broth."

"Ach, Vrouw, but I had a dreadful dream," Joris mumbled. "Some strangers had come to me in the yard and told me they were Willem's men and were bringing a parcel of Beggars to live in our inn. Then Dirck's son came after them and told me they were not patriots, but Spaniards. He said we'd have to pack up our valuables and move into the city because the burgemeesters were coming to raze the inn. It was awful, Vrouw, something awful!"

She was smoothing his forehead with both hands. "Rest, rest, husband. *Ach* me! How did I ever leave you alone to roam around the place?"

He closed his eyes again and felt the worry and fear drain away. When he smelled the aroma of broth, he looked up at Tryntje's cherubic cheeks and saw childish anxiety in her wide blue eyes.

"Bless you, child," he murmured.

If only he could just get well again. *Ach*, but he never should have gone to Ghendt. How much sorrow and pain it had brought to them all. And with the stable gone . . . and his "new faces" . . . *Nay!* But he would find a way.

He let Hiltje hold his head up with her arm and sipped the broth she put to his lips. Never had broth tasted so delicious or felt so warm and soothing going down! Did it presage better days?

———

Once Pieter-Lucas had rolled Joris into his bed, he lingered, standing behind Hiltje, just long enough to see the man open his eyes. Then grabbing Christoffel by an arm and moving him along with him, he rushed to the other end of the inn to round up his own family and prepare them to leave.

Christoffel protested, trying to pull away. "Where are you taking me?" he asked.

"I need to talk to you!" Pieter-Lucas answered. "I must give my family the same urgent message. So you follow me and you'll learn what's going on and what you need to do." He knocked on Dirck and Gretta's door.

"What urgent message, and who gave it to you to give to us?"

The boy's saucy tone irritated Pieter-Lucas. Dirck opened the door and Pieter-Lucas said, "Gather up all your belongings and prepare to leave at a moment's notice. Ask me no questions, just get ready. I go for Aletta and the children."

As he turned, he heard Dirck say, "We are ready. . . ."

Without stopping to ask how he knew to get ready, Pieter-Lucas, still dragging Christoffel, hurried across the edge of the dining room. "The message is the same for you, *jongen*," he said. "Your vader is not well enough to do the job of a man here. Your moeder is consumed with caring for him. It's up to you and your sisters to gather up everything of importance and pack it into bags."

"What do you mean?" Christoffel pulled his arm from Pieter-Lucas' grip and stood at the foot of the stairs.

"The burgemeesters are coming to raze this building to the ground, and whatever you do not rescue before they begin, you will never see again. That's what I mean!"

Christoffel stared at him, arms folded across his chest, feet planted wide apart.

Pieter-Lucas grabbed him by the lapel and shouted, "If you value those precious paintings of ships and Beggars and whatever, you will heed my warning!"

Then he took the stairs three at a time and burst into the room where his family lodged. They all sat perched on the edge of the bed, their belongings bundled in a row at their feet. Lucas jumped off the bed and ran toward him, calling out, "Vader! Vader!"

"What's this?" Pieter-Lucas asked, picking up the boy and hugging him. "You're all ready!"

"Please tell us we need not be," Aletta answered.

"I wish I could. Who told you we were going anywhere?"

"I told her," Mieke said, a grin of satisfaction filling her face.

Pieter-Lucas started. Would he never get used to this hole-peeper nursemaid who saw and heard everything and was always preparing everybody's way out of trouble before they even knew trouble was in the air? He stood still for a moment, trying to make sense of it all.

Lucas twisted his hat around sidewise and laughed. "You look funny that way, Vader."

Pieter-Lucas gave him a quick grin, then turned to Mieke. "Go help Dirck and Gretta get ready."

"I already has," Mieke said, clasping hands in front of her and swaying her body nervously back and forth. "Want us to take th' bags down?"

Pieter-Lucas gaped at her. "*Ja!* Pile them by the door to the kitchen. Then help Christoffel and his sisters round up their things."

He set Lucas on the floor, and the whole family sprang into action, carrying bags down to the appointed meeting place, then rushing off to help Christoffel and his sisters.

No sooner had he entered the kitchen than he heard noises coming from the yard. "Great God," he prayed under his breath, "let it be the burgemeesters, not the traitorous Spaniards." Rushing from the house, he found himself surrounded by more mounted men than he could count in the half darkness. Their faces glowed like spirits in the light of the pitchy torches they carried. Straight in front of him stood the same three men who had apprehended him earlier in the town hall. He sighed his relief.

"It's time," the leader said. "The Spaniards will be here before morning. Where is the innkeeper?"

"In his bed. His vrouw hovers over him like a mother hen over an unhatched egg."

The three men conferred briefly. "We must set him on a horse in the center of the company."

"Don't try to separate him from his vrouw, I warn you," Pieter-Lucas said.

"How many more are you?"

"Four more full-grown ones, four large children, one little boy, and a baby—beside myself."

"So many?"

"I can go get our coach," Pieter-Lucas offered.

"*Nay*, no time for that. Time is life! Who knows at what moment the soldiers may arrive?"

"So what, then?"

"We load the people onto the horses and ride all of us together in a group."

"Very well. I shall get the innkeeper," Pieter-Lucas said, not letting the men cross the threshold. "His vrouw knows nothing of what is going on, and if you rush in uninvited and unannounced, she'll fight you off."

Pieter-Lucas crept into the sickroom, where he found Hiltje pacing the floor beside her sleeping husband. He tapped her on the shoulder. "Vrouw Hiltje, you and Joris must come with me."

She stared at him, frowning, but not saying a word.

"You need to know, Vrouw Hiltje, that the burgemeesters of Leyden are even now on your back doorstoop awaiting my signal to come and carry you to safety into the city."

"I knew they were coming. But so soon? The girls are still packing up our valuables."

"How did you know?"

"Joris told me he had dreamed it, but I knew it was no dream. That little elfin nursemaid of your vrouw's, she's been here warning me. I hoped she was wrong, but I knew . . ."

"I go for help with Joris," Pieter-Lucas said, then ran for the burgemeesters.

The next moments were a blur of movement and strange sounds as the men from Leyden emptied the old inn of all its people and prepared them for their journey. Joris was awakened by the hubbub when they lifted him out of his bed. While he screamed and thrashed about in protest, he had little strength to resist and was soon securely settled on horseback with one of the burgemeesters.

Pieter-Lucas scurried about matching riders and bags with horsemen. He committed little Lucas to the care of his grandvader on his own horse. Then he went from horse to horse, searching each face in the light of a lantern, until he'd accounted for every member of both households. Finally, settling Aletta and the baby on Blesje, he climbed on behind them.

Just as the company prepared to start, Joris cried out, "Christoffel . . . the pictures!"

"Hush, Joris," Hiltje said from beside him. "He has them."

"I hope she's right," Pieter-Lucas muttered to Aletta, "because what's not rescued now will not be here in the morning."

The procession began, leaving behind a trio of men with blazing torches and fast-riding horses. A mistlike dew gathered on their coats and hats and slickened the trekpath. An ominous crackling sound came from behind, and the call of a long-horned owl sounded like a funereal trumpet that followed them nearly to the Rhine.

Pieter-Lucas held his wife and Kaatje fast in his arms ahead of the saddle and guided Blesje gently. He drew strength and courage from their warmth. Not until they turned west just outside the city walls did he look back. Huge tongues of bright orange and gold reached up toward the heaven, and Pieter-Lucas imagined he felt their warmth as well.

He heard Hiltje's voice cry out from the center of the pack. "She's seen the flames!" he whispered. He tightened his grip on his vrouw and drove Blesje onward.

"Is the inn gone?" Aletta murmured from the hollow of his chest.

"All gone," he answered and soon heard and felt the clatter of horses' hooves on the wooden bridge at the Zyl Poort.

————————

In the pale light of a moon obscured by fleeting clouds, Christoffel climbed the stairs of the old citadel. He brought along Vader's paintings in a long roll and as many of his own belongings as he'd salvaged from the inn, wrapped in his feather bag.

"If Leyden's in so much danger that we had to abandon the inn, then just maybe the citadel door might be open," he mumbled. At the thought, his hands oozed moisture and he quickened his pace.

He hurried to the top where everything looked the same as always. But as was his habit, he shoved against the door with his shoulder. Was that a movement he felt—or did his imagination will it to be so? He shoved again, this time harder. No doubt about it now. The door yielded to the pressure and, with a loud creaking sound, scraped across the grass.

Ecstatic, Christoffel followed it inward until he stood in the middle of a grassy circle. With so little light, he could only make out the faint outline of the heavy circular wall. He headed toward it and found himself in what appeared to be a small alcove with a roof of sorts.

Here he rolled up in his bag and spent the rest of the night pondering the tragedy that had forced them out of their home and the miracle that dangerous times had opened up a door into his fondest dreams. Sometime in the night he drifted off to sleep and knew nothing till morning splashed his face with light and stiff cold breezes stirred around him in his make-shift shelter.

"Oh!" He let the word escape softly from his lips. "It's just the way I always knew it was. The wall is full of arrow slits!"

Then throwing back the feather bag from his shoulders, he scrambled to the edge of the wall behind him and pressed his face up against the slit nearest him. It did make a wonderful frame!

What he saw through his frame took his breath away. In the distance, thin sporadic plumes of smoke rose from a wide space of darkened earth.

"*The Clever Fox Inn!*" he gasped and swallowed down a small disturbing lump.

A closer look told him there was more to gasp about. Marching about in ominous formation, just beyond the city wall, were many regiments of soldiers.

"Spaniards!"

For a long breathless moment he stared at them. Then jumping up, he ran around the whole wall, stopping to peer out of each arrow slit. On every side the sight was the same. Soldiers rimmed the entire city!

He crawled back into the alcove and pulled out a long rolled package. Carefully he unrolled it and looked at each picture.

"They're all here—the ones that count," he mused, "my collection of ships, the Zyl Poort, Vader's landscapes, the Beggar, Abraham and Isaac . . ."

He gulped, then took out a blank canvas from the bottom of the pile and pulled a stick of charcoal from the bag tied at his waist. There would be no more of these from Vader's charcoal oven, he remembered with a sigh. He held it thoughtfully in his hand for a long while.

Settling himself on a large flat stone beside the arrow slit that looked out on the smoking ruins of his home, he lay the canvas across his knees. He scrawled across the top, "The Siege of Leyden Has Begun."

"And there's not a Beggar in sight," he mumbled to himself.

He reached for the picture of his Oude Man Beggar and propped it up before him. "They'll come yet," he muttered.

From inside, way at the back of his mind, he heard a voice prodding, *Go to the warehouse where your family spent the night. They'll be worried about you by now.*

After a while, he told his annoying conscience. *Besides, Vader knows where to look for me.*

Then peering through the arrow slit, he began to draw.

How good the feel of charcoal once more in his fingers! It had been

too long—far too long since he'd picked up even one piece of this precious stuff. The horizon, the trees, the plumes of smoke, city gates, and
soldiers marching—and through an arrow slit! How could one painter feel
so much happiness in his fingers, his eyes, his heart?

PART THREE

Renovated Masterpieces

We learn to trust in God with our
whole hearts
and help each other along the thorny,
muddy, robber-infested ways
we cannot avoid.

—Jakob de Wever
Fictitious Anabaptist leader of Leyden

You ask if I have entered into a firm
treaty with any great king or potentate,
to which I answer, that before I ever
took up the cause of the oppressed
Christians in these provinces I had
entered into a close alliance with the
King of kings; and I am firmly
convinced that all who put their trust in
Him shall be saved by His almighty
hand.

—Willem van Oranje, in a message to
Diedrich Sonoy, Lieutenant-Governor
Province of North Holland, Fall 1573

If the little province of Holland can thus
hold at bay the power of Spain, what
could not all the Netherlands—Brabant,
Flanders, Friesland, and the rest
united—accomplish?

—Willem van Oranje
Message to Estates of the Netherlands,
September 1573

CHAPTER FIFTEEN

Leyden

31st day of Wine Month (October), 1573

*T*he golden glow of morning turned gray before it had passed through the wavery leaded-glass window panes into the drafty old building where the refugees from *The Clever Fox Inn* had spent the night. Pieter-Lucas awoke on his straw-filled mat on the floor of the warehouse and looked at his vrouw beside him. Blinking at the new day, she looked as bewildered as he felt.

"At least we're together," he mumbled, reaching out a hand to caress her cheek.

"And safe, with our children at our side," she added, her voice a whisper.

"Later on today we can move into the upper story with the printery," Pieter-Lucas said, stroking his vrouw's arm.

"Is there room for us up there among the presses and correction tables? And is it warm enough?"

"I haven't looked myself, but your vader assures me it will work. There are two rooms—one for us and the other for your family. That way the innkeeper and his family can have the ground floor."

"Will they have always to sleep on this cold floor?" Aletta, the *physicke*, frowned.

"*Nay*. The plan has always been to build in a few cupboard beds. I'm sure the men who have so far concentrated on preparing the printery will now do them."

Aletta sighed. "Ah, my dear husband, how many strange and fearful obstacles have lain in our pathway! Things we never dreamed when we were children playing in the wood across from Prince Willem's *kasteel* in Breda."

"Youth does not include nightmares in its dreams for the future."

"Nor do they know how faithfully their Vader in the Heaven can take care of them."

Pieter-Lucas raised himself on an elbow and looked about the room, taking a mental count of bodies on the floor. Except for Mieke, who always slept in the out-of-doors, everyone else seemed to be still resting. Dirck and Gretta and Robbin, and on the other side of the room, Hiltje and Joris and two lumpish, child-sized bodies. *Nay*, but there should be three. Who was missing?

At this moment Hiltje raised her head and looked over her family. She grabbed her husband, shook him, and shrieked, "Joris, your son is gone!" Her voice bounced around the tall walls and high ceiling of the big room.

Pieter-Lucas held Aletta by the hand, as if she needed his protection from the unhappy voices cannonading the air about them.

Hiltje scrambled out of her place and began rummaging through the feather bags beside her, muttering, "Christoffel, where are you?" Girlish voices protested.

Joris raised himself quickly to his elbows and asked, "And the pictures?"

"Is that all you can think about?" she retorted. "What about the boy?"

"He's at least big enough and smart enough to take care of himself, but . . . if the pictures are gone . . . *Ach!* Vrouw, you have no idea . . . no idea at all."

Hiltje smacked her hands together and squatted down beside him. "You're right. I have no idea why you can't forget the paintings for once. All they have ever done is to get us into trouble. Now tell me, where might Christoffel be hiding out?"

"Among the trees at the foot of the citadel. Oh! I must go see what he's done!" He started to get up but lay immediately back down.

"I'll go for him," Pieter-Lucas called out.

Hiltje looked at him as if she'd not known he was in the room until this moment. "Bless you," she stammered.

"You sure you know where the citadel is?" Joris mumbled.

"That much I cannot miss," Pieter-Lucas assured him. He nudged Robbin, who was wriggling farther down into his bed. "Want to come along? You'll know exactly where he is, I'd wager."

Robbin yawned and ran fingers through his mussed hair. *"Ja,"* he groused, "I'll go."

Pieter-Lucas gave his vrouw a squeeze about the shoulders and whispered to her, "I do believe that man is the painter his son told me about." He shook his head slowly. "Nobody but a painter talks that way about lost paintings. We'll be back shortly."

Minutes later Robbin and Pieter-Lucas were hurrying through the streets. A more pleasant autumn morning one could not imagine. Neither foggy nor raining, not hot, not cold. Leaves of red and gold and crackling dry brown drifted gracefully to the ground all around them, brushing their heads and shoulders.

"I wonder how far away the Spaniards are," Pieter-Lucas said, breathing deeply of the refreshing air.

"What'll happen to us when they come?" Robbin asked. "Will we starve?"

Pieter-Lucas shrugged and put down the tiny wave of fear that begged his attention. "Leyden has been preparing for this for a long while," he said. "They have a whole shipload of extra food stored away. It was bound for Haarlem's relief and never got through."

"How long will it last?"

"You're talking like we already have a siege."

Robbin shrugged. "How do you know we don't?"

Pieter-Lucas felt a somersault tumbling in his chest. How did he know indeed? Prodded by a fresh urgency, he sped up his pace. "Siege or no siege, we must find your friend. Do you think he'll be up there by the citadel?"

"*Ja!* He likes it up there. Until the rumors kept us out of the city, he used to run in here every day and look down on the city. He called it his 'window on the city' and was always talking about how he hoped one day he'd see the Beggars defend Leyden through the slits in the citadel walls, like Leyden's armies used to do in the long-ago days."

Pieter-Lucas shivered. "I hope we don't have to see such a thing. You never know how ugly war and fighting are until you see it once. Nothing glorious about it at all! There's a lot of good reasons why our Children of God refuse to carry arms. War can't be God's way—just can't be."

"Not even when Alva comes waving a sword at you?"

Pieter-Lucas sighed. "I've been struggling with a good answer to that one for almost as many years as you've been alive. I still don't know for sure."

They were climbing the stairs toward the citadel now. Halfway up, Pieter-Lucas stopped short and took Robbin by one shoulder. "Tell me, Robbin," he begged, "this boy, Christoffel, he really is a painter, isn't he? I mean, if the work he showed me was his own, he is a painter."

"*Ja*, he's a good painter all right."

"Is his vader his *meester*? Did they have a studio at *The Clever Fox Inn*?"

"He always told me that was true. And once his vader went away,

Christoffel said he wouldn't paint anymore. He never would explain, refused to talk about it."

"Did you ever see the studio?"

Robbin looked about as if fearful someone might hear and answered in a whisper. "He never took me there. Said his vader wouldn't allow it. But one time when I was walking around the buildings, I peeked through the windows of a room at the end. Inside I saw tables and easels with paintings on them. There were pictures hanging on all the walls, like I never saw before, and all kinds of bottles and painter's palettes. If that wasn't a studio, I don't know what else."

Pieter-Lucas sighed. "Aha! So it must be true. Then Christoffel is hiding out up here somewhere with all the paintings. I wonder what Joris paints that he doesn't want the rest of us to see."

They moved on up the stairs in silence and were just ready to go around to the backside of the old tower when Robbin gasped and stopped short.

"Look!" he said in a loud whisper. "The door is open!"

Pieter-Lucas stared at the old weather-scarred door standing ajar. "You think he went inside?" he asked.

"No doubting that. Every time he climbs these steps, he pushes on the door before he goes around to the backside. 'One day I'll find it open,' he says, and looks like he did this time."

Robbin shoved the door wide open and edged through. Pieter-Lucas followed him into a large grassy enclosure with a handful of trees and a well in the center. A stairway led to a high walkway that ran all the way around and formed a circle of alcoves beneath, where the wall was indeed pierced at regular intervals with narrow slits.

Several groups of people stood on the upper walkway, talking, pointing out across the countryside. To Pieter-Lucas' and Robbin's right, in an alcove partially hidden by the stairway, they saw Christoffel. He was sitting on a large stone, peering through an arrow slit and drawing on a canvas. They crept up behind him until Pieter-Lucas could read the large letters across the top of the sheet: THE SIEGE OF LEYDEN HAS BEGUN.

"How do you know the siege has begun?" he asked.

Christoffel answered as evenly as if they'd been standing behind him for hours. "Look for yourself and you'll see."

Pieter-Lucas stooped down and looked through the long narrow hole in the stonework. "Spanish troops everywhere!" He whistled. "It's a siege all right."

He stepped back to watch the young artist at work. Propped up beside the canvas was a large painting of a Beggar with the title underneath, "The

Storyteller," and another of the ships in the harbor. He was using them as models, adding a boat full of the rowdy patriots coming on to the scene from the upper right corner. Pieter-Lucas examined the Beggar carefully, then sucked in a quick breath. It was an amazing likeness of Hendrick van den Garde!

"Is that your special beggar friend?" Pieter-Lucas asked. "The one your vader didn't want you to paint?"

"What if it is?" Christoffel defended without interrupting his work.

What indeed? It meant the man was still alive. Often Pieter-Lucas had wondered. The last time they had met was out on the shores of the Ems River, after the disastrous battle of Jemmingen—not a happy meeting at all. Since that time, so many battles for the Beggars had occurred that they'd set Pieter-Lucas' mind to wondering whether the crusty old warrior had survived.

He rubbed his hands together and shifted from one foot to the other and back again. *Be gentle*, he told himself. Slowly he stooped down again, this time sitting on the rock beside Christoffel. "Tell me what it is you like most about this man?" he asked.

The boy said nothing for a long while and didn't look at Pieter-Lucas. Finally he said, "He's strong and brave and tells the best stories I ever heard. If he'd just come back to Leyden, I know he could save us."

"Did he ever tell you about the image breakings in Breda, when he sliced his vader's painting to shreds, then attacked the boy he'd always called his son with his knife when the boy tried to stop him?"

Christoffel rolled his eyes in Pieter-Lucas' direction. Pieter-Lucas felt fire mixed with pain in the glance. "You don't know anything about my storyteller Beggar!" he spouted.

"I wish I didn't," Pieter-Lucas responded. "You know, you've painted an excellent picture of my stepvader here."

"Your stepvader?" The boy glared at him, disbelief burning in his eyes.

Pieter-Lucas nodded. "You heard me, *jongen*. Now, watch out for him. He can be dangerous. I do know." Then pointing once more to the scar below his eye, he added, "He carries a sharp knife and isn't afraid to use it on any artist that gets in his way."

Christoffel frowned. "He didn't ever hurt you!" he snapped.

"He was the very one. Made a deep gash in my leg too. I'll limp from it the rest of my life."

"So now you hate him!"

Pieter-Lucas watched anguish rankling in the boy's eyes. "*Nay*," he answered, thinking each word into being with care. "I forgave him long ago."

"You still remember!"

"I can never forget an injury that makes me limp and sometimes causes great pain. But I feel pity for him, not anger."

"Pity?"

"He's a hard man, Christoffel, and fearful and angry—and lonely."

"Then why have you been trying ever since I first met you to turn me against him?"

Pieter-Lucas swallowed hard. What could he say to spare this boy the grief he knew lay ahead for him if he set his eye to following after the ways of the wild and reckless Beggars? At last he said carefully, "Would you rather I let you go on playing with your charming wolf-in-shiny-coat and never warn you of the dangers of his bite?"

Christoffel stared at him, a mystified expression across his face. Then he pulled away and went back to his sketching. After a long moment he asked in perturbed tone, "Why'd you come here?"

"Your vader and moeder are worried about you," Pieter-Lucas explained. "You didn't ask their permission to spend the night here. They could only guess where you were. For all they knew, you may have met with a knife-toting Spaniard—or Beggar."

Christoffel stared at the ground and answered with an impudent reserve, "I can take care of myself. Don't need to go sleeping with everybody else in that awful old building."

"I suggest you come with us, Christoffel."

"I'm not through with my picture."

"Once you've talked to your parents, I'm sure they'll let you come back and finish. Your vader is a sick man, and your moeder is sick with worry over you. Your vader worries, too, about the paintings. Did you bring them with you?"

Christoffel looked at Pieter-Lucas with a cold agonizing stare. "I can't tell you."

"Your vader is desperate to know," Pieter-Lucas said. "He's been asking about them since before we left *The Clever Fox Inn*."

"If he comes here, I'll tell him."

"You know he can't come here, Christoffel."

"Then send my moeder. I'm not leaving this place—not for anything."

Pieter-Lucas peered over the boy's head and into the shelter of the alcove behind him. Back in the corner, under the stairway, he spotted a crumpled feather bag with the end of a long rolled package protruding from one corner. So that was it. The paintings were there, and Christoffel was hiding them.

"It's going to get cold sleeping out here, *jongen*," Pieter-Lucas said.

"I got my feather bag and a roof."

"What about food?" Robbin spoke at last.

"I brought some with me from home," he snapped. "Now go away and leave me to draw my picture." When they didn't move, he repeated, this time with a vigorous shout, "Go away!"

Pieter-Lucas nudged Robbin's shoulder and together they returned the way they'd come.

"I think I saw the roll of pictures," Robbin whispered when they had reached the street below the hillock.

"That's our secret right now, can you remember?"

Robbin looked up at him, his eyes jumping with question marks. "What'll happen if we let it out?"

"We'll make an enemy out of the boy, that's what."

"*Ach!* He's not nice to us anyway."

"He's afraid, Robbin."

"Of what? We didn't threaten him."

Pieter-Lucas thought a bit before he said more. "There are some things we don't know about this boy or his vader."

"Like what?"

"I don't know, but I think if I did know, his actions might make perfectly good sense. Now, Robbin, you say nothing to anyone, do you hear?"

Robbin shrugged. "If you insist."

By the time they'd reached the warehouse, the streets were filling with people. Some stood in tight little groups and mumbled in serious tones. Others ran together and shouted hysterically. All were excited, and the mood was decidedly black and heavy. Two words seemed to be on every lip—"*speken*" and "siege"!

Pieter-Lucas felt Robbin moving closer to him as they walked. The boy tugged on his sleeve and asked, "What are *speken*?"

"It's a nasty word for Spanish soldiers," Pieter-Lucas explained. "They are our real enemies here. Christoffel and his family are our friends. No matter what you hear or see, always remember that!"

Robbin didn't answer.

He's not so sure, Pieter-Lucas decided.

———

Hiltje made her way through the crowded streets of Leyden, looking straight ahead. Not once did she hear the dreaded word *marrano*, as she had heard so mercilessly cast at her the last time she walked here. Instead, the whole city was abuzz with gossip about the Spaniards who guarded the city. In her mind she could picture them clearly—helmeted and corseted, with broad shiny swords and dark bushy mustachios, blocking the passage of any who would go outside the walls.

"We're captives!" she mumbled to herself as she prepared to climb the steps at the bottom of the citadel hillock.

For how many weeks had she been unwelcome in the city, afraid to set her foot inside the gate? And now she could not go back out. Strange and frightening it was. They might starve to death before this thing was over. She shook her head as if to put it all from her and climbed on.

At the top, inside the doorway, she stopped and caught her breath. How often she'd heard stories about this place. Never had she actually stood inside these walls before. "Only in times of danger!" She looked about the ancient courtyard, remembered, and shuddered.

She moved softly toward Christoffel until she stood behind him. For a long while she said nothing but studied the sketch he was creating. Formations of soldiers spread out in circles beyond the city walls, and in the distance, a fleet of beggar ships sailed down the Zyl River where it ran past a blackened piece of ground with small plumes of smoke rising up.

"Is that what you see through your arrow slit?" she said at last.

Without turning to look at her, Christoffel replied, "Look for yourself."

Not at all sure she wanted to see it, she crept forward, then stooped down and gazed through the arrow slit. There were no beggar ships, but otherwise it was as he had sketched it. Her eyes were drawn to the line of trees along the riverbank trailing off into a haze. Everything in her refused to believe that the black swatch of color out there was the spot where she'd been born, grown up, raised her family.

A shiver ran down her backbone. It couldn't be. Ignoring the lumps rising in her throat and threatening to bring tears, she turned to face her son. For a long moment she shook her head and stared at him, putting on her sternest possible scolding countenance.

"Whyever did you leave us all and hide out here?" she demanded. "Your vader and I were worried that something dreadful had befallen you."

He motioned toward his feather bag pile and said without a show of feeling, "I had to save the paintings. You told me never to let anybody see them, and I couldn't keep them a secret in that big building with so many people."

"Son," she began at last, "right now we have more to fear than the discovery of your vader's paintings." If only they had left them in the inn and let the flames consume them. Must Joris always be so tied to those fanciful pictures? *Ja*, he must. If she'd had any idea, years ago, what it would be like to be married to a painter, she might never have done it. Not marry Joris? *Ach!* The most impossible idea of all!

Christoffel's scowl told her he was a true son of his vader. Neither could he see anything more important than the paintings.

"I think that at this moment your vader's accusers are far too busy worrying about the siege and what it will do to them to bother about him anymore. Besides, the people we are living with are our friends."

"What makes you so sure?" Christoffel asked, his voice tight.

"From the day they came to stay with us, they have shown us every kindness. Aletta has spent her days searching out herbal cures to restore your vader to robustious health. Mieke has come into the city every day to buy bread for us. When Pieter-Lucas was warned of the trouble from the *glippers*, he could have hastened to take his family out of harm's way and left us to our own plight. And Magdalena and her friends took us in and gave us a place to lay our heads."

"Pieter-Lucas doesn't like Oude Man," Christoffel said sulkily.

"Who's Oude Man?"

Christoffel threw a startled glance at her. "The Beggar that tells all those wonderful stories. Here he is!" He held up a painted portrait of the surly old man. So many times Joris had complained about it that she felt she must have seen it, though this was her first glimpse. A perfect likeness indeed!

"Why doesn't Pieter-Lucas like him?"

"Says he's attacked him once with a knife. I don't believe it, do you?"

Hiltje sighed. "Attacking people is what Beggars do, you know. They're soldiers, but Pieter-Lucas is supposedly from the same army, so why would a Beggar attack him?"

Christoffel shrugged. "He said it had something to do with a painting. He's a painter too. Did you know that?"

"So I've heard. I suggest you take Pieter-Lucas' warning and watch out for any man that wears a uniform and carries a sword." She reached for his feather bag, adding, "Right now you are coming with me."

He snatched the bag from her. "I like it out here!"

"*Nay!*" she insisted, standing to her feet and grabbing the bag back. "Now, hand me the roll of pictures. You bring the rest and follow me home."

"We've got no home," he muttered.

Slowly he handed her the long rolled package without looking at her. She encircled it with the feather bag and trudged out around the well, down the stairs and through the streets. She didn't look, but she knew the boy trailed behind her. She could hear his shuffling feet, his heavy breathing, and something that sounded almost like restrained sobs. She swallowed a few sorrowful lumps of her own and moved on.

————

Christoffel lagged behind his moeder—not far, but always behind. Not that he didn't know where she was going or how to get there. *Nay*, she had the pictures, and right now he was not at all sure what she might do with them. He had to guard them.

The building she entered was big and stern-looking, with a brick facade and only four windows across the front—two on each level. He'd seen it many times from the street but never been inside. He knew it would be dark and glowering and unwelcoming. He walked through the door that Moeder held open for him and lowered his head, as if expecting some heavy cloud to envelope him.

He found himself in one large room with bags and sleeping mats scattered around the floor. Moving about among them were all the people he expected to find here. A fireplace on the back wall held a low-burning fire, where his sisters and Mieke were cooking something in a large pot. Beside it ran a stairway to the upper story. No cupboards for beds or anything else to make it look like a home. He would go back to the citadel at night, he decided. At least there he could breathe the fresh air and get away from so many people.

In the middle of the room, Vader was sitting up on his mat and looking in his direction. "Come here, son," he called out.

Christoffel left his street shoes at the door and picked his way across the cold floor, feeling the pointy rushes through his stockings and wishing with his whole heart that he was back at the inn. Vader reached up to him and without smiling asked, "You did bring the paintings, did you not?"

"Moeder has them, wrapped up in my feather bag," he said, motioning toward her where she stood on the other side of him.

"Let me see," he told his vrouw.

When she'd removed the long roll, wrapped in a sheet of heavy brown paper, she placed them in his outstretched hands. Christoffel watched him take them, a smile of pleasure and almost worship lighting up his face.

"They're all here?" he asked Christoffel.

"All the important ones," he said.

"How do you know what's important?"

Christoffel bristled. "The ones you had on the walls and the easel and . . ." He knelt down in the rushes, looked directly into the man's watery eyes, and added, "And the one without a face."

"*Ah!*" Vader sighed and drew the package up in both arms, hugging it to his breast.

For a long moment Christoffel stared at his vader. He knew he'd grown thin since his illness. But this was the first time he'd looked at him up so close. How old he looked! Almost like Opa—and the Oude Man Beggar. The familiar face was wrinkled and layers of saggy skin hung loosely around his jowls and cheekbones. It frightened him.

He glanced up to see that Moeder no longer stood over them. Then leaning toward his vader, Christoffel asked, "How we going to keep them hidden in this place with all these people?"

Still clutching the pictures, Vader looked around the room and sighed, "I still don't understand why they took us away from our home. If we're lucky, it won't be long and we can go back to *The Clever Fox Inn* again."

Christoffel felt something stick in his throat. Vader didn't know the inn had been burned? Nor was he going to be the one to tell him.

"I had a good hiding place out in the citadel," Christoffel offered, "where I could sleep at night and keep the pictures all wrapped up in my bag in the daytime."

"You can't stay out in the cold, *jongen*. What happens when it rains?"

"My spot was hidden from view, dry, sheltered from the weather." He leaned over and whispered into his vader's ear, "It was inside the citadel!"

Joris started. "Inside the citadel?"

Christoffel stared at his vader. He looked for all the world like some pitiful, half-witted old man. How could he tell him the truth? Yet how could he not?

"It's a time of danger," he said to the rapid beating of his heart. "Leyden's under siege!"

The man's eyes grew wide, and he began stuffing the package down under his bedcovers. "*Ach*, my son," he wailed. "If the Spaniards are at the gate, our danger is much greater than you know. They threatened me, you know."

"Who threatened you?"

"Those men—*glippers*—what came to me at the inn before we left."

Christoffel frowned and probed his memory for any such event. "You were dreaming, Vader," he said.

"*Nay*, it was real. They told me if I didn't let them put their soldiers in the inn, they'd lock me up in the tower dungeon—in a special cell reserved for . . . *Ach!*" He crawled down under the covers, and all Christoffel could hear was his muffled voice, moaning, "*Nay*, they cannot find me here, don't you tell them. . . ."

Christoffel stood to his feet and trembled. He felt an arm on his shoulder and looked up into his moeder's face. "Is he mad?" he asked in a whisper, afraid to hear the words. It was bad enough just to think them.

Moeder looked brave, he decided, but he knew she was fearful too. She patted him on the arm and said in a quavery voice, "He says strange things, *jongen*, because his head was injured."

"Moeder, we must find a place to hide the pictures—and Vader. If only we had a bed cupboard."

"The men that own this place are going to build cupboards."

"They'd better make it soon!"

Together they looked down at the lumpy form still wriggling under his covers and moaning, *"Nay!"*

Christoffel felt fear well up inside. If only he were a little boy again and could hide in his moeder's apron and cry. Instead, he felt her grab him by both shoulders. "Promise me, son," she said earnestly, "that you will not run away again. I must count on you to be a man and protect me."

He felt her arms hugging him, and he was hugging her back, even letting a few tears dribble onto her dress. Whatever else might happen, he now knew he could not go back to the citadel to sleep.

CHAPTER SIXTEEN

Leyden

3rd day of Tallow Month (November), 1573

Toward the middle of a wearying afternoon, Aletta sat on a stool beside the warm chimney on the upper floor of her warehouse "home." She nursed her baby at the left breast and tried to console a whimpering Lucas who draped himself over her right knee. The boy sniffled and whined without stopping.

"*Moeke*," he wailed, "my throat, my throat—it pains."

Lucas had fretted off and on through half the night and carried the same unhappy mood all through the day. Aletta filled him with horehound syrup and honeysuckle water. Pieter-Lucas tried calming him, and Mieke later on, but he seemed only to want his moeder's knee.

"Sick *jongens* are jus' like that," Mieke sputtered and went on about her business of cleaning and shopping and helping Hiltje with the preparation of the day's meals for the three-family household.

Great God, Aletta prayed silently, *I give Thee thanks for herbs and a sheltered place with a warm and cozy chimney running through.*

She sent her mind on a quick run through the list of herbal cures for soreness of throat she'd used frequently over the years—licorice, peppermint, St. Jakob's herb, throat herb, gypsy miracle herb, goldenrod. She would try them all. If only Kaatje's twisted foot could offer so many solutions.

Aletta swallowed down the tears that threatened to well up and choke her. She looked down at the slumbering infant on her breast, a stream of milk trickling from her mouth. She helped Lucas to stand, then laid Kaatje in her cradle bed.

Next, she gave Lucas another spoonful of syrup, then opened her arms and let him crawl up into them. For a warm and cozy hour, she rocked him, sang "*Suja, suja, slaap*," and treasured the pressure of a little hand wrapping itself around her forefinger. By the time he'd fallen asleep, a faint pattering of raindrops fell on the roof just above her head. She put him into his little makeshift bed, covered him with a blanket, and stood watching, listening, praying.

"Thank Thee, God, for horehound and licorice and peppermint . . . and the unknown cure for twisted limbs."

She heard footsteps on the stairs and, wiping away a pair of tears from her cheek, turned abruptly to see Pieter-Lucas' blond curls and brown tam rising up to greet her. She raised a finger to her lips and walked to meet him.

"Lucas sleeps?" Pieter-Lucas whispered.

"Both sleep. The music of raindrops on the roof sings a lullaby." She took him by both hands and, pushing down the sadness, smiled up at him.

"He will be well soon?"

"Soon," she reassured him, and in her heart she knew it had to be so.

"I am sorry, my love, to say so, but the burgemeesters are sending me tomorrow to Prince Willem again," Pieter-Lucas said.

"The Spaniards will let you out through the gates—with a message for Willem?" she whispered, tightening her grip on his thick fingers.

"I can find a way now. And of course they'll have no idea what I carry in my knapsack—or my shoe."

She wished he'd said *"nay."* Yet she knew he wouldn't. He worried continually about Prince Willem. No messages had passed from inside the city since the siege began four days ago.

"I must get through the gates and tell him that the people of Leyden are strong enough to make it through this siege!" If he'd said it once, he'd said it ten times every day since they'd been locked up by the Spaniards. "Willem can't see inside our walls. He doesn't know that we've plenty of food and our spirits run high," he always explained.

"How will you get through?" Aletta asked.

"The Spaniards are busy building a ring of fortifications around the southern border of the city and are not as watchful as they were in the beginning. If we watch our chances, we can now slip through."

"Oh, Pieter-Lucas, that sounds dangerous!" Aletta felt her whole being shudder.

"No more dangerous than some other things I've had to do—and never told you about." He patted her arms with his large warm hand. "Tomorrow I go out disguised as one of the workmen that meets at the town hall at five of the clock each morning. Mostly men from outlying villages that have come into the city for refuge, they are helping to build a fortress in Lammen, just south of the city."

"The Spaniards let them do it?"

Pieter-Lucas raised his eyebrows and half chuckled. "Why not? It saves them the work and expense, and once it's finished, they'll stage a battle and take it away for their own use."

"Our burgemeesters can't see the foolishness of the action?" Aletta felt a sudden fear, as if she doubted she could trust the men in whose hands the safety of her little family must rest these days.

"They didn't ask my counsel," Pieter-Lucas said. "The men who rule this city are an odd mixture of loyalists and patriots and mostly men who simply refuse to declare any allegiance lest it get them in trouble."

"Oh, Pieter-Lucas," she gasped.

"The same as in every other Lowland city. They all have those who stand for a vision of freedom, and when they light the fires of revolt, we shall see that even Leyden is not of a mind to surrender to Alva's men. In any case, the building of Lammen gives me a way to escape."

"And return?"

Taking her in his arms, he nuzzled her hair with his nose and murmured, "And return. I cannot say how soon or how many days and other journeys may lie between my departure and that return. Only know that I shall return. Wait, my love, with daily hope!"

———

10th day of Tallow Month (November), 1573

The wind whipped at Aletta's skirt and tugged at the shawl she used to protect herself from the cold on the doorstoop of the Beguinage. She pulled on the heavy chain attached to the door knocker, then stared up at the old scarred oak door towering over her.

A shiver ran down her spine. This was the first time she'd been in a Beguinage since she left Breda, way back before she and Pieter-Lucas were married. What would she find on the other side of this door? In Breda, she was the neighbor girl who'd known the Beguine sisters all her life. Tante Lysbet, who cared for her moeder, was a Beguine, and when Aletta went there to gather herbs for her they never asked questions.

But this was Leyden. The community of lay sisters here did not know her for any reason. In these days, with Spaniards guarding the gates and traitorous *glippers* slipping in and out among the citizens, nobody knew whom to trust. Who was on which side in this revolt, anyway? Taking chances could lead to disaster.

Whichever way she went, though, today, she had to take chances. She had to have a fresh supply of herbs for her Lucas, who was lying at home with a *heatte* that sapped all the strength from his little body. A week ago, when Pieter-Lucas left for Delft, Aletta had been so certain the boy's soreness of throat and irritating cough would be short-lived. She'd kept him warm and filled him with broth and all the right herbs and syrups. Yet he seemed each day to grow more ill than the day before.

"Great Vader in the Heaven," she whispered into the shawl wrapped around her neck, "please let them have the herbs I need—and the willingness to sell them to me."

The bolt was being drawn. Aletta held herself erect and as stately as possible. The door opened a wedge, and she saw a round pleasant face framed by the familiar plain white shawl-like hood of the Beguine order.

"Good day, young woman," the Beguine offered. "You come with a need? An ill child, perhaps—or husband? Not begging food, I trust, as there is little to spare these days in all Leyden."

"Nay, I come not in search of food," Aletta stammered. "My name is Aletta and my family is boarding these days near the Koe Poort. My son lies ill with a *heatte*—some sort of ague. I have nursed him carefully for days now, and my supply of herbs wanes quickly."

"Come in to our haven, if you please." The Beguine led her through the door and across the courtyard filled with a neatly ordered herb garden. The courtyard was larger than that of Breda, and there were more short, narrow little houses around the circumference, but otherwise, it looked much the same.

A chill of excitement gripped her as she followed the white-hooded woman into the dispensary. Larger than the houses, the place was redolent with drying and brewing herbs, and a whole flock of sisters busied themselves with the various stages in the preparation of herbal cures.

"The sisters here can help you," her guide said, then left her with an older sister. Stiff, sober, almost foreboding, the woman towered over Aletta and did not smile. "You need healing for a child?" she asked in a heavy grating voice. Aletta sensed her probing gaze and trembled.

She nodded. "I am an herbal healer newly come to Leyden. My young son has suffered many days with soreness in his throat, coughing, running of the nose, and now a *heatte*. I have exhausted my supply of the herbs I need to produce a cure."

"What sort of herbs have you need of?" the woman asked, not taking her gaze off Aletta's face.

"Wormwood, along with chamomile, marsh parsley, masterwort, or hops."

"Wait here." The woman indicated a stool near the door and walked into the busy company of healing sisters.

Aletta sat staring about her, sniffing the aromas, watching the women doing the thing she loved most on earth to do herself. In this place with all the herbs and fragrances that she knew and loved so well, she should feel more at home than anywhere else in Leyden. Yet the sister had treated her like an unwelcome annoyance. What was it all about? Weren't all herbal healers friends of all other herbal healers?

The wait went on and on until Aletta felt a tightness in her joints, and her back and shoulders began to ache. Just when she thought she could not sit still one more moment, a sister came walking toward her, carrying a small package in her hand. Her habit told Aletta she was not a Beguine.

"Ah, 'tis you," the woman said, laying a hand on her arm.

Aletta gasped. Once she'd seen her eyes and heard her voice, she knew it was the short pleasant hermit sister who had given her the borage at the cloister out by the Zyl River. "I never thought to see you here!"

"Before they burned *The Clever Fox Inn*, they came for us as well."

"They burned your cloister and the herbs?" Aletta gasped.

"*Nay*, they dismantled the house and allowed us to harvest the herbs. Some we cut, others we dug up and brought here to put into the ground. Hard to tell how many will live. Not the best season for moving them, but . . ." She lifted her eyebrows and gave a loud sigh. "You must follow me." She was motioning Aletta, who rose, glad to be on her feet.

"I need to return to my son," Aletta protested.

"All in good time, young woman," the sister said.

"But . . ."

She took her by the arm and led her out into the brisk afternoon air.

"In this place, I never dispense herbs without a moment in the chapel with my patients," she explained.

The chapel? Aletta followed, wondering. As her guide opened the door it creaked, and in her mind's eye, Aletta fancied she saw Opa's painting, "The Healing," that hung above the altar in the chapel of the Beguinage of Breda.

As clearly as if it were real and not imagined, she saw in her mind the little crippled girl being touched by the hand of Jesus. She remembered the bright colors and the kindness on the face of Jesus and how every time she'd looked at that picture she imagined she was the girl with the crippled leg. Never in those days so long ago had she dreamt she would one day have a child with just such an infirmity.

On this afternoon so far away in time and miles, she realized she was kneeling at a railing just before the altar, next to a stranger. Still she felt like the girl with the twisted limb. As if from some distant place looking on, she heard the woman begin to pray.

"In the name of the Vader, Son, and Holy Ghost, we approach Thee, Almighty God, and beseech Thee to reach out Thy powerful hand and heal this woman's son of his *heatte* and ague and whatever else it may be that plagues him. And touch the heart of the moeder with the gentleness of Thy peace. Amen."

Both women stood to their feet. Aletta did not want to go.

"Long years ago," Aletta said to her companion, "I used to think God would miraculously touch our bodies—twisted limbs and aching throats—and make them whole. He did it once when He lived on earth, I know. My husband's grandvader painted a picture of it, and it hung in the Beguinage where I lived then." She paused.

"You no longer believe in miracles?" asked the sister.

Aletta pondered the question for a long while. "Since I've become a healer lady, I've come to understand that God more often heals through the herbs He causes to grow in our gardens than through miraculous touches."

"Does that not seem enough for you?"

"It has seemed so . . ." She mustn't say more.

"It has but does not anymore?" The woman was looking at her with an expression so intense, compassionate, and probing, all at once, that Aletta knew not whether to run or to pour out her heart.

" 'Tis just that right now it seems simple enough when it's a runny nose and a throat in need of horehound syrup or chamomile," Aletta mused, forgetting for the moment that she had an audience for her words. "But when it is a misshapen foot, perhaps that's quite another matter."

"Whom do you know that has a misshapen foot in need of curing?"

Aletta gasped. From the moment she'd met this woman, she'd been eager to tell her about Kaatje, ask for her help. Yet now, something in the woman's tone of voice—or was it in the expression in her eyes?—whatever, it gave rise to fear.

"I've known several such persons," Aletta said quickly. "Thanks to you for your kindness and the herbs for my son. I must go to him now before they are too late to do their work." She pulled the coins from her waist bag and exchanged them for the package of herbs.

" 'Pray and it shall be given you; seek and you shall find; knock and it shall be opened unto you,' " the sister said as they parted.

The words were soft and gentle and compelling. But there was no time to stop and ponder them. Aletta fled through the gate and up and down the cobbled streets toward home.

All the way, she felt warmed by the hermit sister's prayer and a continuing vision of the painting. Again and again, the question ran through her mind, *Is it possible God might touch my Kaatje as He did the golden-haired girl in "The Healing"? Do I dare to pray, to seek, to knock?*

Delft

13th day of Tallow Month (November), 1573

Pieter-Lucas pressed through the noise and confusion of a midday market just as the clock from the Nieuwe Kerk tower struck ten times. Only a few streets now to the old St. Agatha Cloister where Willem's headquarters for the revolt were housed. He'd traversed the trekpaths between Delft and France many times in the days since he'd left Leyden. Surely this time, when he would deliver the message to Willem from Ludwig down in France, he could go home.

His heart beat rapidly at the thought of Leyden, where fortresses were growing in the surrounding fields while mustachioed guards with flashing shiny swords marched in formation around the city's rim. And inside the walls, his vrouw and children awaited his return.

His path led through the market of Delft, where aromas of frying fish and baking waffles teased his nostrils and stirred the growls in his stomach. He purchased a flounder and a waffle with syrup, both hot from their pans. He gobbled them hastily as he rushed past the myriad of tempting stalls.

In the cloister he found Willem, head bowed low over his writing table, pen in hand and deep in thought. "Aha, Pieter-Lucas," he exclaimed without looking up. "What for news do you bring today?"

Pieter-Lucas laid his message before him. "Ludwig is in good spirits, Excellency. He and Jan are raising troops, though the progress is slow."

Willem sat erect and opened the message before him, reading it quickly through. Without comment, he picked up his pen once more and began scribbling across the paper before him. As he wrote, he talked. "Latest word from Spain is less than cheering. While the Duke of Alva will soon be departing for Spain, his replacement, Don Luis de Requesens y Cuñiga, is even now on his way. He will be in Brussels any day." He paused and gave full attention to his writing.

What sort of tyrant might this Requesens be? Pieter-Lucas wondered. Surely King Philip would not send a soft man to follow the iron-fisted Alva.

Willem was speaking again. "Now I receive messengers from the Spanish commander, Romero, that Requesens comes bringing strong overtures for peace and amnesty."

"Peace and amnesty?" What could such words mean from Romero, who in the past year had led the siege and ensuing slaughter of one Lowland city after another?

Willem looked up at Pieter-Lucas and said nothing for a long thoughtful moment. Then, pen still in hand, he said, "Peace, to King Philip's men, means all Lowlanders giving absolute allegiance to the rule of Spain and the Holy Catholic Church."

He scribbled furiously for several moments. Then folding his missive and sealing it with wax, he handed it to Pieter-Lucas. He looked him full in the eyes and said, "Nor do we change our goals—freedom, both from the rule of foreign tyranny and from the absolute position of the Holy Catholic Church. Van der Werff and his unstable bunch in Leyden must never forget it."

Pieter-Lucas took the message, slipped out of the room, and headed with all possible haste for Leyden. Without a horse, the way was slow, and the closer he came to Leyden, the more nests of Spanish soldiers he found guarding little villages, building fortresses, patrolling the roads and waterways. Repeatedly he resorted to running through fields, dashing from barn to barn, pole-jumping the rivers and canals that threaded their way across the vast flat pastures, tilled garden plots, and hay fields.

Once he reached Lammen he could return home with the fortress builders. When he neared the nearly completed fortification, however, he saw no signs of life.

"They've already gone home for today." He sighed, looking out across the fields to the towers and walls of Leyden shimmering in the setting sun. "In an eyeblink the sun will be over the edge of the world, and I can move on in the dusk and oncoming darkness with more safety than broad daylight would afford."

One look at the road into Leyden, though, and he knew that would not work. The way swarmed with soldiers, their heavy boots thudding like thunder on the packed dirt, their swords and halberds and spears clashing, metal against metal, as they marched and jostled one another. The sound reminded Pieter-Lucas of Jemmingen where the Spaniards slaughtered Ludwig's troops, then hunted down the few that escaped, slaying some with swords, tossing others into the river, setting fire to those who hid in thickets.

He hurried across the nearest field and up across a dike, one of a vast network that provided channels for the swiftly rising waters at high tide and storm times. He pole-jumped the channel, then dropped to the ground and made his way by crawling, nearly on his belly. Unfortunately the crops had been harvested and no place remained for him to hide himself. The rows of weeds that grew beside the dikes offered him only scant refuge.

Halfway across the fields, he found himself not far behind a handful of farm workers carrying hoes and rakes and headed for the Koe Poort. They might provide the cover he needed to get into the city. Unless things had changed since he left on this mission, these men would be allowed past the guards without a contest. If the farmers saw him, however, they would no doubt think him to be a Spanish spy and attack him with their implements. So he stayed low and out of sight and followed along at a safe distance, puffing at the effort and praying for an impossible miracle.

By the time they'd reached the gate, the darkness had deepened sufficiently that Pieter-Lucas found it possible to slip in among the milling farmers unnoticed. Breathing a sigh of profound relief, he passed through the Koe Poort and scampered quickly away from the farmers and toward the town hall.

"Thank God!" he whispered, shaking his arms and shoulders and stomping his feet as if to loosen up all the bindings that had held him captive ever since Lammen. "One more message saved from enemy eyes! And one more chance to go home!"

29th day of Tallow Month (November), 1573

At daybreak on a Sunday morning, Hiltje felt her husband stirring beside her and moaning. She'd already lain awake for what seemed like half the night. Her mind roamed about to every possible corner of the world she knew about—from her children to their former home in Brussels to *The Clever Fox Inn* to their secrets. She lingered long on thoughts of Joris' trip to Ghendt and her own secret wish of going with Magdalena to the Bible reading that went on in her attic room on Sunday mornings.

"Joris," she began.

"*Ja?*" he sputtered in his early morning voice.

"I go to church this morning," Hiltje ventured.

"Not to the Pieterskerk to listen to the *glipper!*"

"There are other places to go in this city. I know. I visited them while you were in Ghendt."

"Where this time?"

"I think I shall go with Gretta and her family."

"Where is that?"

"Somewhere nearby—where Jakob and Magdalena de Wever go." She didn't dare to tell him they met in the weaver's house. The whole world knew this was the way the dreaded Anabaptists worshiped—in "hidden churches" behind secret wall panels and in dark dank cellars or crowded cobwebby attics, doing who knew what kinds of strange things.

"What sort of church is it?"

"It seems to have no name. I only know they read the Bible there, and . . ." *Ja*, what more did she know?

"The Bible? You mean they read it aloud to the congregation?" The tone of his voice said he couldn't quite believe it—or maybe he didn't want to believe it.

"That is what they do in the Marekerk these days," she said, then hurried to add, "I took the children there with me when you first left. Ah, Joris, but it is wonderful to hear the Bible reading! You should go hear it too."

"Humph!" he grunted. "Sounds like a hole of Anabaptists to me. Remember, Vrouw, they're a dangerous bunch of polygamists, deluded madmen, *dopers*. You're likely to go in all innocent and trusting and come out with your mind beguiled, and next thing you'll be letting them baptize you and . . ."

"*Nay, nay*, stop! I didn't say they were Anabaptists. You just jumped to the wild idea. I don't know what they call themselves, Joris. I only know they're good people, every one of them. While you were gone, Magdalena was the only person in Leyden to treat me kindly when all my other friends turned their heads." She gasped. What made her say that for his ears to hear?

"What?" He sat up in bed and grabbed her by the shoulder. "Why would your friends turn against you?"

"Who knows why?" She pushed him back down into the bed and patted the feather bag under his chin. "The important thing is that Magdalena always proved to be a true friend. And you've seen how they gave us this place to stay and never a day goes by that they don't do something for us that needs to be done." Not wanting to pause long enough for him to answer, she went on. "I don't know what you think about religion, Joris. You've never told me, and I suppose I don't really need to know."

"I never thought you cared," he mumbled.

Hiltje went on, pretending he had not interrupted her. "I only know that since the religion of these people makes them treat the rest of us with such kindness and still read the Bible and talk with God as if He were a friend, I want to know more about it. So I intend to go there this morning."

"But, Vrouw . . ." he sputtered.

She didn't listen. She was letting herself out of the bed, beginning to dress for the day, giving him instructions. "I shall leave the children here to help you if you need anything. Christoffel will know where to find me, and you need not know or do a thing, and when your vrouw comes home she will be jovial and carefree, and won't you love that?"

She hurried off to waken the children and stir up the fire, leaving Joris mumbling and disentangling himself from the feather bag. "Not fully like himself again today," she said aloud over the rekindling embers of yesterday's hearth fire. "When will he ever be?" She shook her head and blinked at the sight of the fresh and delicate flame curling around a chunk of peat she'd just put down.

Christoffel shuffled to her side, yawning and wiping at his eyes.

"When the church bells ring, I go," Hiltje told him.

"And what am I supposed to do?" the boy asked.

"Just watch your vader and make sure he doesn't get into something harmful or go out the door."

Christoffel laughed. "Go out the door? He hasn't done that since we moved here. He shouts at me every time I even open it."

Hiltje groaned inside. It was true. The poor deluded man had some sort of an unreasonable fear running around in his head and turning his heart bottom side up. In his dreams and sometimes even when he was awake, he often cried out in terror, "They're coming to take me to the dungeon and put me in the cell for . . ." He'd never finish the sentence, and she couldn't imagine what the unsaid words might be or where he'd gotten this fearful idea.

"Then your job should be easy enough," she told Christoffel.

She scurried around putting everything in order, giving the girls instructions what to do while she was gone. Last thing before she left, she took Christoffel by the shoulders, made him look at her, and said sternly, "One more time—don't let him out the door, now, do you hear?"

"I hear," he said, wriggling to free himself from her grip.

To the sound of persistent church bells, she hurried out into the fresh misty morning. Moments later she was climbing into the crowded windowless attic room of the Wever's home and setting up her chair next to Gretta on the end of the row nearest the stairs.

The room was chilled enough that she could see little puffs of vapor rising from each person. She held her arms together and wrapped her hands snugly inside her shawl—the brown woolen shawl with the bright darts of sunlight scattered all around. It was one of the few treasures she had saved when they'd pulled her away from the inn.

The priest—here they called him an elder—stood behind a small table reading from the big Bible. His wavy snow-white beard seemed almost to ripple in the flickering candlelight, and his voice sounded, too, like the rippling of a full fast-flowing brook without stones to stumble over or send stray droplets flying.

"Words of Jesus from the mountain," the elderly man explained, then read the most amazing things. Hiltje had never heard the likes.

> Blessed are the poor in spirit, for to them belongs the kingdom of the Heaven.
> Blessed are those who grieve, for they shall be comforted.
> Blessed are the gentle-spirited, for they shall inherit the earth.
> Blessed are those who hunger and thirst after righteousness, for they shall be satisfied.
> Blessed are the merciful, for to them shall mercy be done. . . .

The smooth sonorous flow was interrupted by the feel of her elbow being shaken and the sound of her son's excited whisper in her ear, "Come, Moeder! Vader is gone!"

"What?" She stared at the boy, not believing what she heard.

Christoffel did not answer but started back down the winding stairs. Reluctantly Hiltje stood to her feet. Just as she placed her foot on the first step, the elder read, " 'Blessed are those who are persecuted for the sake of righteousness. . . . ' "

"Blessed?" she mumbled and shivered as she descended out of the cozy room of the Bible reading. She heard footsteps and turned to see both Dirck and Pieter-Lucas close behind her.

"Is there trouble?" Dirck asked.

"Vader has disappeared," Christoffel said.

"How did you let him get away and how long has he been gone? Weren't you watching?" Hiltje babbled, near to hysteria.

"I . . . I don't know what happened, Moeder. I thought he was sleeping. When I realized I did not hear him snoring, I went to look—and he was gone."

"Where have you searched?" asked Pieter-Lucas.

"All through the building, I hope," Hiltje said, her mind running through the whole place. "Upstairs and down? Behind every screen and in all the beds?"

"Ja, ja, Moeder, and on the streets nearby, all the way to the harbor."

"You looked in the citadel?"

"Ja."

"In every alcove, behind every stone?"

"Moeder, he is not there!"

"The brothers will help," Dirck offered and started toward the stairs.

"You cannot disturb the service," Hiltje protested.

"When a brother is in trouble, nothing's more important than helping him," Pieter-Lucas called back over his shoulder.

A brother? That's what these people called each other, but Joris was not one of them. Before Hiltje and Christoffel had reached the door, they heard Dirck's voice shouting out, "Come, brothers. Joris needs help!"

The sound of feet thundered across the floor and down the steps. In no time, Dirck and Pieter-Lucas had dispatched their friends in every direction, with instructions to search for the missing man.

"With or without him, we'll meet back here as soon as we hear the clock chime again," Pieter-Lucas added.

At least ten people spread out across the streets and bridges of the city. Spotting him should be simplest at this hour when most of the people were in church. But there were hundreds of buildings and alleyways where he could take refuge.

Hiltje and Christoffel headed west along the large canal that curved northward. They didn't talk but looked in every direction, stopping to search out each obscure corner and under every bridge where a spot of dry land lay beside a waterway beneath.

All the while Hiltje carried on a mumbling dialogue.

"You never should have left him," she scolded herself.

"Why not?" she protested. She'd done it many times before and always he'd cowered inside the old building as if he thought a lion awaited him in the street. No one could have forced him, even at sword's point, beyond the threshold. What, then, could possibly have prompted him to venture out this morning?

Hiltje and Christoffel had passed the Beguinage and were nearing the square corner of the city wall where the Rhine River flowed under the wall when Christoffel pointed toward the grain mill just inside the Witte Poort and shouted, "Look, Moeder! The *molen* is on fire!"

Hiltje gasped. Stunned, she watched the bright orange flames reaching high into the air, licking at the clouds. Memories of a burning stable and flames in the night where once her home had stood tore at her heart.

A crowd of people were gathering in the streets now, and a bucket line was forming between the river and the *molen*. From all around came loud shouts of "The *speken* are burning our grain *molen*!"

Grabbing Christoffel, she shouted, "Let's go!"

They turned to go east along the Rhine, just in time to see Joris stumbling toward them.

"Joris!" Hiltje shouted.

He stared past her toward the burning mill and burst into a storm of loud howling sobs. He covered his head with both hands and cried out inconsolably, "Oh! Oh!"

Hiltje took him by an arm, Christoffel staying close beside her. "Come, let us go home," she urged.

"*Nay!*" he wailed and refused to move. "They're after me. Great God *Yahweh*, provide a ram! Have mercy! *Yahweh*, I shall serve you till I die. Oh! Oh!"

Hiltje felt her heart racing as if it would spring from her bodice. What dangerous words he spoke out here in public. Had it not been for the fire, he would surely have become the instant center of attention. Maybe indeed he was. She refused to look about her. Instead, she tugged at her husband's arm and urged him with all the calmness she could put into her voice, "Joris, we must go home. In no other place can you be safe. Come, Joris, come."

He ignored her as if she were not there. What more could she do? Oh, for a strong man to come to her aid. Where were the brothers who had set off in search of him?

"Joris, come." She followed the sound of a man's voice and looked up at young Pieter-Lucas, standing already with both hands gripping her husband's shoulders. "We've come to guide you to the safety of home."

Joris turned to him, "Frans," he cried out, "have you brought the ram?"

"I have . . ." Pieter-Lucas began without finishing.

Joris heaved a tremendous sigh, then yielded to the strong hands that led him through the streets and away from the hubbub. All the way he moaned, asking a hundred questions about the ram and occasionally bursting out with the name *Yahweh!*

Hiltje followed along, holding tightly to her son.

"What is he talking about, Moeder?" Christoffel asked.

"Your vader has his head in a sock. Nothing he says makes any sense," she told him. In her heart she wished all she said could be true and actually found herself doing something she'd never done before—praying.

"God, whoever and wherever you are, please keep away the soldiers who would put him in the prison cell he fears so much." She had no idea whether her prayer had been heard, but just saying it calmed her enough to get her home.

At home they tucked Joris into his bed. Dirck and Pieter-Lucas stayed close by until he fell fast asleep.

"Tell me," Hiltje asked Pieter-Lucas, "how far did you follow him?"

"From the Marekerk."

"The Marekerk? Whatever was he doing there?"

"Attending services, perhaps?" Pieter-Lucas suggested.

"Nay, he wouldn't do that," she protested.

Pieter-Lucas shrugged. "I only know I saw him come out of the church with the rest of the people when shouts of 'Fire!' filled the streets."

She stood stunned, remembering. "This morning I told him I'd heard them read the Bible in the Marekerk and that he should do the same. Do you think that's what he did?" Dirck smiled, and for the first time Hiltje noticed how warm and kind his gray eyes were.

"Stranger things have happened," he said. "Stranger things, indeed."

Chapter Seventeen

Delft

10th day of Winter Month (December), 1573

A swirling storm was turning all Delft into a gigantic shapeless snow-bank when Pieter-Lucas found his way at last to the old convent on the St. Agathaplein. He shoved his way through the gate and into the shelter of the dull gray stone walls, shaking the damp load of snow from his outer garments and fighting the cold that seeped into his bones.

In Willem's little room on the upper floor, a chunk of burning peat on the hearth behind the table reached out its radiance to welcome the travel-weary messenger.

"Come and thaw your bones," the prince invited. He leaned back in his chair and motioned toward the hearth.

"Hearty thanks, Excellency," Pieter-Lucas said. He moved to the fire, pulling off soggy gloves and spreading benumbed fingers out trembling toward the warmth.

"What is the news from Leyden?" Willem asked, his facial expression weary.

Pieter-Lucas shivered and his teeth chattered as he spoke. "Yesterday the Spaniards took the fortress at Lammen and burned the *molen* at the Koe Poort. They burned the village of Huis ter Warmond the day before."

"*Ach!* So is there a village or fortress in the environs of Leyden left in our possession?" The prince wrinkled his brow and stared at Pieter-Lucas with an earnestness that burrowed into his soul.

"I know of none."

"How are things in the city? Are the people still in good spirits?"

Pieter-Lucas turned his back to the fire, clasping the fingers of both hands behind him. What he wanted most to say was that his own son no longer coughed, nor was he afflicted with that dreadful *heatte* that had sapped his strength and drained all the color from his cheeks. *Yet I fear for his life*, his heart cried out, *when there's not enough food to go around—or peat for the hearth in the warehouse-printery—and the least illness floating through the air will find in him a ready victim.*

But Willem had asked about the citizens of Leyden, not about little Lucas. So Pieter-Lucas swallowed down the anguish lurking always just below the surface and said, "Leydenaars are tough, Your Excellency. Not always of one mind about how things are to be done, but they do not give in easily to despair."

"Their *molens*—do they work yet? Or have they all been burned along with the one outside the Koe Poort?"

"Only the Witte Poort *molen* has been torched—ten days or so ago. The corn mills grind on, and the bark mill as well. But the supply of grain is dwindling now that harvest is past, and the streets swarm with refugees from the neighboring villages and with swaggering freebooters who expect us to feed them as payment for their services."

"What services?" Willem asked.

"They brag about protecting us, fighting for us, freeing us. But they pay no attention to the burgemeesters nor to the men who try to bring some sort of order to the resistance. I've heard them talking about attacking the Spaniards in their own fortifications. Fiery self-styled fighters they are, like the Beggars, only worse."

Willem sighed. "Good loyal soldiers with ambitions only for their vaderland are not easy to come by. Did the burgemeesters give you a written message for me?"

"*Nay*, only this report of my lips. Too much risk now, with the city so tightly invested."

"Do you fear for your life—passing in and out of Leyden so often?"

"What man does not fear for his life in these days? Surely none has more reason than you. Yet you do not desert us, so how can we do less than push on past the guards and spears? What our men need most are your words of encouragement—any possibilities that the end may be in sight. I think our freebooters especially grow weary of the long silent wait when no cannons explode or swords wave. They begin to suspect that the slow strangulation of a city is at least as painful as a swift and bloody battle."

"Do they speak of compromise with the new governor?"

"Only the *glippers* speak so. The rest jeer them down and harry them from their council meetings. I'm sure many of the citizens would be likewise inclined, given the opportunity—and empty bellies or a ravaging plague." Pieter-Lucas lowered his voice and leaned close to Willem, as if he feared the walls might hear and shout his words from the church steeples. "I fear that not until our bellies pinch and our children die in our arms will most Leydenaars believe this siege could be as devastating as Haarlem or Naarden."

Willem nodded slowly. "Exactly what the new Governor Requesens is counting on. While Alva doubled his fist with each new encounter, this man plays instead a game of feigned softness. 'Tis the way of intimidation—and deadly. This you must tell the burgemeesters and councilors from my lips. 'Be not deceived by the apparently kind inattention of your besiegers. Turn deaf ears to the *glippers* and never, NEVER entertain so much as one conversation about amnesty. That is no answer.' "

"When they ask what are your plans, Excellency, how do I answer?"

Willem tapped his fingers slowly on the table before him. With cautious deliberation he said, "Tell them I gather my army, and Ludwig and Jan gather theirs, with all possible haste. You know. You have seen their efforts. We shall push the enemy first from Leyden's walls, then from our vaderland's shores."

Pieter-Lucas nodded. "That shall I tell them, and may their ears be scrubbed to hear it well." He rubbed his hands together briskly, happy to feel them soft and pliable and warm. He headed toward the door.

"First take a good night's sleep," Willem said. "Then arise with strength, travel with good fortune, and enter the city with caution. Now, good night."

"Good night, Excellency," Pieter-Lucas echoed. He slipped out of the man's presence and down the hall to a waiting sleeping mat and a night of uncertain dreams.

———

Lammen

11th day of Winter Month (December), 1573

Pieter-Lucas' trek back to Leyden led across a wonderland of glistening white fields and waterways frozen along the banks like thick rolled hems on ribbons of silver. No flakes of fresh snow fell, and a brush of fleeting stringy clouds chased a pale watery sun swiftly to its early horizon. The wind whipped around him like a dreary cape, and each labored step of his shoes left its telltale imprint in the freshly crusting snow.

Pieter-Lucas had taken the shorter way around the fortress at Lammen, hoping to arrive in the enemy-infested countryside before dusk. Thanks to the accumulation of icy snow and a pain in his lame leg, the journey took longer than he expected. By the time the sun had slipped, first behind a drift of darkening clouds and then below the snowbanks, he could barely make out a handful of faintly flickering lights in the fortress of Lammen.

In daylight and with clear roads and fields to pass through, reaching Leyden was tricky though not impossible. Now, on this moonless night, the dusk had turned swiftly into stick-darkness, and the cold was far more bitter than he had imagined. He knew the roads were guarded by soldiers, but he could not pick his way across the fields piled high with drifted snow.

He stumbled on, guessing where the trekpath lay by the trickle of water still flowing through the Vliet River to his left, keeping the lights of Lammen always just to his right. If only the fortress still belonged to Leyden, he might find shelter there for the night.

"Great and merciful God," he cried out, his voice muffled by the cape with which he'd wrapped all but his eyes, "lead me home that I freeze not to death in this deadly iced world."

Scarcely had he uttered the words when he heard a noise of metal against metal springing on him from the right. Strong arms grabbed him from all sides.

"Let me go!" he screamed, wrenching at the restraining hands.

His captors held him fast and a pleasant voice answered through the wind, "We come to save your life."

"To save my life? Or to take it?" How many captors were there? Pieter-Lucas strained to see in the eerie glow of a single torch. All he could determine for certain was a circle of helmeted heads and heavy beards surrounding him on all sides.

"You trust us not, *qué no?*" one man sneered and fastened a chain about his wrists.

Spaniards! Why should he trust them? They were Willem's enemies! Probably the ones who had taken Lammen by storm from the soldiers Leyden hired to guard it. All too well he knew their intentions. They would try him as a hole peeper and string him up alongside the road. More than once he'd seen a lifeless body dangling from a tree branch spreading out over the roadway. Remembering sent shivers along his backbone.

From somewhere at a muffled distance he heard a hollow mocking laugh, followed by an earsplitting shout, "We've caught him at last, the traitor who limps!"

"And carries messages for his 'prince' in his shoes!" came another voice from a different direction, spitting the word "prince" as if it were some great deception.

Numbness gripped him—body, mind, and soul. He tried to struggle for freedom, but fear had turned his arms and legs into chunks of boneless meat. Unable to feel the sting of the cold or the chafing of the chains, he was vaguely aware that he was being dragged along—to where, he could not even think. A sudden flood of warm liquid trickling down his legs told him he'd lost all control of his body.

They were beating him with sticks and dragging him into the fortress. Not until they had dumped him onto the damp earthen floor of a dungeon cell and chained his arms to the wall did his body begin to regain any feeling.

With ruthless hands the men stripped him of his shoes. Not finding the message they sought, they swore a long chain of loud Spanish oaths.

"Where are your messages from *Prince Willem*?" they demanded, pronouncing the prince's name with a sneer that made Pieter-Lucas' stomach churn.

"I carry no messages. I am a painter," he managed, his own voice sounding pinched and far away.

One soldier slapped him across the face—first one side, then the other. "Painter indeed!" he sneered.

Another landed a gnarly fist under his chin and added, "Lie to us, will you?"

The rest tore at his clothes—scraping into his flesh with clawing fingernails, removing his cape, hat, stockings, breeches, and ripping holes in his doublet. In a final desperate move, one soldier reached inside his nightshirt and felt over his entire body with rough cold hands.

"Aha! What do I find here?" he cried out. He was wrenching Pieter-Lucas' little bag of painting tools from around his waist.

Pieter-Lucas strained at the chains that manacled him to the wall and cried out through chattering teeth, "My paints!"

"Paints indeed!" came a mocking voice, followed by a round of raucous laughter.

"Open it up and let us see what sort of messages he paints," called another.

The leader of the group snatched the bag, and another soldier shoved a torch near to him. He yanked at its cord and reached in, pulling out a pot, removing its stopper. He sniffed at the paint it held, then dumped it out on the floor. With unbridled glee, he stomped on it, grinding it into the packed dirt beneath his feet while his companions roared their pleasure.

Pieter-Lucas felt a lump in the pit of his stomach, cold, hard, and heavy. *Great God in the Heaven*, he prayed, *do you not see? Do you not care?*

The whole pack of soldiers ripped at the bag now, grabbing charcoals, brushes, the miniature palette and paintpots, tossing them out across the cell, grunting and laughing.

"Is that all?" screamed the leader.

The man who'd searched his nightshirt went back to his despicable work, examining every fold of his doublet as well. "Eureka! I have found it!" he shrieked. In both hands he held up a stack of tiny canvases.

"*Nay*, not those," Pieter-Lucas cried out, thinking of the two paintings he carried with him always, along with empty canvases to use along the way. One bore a portrait of Aletta, the other little Lucas' lamb. Small pieces of his beloved ones they were, tucked away close to his heart. He often pondered what would happen if his enemies confiscated them. Should he leave them at home in a safe place? *Nay*, he couldn't. It had always seemed worth the risk.

"They are not messages," he protested with a stoic reserve that seemed to tear at the depths of his gut.

"Aha! This one is a beautiful *vrouw*," shouted the man with glee. He kissed it, then held it up for all to see.

"Your *vrouw*?" The leader taunted Pieter-Lucas. "What a pity you did not stay by her side!"

The pack descended on the man who held the pictures. The men tussled with one another, all trying at once to find hidden messages.

"What do they say?" they asked of each other.

"Nothing but pictures and empty sheets," said one man. He grabbed the canvases, crumpled them in his hand, and tossed them to the far corners of the cell. For a gut-wrenching moment he hovered over Pieter-Lucas and spit on him. Then stooping down, he looked at him over the bridge of a long well-rounded nose.

"So, our testy little traitor," he mocked, haughtiness dripping from every word, "what message do you carry in your mind?"

Pieter-Lucas stared hard at the faintly illuminated patch of floor on which he sat nursing his grief and did not give an answer.

The soldier stood and kicked at him, landing a nasty blow to the bony ridge of his shin. "You choose not to talk without pain?"

What more did the man have in mind for producing pain—the rack perhaps? Pieter-Lucas shuddered uncontrollably. Many were the terrifying stories he had heard about the rack, one of the cruelest instruments of torture ever invented to induce one's enemies to talk. It was a long hard bench where the body was stretched out fully. By means of a system of pulleys and weights, the arms and legs were pulled farther and farther apart, often dislocating them from their sockets.

The man laughed. "We know you carry messages to the burgemeesters of Leyden."

"*Sí, señor,*" said another, "we've seen you jumping canals and slinking through fields many times before."

"And always on the roads you limp," added a third, triumph in his voice.

Pieter-Lucas' palms were sweating, while the rest of his body trembled with shivering. "Your eyes do not see so well in the darkness," he stammered. "I am no such hole-peeper, field-runner, nor jumper." To tell a lie always set his heart to racing, but never had it paralyzed him as it did now.

"You lie not in a convincing manner, *señor.*" The soldier kicked at him again, this time hitting him on the other shin. The warmth of fresh blood trickled over his foot and left it smarting.

"We shall leave you here to your deceitful thoughts," said another soldier. "When you've shivered through a few more hours, perhaps you shall be more willing to tell us the truth."

Pieter-Lucas pulled his arms to his side as tightly as the chains would allow and folded his bare legs and shirttail up into his belly. "At least give me back my breeches," he begged.

A volley of hollow laughter erupted. He felt stinging blows to his head and a mocking voice called out, "Poor little half-naked boy!"

The next thing he knew, Pieter-Lucas felt the breeches landing on his head. He smelled the strong aroma of urine and shook his head repeatedly until the garment fell to his lap.

"Ah, give the man his shoes too," called out one more man with mock concern. "We would not want his feet to freeze so that he could never walk again and carry messages for his beloved prince."

The man who had kicked him stooped over, picked up the requested items, and dropped them into his lap.

"Now put them on, if you think you can!" he ordered. The Spaniards laughed and called out words in a language Pieter-Lucas could not understand. Their tone told him that they were jeering taunts, and their mocking voices seemed to fill the dungeon cell with demonic presences.

The soldiers shuffled from the room, closing the heavy door with an enormous clanking of metal chains and locks. Pieter-Lucas strained at the manacles on his arms, but it was useless. He could not reach the shoes. Stunned, daring not to lean against the slimy wall, he maneuvered his legs and torso around until he finally sat on his soggy breeches like a cushion. His whole body ached and shivered.

"*Ach!* My Aletta," he moaned. "You warned me not to leave you this time. If only I had listened! But I couldn't. . . ."

He pulled his legs up as far as they would go and leaned his head against his chest, then closed his eyes and tried not to think. Suddenly, out of the stillness of the dark, he heard a moan from a far corner of the cell, followed by sniffles from another corner and a snore from another.

Ach! There are other prisoners here! Oh, Aletta, Aletta, pray God to deliver me soon . . . soon . . . soon!

He'd scarcely let the thought pass through his confused brain when he heard a movement nearby and felt a hand on his foot.

"Who goes there?" he demanded, drawing up his foot farther under his leg.

"Shh!"

He felt a warm breath in his face.

"Let me put your shoes on for you" came the whisper in his ear.

Pieter-Lucas strained his eyes in the pitch blackness, eager to see the prisoner who posed as an angel of mercy. Instead, he felt the act of mercy—first the stockings, then the shoes, being tugged onto his feet, still sore and swollen from the kickings in the shins. Finally he felt a warm garment being laid across his aching bruised shoulders.

"God bless your merciful hands," he whispered.

The man said no more and slipped shortly out of reach, leaving Pieter-Lucas with a brain filled with questions. Who were his companions in this place? How had they been captured? What would the Spaniards do when they returned to him in the morning? Would they wreak revenge on the man who had helped him?

Pieter-Lucas spent the rest of the night shivering, writhing against the chains that bolted him to the wall, at times moaning or screaming out with excruciating pain. The continuing sighs and snores all around him told him he must have many companions. He decided it was their breath that kept the cold from turning his exposed legs and nose and shackled wrists and hands to ice.

The first shades of pale daylight creeping in through the single window high above his head confirmed his suspicions. The floor was covered with bodies, each man curled up into a tiny ball. And every one wore a soldier's uniform. Must be the soldiers who were guarding this fortress when the Spaniards took it.

Pieter-Lucas shuddered. He closed his eyes and tried to imagine it all away—the cold, the pain, the numbness, the crowd of cellmates. No matter that his body had never felt more exhausted, sleep would not come. Just when he was beginning to feel something akin to warmth, a shout came from the far corner of the cell.

"So we have a hole-peeper among us!"

"*Nay!* He's an artist!" shouted another, and several men laughed.

"Here's a pot of his paint" came a third.

"And look at this old brush! Must have belonged to his opa."

Pieter-Lucas cringed. By now he could see hands waving the contents of his painter's bag in the air all around him. Would they return them to him? These men were soldiers, probably not sympathetic to his painter's blood. In this place he couldn't even tell them that he was on their side, that he ran messages for their prince. How many of the men were patriots? How many were mercenaries?

"*Hei!* This is a right pretty vrouw you got," shouted another, a lusty delight tingeing his voice.

"Let's see!"

Pieter-Lucas watched the portrait of his Aletta being tossed from one pair of grimy hands to another all around the cell. "Let me have it back," he screamed out.

Such a pandemonium of excited shouts now broke out that he could only catch an occasional intelligible word until the man nearest the door began waving his hands in the air. A hush settled over the crowd, like the stillness at the end of a spent rain shower.

He heard the jangle of keys and a clunking sound in the lock of the door. The door opened with a shudder, scraping the straw from the floor as it went. Three Spanish soldiers marched through with drawn swords and scowling faces.

"What is all the noise about?" the leader shouted. No one answered. One at a time he glared at every man in the room until they sat immobile under the spell of this Spaniard with an intimidating air.

He stared at last at Pieter-Lucas. A sneer lifted the corners of his mustachio ever so slightly, and Pieter-Lucas looked down.

"Look at me, hole-peeper!" he shouted.

He lifted his head but fixed the gaze of his mind somewhere out and beyond the dungeon.

"Are you ready to give us your message?" the soldier asked.

"I have no message to give," he said. It was true, in one sense. All Willem had given him to say to the burgemeesters were words of encouragement which any Spaniard could guess—not really secrets at all. The fact that both Willem and his brothers were raising troops to further their cause—the whole world knew that.

It was also a lie. For the real thing the soldier wanted to extract from him was an admission that he was a hole-peeper, that he carried messages for Willem at all. And *ja*, he did carry messages, but *nay*, at least on this mission he was no real hole-peeper searching out the enemy's secrets and passing them on to the planners of the war.

"Come with us," the man growled. Then he nodded to his men, who quickly went to work freeing his chains from the wall and raising him to his feet.

"*Hei* here!" the leader roared, staring at Pieter-Lucas' feet. "How did you manage to put on your stockings and shoes? Your arms were fastened to the wall all night!"

"My shoes?" he stammered, looking down at them.

"I suppose some angel came down from Heaven and did it while you slept." The man grinned ominously at him.

Half believing it could have been so, he stammered, "God has always a way to lend comfort and aid to the innocent."

"Innocent? Bah!" The soldier slapped his cheek. He pointed at the men on the floor and roared, "Which one of you played delivering angel in the night?"

When the men remained silent, he pointed directly to one little man near Pieter-Lucas, "Gerard, it was you again, was it not?"

Gerard lowered his head and said nothing.

The Spaniard stepped over three other men and grabbed him by a lapel, raising him to his feet before him. He trembled with rage and stormed at his latest victim. "Whoever told you you were a soldier, you spineless weak-livered savior of all who suffer?" The words poured out of the Spaniard's mouth, a tirade of impassioned sarcasm.

After a long and ominous pause, he ordered, "Take off the shoes you put on this prisoner's feet in the night."

"I cannot do it," Gerard said, trembling.

"Then neither shall you lessen the pain of one more man to whom justice is being served," the Spaniard roared. He turned to one of his men and ordered, "Bind Gerard to the wall and remove the shoes from his feet. See to it he has nothing to eat all day."

To the other soldier, he said, "You, remove the shoes from our hole-peeper here before we lead him to his own solitary cell. Bring them along. I have plans for them!"

The obedient soldier stooped down, stripped off Pieter-Lucas' shoes, and handed them to his superior. Then they secured his chains to both soldiers and dragged, shoved, and kicked him out the door, up a long flight of cold rough stairs with flinty outcroppigs that cut into his feet and toes. When they'd reached a high rampart, they were surrounded by a regiment of Spanish soldiers, all laughing and jeering his arrival.

His captor led him to the edge of the wall. He could see Leyden sparkling like a fairy city in the sunlight. So close he'd come. If only he could have plodded on a little longer—a few minutes more—he would have reached home and Aletta instead of this awful place. Everything in Pieter-Lucas' innards sighed.

" 'Tis a beautiful city indeed," the commander of the regiment taunted. He put his forefinger under Pieter-Lucas' chin and lifted it just so he'd have to look him squarely in his angry eyes and gloated, "And it's ours, all ours! Without those vital messages entrusted to your care, it will stay ours now and forever!" He laughed, then held both of Pieter-Lucas' shoes out over the edge of the wall and went on. "If you'll just tell us about the message in your brain, we'll give you back your shoes, even consider letting you go back to Leyden." He laughed, adding, "Someday!"

Pieter-Lucas held himself like a statue and fought down the overwhelming grief rising up in his throat. With a calm reserve he did not know he possessed, he responded, "I have no messages to give to you."

With a mad mixture of anger and glee, the man flung Pieter-Lucas' shoes out over the edge, laughing and shouting, "They'll get closer to Leyden than you ever will again."

A loud cheer rang from the crowd of soldiers. They raised beer tankards high into the air and shouted out a toast to "Willem's Leyden hole-peeper!"

Pieter-Lucas fixed his eyes on Leyden before him and found himself crying out from the depths of his heart in silent prayer. *God, if you're there and listening, then at least protect my Aletta and Lucas and Kaatje.*

"Too bad your vrouw with the beautiful face will never see you again." His tormentor was speaking and fingering Pieter-Lucas' hair. "I'm sure she would miss these golden curls."

My curls? Instinctively Pieter-Lucas tightened every muscle as if to protect himself. He looked up to see a wide grin of mischievous satisfaction spreading over the man's oily face, and the glint of a polished sword in his hands. All the soldiers were laughing again.

Pieter-Lucas strained against the chains and every restraint, but it was no use. He closed his eyes, unable to look again at the glee his shearing would bring to these evil men. Then he felt the great sharp implement pulling at the roots, severing his hair like some gigantic saw, hacking limbs from a noble fir tree set for palace decoration.

The man took them slowly, one at a time, and tossed them to the winds. He celebrated each new cut with the fanfare of laughter and one more offer of clemency if only Pieter-Lucas would but tell his secret messages. When he refused to speak, they descended on him like a pack of hungry wolves, snarling, hissing, and once more pummeling with their iron fists, slapping his ears.

With eyes shut tight and his mind in a confused jumble of unstoppable anguish, he finally realized that they were dragging him down another flight of stairs and shoving him into a cell so tiny he had to turn sidewise to enter it. The high window was covered with a dark material of some kind, and there was no room to stretch out on the straw to sleep. They gave him his breeches and did not fasten either arm to the wall.

His tormentors left him alone, but not before the commander had spoken to him through the nearly closed door, his voice so sickly sweet that Pieter-Lucas held both hands over his ears to block it out. As if in a heavy fog he heard it anyway. "May God's delivering angel bring you out of this one. If not, we will be back and give you one more chance to save what remains of your curls."

Pieter-Lucas ran his fingers over his head. The stubble felt like knife blades brushing his fingertips, every part of his battered body ached, and he had to fight down an almost irresistible urge to vomit.

He pounded on the slimy walls with his fist and screamed as loud as he still had voice to scream, "What will Aletta say? Or will she ever know?"

CHAPTER EIGHTEEN

Leyden

Christmas Day, 1573

*T*he crisp cold air of early Christmas morning sent the antiphonal sounds of jubilant church bells bouncing about from corner to corner all over Leyden.

"Unto us a Savior is born!" they seemed to say.

The old familiar message bore a special meaning to Leydenaars this year. With soldiers all around they knew how desperately they needed a Savior! On all other days they might chafe and fret at the borders of Spanish soldiers ringing them in behind their walls. And they would threaten the men who sat at council tables in the town hall. Today, though, they would take time out to rejoice and do their religious service. Calvinists, Catholics, loyalists, *glippers*, and patriots—all would tell themselves they hoped in God to save them because they were standing for whatever they saw to be His cause.

In the old warehouse freshly turned into a center for refugees, Joris lived in a cocoon, largely unaware of what went on in the streets of the city, fearful of finding out. Neither was he aware it was Christmas morning, nor was he thinking of religious services or a savior. He sat on the edge of his cupboard bed, feet dangling above the floor, hair mussed, struggling simply to come fully awake. He looked up at his vrouw, already dressed and with her hair tied up neatly beneath her headdress.

"Why all the bells?" he asked.

"'Tis Christmas morning and the girls and I go to church!" She smoothed out her skirts and rested both hands on her hips, looking at him with stars of triumph shining in her eyes.

"Not to the Pieterskerk!" he retorted. Pain pierced his innards at the mention of the name. Never could he forget the priest's invective against Willem's supporters as *marranos*! Nor could he ever forgive!

"We go today in search of candles and swells of organ music," Hiltje said. "It's Christmas, Joris! And strange to say, I feel a yearning in my soul to hear the mass and feel the wafer on my tongue. . . ." Her voice trailed off and she raised her eyes heavenward.

Joris shook his head and frowned. "Whatever has happened to you, Vrouw, that you speak such words?"

"Who knows?" She shrugged and didn't look him in the eye.

He stared hard at her. "After all these years, Vrouw! Never has Christmas made a difference to you before."

She lifted her eyebrows and asked, "Would it be so awful if your vrouw decided to care about religion for once? I thought you would be glad!"

"Too late for that," he mumbled, "too late."

"What do you mean?"

"You wouldn't understand if I told you." Something inside Joris began to quiver. After so long of holding his deep secret, he could not tell her now. *Nay*, he couldn't do it.

Hiltje edged up close to him till her elbow nudged his arm and he felt her breath hot on his forehead.

"So I don't understand that you are indeed not the Christian you have so long pretended to be?"

"Who told you that?" Joris grabbed at his chest and felt his heart racing beneath the ribs.

"You've said it in more ways than you know, ever since you came home," she said, her voice registering a strange combination of triumph and fear.

"How?" he demanded. Surely he hadn't told her a thing.

"In all your callings upon *Yahweh* and your delirious ravings about being a Jew—and that painting of Vader Abraham that you buried in the bottom of your chest."

Joris gasped. "Great *Yahweh*, indeed!" Reaching out to her with both hands, he pleaded, "Oh, my vrouw, turn not against me. I cannot help what I was birthed to be. I've tried all these years. God only knows how desperately I've tried to be a Christian. . . ." He felt his energy trail off into weakness.

Smiling, she took his outstretched hand in her chilled and bony hands all roughened by years of innkeeping. As she pressed his fingers, he felt the same tenderness in her touch that he had felt back when they were young and passionately in love.

"When I first knew your secret, I was fearful and angry," she said softly. "But I watched you struggle for life and saw you strengthened by your faith in *Yahweh*, and my fear began to give way to acceptance. I now know that you are no less my husband just because you were birthed a Jew."

What did she mean by all that? He took her by the arm and squeezed with what little strength he had left. "You must keep it as our secret, my vrouw," he whispered.

"That I can do. In exchange, I ask that you let me go now. I know not why, but something is burning inside me, and I must go, Joris."

He sighed. "Only stay away from the Pieterskerk."

"I shall take care," she said. "And you shall trust me." She kissed him on the forehead, then pulled free and was soon gone.

Hiltje had scarcely closed the door when Joris suddenly felt a heavy drowsiness overpowering him. He no longer remembered why he was worrying or where his vrouw had gone—nor did he care. He crawled back into his bed and drifted off into an uneasy sleep.

He dreamed that Hiltje was dragging him through the doors of the Pieterskerk, where they were greeted by demons with flaming eyes and carrying long forks. The creatures snatched him up and carried him to the altar. Here the *glipper* priest bound him with strong cords and raised a knife above his head. The dreaded clergyman was laughing an evil laugh, and Joris was cowering, searching for a way to burrow down through the altar and escape. He felt his whole body shudder, and then someone was shaking him and shouting, "Vader! Vader! Wake up!"

Joris grabbed at the hand that shook him and screamed out, "Help me, save me from the demons and the *glipper's* sword! *Ach!* God have mercy!"

"There are no demons or *glippers* here, Vader." The voice was Christoffel's and the altar beneath him felt like his bed. Joris pried open his eyes. The lids were heavy and sticky and resisted his efforts. At last they yielded, and he saw his bed curtains framing the face of Christoffel.

"You had a bad dream, Vader," the boy said.

"Am I safe now?" Joris felt a quaver in his own voice.

"Aren't you always safe in this building?" Christoffel asked.

Joris sat upright with a start and looked out through the bed curtains. "Where's my vrouw?"

"She and the girls went to church. Remember?"

Joris mussed his hair with one hand. "That must be why I dreamed about altars and a priest with a knife," he moaned.

"An altar with a priest and a knife?" Christoffel stared at him wide eyed. "Like your picture, Vader? Was the man you drew—the one without a face—was he the priest from the Pieterskerk?"

Joris shrank back away from Christoffel. "*Nay*, never! I do not draw priests. Priests are angry men, son. They call us by vile names."

"Like *marranos*?"

Joris gasped and cowered back into the corner of his cupboard. "Never say that word into these ears, do you hear? Never!"

"What does it mean, Vader?"

"It's a very bad word, and long ago and far away when the priests called my opa by that name, they chased him from his home. That's always what it means."

"What? That they are getting ready to chase you away?"

"*Ja*, that's always what it means."

"Why would they chase your opa or you?"

"Stop!" Joris shouted, then turned to the wall, where he dug under the edge of his featherbag and pulled out the roll of pictures. He took them in his arms and held them to his breast.

"Was your opa the man with the knife?" He heard Christoffel's voice.

"*Nay!*" he responded, his heart beating a heavy rhythm, his head beginning to throb with the pain that had come to be his familiar companion ever since he came home from Ghendt.

"Who was he, then?" Christoffel went on.

As if in a fog, Joris heard himself answering, "Abraham, Vader Abraham!"

Christoffel climbed up into the bed beside him and grabbed him by the arm. "It's the same one!"

Joris pulled away from him and frowned. "Same as what? There's only one Vader Abraham!"

"While you were gone, Dirck read to us from his big book, the Bible, about Abraham offering his son on an altar and an angel stopped him and there was a ram in the thicket."

Joris felt his breathing stop and gasped. "It was a Bible, not a Torah?" He felt himself in a faraway daze.

He heard Christoffel ask in a quickly fading voice, "What's a Torah?"

Unable to answer, unable to think about anything else, Joris hugged the picture in his arms and rocked back and forth on his knees. "*Ach!* Vader Abraham!" he moaned. "I have betrayed you. *Ach!* Can you forgive?"

Christoffel was shaking him and shouting something, but Joris did not know what the boy said. All he could do was hold the picture tightly and go on rocking on his knees while he felt hot tears rolling down his cheeks.

"Vader Abraham!" he wailed. "Vader Abraham! Ah, Vader Abraham!"

———

Before the bells had stopped their ringing, Hiltje and her girls made their way into the Pieterskerk.

"Why do we not go to the church in de Wever's attic?" Tryntje asked.

"They have no celebration on Christmas day," Hiltje said. "And just once more I must hear the big organ and take the mass."

"But Vader said we must not go there again," Clare insisted, her eyes big with concern.

"Your vader is not well." Hiltje took them each by a hand and they followed.

With renewed determination she led the way to the old familiar church with its high steeple and colored-glass windows. They set up their seats in a spot near where the family always used to sit.

Aware of disapproving stares from people who once were her friends, Hiltje looked straight ahead. In a way that never had happened before, the grandness of the old place, the deep strains of the organ, and the choir chants gripped her soul. She followed the rituals with her mind, for once, and recited each prayer with a devoted attention to match that of both Tryntje and Clare.

The recitation of the mass stirred something new in her. What that something was, she couldn't say. She only knew it welled up inside, and she thought she saw Jesus himself standing there at His altar, with arms outstretched.

She knelt before the priest, for once eager to receive the wafer on her tongue. But he reprimanded her with his eyes and passed her by. She read in the movement of his lips that dreaded word, *marrano!* In the eyes of her mind, the priest had shoved Jesus back into a corner and loomed over her as a stern judge.

Dear God, her heart cried out from a sense of the most excruciating desolation, *never before have I seen myself as a sinner when I knelt in this place. Today it shouts at me like a million angry voices. It stares at me like eyes filled with raging fire. Oh, turn me not away. Even if my husband is a Jew, I beg for your forgiveness for my many sins.*

Did the Jesus she had envisioned moments ago still stand with arms outstretched, even though the priest now stood between them? For all his arrogant self-importance, this *glipper* priest could not change the heart of God. How she knew that, she didn't know, but she knew it. Was there some word she'd heard in one of the Bible readings that told her this?

"Come hither to Me, all you who are weary and burdened down, and I will give you rest."

That was it! The words echoed through her brain and seeped down into her heart. Nothing here about the need for a priest to decide whether God would let her through or block the way. He didn't even say, "Unless your husband is a *marrano* or a Jew, you can come to me." For a long moment she let the wonder of this newly discovered truth fill her with a kind of joy she'd never dreamed existed.

When the priest tapped her on the shoulder and scowled down on her, she rose to her feet. With head bowed, she walked down the long aisle and out through the doors, her daughters close behind. She paused on the threshold and looked back at the imposing altar. While she could not see Jesus standing there, it didn't matter any longer. In a way she could not explain, it seemed that He was walking out the door with her.

In the street, Clare said, "Vader was right. We never should have come here."

"Why not?" Hiltje asked.

"Because the priest wasn't kind to you."

"And he didn't read from the Bible," Tryntje added.

"If we had not come, we would not have known for sure that the service of the *glipper* priest at the Pieterskerk is no place for us." Hiltje looked down at her girls and began to hope that they would never lose their religious fervor.

"Moeder," Tryntje said at last, "is there a story about Christmas in the Bible?"

"I . . . I never thought about it," Hiltje stammered. "It must be there." As if a ray of light had flashed through the darkness of a winter night, she saw how terribly important it was to know what the Book said about the Jesus she had seen standing at the altar.

"Can we ask your friend?" Tryntje suggested.

"You mean Magdalena?"

"*Ja!*"

Hiltje hesitated.

Clare grabbed her moeder by the hand and begged, "She is kind to us, Moeder. She would tell us."

"And not grow angry," Tryntje finished.

Hiltje straightened her shoulders and breathed deeply to recapture her moederly air. "First," she said, "we go to see how your vader is doing. Then later we pay Magdalena a visit . . . and maybe Jakob might read to us what God's Book says about Christmas day. But we shall not ask them why they do not celebrate it in their church, do you understand?"

She looked each girl in the eye to make sure they got her message. What she saw there were mystified expressions. What she heard were two solid promises. "*Ja, Moeder, we shall not ask.*"

The church bells had fallen silent when Aletta stepped out into the streets, wrapping herself and Kaatje in the warm snugness of her cape. The city lay frozen beneath a cloud-free sky. Icicles hung from every wide overhanging roof, and piles of old snow cowered in doorways and corners. A howling wind whipped around the hems of Aletta's skirts and tugged at her cape. She drew it tighter around herself and Kaatje and grabbed at the low-hanging bellpull outside the gate of the Beguinage. The bell sounded from the other side of the wall, as clear and crisp as the frame of sparkling ice crystals that glistened in the archway above the gate.

No answer came. Three more times she pulled on the bell before the old gate shuddered open, scraping and complaining in its track, and a Beguine appeared in the opening, her eyebrows pinched into a tight half frown.

"*Ja?*" the little lady questioned.

"May I come in and pray in your chapel?" Aletta asked.

The Beguine's frown deepened. "The Beguines are in their Christmas mass. Have you no church of your own?"

Aletta shifted from one foot to the other, nervously trying to keep the cold from seeping through her street shoes. What could she say? Surely not that her church met in an attic and did not observe Christmas! "I come here often for herbs," she said, "and always the sister leads me to your chapel to pray. I feel near to God here in this place of healing. Besides . . ." *Nay!* The things that broke her heart this day could not be divulged to an unknown Beguine with a scowling countenance.

"Besides, what?"

Aletta gulped and fought down the anguish she felt rising in her. "Besides . . . when the mass is over and the hermit sister—I know not her name—is free, I need a fresh supply of herbs as well."

An expression of discontent gripped the face framed by the woman's Beguine habit, and Aletta felt a distinct air of resignation combined with disapproval. Without a word the Beguine opened the gate just wide enough for her to pass through and motioned her in. Then walking ahead she led her the full length of the courtyard and into the chapel. Never once did she look back, nor did she speak. Inside, the sister showed her to a seat in the last row at the end farthest from the door.

"You may go no farther," she whispered, "and keep that baby quiet." She hurried off to her place among the others.

Aletta slipped onto her knees on the kneeling bench, clutching the child to her breast and leaning her forehead on the rail before her. With eyes closed, she smelled the aromas of old wood, bodies, burning candles and incense, and heard the droning intonations of the priest saying mass.

How very, very long it had been since she had attended a Christmas mass—a mass of any kind. In fact, if her vader could see her now, he would not be pleased. Nor would her moeder. And Pieter-Lucas? Who knew what Pieter-Lucas would think?

"Great God," she cried out, "where indeed is my Pieter-Lucas on this morning? So long he has been gone. Not that it does not often happen so. As long as he is on business for the prince, I never know when he will return. This time, though, something in my spirit tells me all is not well."

Always, fear gripped her at the moment when Pieter-Lucas left on one of Willem's missions, but this time she had soundly warned him not to go. As always he had tried to soothe her fears while insisting on the absolute necessity of his mission. He left, reassuring her that no matter how long it took, he would be back.

This time the fear had not loosed its grip with the passage of time. Instead, with each day it grew more intense, until now, more than two weeks later, her whole inner being was bound up by it. Besides, there was little Lucas—still so thin and wan and listless—and the never ceasing burden over Kaatje's twisted foot.

She wiped her eyes on her cape and gave way to a wordless mourning, made gloomier by the continuing recitation of the Latin words and the chanted response of the sisters. She had forgotten how sad a mass could sound—and on this Christmas morning, her breaking heart sought desperately for some words of comfort!

Just when she thought she could hold no more grief and hot tears were gushing over her cheeks, Kaatje began to stir. Aletta moved to a sitting position on the bench behind her and, under cover of her cape, opened her bodice and offered the child a breast. Her mind now a blur of nothingness, she heard the priest recite a line of words she had come to understand.

"Benedicat vos omnipotens Deus, Pater et Felius et Spiritus Sanctus."

Vader had once told her long ago when she was a child in the Great Church in Breda that it was a benediction: *"Blessed be thou of the Almighty God, Vader, Son, and Holy Ghost."*

"Amen!" the sisters added in chorus.

"Blessed be thou," she whispered to Kaatje. Where that blessedness would come from when the child began to try to walk, Aletta could not imagine. What could the name of the Vader and the Son and the Holy Ghost have to do with it? Certainly there was no blessedness for herself in all of this.

The Beguines filed out of the chapel in silence. Aletta turned her face toward the wall and hunched over her nursing child, wiping the flowing tears on her cape. When the rustle of stiff black skirts had ceased and the chapel stood empty and silent, she raised her head and looked toward the altar where a towering wood-carved crucifix hung, illuminated by the flickering light of a crescent-shaped ring of fat fragrant candles.

Drawn by some irresistible warmth, she walked to the front of the chapel. Standing with her toes nudging the edge of the platform that held the altar, she pulled Kaatje's little body out from under her cape. Slowly she unwrapped the misshapen foot and held the girl in outstretched arms, presenting her to the Christ hanging on the cross above her.

"Great and merciful God," she prayed aloud, "how often have I asked Thee to heal this tiny foot, whether by herbal cure or a special touch. Yet still it dangles helpless and foreboding. On this Christmas morning, when the priest has spoken of blessedness, I hold Kaatje up to Thee and ask again for a healing touch like Jesus gave to the girl in Opa Lucas' painting. I bid Thee, as well, to bring my Pieter-Lucas home that he might see the miracle I seek from Thee and be a vader to his daughter—and son."

The statue of Christ did not look at her. The thorn-pierced head drooped against his naked unmoving breast, and the eyelids did not flutter open.

Aletta held Kaatje close and let her own tears drizzle over her. "Vader in the Heaven," she prayed between sobs, "art Thou as blind to my plight and as deaf to my cries as this dead wooden Christ on the wall?"

The pressure of a gentle hand lay on her shoulder. She tightened and turned quickly to see the hermit sister looking at her, the embodiment of compassion.

"Let me see the crippled foot," the sister begged.

Aletta started, pulling the child tightly to her breast. In a moment of unguarded grief, she had divulged her secret—the one she'd up until now so diligently kept hidden. The realization terrified her. But the warmth in this quiet little woman was so gentle she felt her heart melt before her. Without speaking a word, Aletta held the leg out. The sister took it in both hands and examined it with care.

"She was born with this malady?"

Aletta nodded, the memory of her moment of discovery twisting like a sharp dagger in her heart.

"You have tried herbal cures?'"

"All of them in my book, and all that the Julianas found in all their books."

"Nothing has helped?"

"Nothing." She had no heart to find more words, no energy to speak them.

The sister tucked the leg snugly into its wrapping, saying, " 'Tis a curse!"

Aletta gasped, grabbed the child free from the woman's touch, and began to retreat. The sister took a firm hold on her arm, thrust her face up into Aletta's, and went on, "Tell me, what vow have you broken?"

"I make no vows and have none to break," Aletta stammered, pulling free from the tight grip of fingers no longer feeling gentle to her touch.

"Payment of a vow will be required, whether your own or that of another," the sister said.

Stunned, gasping as if for air to breathe, Aletta fled across the chapel from a voice no longer soothing to her ears. Kaatje was crying inconsolably beneath her cape. Mad with a helpless frenzy, Aletta shoved open the door and stepped out into the frosty morning sunshine.

In an instant this cozy place had turned from a sanctuary into a prison of terror. How could she have forgotten about the dread of the popish world of curses and vows from which she had been rescued when her family took refuge among the Children of God? Scurrying across the Beguinage grounds, her confused brain threw up to her the dreadful image of the "Eye of God" in the ceiling of the Great Church staring down at her in every service, reminding her of her many misdeeds.

She started through the gate, only to hear the piercing voice of the stranger who had admitted her with reluctance. "Did you forget your herbs?"

Without answering she moved ahead out into the street. Here a quickened memory assaulted her with the terrifying image of herself sitting at the deathbed of Pieter-Lucas' moeder, Kaatje, listening to her tell of a vow made in her youth. After her first husband's death on a long-ago Christmas morning, the woman had entered the Beguinage of Breda, taking her infant son, Pieter-Lucas. She'd vowed to give the rest of her life to this religious order but later allowed Hendrick van den Garde to woo her away and marry her.

All her life since, she'd conceived many children but lost them all, either before or at birth. As she lay dying, she urged Aletta to help Pieter-Lucas keep her vow by giving himself to the priesthood, lest something worse befall him. Aletta could never forget the woman's final words to her. "God will always win!"

The Children of God had taught her that vows were popish things, neither born nor honored in heaven. She and Pieter-Lucas had disregarded the woman's warnings and married. Aletta had born three children. Her firstborn, Lucas, had been robustious enough until they came to Leyden and he met with some affliction that left him weak and sickly.

Her second, a daughter, died while being birthed. The third she held even now against her bosom. She was living, breathing . . . crippled.

"You are not cursed, my child!" Aletta cried into the bundle in her arms.

———

All day long Hiltje found reasons not to go to Magdalena's. Not that she didn't want to hear the Bible account of the birth of Jesus. Never had she wanted anything more. In fact, she sensed in a surprising new way that He was a real person walking beside her. Way down deep inside she felt a growing desire to learn all the Book had to say about Him.

The truth was she feared talking to Magdalena, lest she would learn that these people she had come to trust might indeed be Anabaptists.

But her girls prodded her continually and reminded her of her promise until, in late afternoon, she told Joris and Christoffel they were going to Magdalena's for a short visit and would be home soon. On the way down the street, around the corner and over two more streets, she reminded the girls of their promise not to ask the wrong question.

They found Magdalena cheerful as ever and soon were seated by the low-burning fire and sipping a weak vegetable broth.

"My girls and I have a question," Hiltje began, her palms sweaty and her voice a bit unsteady.

Startled, Magdalena looked from face to face and laughed lightly. "You think I have answers?"

"We are sure of it. We want to know what the Bible says about the Christmas story."

"*Ah*, so!" the plumpish woman said with a sigh of relief. "Indeed I do know the answer to that one. You probably wonder why we Children of God do not celebrate His birthday nor call this day Christmas."

Hiltje felt the woman's eyes staring at her as if expecting a response. She saw her girls sitting silently with heads bowed over the hands folded in their laps. Ever so slightly she nodded her head.

"Christmas is a popish name—the mass of Christ," Magdalena explained. "Because the popish church has turned the celebration into an almost pagan rite, we observe not the day as such."

"Is it a sin for you, then, to read the story to a neighbor on Christmas day?" Hiltje couldn't believe the eagerness beating in her breast.

Magdalena smiled. "'Tis never a sin to read from the Book. Shall I call my husband to do it for you?"

Clare and Tryntje were nodding and wriggling with an enthusiasm Hiltje knew she was feeling, though she dared not to show it the same as they did. With a studied effort at control, she said, "If you please."

Magdalena beckoned to her husband, and he was soon seated at the long table by the hearth, with a candle shining on the big old Book.

" 'The birth of Jesus was now in this manner: for when Mary, His mother, was betrothed with Joseph, before that they had come together, she was found to be with child by the Holy Ghost. . . . ' "

The warm deep voice and the incredible words set a fire to glowing and growing in Hiltje's heart, more intense and more consoling than she had guessed could ever be. She and her girls sat in rapt silence, listening to the old story in new words. In what seemed no time at all, she heard him read, " 'But Mary treasured up all these words together, meditating over them in her heart. And the shepherds returned to their fields, glorifying and praising God for all things they had seen, just as the angels had spoken to them.' "

He paused and opened his mouth to speak. But he was interrupted by a flurry at the door. It flew open and in burst Mieke, arms flailing, sharp voice calling out in distress, "Help, help! Vrouw 'Letta's *jongen's* done swooned near to dead away an' his body's a-burnin' with a dreadful *heatte*. Come, Tryntje an' Clare, with me along to the Beguinage. We have to fetch the hermit sister an' her herbs."

"Great and merciful God!" Magdalena cried out.

Without another word the women and girls scattered, leaving Jakob with his Book.

Hiltje and Magdalena found the young moeder with her son just as Mieke had said. Both Aletta and her moeder, Gretta, bent over the boy, washing his body with cool moist cloths, splashing drops of water on his crimson face.

Hiltje went below for water to replenish the dwindling supply. All the way down the stairs and back up she mumbled again and again, "Christmas is for birthing, not for dying. Great God, have mercy! Have mercy!"

Magdalena met her at the top of the stairs and exchanged the pitcher of water for a tiny crock of aromatic liquid. "Can you heat this over the fire so she can give it to him when he wakens?"

Hiltje returned to the fire, poured the healing brew into a cooking pot, and heated it. Christoffel was sitting at the table, tapping a finger restlessly on its rough surface.

"I thought the *jongen* was well," he said.

"Though his cough and rattling in the chest were gone, since the day he first took ill, he's been listless, pale, and sickly looking. Suddenly the *heatte* returned. If only his vader would come home." A pain shot through her, remembering how it had felt when her Joris was off to Ghendt. She had no idea why or for how long—but at least an idea where. And there were no soldiers lined up between her and her wandering husband.

"Here, son," she said to Christoffel, handing him a water bucket. "Go for some more water. We're going to need it—all we can get."

By now the liquid was warmed, and Hiltje started up the stairs just as Mieke returned with the girls and a bulging bag. They passed her on the stairs, Mieke mumbling, "Th' sister says there's a curse on this place—she's not about to come near it."

A curse? Hiltje bristled! "Sounds more to me like a sister that won't interrupt her celebration, that's all," she mumbled to herself.

Aletta was waiting. "His eyes are fluttering. Awake enough to take tiny sips." She took the crock, then went to the *jongen*. She lifted his head on her arm and cautiously poured the healing liquid through parched lips, whispering, "Sorry it's so bitter, son." For a brief time, he strained to consume it, until he'd nearly drained the crock dry, then laid his head back on his sleeping mat. For one brief moment, Hiltje watched him look up at his moeder with tired sad eyes. In another instant the eyes were closed, and he'd drifted off to sleep.

Aletta did not leave his side but conferred with Mieke about the contents of the bag of herbs sent by the Beguines, then gave instructions to each woman around the circle.

"Mix this powder with a cup of wine and heat it on the fire."

"Rub his feet with this salve."

"Find a leather thong to hang this little root around his neck."

Before Hiltje could receive her instructions, she heard an infant's cry. Rushing to the cradle, she picked up the baby. She held her to her breast and rocked her gently till she ceased her crying.

Then looking back at the scene of great sorrow at the moment, she saw a circle of women and girls on their knees. They were pressing their faces to the floor, and Magdalena's loud clear voice was ringing out, "Great and Merciful Vader in the Heaven, this *jongen* is Thy gift to Aletta and her dear peace-loving husband. Little Lucas, here, is Thy child, as well, beloved by Thee, created by Thee, protected by Thee. We beg of Thee to make these herbal ministrations effective to the restoration of this *jongen* to robustious health, and in the waiting time speak peace to his moeder's brave heart. In the name of Thy precious Son, Jesus the Christ, Amen and Amen."

Hiltje wiped a tear from her eye and rocked the sleeping baby, praying in her own way, " 'Tis Christmas, ah, Lord God—a day for birthing, not for dying."

The tear was replaced by another and another. Underneath the pain she knew the Jesus who had come home from the church with her was still here.

Ever so softly she kissed the baby in her arms and whispered over her, "Your Vader in the Heaven will not go away, child. Never, *nay*, never!"

CHAPTER NINETEEN

Leyden

26th night of Winter Month (December), 1573

*A*ll through the night, Aletta wrestled for the life of her son. She had neither eaten nor slept since the *heatte* had grabbed him. Hovering over the sickbed of her firstborn in flickering lamplight, she bathed his feverish brow and administered every herb she knew to apply to the heavy humors in his little chest. She spoke sweet soft words in his ears, even when his eyes were fast shut. She smiled through her tears whenever his eyes fluttered open and his hot fingers squeezed her hand ever so slightly.

Almost from the moment she discovered his *heatte*, she struggled against the persistent voice of her mother-in-law ringing through an unwelcome memory, *"God will always win! God will always win!"* On and on it went, the relentless accusations of an inescapable curse.

Halfway between sundown and sunrise, Aletta sat suckling Kaatje. Even here she was tormented. *Kaatje, indeed!* Her imagination conjured up pictures of Moeder Kaatje scolding her. *"You disregarded my warnings, then thought you could sidestep the consequences by giving this child my name. Is it your intention to give her up one day to fulfill my vows as a Beguine sister?"*

"Great God," Aletta cried out as Kaatje ceased to suckle and fell into a calm and quiet slumber. "I once promised to keep the vow myself, so Pieter-Lucas could be free to marry. Instead, I am indeed married to the man, and I love him with all my heart. I've borne his children, and he tells me that the memory of my arms and my heart sustain him in the duty he is forced to do. What, then, can I do?"

"God will always win!" The sole answer droned on, an increasingly sharp finger pointed at her breast, where the sleeping child no longer caused its milk to flow.

"God, I cannot go to the Beguinage with its lifeless Christ and accusing sisters. Whatever would happen to Pieter-Lucas? Do you not care that I would break his heart? And my children?"

A host of tragic thoughts burst upon her, one after the other. She saw Pieter-Lucas lying facedown and unbreathing in the snow with blood pouring from his head. She saw little Lucas' still cold body being buried in the ground. She imagined she saw Kaatje struggling to walk, never succeeding—and weeping, weeping, weeping, while a flock of Beguines gathered round and screamed at her to walk!

She clasped the baby in tight arms and wept, rocking back and forth on the edge of the bed, chasing the pictures from her brain and crying softly, "Great God, be merciful, be merciful! Ask me not to go from this room—or to desert my husband."

Lost in her anguish, she was only faintly aware that Mieke had come and sat beside her perfectly still, as if awaiting orders. Aletta felt herself drowsing into a half sleep when Lucas broke into a fit of coughing.

In an instant she rushed to the boy's side, handing the baby to Mieke to put in her cradle. The cough went on, growing steadily more deep and heavy, and in no time the phlegm he spit up turned to a dark color.

"Blood!" Mieke gasped.

"Wrap Kaatje," Aletta ordered. Already she was wrapping Lucas in his feather bag, then wrapping her cape around her own shoulders.

"Where we goin' in th' middle o' this freezin' cold night?" Mieke asked.

"The Beguinage, where the sisters can give us help."

"What kin they do what ye kin't?"

"Mieke," Aletta said sharply, "this is no time to dispute with me. Just wrap that baby and come."

At the head of the stairs, she paused long enough to look back on their temporary home. "God, You have won! If You will save my son's life—and if You insist—I shall not return to this place," she mumbled into the coughing bundle in her arms. "Please take care of Pieter-Lucas for me."

Blinded by hot smarting tears, she made her way uncertainly down the stairs and out into the freezing night.

Lammen
30th day of Winter Month (December), 1573

The dungeon in the fort at Lammen was warmed only by the crush of more bodies than the cell could comfortably hold. A single pitch torch burned low on a rack on the wall.

Pieter-Lucas sat in his allotted space and hugged his knees and leaned against the cluster of bony backs that warmed and held each other up with what little strength remained after the long weeks of the prisoners' ordeal. He closed his eyes and longed for sleep.

Deep down inside he sensed a surging flood of unexpected gratitude. In a place like this? One after another, reasons suggested themselves. For at least three days now, he had been freed from the solitary cell where he could neither lie down nor curl into a ball. In that cursed place, his whole body had ached from the daily beatings. Often he went without bread or water or the sound of another human voice. Some days he'd even welcomed the company of his interrogators as a break in the maddening solitude.

Once more restored to this larger cell where captured soldiers crowded up against one another's squatting spots, he never lacked for company, though he often wished for a different sort. Loud explosions of bravado and anger, wails of self-pity, endless hours of senseless chatter, occasional philosophical arguments—all robbed him of any silence, especially in the deep of night. Even then there were moans and snores.

He could also be grateful that since that first night of his arrest, he was no longer chained to the wall. Further, the Spaniards had not tortured him on the dreaded rack—and he had not broken down and given them what they wanted.

Most important of all, he was still alive—more than could be said for some of the men who had been imprisoned in this place. Besides, his captors had left him yet with one golden curl. He reached up and fingered it, imagining that once again his head was covered with the curls, that Aletta was combing them with her fingers. . . .

From somewhere in that haze-filled land between self-induced dreams and real ones, Pieter-Lucas was jarred back to reality with the sound of an enormous racket clanking down the stairs and ending with a loud grunt and a solid thud against the cell door. The cellmate they called Gerard nudged Pieter-Lucas from his position behind his left shoulder and mumbled, "Did you hear that?"

Pieter-Lucas shook himself and stared at the door. "What was it?"

"We'll soon know," Gerard answered.

By now a key was turning in the lock and the door creaked open. The ominous forms of a handful of men burst into the cell, carrying torches and shouting, "On your feet and follow us—NOW! We've taken the fortress from the Spaniards. Hurry! Flee for your lives! Hold your peace! Not a word!"

"Freebooters!" Pieter-Lucas muttered as he struggled to his feet. What mischief would this end in? These men never played by Willem's rules—

or the burgemeesters'. They swaggered about Leyden boasting of their great value, then planned wild forays that could not be executed or else ended in dismal failure and danger to the well-thought-out strategies of reasonable men.

The whole cell turned into a gigantic commotion. The dumbfounded men grunted and shoved and tripped over one another, squeezing through the door and up the stairs. Along with many others, Pieter-Lucas stumbled, aching and unsteady on his feet after so many days of cramped confinement and continued beatings. Further, the shoes he wore had been salvaged from a dead cellmate, and they were far too large for his feet.

At the top of the stairs, each man was handed a weapon of some sort, ordered once more to keep silent, and herded out into the frosty night air. Pieter-Lucas stared at the long spear in his hand and heard his heart crying out, *Great God, You know how many times I've vowed never to bear arms in battle. Ask me not to use this spear in this foolhardy mission that was sanctioned neither by Willem nor by the burgemeesters. Everything about it tells me it is doomed to failure. But for the love of Aletta and for my part in Willem's cause—and the lives of my cellmates—bring it to success.*

Pieter-Lucas struggled to walk in his borrowed shoes through the pitch black night, across the icy roadway. He kept to the center of the throng, where shoulders jostled and feet slipped on the ice, and weakened soldiers held one another up. Fortunately the way was short to the city, and the freebooters did indeed keep the way mostly clear.

Not until they'd reached nearly to the Koe Poort did they begin to hear Spaniards shouting at them, shots ringing in the night, arrows whizzing toward them, mostly falling short of their targets. The patriot soldiers who guarded the gate unlocked it and ushered them quickly through to safety. When the last man was through, they followed and bolted the gate.

"Freebooters dressed in Spanish uniforms, God's angel guards?" Pieter-Lucas mumbled.

Outside the wall, Spaniards screamed at one another, while inside, the liberated captives raised their fists in triumph, then made their way to beds and waiting families.

Pieter-Lucas approached a freebooter and handed him his spear.

"Keep it for your next duty," the burly man said.

"I am no soldier," Pieter-Lucas protested. Then without listening for an answer, he crept through the streets toward home.

When at last he reached the old warehouse, he stood before it for a long moment and pondered. Never had even the *kasteel* at Dillenburg looked so inviting. In moments he'd be creeping into bed with his precious Aletta.

"Pieter-Lucas, God brought you home!" He could already hear her voice, like music from heaven.

"And gave me one more chance to tell you how terribly much I love you," he'd answer as he entangled his fingers in her silky hair and kissed her and dared to hope she would not notice how bearded he had grown, nor that his curls were missing, his face smudged, his doublet ripped. Come morning, when the whole world could see, she would have questions and he must give answers.

It was not morning yet. One thing he could do this night before he went to her. Hurriedly he knelt beside the doorstoop. With both hands he scooped up the snow and smeared it over his face. He yanked the old tam from his head, then gathered up more snow and rubbed it into his fresh growth of hair. He ran stiff fingers through the stubbly promise of new curls and replaced his cap, mumbling, "That's enough for tonight!"

He hurried up the stairs and went for the bed as fast as his stiff and weary legs would allow. But in the faint light of a low-burning lamp, he could see that Aletta was not here. Shock turned to disbelief.

"She must be here!" He rummaged through the entire bed with trembling hands. He pulled back the unrumpled covers and found everything lying in precise order—flat, smooth, cold.

Lucas' bed and the cradle also stood empty! Like his head and his heart. He went to the table where he found, beside the lamp, a piece of rough paper with four lines of words inscribed:

Moeder Kaatje said, "God will always win."
God has won.
I shall love you always.
Aletta

He grabbed the note in his hands, then sank into a chair. He stared at it until his eyes grew too bleary to read it again. What did it mean? Where had she gone? Why?

He pounded on the table with a tight-knuckled fist and cried out, "What have you done to her, God, while I was out doing your bidding? Running messages across a snowy countryside infested with *speken* was never my idea, as you right well know. Where is she, God? *Ach! Ach! Ach!* I must have her back. . . ."

For a long moment he stared into the emptiness of what had become a world laid waste. Too numb for pain, too shocked for thought, all his mind would give him was a clear warm image of her face. It tantalized him until he thought he would go mad. With a sudden burst of energy, he stood to his feet, jabbing at the air behind him with fierce elbows and knocking the chair clattering to the floor.

"Aletta, my Aletta," he wailed, as if pleading with her to come to him out of the shadows. "I cannot live without you."

Finally he threw himself on the bed, buried his face in the feather bag, clenched his teeth and fists, and howled, "Where did you take her, God? Where? Where?"

"Try the Beguinage" came a clear masculine voice from above him. God was talking to him? He froze to his spot and waited for another word. Instead, he felt the bed move and turned to see Vader Dirck sitting beside him. He shoved himself up onto his elbows.

"When did she leave?" he asked.

"Four nights ago."

"Why?"

"Lucas has been very ill again."

"*Nay*, not my Lucas too!"

Dirck sighed. "That night he coughed worse than ever. We heard the coughing, but by the time my vrouw had come out to help, they were all gone—Aletta, Mieke, and both children."

"And you didn't go to bring them back?" A tightness was growing in his chest.

"I tried," Dirck insisted, "but the sisters refused to let me in. I sent Joris' daughters, but they refused them too. At sunset today, Mieke came back."

"What did she say? How is Lucas?" Pieter-Lucas felt trapped again, the way he'd felt in the solitary cell in the dungeon.

"Mieke said he's better today. The *heatte* is nearly gone and he's no longer coughing so violently. She left a note for you on the table but told us that Aletta won't talk to anybody—not even to her. When she's not hovering over Lucas, she's off by herself praying in the chapel."

Pieter-Lucas sat up. "I must go to her."

"Be not surprised if they don't let you in."

Pieter-Lucas felt a rising indignation. "She's my vrouw, and they're my children—they cannot deny me entrance."

"Wait at least till daylight," Dirck urged.

"And lie here in this cold abandoned bed with smashed dreams and ghosts that offer the thing I seek, then sprint devilishly out of reach?"

Dirck shrugged and said, "I pray you Godspeed."

Pieter-Lucas headed for the streets.

———

The Beguinage lay utterly still and shrouded in darkness as Aletta made her way around the courtyard toward the chapel. Both children were sleeping again, and Mieke kept watch so she could slip away to pray. She had so much to learn about begging forgiveness, deepening penitence, and seeking a way to atone for the breaking of Moeder Kaatje's vow. The sight of the lifeless Christ at the altar brought despair to her heart, but in time she trusted the load would lighten. Her Anabaptist years, filled with images of the resurrected Christ, had made her nearly forget the need for sacrifice, the value of self-denial and examination, and that dreaded word, penance.

She was not more than halfway to the chapel when the bell at the gate began to ring. Something in the urgent pace and volume told her that the person who rang it, at this unlikely hour, was desperate to be admitted.

"Pieter-Lucas!" Her heart beat so hard it nearly leapt into her throat, and she rushed on to the chapel. She dared not to look into his face to see the hurt mixed with love in his eyes, to hear the passion in his voice, to let him touch her. She could not be his vrouw anymore. This exercise in Beguine sisterhood was difficult enough without the tug and pull of the man she loved more dearly than her own life. At least Lucas was healing at last. This must be the right thing to do, no matter how it pained!

"*Ach* me! I must never see him again," she whispered to herself. She hurried into the suffocating sanctuary and shut the door, trying to block out the continuing sound of the bell.

She fled all the way to the altar at the front of the room, fell to her knees on the kneeling rail, and held both hands tightly over her ears.

"Great and merciful God," she prayed. No sooner had she begun than the tears began to flow. "Teach me all Thy ways of penitence and self-resignation that the lives of my children and my husband may indeed be spared, that they may one day know the smile of Thy face warming their bodies, their steps, and their hearts." She forced out the words—maybe not the proper words to express the thoughts she must learn as a Beguine. For now, they were all the words she knew.

"Give to my husband a holy happiness and a release from pain and anguish." She burst into such a torrent of tearful anguish of her own that she could go no further. For a long while she leaned against the mourner's rail and wept. Not the way it was supposed to be, but she could do no other. If only she had never married Pieter-Lucas in the first place, it would have been so much easier. For marriage to a good and honorable man with a passionate and single-minded love cannot be so quickly tossed into the sea of life's turmoils and religion's demands.

"Dear God, give me time to learn, and chastise me not overmuch for my tears and the passion of my married heart. In time I shall learn to give all the passion to Thee, that I might make atonement for the ones I love, but for now. . ." She gave herself to the sobbing and tried not to think, falling finally into a sound sleep.

31st day of Winter Month (December), 1573

Pieter-Lucas rang the bell at the Beguinage with the urgency of a dying man. He couldn't let anyone keep his vrouw imprisoned outside of his aching arms. He rang, then paced back and forth across the uneven cobbled street. He rang again, then paced and rang and paced and rang until at last the weathered wooden gate creaked partly open and the sleepy countenance of a Beguine sister frowned out at him.

"Have you no regard for the peace and quiet of this holy place? May God bring you to holy shame for such rude disturbance."

"I need to see my vrouw," he demanded, shoving against the door. She held him back.

"Vrouw? We are not married women in this sisterhood," she said with ice in her voice.

"My vrouw is here. She came while I was away, bringing our son who has been deathly ill. I must see them both."

"Your vrouw is performing penance and will not speak with anyone."

"Penance? Not my vrouw! She has nothing to pay penance for. You have deceived her into believing so. And my son, what penance does he perform that he is not allowed to see his own vader?" He knew his voice was rising in volume; he could feel it in the tightness of his knuckles, the pressure on his temples.

"You will go on your way and not come back until your vrouw calls for you," the Beguine said firmly and slammed the door in his face. He reached up to tug on the bell cord once more, only to discover it had been pulled inside, beyond his reach.

He swung his foot back and landed a solid kick on the door. He'd forgotten about the oversized shoes he wore, and as he kicked, they cut into the shin still sensitive from the soldier's kicks in the prison. Prison? It seemed so far away, and yet his body screamed out in every joint to tell him that he had only left it a few hours ago. Weary, aching, and feeling a bit of dizziness in the head, he began to wander aimlessly through the streets. The borrowed shoes slipped on icy cobblestones and turned his ankles.

Daybreak found him sleepily staggering past a row of red brick stepped-gable houses with the clumsiness of a drunken freebooter. He yearned for a bed, but the one bed in this city that was his to claim was too full of ghosts to let him rest. In fact, he doubted that he could ever rest again, anywhere, without Aletta. The toe of his oversized shoe tripped on a protruding cobblestone and sent him sprawling to the ground. He lay there, facedown in the ice, for a long moment before he gathered strength to push himself to a sitting position. He slumped his back and head against the door of the building behind him, then felt his eyelids close and was soon drifting off into a light and unsettled sleep.

The next thing he knew, he awoke with the strong feeling that someone was looking at him. Kneeling in front of him, tapping him on the shoulder, was Mieke. He snapped to life.

"Is my vrouw indeed in the Beguinage?" he asked.

"That she is."

"And is it true that she does penance and will not talk with anyone?" He searched her eyes for the least flicker of shiftiness.

Mieke shook her head and sighed. "I fear 'tis true, an' I kin't git her to tell me what th' difficulty is. She's not a-talkin' to th' sisters, not even to me. She watches Lucas, feeds Kaatje, an' prays. One o' the sisters found her a-sleepin' in th' chapel this mornin' already, her beautiful head a-lyin' on th' mourner's rail an' her hair soaked with tears."

"She hasn't said anything at all about why she ran away or when she'll be back?"

"Lucas was awful sick. The *heatte* done sapped all th' life out o' him, an' she said we had to git help fer him. I told her I thought she could do anythin' fer him at home what th' sisters could do. She snapped at me then, an' b'fore I knowed what was a-happenin', we was off and gone."

"She said nothing more?"

Mieke furrowed her brow and thought. "*Ja* . . . one thing she keeps a-sayin' over an' over like as if she's off in a trance."

"What is it?" Pieter-Lucas grabbed her by the arm.

" 'God will win!' " A perplexed look spread over the woman's face. "I'se never heared her talk like that b'fore. Kind o' mournful 'tis. . . . I jus' figured it was b'cause she hadn't gone to bed fer a good sleep ever since Lucas' *heatte* comed back—an' that horrible awful cough! Ah me! When folks doesn't sleep, all sorts o' fanciful things comes out o' their mouths, ye know."

"How long ago was that?"

Mieke shrugged. "Th' night after Christmas, 'twas. She'd been jus' a-hoverin' over that *jongen* day an' night an' wept an' rubbed him an' gave us all orders about fixin' herbs. Later she was a-sittin' on th' bed a-rockin' Kaatje an' a-moanin' an' a-mumblin' to herself, mostly words too soft to figure out, except 'God will always win!' She looked so sad. I never seed her so sad lookin' b'fore."

God will win! Pieter-Lucas turned the phrase over and over in his mind. That was what his moeder said to her when she told her about her vow to be a Beguine and how she'd broken it and wanted him to keep it for her by being a priest.

A great horrible shudder flashed through his whole body from head to toe. Surely she couldn't be thinking she had to fulfill his moeder's Beguine vow in order to save Lucas' life!

"Mieke!" He grabbed both of her arms now and pulled her face up to where she could not but look him straight in the eye. She struggled, but he held her tight. "Mieke, you have to get her out of that place and bring her to me."

"How?"

"Nobody needs to tell you how. That's the sort of thing you do best. Listen, if you don't get her out of the Beguinage now, she'll never come out again. Do you hear me? Never again, and neither will she—nor any of the sisters—let my children out."

Tugging hard against his grasp, the little woman trembled as much as Pieter-Lucas' stomach and hands were trembling right now. "I do whatever Mieke can do. Jus' r'member, not even Mieke kin make yer vrouw go where she sets her mind not to go."

"Nor can anybody stop Mieke from doing anything she puts her mind to do," Pieter-Lucas said. Then gripping her more firmly yet, he said, "You bring her to me—or show me a way into the church where I can find her when she prays. If I do not see her and the children, I shall not live to see the siege lifted from this place. For without Aletta, I've no reason to live. Now be on your way!"

He let her go and felt the last of his strength drain from him. Exhausted, he rested back against the door again. Newborn hope trembled at the pit of his stomach and sent little flutterings all through his belly. Surely once he could get Aletta to look him in the eye and let him hold her in his arms, she would follow him home. But would she meet him? Or would he have to invade the Beguinage and take her by force?

He stared straight ahead, not seeing, for a long while. Then, as if a bolt of lightning had illuminated the scene before him, on the doorway directly across the street from where he sat, he saw a sign carved into the lintel: St. Jan's Hospitaal.

"The poorhouse where Christoffel told me Lucas van Leyden's painting is," he mumbled. "How long I've waited to find it, to look on it, to study it." He stared hard at the building. " 'The Last Judgment,' " he mused. "Nay, not now! I've all I can do to handle God's present judgment without thinking about the future." The words sent wild dreams into his head. He shook them away. He unfolded his aching body and stood to his feet, finishing, "Besides, Christoffel said they would not show it to me."

In a deep fog he stumbled up one street and down another, shivering all over. "Great God," he pleaded, "must you always win? And when you do, can you ask no other victor's prize than my vrouw and my children? Nay, God, nay! I will not give them up to any Beguinage!"

How long he wandered, he had no idea. The heavens were draped with a dreary gray gauze of fog clouds, and he couldn't even tell where the sun was. Not until he found himself at the bottom of the citadel hill did he even notice where he was.

"Ah, so," he sighed and took the measure of the stairs with a weary eye. "At least a spot to rest," he mused, putting one tired foot above the other, climbing as slowly as an old man. Once in the flat *plein*, with its oak tree beside a well, he paused, then climbed some more to the upper level where he could circle round and see all that lay below.

He looked out at the Zyl Poort and the Zyl River and the place where *The Clever Fox Inn* had so long stood. He gazed out at Lammen, where he saw a Spanish flag hanging limp in the damp unbreathing air.

"They've recaptured it," he murmured. "Thank God I was set free when I was. Or maybe 'twould have been better had I perished there. Without Aletta waiting for me, caring . . ."

He moved quickly on around. The Beguinage lay just on the other side of the Pieterskerk. All he could see was the chapel steeple. "Dear God, does she kneel there at this moment and pray? What does she pray? If only she could see me and know how my heart is wounded beyond repair!"

A perpetual wind stirred about his ears and caught at the corners of his cape, tossing them back and forth. He stared across the vast expanse of buildings, walls, fortresses, and soggy pasturelands laced with waterways and dikes holding the waters back. So this was Leyden!

All his life he'd lived to come here. Opa had held it up to him as the great golden city of promise and the fulfillment of all his fondest dreams. Here he'd find a meester to teach him all the secrets that would make him as great a painter as Lucas van Leyden. Here he'd find safety and quiet and abundance and peace for Aletta and the large flock of strong and healthy children she would bear him.

If only it could have been so. Instead, Leyden had taken everything from him—the strength of his youth, all hope of finding a meester, the health of his children, safety from the ravages of war and famine, the love of his vrouw. . . . One thing remained. What the Spanish soldiers and wild mercenary soldiers in the dungeon had not destroyed of his painting sup- plies he had wrapped in their torn bag. His fingers, now chilled and stiff, moved uncertainly toward the bag hidden beneath his doublet, next to the miniature paintings and empty canvases he'd also recovered. He pat- ted them protectively.

But of what value were these tools now that all else was gone? Long ago his opa had reminded him over and over, *"This passion to paint is a monster in your blood. Without the hand of God and a good vrouw to check and soothe and prod and guide, it will consume your heart and mind and leave you with nothing but ashes on your palette."*

Once, these words had prodded him to paint a picture for his wed- ding. Today they mocked him and turned his innards cold and lifeless. In between he'd known years of running messages, fighting just to be allowed to spend one hour with his vrouw beside him, worrying con- stantly about her safety, watching her bear a dead child and care for two living, sickly children, watching painters slip elusively from his own grasp. The anguish of it all had cooled his passion for the paint that, until this moment, he'd always believed ran in his blood.

With difficulty and determination, he pulled the bag from his doublet and laid it out before him on the stone wall of the citadel. He untied the cord that held it shut, then lifted out the one remaining pot of paint, removed the stopper, and shook its contents into the winds. Flecks of bright red color flew away from him, like blood. Next he threw out his charcoals. Then he took the tiny piece of wood he used for a palette and flung it, skipping across the currents, like he'd often sent a flat pebble skipping across the river.

He felt in the bag. Only one piece left—Opa's brush. Could he throw it to the winds as well? He stood a long while feeling the pain pounding in his chest. Then he lifted out the old worn brush. He turned it over in his hand, now sweating, even in the cold.

One other time he'd sweat in agony over this brush. That day his vrouw had made him promise never to give up the painting gift for any- thing. But she stood beside him then. For a long while he listened to his heart as it argued with his heart.

"Do it, *jongen*," he prodded himself and raised his hand, prepared to aim it straight to the Beguinage.

Nay, he couldn't! Even if he never painted another stroke, it was all he had left of Opa and the dream that old man had inspired. He might yet pass it on to his Lucas. He shoved it into the bag.

Reaching into his doublet, he felt the tiny canvases next to his heart. Slowly he lifted them out. The empty canvases he tossed into the air and watched them billow on the wind, a piece of his heart blowing away with them.

Finally, he smoothed the wrinkles from Lucas' drawing of the lamb and the portrait of Aletta, defiled by the crude kisses of thirty men in a dirty prison cell.

"*Nay*, not these too! They must always lie next to my heart."

A sense of horror gripped him as the wind tugged at the corners, begging to snatch his treasures away. He gathered them to his chest, then lowered his head and wept. The stiffening wind blew away his tears. "Take my tears, mixed with the paints and charcoal ashes and empty canvases, to the Beguinage," he cried out.

Never had he felt so hollowed-out, scraped clean of every morsel of life, drained of every oozing drop of blood.

CHAPTER TWENTY

Leyden

31st day of Winter Month (December), 1573

Christoffel curled his legs around each other and tucked them under his chair, which he had scooted as close as possible to the scant fire. Not enough peat to go around these days. Moeder said it was because of the siege. He lifted his dented cup up for her to fill with the thin vegetable broth that he knew would hardly stick to his ribs till he could have more. Also a part of the siege. At least they still had bread to go with it.

He heard a noise and looked up to see his vader crawl out of his bed cupboard and land on the floor with a thump. He was toting his roll of pictures under his arm and walking to the table, nightcap and strings of hair obscuring half his face. "Today is the day!" he announced.

"The day for what?" Moeder asked, cocking her head to one side and frowning.

He grinned like a silly child, raised the roll above his head, and shouted, "I take my picture to the citadel and paint in the sunshine."

Christoffel and his sisters giggled, suppressing outright guffaws. "It's the dead of winter, and you expect to find sunshine?" Christoffel taunted.

"Who says it's winter?" Vader scowled at him.

"Can't you feel it in your bones, standing there in your nightshirt?"

Christoffel didn't dare to look at his moeder. She'd be glaring at him. She was always making him be nice to Vader. *"He is your vader, and it's not his fault his mind doesn't work like yours does,"* she'd always remind him. He dipped his bread in the broth, then tore off a hunk with his teeth and chewed and sucked on it and didn't look at anyone else.

Vader was making funny mumbling sounds, then saying with steadily increasing loudness, "Well, so maybe it is winter, but I feel like painting— and out in the citadel—and you will go with me. Do you hear me, *jongen?*"

Christoffel nearly choked on the bite he was trying to swallow. He looked up at his moeder, hoping she'd intervene for him. Instead, she ladled more broth into the cups and said to her husband, "Take your heaviest woolen cape and gloves for your fingers."

"Can't paint with gloves on," Vader complained. He headed back to the bed and pulled on his clothes, muttering, "My fingers are restless to go to work." Then with his clothes all on askew, he came back to the table and said aloud, again in the manner of an announcement, "Today I put a face on Vader Abraham! And you, *jongen*," he said, smiling at Christoffel, "will be sure to bring the charcoals and paints and brushes. Now, hurry along with me before the sun goes away."

He pulled his hat on, making sure the earflaps covered his ears snugly.

"Don't forget the easel," he called out, his voice now bright and cheerful, as if he hadn't a thing in the world to cause him to fret and the sun was shining in the middle of the brightest summer day. At the door he slipped into his street shoes and motioned to Christoffel impatiently.

Christoffel gulped down the last of his broth and stuffed the rest of his bread into the bag that hung from his waist. He laid a hand on Moeder's arm and pleaded, "Do I have to go with him today?"

"Can't let him go alone" came the brusque reply.

"Not on a day like this. Moeder, you have to stop him."

Moeder rested one hand on her hip and looked directly at Christoffel with sad eyes. "We have to go along with him, son. It's all the joy he's got left. When he gets out there and finds out how cold it is, he'll come back in. Now, get along."

Disgruntled, Christoffel dressed in his warmest clothes, then gathered up a bag with a handful of charcoals and paints, and a board that he used for an easel. At the door he pulled on his own cape, then draped another cape over Vader's head, grousing all the while, "This is a foolish idea. It's cold out there—probably wet and foggy. Remember the last time you decided we should go to the citadel?"

Vader fidgeted with his cape, arranging who-knew-what beneath it. "Can't be that cold," he argued. "Besides, we haven't done this before. I've only talked about it, dreamed about it. Now, come on, let's get going before the whole city comes out to greet us."

It would do no good to remind him of the day not long ago when they had gone out just like this. *"I feel like painting today,"* he'd said that time too. Christoffel had taken him for the first time inside the citadel, where he grew frightened of whatever it was that always frightened him these days. Something about the *speken* putting him in a dungeon reserved for somebody, he never would say who. He had hunched down under the stairs and begged Christoffel to hide him behind his cape. Christoffel had

had a dreadful time getting him out of the tight little alcove and back home again. All the way, he vowed he'd never do it again, but today his moeder left him no choice.

Outside, the world lay gray and silent. They found neither fog to impede vision nor ice to impede movement. Just that ever present damp cold that penetrated every garment, chilling all the way to the bone and carrying all breath away in white steamy vapors. Christoffel eyed the sky, spread with a layer of thin fog clouds, the kind that could give way to a piercing ray of sunshine before long. He followed alongside his vader. Vader ambled up the stairs without even stopping to rest till they'd reached the top. Then he sat on the edge of the well and spread his arms wide just as a ray of sunshine did burst through the cloud cover.

"Didn't I tell you it was the perfect day?" he said.

Christoffel cringed. Little matter that the well was covered. If there was a rotten board, he was sure Vader would fall on it, and he had no desire to fish him out of that deep dark wet hole.

"Best sit over here on my painting rock," he offered, leading the way to his favorite spot beside the stairs that led to the walkway.

"Just let me stay in the sun."

"It's gone again, Vader," Christoffel noted as he helped the man prop up the makeshift easel on his lap and roll out his canvas.

"It'll be back. Now! Aha! Give me a charcoal. I have the perfect image at last."

"Perfect for what?" He handed him the charcoal, then hugged himself for warmth and pranced and wiggled his toes, trying to chase the cold dampness away.

"For Vader Abraham's face."

"Where do you see it?" Christoffel looked all around, seeing no one.

"Here," Vader said, tapping his head and then bending over the canvas and drawing as he babbled on. "It's my brother, Frans—best Jewish face I ever saw—and as clear as if he stood right where you are. One thing about doing faces, *jongen*, you got to remember this. Never do a face till you can see it either with your eyes or in your mind."

Christoffel stood behind his vader now, looking over the man's shoulder at the work before him. Amazed, he watched the lines flow from the charcoal. A sober face emerged in the space that had gaped so ominously for who knew how many years.

"That's a Jewish face?" Christoffel asked.

"A most wondrous patriarchal Jewish face, and see, the sun shines on it!" Vader chuckled and viewed his work with an air of rare enthusiasm.

"What's a Jew?" Christoffel asked. Years ago, just before she died, he remembered his grandmother telling him, *"We are Jews. Don't you forget it."* When he asked her what it meant, she said simply, *"Ask your vader."* But every time he'd asked, Vader always refused to give him an answer.

This time, though, Vader stopped drawing and looked down, holding his hand with the charcoal poised above the canvas. "Abraham was a Jew," he said finally, then went on drawing. "Moses was a Jew. Jesus was a Jew. My opa was a Jew. My vader was a Jew. My moeder was a Jew. . . ." His voice floated off into that sort of strange nothingness that had come and gone so often, ever since the day he came home with his head bleeding.

"Are you a Jew?" Christoffel asked, paused, then added, "Am I a Jew?"

Vader ignored him and went on drawing. "How long have I been waiting for this face to come clear so I could draw it? The robbers stole my sketch, you know." He spoke again in that dreamy far-off voice belonging to the strange person who lived in Vader's body but was not quite like Vader.

The silence that followed was broken by the sound of feet on the stairs that led to the upper walkway. Christoffel felt a shiver run down his backbone. He looked up and gasped. "Pieter-Lucas! What are you doing here?"

Had he been up there all along? Heard all they'd said? Christoffel moved to shield his vader's picture from view. Pieter-Lucas was not quite a stranger. Still, Vader always acted as if he didn't trust him, not letting him into his studio, and . . .

"Come have a look!" Vader was inviting without glancing up. "Does it look like Vader Abraham?"

"Vader." Christoffel laid a protective arm around his shoulders. What was the strange monster that had changed the man so? One day he was too fearful to poke his nose outside the door. The next day he was showing off the sketch of his secret painting.

"This man is our friend," Vader said. "He saved my life out there in the thicket. Can you forget? Besides, I hear he is a painter too."

Christoffel glowered at Pieter-Lucas, who was already standing behind Vader's other shoulder. His curls were gone! Whatever. . . ?

"You are the painter here, Joris," Pieter-Lucas muttered. Christoffel heard awe in his voice and saw it in his eyes. "And should I know what Vader Abraham looked like?"

"*Ach*, me!" Vader chuckled and put the finishing touches on the long beard with its stray hairs blowing in the wind. "Of course you wouldn't know. You're not a Jew!"

"I do know the story, though."

"That's because you're not the *glipper* kind of Christian. You have a Bible in your house!" Vader was continuing to sketch in little lines, now embellishing the ram in the thicket. "I used to call myself a Christian, you know. But I never was one on the inside like you."

Pieter-Lucas acted as if he hadn't heard Vader's last words. Instead, he was leaning forward, hands on his knees, examining the sketch. "I know one thing you are inside," he said. "You're a *meester*—with a wide stream of paint in your blood."

Vader puffed out his chest, chuckled, and protested mildly, "*Nay*, not a *meester*—just an old dabbler in paints—mostly landscapes and portraits."

"If I ever paint again, you can be my *meester*," Pieter-Lucas said.

If he ever paints again? Christoffel wrinkled his brow into a frown and studied his face. The eyes were sad and puffy, and dried tears ran in streaks across the unshaven cheeks. What had happened to him?

Vader turned and pointed a stick of charcoal directly at their visitor. "You don't need a *meester*," he said, "but someday I can take you to Ghendt to study the Van Eyck brothers' famous painting, 'The Adoration of the Lamb.'"

Pieter-Lucas sighed. "That's what my opa used to tell me—"

"Ah, it's beautiful and more wonderful than you can imagine," Vader interrupted. "Twenty-four panels in all!"

"Twenty-four panels in one painting?" Christoffel suspected Vader was exaggerating.

"I counted them myself. Masterpieces, every one. 'Tis the one in the middle what draws every eye. It's a Lamb on an altar. There's blood bursting from his breast and filling a chalice. He's standing and alive, with a crown of gold sparkling on his head—and a world full of people bringing him their adoration."

"What kind of people?" Christoffel asked.

"Priests, kings, peasants, soldiers . . . even angels."

"And Jews?"

Vader hesitated. "Who knows? In a Christian painting, just like in a Christian world, a Jew must always hide."

"Why, Vader?" This new idea took Christoffel's breath away. He remembered all those times back in Brussels when Vader used to hustle him quickly into a dark alley or back to home. He was hiding—because he was a Jew?

Vader looked at him with a most curious expression. "A Jew hides to keep his head attached to his neck." He hung his own for a brief moment, then put his hand on Christoffel's arm and turned to look again at Pieter-Lucas.

"Painters from all parts of the civilized world who want to be great flock to Ghendt to study from this greatest of all *meesters*—'The Adoration' itself. Then Christians go home and paint a 'Procession to Calvary' and thank God every day for the Lamb of God that takes away their sins."

"And what do you Jews do?" Pieter-Lucas asked.

"We are left with 'Vader Abraham and the Ram.' It tells us that human sacrifices are not God's way. We must bring an animal ram—never a son."

We? Christoffel mused. *Like Oma said, we are Jews, whatever that means.* He felt a pounding in his heart and a sudden desire to curl up in his vader's arms and beg him to teach him what being a Jew was all about! But Vader was still talking. Christoffel listened.

"Our temple's gone, though, and no rabbi can offer a lamb to cover my awful sin of pretending to be a Christian. I had to pretend, you know, just the way my vader taught me. There is no other way in a Christian world."

Pieter-Lucas' voice turned soft now. He squatted down before Joris and looked up at him, then at Christoffel. "What can you do for a ram?"

"Go on waiting and painting the Torah and Abraham and the ram in the thicket," Joris said dreamily. "Someday *Yahweh* will put a ram in my thicket, and until then?" He shrugged. "At least I will not have to sacrifice my son. The Jewish God will never ask that again!"

Pieter-Lucas stood and rubbed his hands together briskly, blowing on them. Christoffel watched puffs of white breath wrap them all around and heard the man ask in the most forlorn voice he'd ever heard, "How about a daughter—or a vrouw?"

Joris looked up at Pieter-Lucas and said simply, "*Nay, Yahweh* will ask it no more than your God. They are the same, you know. Only you say He had a Son and sacrificed Him as your lamb."

Pieter-Lucas grabbed Joris by one shoulder and squeezed it till his knuckles glistened in one more brief ray of pale sunlight.

"I hope you're right," he grunted.

"It's not about killing, you know," Joris said slowly. "It's about saving life."

Nodding his head somberly, Pieter-Lucas turned and walked down the lower stairs to the street below.

"Vader," Christoffel said when Pieter-Lucas had gone.

"What is it, son?"

Christoffel squatted down beside his vader as Pieter-Lucas had done and looked up into his dark troubled eyes. "Can the Christian Jesus ever be the Lamb for Jews?"

Unsmiling, Vader looked him straight in the eye, then down again. "I don't see how. . ." Then looking up again and grabbing the boy by the hand, he added, "I . . . I don't know, son."

"Would you like Him to be?"

"Could be. For now, I grow cold, and I think no more sun comes for today. We go to home!"

31st afternoon of Winter Month (December), 1573

Pieter-Lucas shuffled down the hill and through the streets to the town hall. Somewhere in the back of his mind, he recalled that he did still carry Willem's message. When he walked through the door, the burgemeesters stared at him in amazement.

"So you found your way home!"

"And you look like you've been through a battle!"

Pieter-Lucas pulled his cap down over his hair and rubbed his whiskered chin nervously. "The freebooters freed me from Lammen," he said without enthusiasm.

"You were in that dungeon?"

"For how long?"

Pieter-Lucas strained to remember that other part of his life. "I left you here and went directly to Delft. On my way home the next night, I was delayed by the snow and they captured me."

"You didn't give the *spoken* Willem's message, we hope!"

Pieter-Lucas felt one more dart ripping his already raw soul. Bitter words poured out of his mouth and left him bleeding inside. "Have I ever betrayed Willem? Or the patriots? Or Leyden? I let them take my curls and beat my body into a mass of blacks and blues, but my message? What do you take me to be?" For a long moment, he looked around the room at the arrogant men, silent, ashamed.

"Willem simply says, 'Don't talk amnesty. Hold on.' He and his brothers raise troops, and they will deliver us."

Pieter-Lucas started for the door.

"Wait," called the chief burgemeester.

Pieter-Lucas turned and looked at him, amazed at the momentary feeling of control over them all. "I go not out again on any more message runs for now."

"One imprisonment too much for you?" came a jibe from the far side of the room.

Pieter-Lucas formed his hands into hard fists and felt every part of his body tighten along with them. "My son lies at death's door," he said, "and my vrouw . . ." He swallowed hard and strode out of the room without finishing his sentence.

He stumbled into the dreary morning that could not make up its mind whether to be sunny or gray. He spent the rest of the day wandering in the streets of Leyden, dragging along his oversized shoes, moving always, desperate to keep the cold from reaching to his heart. At one point he remembered that Opa used to tell him Leyden had 145 bridges. He decided to count them, just to free his mind from its uncontrollable anguish.

He had difficulty remembering to count. But as he crossed over the twentieth of his accounting, he heard footsteps scurrying up behind him, followed by the high-pitched voice of Mieke. "I bringed ye a message from yer vrouw."

He wheeled about in the middle of the bridge, and she said, "I kinnot tell ye at all what she's done said in her scribin'. I only knows she will not hear of such a thing as a-talkin' to ye—not yet! But I isn't through with her. So whatever 'tis she's done telled ye', don't pay it no heed. I'se a-goin' yet to change her mind, do ye hears me? There's a new year a-comin' around th' corner, an' I'll bring her home in time for that. Jus' trust me."

She thrust a scrap of folded paper into his hand, adding, "One thing more. Ye needs a fresh doublet—without holes an' blood caked onto it. Can't meet yer vrouw in them rags!"

He only half heard her last advice, so busy was he opening the note, his fingers all abumble. With misting eyes, he began to read.

> My dear Pieter-Lucas,
> Our God has beaten us with many rods. Moeder Kaatje warned me long ago to leave you free to keep her vows to religion. I should have listened, though I cannot imagine the agony of never having been your vrouw. I truly believed all that Hans and the others taught us about vows and penance was true, and I still do. Yet what more could I do than to come here and give myself to performing penance for the sin of disregarding Moeder Kaatje's vow? Indeed it is working. Lucas' *heatte* is now gone, and he grows stronger almost by the hour. The sister here tells me that someday the curse will be lifted from Kaatje's foot as well—if I persist.
> In some way, which I never expect to understand, my coming here was the price God exacted in order to spare your life too. Otherwise, who knows what dreadful death awaits you? I trust you see, then, how it is I cannot leave this place of refuge—cold though it may be without your arms about me—and plunge all those I love to sudden death.

Do not come to visit me. To see your face will only make my agony too intense to bear. When Lucas is fully restored, I send him by Mieke to visit with you. Until then, thank God he is improving and pray for me as I do for you, my dearly beloved one.

Aletta

Pieter-Lucas stared at the water trickling under the bridge between hard walls of grimy old ice. With cold stiff fingers, he crumpled the note into a ball so tiny and so tight that he would never have to read the words again.

"Moeder Kaatje's vows! Deliver me from the God of the Beguinage that demands the sacrifice of a vrouw," he screamed out. He tossed the ball to the currents and added, "What of the vows that we have made to each other, my vrouw and I?"

As clearly as if it were now, he remembered that day in the birch wood in Breda when he'd begged Aletta to promise she would never give her heart to another. *"It is already yours,"* she'd whispered in a tone magical then, almost magical now just thinking about it, *"always has been—always will be!"*

The magic of her promise had carried him through prison cells and gravesite visitations and long months of searching down unmarked and dead-end trails. At last they had stood at a makeshift altar and vowed before witnesses to hold each other for life. Today he needed more than the magic of a promise, more than the memory of a marriage vow.

She loved him yet—of that he was certain. 'Twas Lucas' illness had drawn a veil of confusion over her eyes, pulled her away.

Pieter-Lucas felt a pain twisting in his belly deeper than anything he'd ever known. He leaned over the bridge rail and cried out, "God in the Heaven, where are you—and your Lamb?"

The stream laughed back at him and threw droplets of water into his face.

———

That night when the dusk had not yet grown stick-dark, Pieter-Lucas climbed back up to the citadel. Here he found the feather bag from his and Aletta's bed, along with a candle, a pot of broth, and three slices of black bread tucked into the niche beside the stairs.

He caught his breath! Had Aletta come while he was gone? Where was she, then? He searched through every corner of the old citadel before returning more emptyhearted than ever to his corner. Shivering, hungry, so lonely he thought he could not stand it another minute, he ate the bread, drank the still-warm broth, and wrapped himself in the bag. Then blowing warmth onto his icy nose, he told himself that Mieke would do her best to bring Aletta back to him.

The thought of trusting Mieke set off another chain of tormenting thoughts. It was something he'd had to learn to do over the years while she was changing from street thief to housemaid for his vrouw. But to bring Aletta home? *Nay!* Only God could do that, and who could ever know what He was planning?

"God will always win!" The words replaced doubts about Mieke through his befuddled brain like a nagging demon from a Bosch painting.

Then came memories of Joris, prating in the manner of a simpleton, yet speaking words Pieter-Lucas wanted to believe, *nay*, must believe if he would live, *"You Christians have a Lamb."*

Pieter-Lucas rummaged in his doublet till his fingers rested on the two miniature canvases that had kept his heart warm in so many cold and dangerous places across the Low Lands and Germany. Tonight, fingering the portrait of his vrouw and the outline of the lamb with globs of white-paint wool rising off the canvas only caused the anguish in his soul to grow and swell till he thought his belly would burst with it.

In desperation he snatched the paintings from his bosom and thrust them toward the sky. "God," he screamed out till his chest ached, "if you are merciful enough to give your Son to be a Lamb, then bring my Aletta back to my empty freezing arms."

In the taunting quietness that followed, he began to feel the feather-light touch of cold petals of snow descending on his arms, his upturned face. He pulled himelf back into his shelter and covered his head with the feather bag. For the rest of the night, sleep came and went like some naughty imp, and always when it came it brought dreams of warm feasts and painters' studios just out of reach, filling him with unfulfilled yearnings and empty disappointments. Through every dream, he heard a loud bell tolling slowly, calling out to him as it had years ago when he was searching the country for Aletta. *"Wachten, wachten!* Wait, wait!"

At the end of each dream, he screamed himself awake, then huddled into a tighter ball and chafed at cold feet, aching body, and empty arms.

———

Aletta had stripped off all but her nightdress and freed her long blond tresses from their pinnings. With a cape around her shoulders, and her feet and legs wrapped in the skimpy feather bag the Beguines had provided, she sat suckling Kaatje on the edge of the straw-covered bed in her sparse Beguinage cell.

She looked over at Lucas sleeping beside her, with the flickering of candlelight splashing swatches of light and shadow across his calm and quiet face. Thank God, the *heatte* was gone, and the cough, though still rattly, came less frequently. At least it let him sleep.

She had dismissed Mieke for the night, but the little woman did not leave. She stood at the foot of the bed, her head slightly down, her fingers twisting the fringes on her worn shawl. "I done tooked care o' yer husband t'night," she said.

Aletta felt a jolt in her heart. "You did what?"

"After I gived him yer letter an' heared him screamin' an' watched him throw it into th' river, I tooked the feather bag off yer bed in th' print house, along with a pot o' Vrouw Hiltje's broth and three hunks o' black bread, an' I stuffed them away in th' niche in th' citadel where I knowed he'd be a-goin' fer th' night."

She gasped. "He can't sleep out there. He'll freeze to the bone!"

"Ye kin't expect 'im to climb into th' bed all a-crawlin' with th' ghosts o' his vrouw an' marriage vows, now, can ye? 'Specially when she tells him she's a-turnin' into a Beguine an' a-leavin' him all to hisself fer th' rest o' his days."

"Mieke," she cried out at last. "Go now! I cannot listen to your prattle."

The little woman stood silently for a long moment, continuing to twist the fringes of her shawl. Her body began to shift from side to side. "Very well, I go." She moved across the room, where she laid a hand on the door handle and said simply, "Jus' seems to me like as if God might be a-thinkin' more about yer vows with yer Pieter-Lucas than his moeder's vows what was never intended fer ye at all." Quickly she slipped out.

The thump of the closing door echoed around the room and beat against Aletta's ears. *Which vow? Which vow? Which vow?* the ominous sounds said over and over and over.

A flood of hot tears splashed over her fingers as she held the limp hand of her now sleeping baby. She remembered back to that day so long ago when Moeder Kaatje died. She'd heard this same question echo around the death chamber. 'Twas her heart taught her that the vow she and Pieter-Lucas had made in the birchwood was hers, not Moeder Kaatje's. Later, the Children of God had confirmed all her heart said so persistently. If it hadn't been for Lucas' illness, the first Kaatje's death, and the second Kaatje's lame foot, she never would have doubted.

"Great God," she cried out, "have you really asked me to do this awful thing? Without me, Pieter-Lucas—*my* Pieter-Lucas—will shiver and die out there in the citadel. Besides, every day I find new reasons to think you have set yet another child of Pieter-Lucas' to growing in my *wombe*.

It cannot be that you would hold me here, fettered to a vow not my own, while my Pieter-Lucas bleeds from the heart out in the cold. Oh, Vader in the Heaven, please, please, let me go home."

She walked to the window and gazed out. A shaft of clear moonlight burst through the clouds and crept toward her. It sprinkled diamond sparkles across the snowy rooftops and herb garden. The voice of Moeder Kaatje died away and in its place she heard Pieter-Lucas' voice on the morning of their betrothal, *"God gave you to me to be my flesh-and-blood Christmas rose."*

And a Christmas rose is for healing, not for cursing, her own heart responded. The Children of God were right, Mieke was right, her own heart was right! She must be free at last to do the thing her heart had begged her so insistently to do.

She laid Kaatje in the cradle, then pulled on her clothes, fastened up her free-hanging tresses loosely under her headdress, and arranged the curls as best she could around her temples. She leaned over and planted a kiss on Lucas' forehead and squeezed his hand. He squeezed back, then opened his eyes and asked, "When can we go home, *Moeke*?"

"In the morning, *jongen*," she whispered.

"Will Vader be there?"

"He will. But you must sleep some more first." She smoothed the curls back from his face. They exchanged smiles, and he closed his eyelids once more.

When his breathing had returned to its slumber rhythm, Aletta moved out into the crisp night air. She nudged the form of Mieke sitting propped up against the wall just outside the door.

"I go," she whispered.

Mieke sprang to her feet, clasped her hands, and squealed her glee. "I knowed ye'd do it," she said as softly as Mieke ever said anything, then hurried into the Beguinage cell, turning at last to give one last word to her mistress. "Take all o' what's left o' th' night. I'll stay here. Oh, an' I'se sorry I couldn't find yer Pieter-Lucas a fresh doublet fer to greet ye in."

The tears that engulfed Aletta now had nothing to do with penance and everything to do with the release of impatient joy!

————

When it was that Pieter-Lucas finally fell into an untormented sleep, he didn't know. Nor why he awoke again, he didn't know. When he did, a ray of light shone full in his face. Looking out, he discovered that the snow had ceased to fall, and the sky was brilliant with twinkling stars and a large full moon. He stared at the sparkling whiteness and felt something akin to peace tugging at him.

"It's a lie," he muttered. "I'll never know peace again. Once, I would have jumped to paint this lovely scene on canvas. Tonight? *Ach!* How cruel of God to torment me with such beauty."

He shut his eyes tightly, wrapped the feather bag over his head, and went back to yearning after sleep. But the sadness only grew, and the pain in his belly threatened to consume him. He decided that sleep was only a fiendish dream.

From somewhere nearby he heard a cackling voice in his ear. *"The paint is gone! You threw it all away. Ha! Ha!"* A chilling laugh echoed about in the shell of his feather bag, assaulting his ears and sending shivers through his body.

At that point, he felt something shake his shoulder. The fiends were swooping down to carry him away! He burrowed deeper into his feather bag and plugged his ears to shut out the noise.

But the shaking went on, not growing fierce yet refusing to leave him. Like the dripping of a water stream on the forehead, it finally became more than he could bear. Throwing back the bag, with wild arms, he yelled out, "Go away!"

Out of the silence that followed, he heard a voice both soft and plaintive and familiar. "Pieter-Lucas, I've come."

Ripples of unbelievable wonder skittered through his entire body. He stared into the swatch of moonlight at his feet. "Aletta! Can it be?" The face was hers, the smile, the curls, all made doubly beautiful by the moon's silvery tinting.

She knelt at his feet in the snow and whispered, "Can you forgive? In my anguish, I listened to the hermit sister and remembered the wrong vows."

"God brought you home, my love," he said, his voice shaking. She was in his arms and surrendering her lips to his. He wrapped her in his feather bag and no longer thought about cold or sleep or words.

When at last he peered out of their unlikely shelter, the horizon was beginning to brighten and the moon shone directly overhead.

"Promise me one thing," he mumbled into her silken locks of hair.

"Whatever you ask," the golden words came back.

"That you will never go away again."

"Never, my love, never! These days of trying to do penance with the Beguines have made me finally understand."

"Understand what?"

"I now know that whatever happens to our children, we can never fear God curses them for the breaking of Moeder Kaatje's vows."

"Then it is true what Joris tried to tell me here this very morning."

"What, Pieter-Lucas?"

"Our Vader in the Heaven gave us His Son to be 'the Lamb of God that takes away the sins of all the world.' And He does not ask us to sacrifice a son or daughter—or vrouw—in appeasement for a sin committed."

"Or another's vow broken. Oh, Pieter-Lucas, the Lamb has paid all the price and freed us!"

He pressed her hard against his breast and, to the pattering rhythm of an excited heart, mumbled, "I must ask your forgiveness."

"Whatever for?"

"I never should have brought you to Leyden in the first place. I—"

She shook her head and interrupted. "We talk not about such nonsense!"

He felt her fingers combing through his stubbly hair and heard her gentle soothing voice, "All is well—" Abruptly she gasped, "Pieter-Lucas, your curls!"

In spite of himself he laughed. All that had happened back at Lammen felt so far away, so unimportant. "They grow out again!" he said.

Helping her to her feet, he led her out into the moonlight and twirled her around in the snow beside him. He held her fast around the waist with one arm and spread the other out toward the eastern horizon.

"A new year greets us with the morning sun already brightening the sky!"

"And we shall gather our children from the Beguinage and begin again!"

They kissed long in the moonlight, and Pieter-Lucas began to feel the paint surge through his blood once more.

EPILOGUE

Leyden

31st day of Wine Month (October), 1574

On a golden autumn Sunday afternoon, Pieter-Lucas and Aletta strolled out through the Zyl Poort Gate with their children. The sun shone in a blue sky, drawing half the city out to soak it up. A chilly breeze sent a profusion of bright yellow and red leaves swirling around them.

Pieter-Lucas held little Lucas by the hand and made sure each step landed squarely on the colorful frost-dried leaves.

"Listen to them crackle, son," he coaxed.

The boy followed his vader's lead, stomping on each leaf and laughing deliciously. When they'd reached the spot where the Zyl River trekpath turned off and went north, Pieter-Lucas and Aletta stopped to rest on a large wayside stone under a grand old spreading oak tree. They watched the children roam through the accumulation of dancing leaves in the field beside the roadway. Lucas leapt from leaf to leaf, shouting his joy. Kaatje half crawled, half rolled after him, laughing in her awkward attempt to do as big brother did.

"Someday she will walk," Aletta said as if she were thinking aloud.

"*Ja*, someday," Pieter-Lucas answered, wishing he believed it with as much certainty as he said it.

"When God wills it," she added with an eagerness he believed was genuine.

He squeezed her around the waist and sighed. She snuggled into the protection of his arm, saying nothing, but warming him. "One year ago, it was, on this next to last night of Wine Month that we fled from *The Clever Fox Inn* along this roadway," he mused.

"And the next morning we awoke to find the Spaniards had imprisoned us within the walls," Aletta added.

"The siege of Leyden had begun!" He felt her hand reach up and smooth the curls back from his face.

"Thank God the sieges are over now," she said. "The Spaniards will not be back. We have plenty to eat, and we all grow stronger every day."

Pieter-Lucas smiled in spite of himself. "If only I had left you in Dillenburg, you never would have known what it was to hunger after the least little mouse skittering through the scant grass around the corner of the house."

Pieter-Lucas shuddered at the awful memory of the months since that beautiful night in the moonlit snow when Aletta came to him in the citadel. How could either of them know it would be a year filled with unforgettable sieges and their tragic legacy of hunger and misery and despair?

The first siege seemed awful enough—five long months, altogether, of restricted access and dangerous river-jumping missions and never quite enough peat to keep them warm or enough food to keep their bellies full. But only a remarkably few of the very old, the very young, and the very ill of Leyden did not survive it. Always they knew that Willem and his brothers Ludwig and Jan were raising an army to come to their rescue.

Then suddenly Valdez lifted the siege. He sent his men south to intercept Ludwig's troops. Willem cautioned the overjoyed Leydenaars that Valdez would be back. But they were too full of joy over their freedom, too confident of Ludwig's victory, to heed the warnings. By the time they learned that Ludwig had not only lost his battle but also his life, it was too late for caution.

Valdez and his *speken* had returned.

This time no extra foodstuffs had been stockpiled. All through the summer months when the fields yielded harvest, Valdez kept them shut up inside the city walls, away from their crops. A few times Pieter-Lucas managed to get through to Willem with a message, and when he did, he smuggled choice morsels of bread, cheese, or fruit back in. But that was months before the end came.

Hunger was followed by the plague. Barely in time to rescue Leydenaars from utter despair, the siege ended in the middle of the third night of Wine Month. The waters were finally rising sufficiently to frighten the Spaniards. When a whole side of the city wall collapsed, the Spaniards' courage broke and they abandoned the city to the stubborn patriots' wills. In the endless waiting time, though, thousands of Leydenaars had perished. Aletta's family had barely survived it. Joris' as well, though on the day of deliverance, both he and Christoffel lay too ill in their beds to greet the Beggars who sailed in on the high tides, bringing food to the famished and hope to the weary.

Pieter-Lucas tossed the leaves at his feet with his toe and said wistfully, "I still wish I had never brought you to this place. I thought it would be a citadel. Instead, it nearly became our burial ground."

"Pieter-Lucas!" Aletta responded, tugging at his arm. "Have you forgotten that I begged you to bring us here to Leyden? I wouldn't give you any rest until you promised, remember?"

"I remember that well. But I am your husband. 'Tis my duty to protect you. Instead, I was so intent on finding a *meester* painter and fulfilling my dreams, and so eager to keep you nearer to me during my travels, that I fear I listened to the wrong cautions."

Aletta took both his hands in hers. "We cannot know how badly things would have gone had I stayed in Dillenburg. At least this way we were together."

"Not all of us." He could say no more, nor did she answer. Surely she was remembering with him that awful night when their second son was born in Harvest month. He came too early and too small, and Aletta had not enough milk in her shriveling breasts to sustain the faint flicker of life. They buried him, and Pieter-Lucas and Aletta wept together that night in their bed. For many more nights they held each other and grieved in silence—and they hadn't even given the boy a name.

"Our son is safe, my love, beyond the reach of pain and hunger and war." Her voice wavered. With obvious effort at cheerfulness, she concluded, "Never will he have to suffer a one of them."

Pieter-Lucas suppressed a sigh. "All the same, it seems that from the moment we set foot in Leyden, God has been destroying our dreams—both yours and mine."

Aletta gasped. "'Twas God sent deliverance to us. Willem's men pierced the dikes and prayed and waited, but God sent the winds and high tides to raise the water and make the wall collapse. God has not destroyed us!"

"I don't know . . ." he stammered.

"And when I'd lost my head and run away to the Beguinage, 'twas God sent Mieke to me with the right words to bring me back. Thank God for Mieke!"

Pieter-Lucas shrugged. "Thank God for Mieke, indeed! Without her out there beside me on that bridge promising to bring you to me, I fear I would have thrown myself into the river along with your note."

"Oh, can't you see it, Pieter-Lucas?" Aletta begged, her smile warm and coaxing. "God has brought us to another new day! Our dreams will yet come true!" Her words formed a tender thread of hope tugging at his heart. How he wanted to yield to them. But he'd put faith in bright new days before, and always their blue skies had filled up with the clouds of God's anger.

"What of my search for a *meester* to teach me to paint? Besides, you have no herb garden since you left the Beguinage. And our children . . ." He stopped and swallowed down one more choking lump. "Oh, Aletta, how much they've suffered!"

"They're young. They don't even remember it now, Pieter-Lucas. Look at them. Lucas gains new strength each day. Kaatje's eyes are regaining their sparkle. My own body feels alive again. And you, my love," she gave him one of her adoring blue-eyed looks. "You have never looked better. Above all else, we have a Lamb!"

The thread was growing stronger. In spite of himself, he chuckled.

Aletta laid her hand on his arm. "There was one other surprising thing God did at the lifting of the siege."

"You mean Hendrick van den Garde?" His heart warmed at the re-minder.

She smiled and shook her head slowly. "I never expected that the sound of that name would ever bring anything but pain," she said.

"Nor did I."

Something in their last encounter had left a lingering ray of unex-pected warmth. It happened the day the wall collapsed and the Beggars swarmed into the city in their flat-bottomed boats loaded with food. Every waterway in the city was lined with starving people, and as the boats passed through, the Beggars tossed or handed food into twiglike fingers. Pieter-Lucas was receiving bread and cheese and a fish from a Beggar when he looked up and saw it was Hendrick.

Even now he had to swallow a huge lump in his throat and fight back the tears just thinking about it. "For the first time since I was a boy the size of little Lucas," Pieter-Lucas mumbled, "that man gave me nourish-ment instead of scorn."

"The look in his eyes," Aletta said, "a mixture of awe and horror. I wasn't sure whether he was angry or just recoiling from all the misery of starving people around him."

"*Nay*, it was something else, Aletta. He's a tough soldier who's seen plenty of misery—caused a lot of it by his own violence—yet he always walked away chuckling."

"I think it was because he recognized you, Pieter-Lucas. No matter how tough a man is, when he sees the man he raised as his own son starving to death, it has to touch him."

Pieter-Lucas rubbed his hands together between his knees and shook his head slowly. "I really think it was Lucas."

"Lucas? What did he have to do with it?"

"You didn't hear Hendrick's question to me when our eyes met?"

"Nay!" She looked at him with startled curiosity. "The boat was moving away in your direction, you know, and I was already breaking the bread and giving a morsel to Kaatje."

"He pointed to Lucas and asked, 'Is he my grandson?' "

"Ah, Pieter-Lucas, what did you say?"

"The only thing I could think to say with my half-starved brain— 'Vader Hendrick, meet my son, Lucas van den Garde.' "

"You called him Vader Hendrick?"

Pieter-Lucas looked down into Aletta' s eyes and saw the wonder sparkling. "I did," he answered, squeezing her hand.

"What did he say?"

"I couldn't understand the words he mumbled, but I'll never forget that he smiled without mocking me."

Aletta covered her mouth with both hands and shook her head pensively. "God put a softness in him, even if it may have been only for that flickering moment."

Pieter-Lucas struggled in silence with the mixture of anguish and hope that the memory inspired. Finally he nodded. "Ah, what would I do without you by my side?" He took her in both arms and held on as if his next breath depended on their embrace.

"May you never need to find out, Pieter-Lucas."

Lucas was running toward them, waving a large gold-veined crimson oak leaf in his little hand. He stopped, throwing himself into Pieter-Lucas' lap. Then holding the leaf up just beneath his vader's nose, he said, "Vader, look, I found autumn! Can we paint it?"

"It's in your blood, isn't it?" Pieter-Lucas smiled down at him. Then he nudged Aletta with his shoulder and mumbled, "And in my blood too. Maybe Joris and Christoffel can spare a few drops of paint."

"You know," Aletta suggested, "Joris is a great painter. He once assisted Bruegel in his studio."

"Pieter Bruegel?"

"Ja!"

"How do you know that?"

"Hiltje told me once."

Pieter-Lucas felt a tremor of exuberance tumbling in his soul. "He could be my *meester* yet."

Lucas was pulling at his doublet tails, begging, "Can we go now, Vader, can we?"

Pieter-Lucas nodded to his vrouw. "I don't know, *Moeke*, can we?"

Aletta scooped up Kaatje, who was clambering at her skirts. "How else are we going to save the memory of this golden autumn day?"

Pieter-Lucas and his son laughed and stomped on crackly leaves all the way home.

ACKNOWLEDGMENTS

Historians frequently talk about the *serendipity* of the research process. Surprise encounters with the right resources at the right time often give them a fateful sense of their subject pursuing them relentlessly.

I consider myself a historian and have experienced probably hundreds of these incredible connections over the past thirty years of studying Dutch Reformation history. But I have another name for them—God's provisions!

In the first two books in this series, I've given credit to the people who have so generously rendered services and encouragement. This time, I want to acknowledge God's part.

God sent our family to live in the Netherlands for three years in the 1960s. Back home in California, God led me to a library to learn about Dutch history. Through two lengthy sets of books by nineteenth-century scholar John Lathrop Motely and some charming volumes by Hendrick van Loon, God introduced me to Willem van Oranje. I knew instantly that someday I had to write about this unusual prince. In the 1970s God gave me incredible opportunities to learn to write and publish and build relationships with editors and writing teachers all over the country. I entered the 1980s with a newly emptied nest (my youngest child went away to college that year) and a surgery that slowed me down for several months.

While convalescing, the thin notebook with notes on Willem and the Reformation beckoned to me from my dream shelf above my desk. Through a series of serendipitous events, I discovered that now was the time to follow through with His vision given to me in the late 1960s.

God had located me within easy driving distance of the University of California at Berkeley Library, home to the largest collection of Dutch language and history books in the country. In those days, for a ten-dollar-a-year card, I had almost unlimited access to all the books, magazines, and maps I could possibly need for my research! I also found generous and helpful access to Dr. Lewis Spitz, a leading Reformation scholar at Stanford University, twenty miles down the road from my house.

In 1985, God allowed my husband to take a three-month vacation and accompany me all over the Netherlands, Belgium, and key corners of Germany and France. We tracked down every artifact we could find left over from the sixteenth century, bought out-of-print books, copied items from books made available to us in archives and museums, collected stacks of brochures and maps, took pictures, recorded sound effects on a microcassette recorder, soaked up atmospheres, filled a journal.

In previous books in this series, I've mentioned many of the treasured "finds" that opened the doors for me into Pieter-Lucas' and Aletta's world. Here I want to tell you about several that belong to this book more than to either of the others.

First is the city of Leyden. Amidst the bustle of a modern university city, we found many of the old windmills, churches, public buildings, and bridges still intact—artifacts of this story. In one museum we saw a stewpot made famous because it was found in the fortress of Lammen, abandoned by Spaniards on the night when a portion of the wall collapsed. We photographed one of the towers left standing from that wall and spent a delightful hour inside the citadel for which this book is named.

When I began this book, I assumed that access to the old fortress was always public. Then I read in a booklet about the citadel that it was privately owned until 1651, when the city of Leyden purchased it. Could it be as accessible to Pieter-Lucas and Christoffel as I envisioned in my story? I searched all the books in my shelves—some new, some old, some English, some Dutch. They gave me no conclusive answer.

I had to read what one of Pieter-Lucas' contemporaries had to say about it. So I pulled out my facsimile copy of Guicciardini's *Description of the Low Countreys*, first issued in 1566. A thick book with gold gilding on the pages, it is one of my prize possessions. God led me to it in a miraculous fashion just three days before the end of our research trip.

Often throughout the writing of the entire Seekers series, I referred to its fascinating double-page maps, which provided birds-eye views of eighty of the old cities of the Netherlands. The map of Leyden was my guide all through the writing of *The Citadel and the Lamb* and became the inspiration for the map in this book. But the text was formidable. Scripted in ornate medieval squarish letters of sixteenth-century Dutch, I found it all but impossible to read. Only as a last resort did I ever consult Guic-ciardini's obscure words.

In desperation I prayed for keenness of mind and meticulously de-ciphered and translated. Guicciardini told me that from the beginning the old citadel was always open to all as "a place of refuge in time of need." Just the detail I needed!

Finally God sent me a character named Joris. For months I'd been casting about in my mind for an artist in Leyden. One day, in my imag-ination, the man approached my desk and said, "I am the painter you're looking for. And I'm Jewish. Now, what are you going to do with me?"

Once more God was launching me, this time into the adventure of researching Jewish history, beginning with the unsavory details of the or-igins of the Inquisition directed against the falsely labeled "Christ killers." The Institute for Historical Study helped me to make sense of the mys-terious discovery that no Jewish artists are known by name in the Ren-aissance time period. Chaim Potok's two marvelous novels about Asher Lev, a Hasidic Jewish painter, opened many doors of insight. An unex-pected invitation to accompany two cousins on a Holy Land tour seemed a final confirmation. I now know I've just begun a lifelong study of the Jewish people and roots of my faith.

I am deeply grateful for God's serendipitous provisions; for the con-tinuing support and prayers of family, friends, critique group, and Sunday school class; for my agent, Les Stobbe, who answers my questions and picks up the pieces when I begin to crumble; for Sharon Asmus, the ideal cheerful and insightful editor; for every member of the expanded team at Bethany House; for you, my readers, who approach this book with hearts and minds hungering to see more of His ways traced out in lives lived long ago.

RESOURCES

I could fill another volume just telling you about all the wonderful books, maps, magazine articles, and pamphlets God brought across my pathway. Here I will mention the most important items in three categories: (1) my mainstays that I referred to continually, (2) an assortment of others that will give you an idea of the scope of the research, and (3) books I suggest to you if you are interested in digging into the sixteenth century for Reformation/Anabaptist history.

My Mainstays

Alfen, H. J. P. van. *Dagregister van 's Prinsen Levensloop.* [Journal of Prince Willem's Life.] No publication information available. Incredible chronological record of details of Willem's entire life (1533–1584)— where he was when, what he was doing and why.

Beenakker, A. J. M. *Breda in de Eerste storm van de Opstand (Van Ketterij tot Beeldenstorm, 1545–1569).* [Breda in the First Storm of the Revolt, From Heresy to Iconoclasm.] Tilburg: Stichting Zuidelijk Historisch Contact, 1971, 187 + pp.

*Braght, Thieleman J. van. *Martyrs Mirror of the Defenseless Christians*, trans. from the original Dutch 1660 edition by Joseph F. Sohm. Scottsdale, Penn.: Herald Press, 1950. First English edition printed in 1837, 1157 pp.

Brouwers, J. A. *Kruiden In Het Bredase Begijnhof* [Herbs in the Breda Beguinage] Dienst Beplantingen in Samenwerking met Bureau Voorliching, n.d. Catalogue of herbs growing in the Beguinage of Breda today with notes about their history and uses.

*Gerard, John. *The Herbal or General History of Plants*, 1597. Complete

1633 edition revised and enlarged by Thomas Johnson. New York: Dover Publications, Inc., 1975, 1678 + pp.

Geschiedenis van Breda, de Middeleeuwen [History of Breda, Middle Ages,] o.r.v. F. F. X. Cerutti e.a. Tilburg: W. Bergmans, 1952.

Goor, Thomas Ernst van. *Beschrijving der Stadt en Lande van Breda* [Description of City and Land of Breda.] 'Gravenhage: Jacobus van den Kieboom, 1744. Mostly archival sources.

Guicciardini, Ludovico. *Beschrijvinghe van Alle de Nederlanden* [Description of the Low Lands.] Haarlem: Fibula-van Dishoeck, facsimile reprinting, 1979. Original, Amsterdam: Willem Jantzoon, 1612, 396 + pp. Built around maps of eighty Dutch cities, mostly completed by 1566.

Hogenberg, Frans. *De 80-Jarige Oorlog in Prenten* [The Eighty Years' War in Prints.] Den Haag: Van Goor Zonen, 1977.

*Motley, John Lothrop. *The Rise of the Dutch Republic*. 3 volumes. Philadelphia: David McKay, n.d. Issued by Harper & Brothers: New York, 1868–1869.

Mulder, A. W. J. *Juliana van Stolberg, "Ons Aller Vrouwe-Moeder."* Amsterdam: J. J. Meulenhoff, n.d., 238 pp. + family chronology chart.

Poortvliet, Rien. *De Tressor*. Kampen: J. H. Kok, 1991, 208 pp.

*———. *Daily Life In Holland in 1566*. New York: Harry N. Abrams Ink Publishers, 1991, 208pp.

Prescott, William H. *History of the Reign of Philip the Second, King of Spain*. 3 volumes. Philadelphia: J. B. Lippincott & Co., 1868.

*Verduin, Leonard. *The Reformers and Their Stepchildren*. Grand Rapids, Mich.: Baker Book House, 1964, 292 pp. Great picture of what made the Anabaptists distinctive from other Protestants of their day.

*Wedgwood, C. V. *William the Silent*. New York: W.W. Norton & Company, Inc., 1944, 1968, 256 pp.

Williams, George Huntston. *The Radical Reformation*. Philadelphia: The Westminster Press, 1962, 924 + pp.

A Sampling of Other Resources I Used

Ach Lieve Tijd: Acht Eeuwen Breda en de Bredenars [Oh, Dear Me: Eight Centuries of Breda and Bredeners,] vols. 1, 3, & 13. Zwolle: Waanders, 1986. Magazine format, highly illustrated history of Breda in 13 volumes.

Archives Ou Correspondence Inedite de la Maison D'Orange-Nassau [Unedited Archives and Correspondence of the House of Oranje-Nassau.] 8

volumes + supplement. Leiden: M. G. Groen van Prinsterer, 1835–1847.

*Bainton, Roland H. *Christian Attitudes Toward War and Peace*. Nashville, Tenn.: Abingdon, 1960.

*Barnouw, Adriaan J., trans., *The Miracle of Beatrice—A Flemish Legend of c. 1300*. New York: Pantheon Books, 1944.

Blok, P. J. *Geschiedenis Eener Hollandsche Stad* [History of a Dutch City—Medieval Leyden] 'S-Gravenhage: Matinus Nijhoff, 1920.

Bonger, H. *Het Leven en Werk van D.V. Coornhert* [The Life and Work of D.V. Coornhert.] Amsterdam: G. A. van Oorschot, 1978.

Brown, Christopher. *Images of a Golden Past—Dutch Genre Painting of the 17th Century*. New York: Abbeville Press, 1984.

Burke, Gerald L. *The Making of Dutch Towns*. London: Cleaver/Hume Press Ltd., 1956.

Chrisman, Miriam Usher. *Strasbourg and the Reform*. New Haven, Conn.: Yale University Press, 1967. Helpful picture of Swiss Anabaptism in the early days of the movement. Shows its early experiments with government and use of force.

Christian History Magazine (*The Radical Reformation: The Anabaptists*.) 4, no. 1 (1985). Several issues were helpful.

Claessens, Bob & Jeanne Rousseau, *Bruegel*. New York: Portland House, 1987—originally Antwerp: Mercatorfonds, 1969.

Coryat, Thomas. *Coryat's Crudities*, vol 3. London: W. Cater, reprinted from 1611. A fascinating travelogue of an Englishman through the Netherlands.

Deventer, Jacob van. *De Kaarten van de Nederlandsche Provincien*. [Maps of the Dutch Provinces.] Wonderful large maps from 1557–1575. I made copies in sections and pieced them together on large poster boards. I also have copies of some of his city plans.

Denis, Valentin. *Het Volkslied in Vlanderen tot Omstreeks 1600* [Folk Music in Flanders Up to About 1600.] Brussels: Museum of Fine Arts, 1942.

Duinkerken, Anton van & P. J. G. Huincks, *Dicthers Om Oranje* [Poets of Orange: Poetry About the House of Orange from Willem to the Present.] Baarn: Hollandia, 1946.

*Ebers, George. *The Burgomaster's Wife*. New York: William. S. Gottsberger, 1882. Novel of the siege of Leyden. Makes for fascinating reading and understanding of what happened.

Einstein, Elizabeth L. "The Advent of Printing and the Protestant Revolt: A New Approach to the Disruption of Western Christendom." In *Transition and Revolution: Problems and Issues of European Renaissance and*

Reformation History, edited by Robert Kingdon. Minneapolis: Burgess Publishing Company, 1974.

Estep, William R. *The Anabaptist Story*. Grand Rapids, Mich.: William B. Eerdmans Publishing Company, 1975.

Fishman, Jane Susannah. *Boerenverdriet: Violence Between Peasants and Soldiers in Early Modern Netherlands Art*. Ann Arbor, Mich.: UMI Research Press, 1979, 1982.

*Foote, Timothy. *The World of Bruegel, c.1525–1569*. New York: Time-Life Books, 1968.

*Frommer, Arthur. *A Masterpiece Called Belgium*. Prepared for Sabena Belgian World Airlines, 1984. Led us to many choice historical sights in Belgium and prepared us to find Pieter-Lucas' and Aletta's footprints there.

Fruin, R. *The Siege and Relief of Leyden in 1574*. The Hague: Martinus Nijhoff, 1927.

Geurts, P. A. M. *De Nederlandse Opstand in de Pamfletten 1566–1584* [The Dutch Revolt in Pamphlets, 1566–1584.] Utrecht: H & S Publishers, 1978.

Geyl, Peter. *The Revolt of the Netherlands*. New York: Barnes and Noble, Inc., 1958.

*Gleysteen, Jan. *Mennonite Tourguide to Western Europe*. Scottsdale, Penn.: Herald Press, 1984.

*Gottschalk, Louis. *Understanding History: A Primer of Historical Method*. New York: Alfred A. Knopf, 1961.

Gray, Janet Glenn. *The French Huguenots: Anatomy of Courage*. Grand Rapids, Mich.: Baker Book House, 1981.

Hale, J. R. *Renaissance Europe*. Berkeley: U.C. Press, 1971.

Halsema, Thea B. van. *Glorious Heretic: The Story of Guido de Bres*. Grand Rapids, Mich.: William B. Eerdmans Publishing Company, 1961.

Hamilton, Alastair, Sjouke Voolstra, and Piet Visser, *From Martyr to Muppy (Mennonite Urban Professionals.)* Amsterdam: Amsterdam University Press, 1994. A historical introduction to cultural assimilated processes of a religious minority in the Netherlands: the Mennonites.

Heeroma, K. *Protestantse Poëze der 16de en 17de Eeuw* [Protestant Poetry of the 16th and 17th Century.] Amsterdam: Elsevier, 1940.

Huizinga, J. *The Waning of the Middle Ages*. New York: Doubleday Anchor Books, 1949. "A study of the forms of life, thought and art in France and Netherlands in the dawn of the Renaissance."

Huygens, Constantijn. *Use and Non-Use of Organ in the Churches of the United Netherlands*. Translated and edited by Ericka E. Smit-Vanrotte (n.d., but Huygens lived from 1596–1687.) Short and fascinating!

Hyma, Albert. *The Christian Renaissance*. New York: The Century Co., 1925. Story of Brethren of Common Life that preceded and paved the way for the Reformation in the Low Lands.

Irwin, Joyce. *Womanhood In Radical Protestantism, 1525–1675*. New York: Edwin Mellen Press, 1979.

Jones, Rufus M. *Spiritual Reformers in the 16th and 17th Centuries*. London: Macmillan & Co., 1914.

Jones, Sydney R. *Old Houses In Holland*. London: The Studio Ltd., 1913.

Kamen, Henry. *The Spanish Inquisition*. New York: New American Library, 1965.

Kossman, E. H. and A. F. Mellink, *Texts Concerning the Revolot of the Netherlands*. Massachusetts: Cambridge University Press, 1974. Documents from the revolt.

Lecler, Joseph. *Tolerance and the Reformation*. New York: Association Press, 1960. Translated by T. L. Westow.

*Loon, Hendrick Willem van. *The Arts*. New York: Simon & Schuster, 1939.

*———, Hendrick Willem van. *Life and Times of Rembrandt*. Garden City, N.Y.: Garden City Publishing Company, Inc., 1930.

*Mander, Carel van. *Dutch and Flemish Painters*, trans. by Constant van de Wall from the *Schilderboek*, 1604. New York: McFarlane, Warde, McFarlane, 1936.

Norwood, Frederick A. *Strangers and Exiles: A History of Religous Refugees*. 2 vols. Nashville, Tenn.: Abingdon, 1969.

Oranje, Prins Willem van. *Brieven* [Letters,] ed. by M.W. Jurriaanse and trans. into modern Dutch by Dr. C. Seeurier. Middelburg: G. W. Den Boer, 1933.

*Pearl, Chaim. *Theology in Rabbinic Stories*. Peabody, Mass.: Hendrickson Publishers, 1997.

Plooij, D. *The Pilgrim Fathers From a Dutch Point of View*. New York: New York University Press, 1932.

Plantin, Christopher. *Calligraphy and Printing in the Sixteenth Century*. Cambridge, Mass.: Department of Printing and Graphics Arts, Harvard College Library, 1940. Translation and notes by Roy Nash. Printed with French and Flemish Text in facsimile from original publication in 1567 in Antwerp. Fascinating little book.

*Potok, Chaim. *Wanderings: History of the Jews*. New York: Fawcett Crest, 1978.

Rachum, Ilan. *The Renaissance: An Illustrated Encyclopedia*. New York: Mayflower Books Inc., 1979.

Renaud, J. G. N. *De Leidse Burcht* [The Leyden Citadel.] Koninklijke Nederlandse Toeristenbond ANWB, 1982.

*Ross, James Bruce, and Mary Martin McLaughlin. *The Portable Renaissance Reader*. New York: Viking, 1953. Good collection of writings from the time period.

Sabbe, Maurits. *Christopher Plantin*, trans. by Alice van Riel-Goransson. Antwerp: J. E. Buschmann, 1923.

Schama, Simon. *The Embarrassment of Riches*. New York: Alfred A. Knopf, 1987.

Straaten, Evert van. *Koud Tot Op Het Bot* [Cold to the Bone.] 'S-Gravenhage: Staatsuitgeverij, 1977. Fascinating book of drawings and painting of winter in the sixteenth and seventeenth centuries.

*Spitz, Lewis. *The Protestant Reformation 1517–1559*. New York: Harper & Row, 1985.

*————. Editor *The Reformation—Material or Spiritual?* Lexington, Mass.: D. C. Heath & Co., 1962.

————. *The Renaissance and Reformation Movements, Volume 2: The Reformation*. Chicago: Rand McNally & Co., 1972.

*Telushkin, Joseph. *Jewish Literacy*. New York: William Morrow & Co., Inc., 1991.

Trevor-Roper, H. R. *The European Witch-Craze of the Sixteenth and Seventeenth Centuries and Other Essays*. New York: Harper & Row Publishers, 1967.

Veldman, Ilja M. *Maarten van Heemskerk and Dutch Humanism in the Sixteenth Century*, trans. by Michael Hoyle. Maarsen: Gary Schwartz, 1977.

Williams, Sir Roger. *The Actions of the Low Countries*. New York: Cornell University Press, 1964. First published in England in 1618. First-person account of the Dutch Revolt by an English soldier who served in Ludwig's army.

Williams, George H. and Angel M. Mergal, editors, *Spiritual and Anabaptist Writers*. Philadelphia: Westminster Press, 1957.

Zumthor, Paul. *Daily Life in Rembrandt's Holland*. New York: Macmillan, 1963.

Suggestions for Further Study

Several of my readers have indicated that Pieter-Lucas and Aletta have enticed them to go back and dig into some church history for themselves but have wondered where to begin.

Start with a basic text and a good dictionary of Church history:

Cairns, Earle E. *Christianity Through the Centuries*. Grand Rapids, Mich.: Zondervan, 1981.
Douglas, J. D., editor. *Dictionary of the Christian Church*. Grand Rapids, Mich.: Zondervan, 1978.

Subscribe to:
Christian History Magazine
PO Box 37060
Boone, IA 50037–0060
1–800–873–6986
Past issues are available as well as a CD-Rom. Visit website at (http://www.christianhistory.net or AOL Keyword:CH)

Pay a visit to the various libraries in your community. Spend some time browsing. It may surprise you what a wide variety of resources you will find there. Read as voraciously and widely on the subject as you can. Don't forget to check the children's section of a library. It is always an excellent source of materials to help you get a good first look at any subject. If you have children in your charge, this will enable you to begin to build into them an appreciation for the great heritage of the Church.

One word of caution about historical novels. Many people think they are a good way to get history in a delectable dessert rather than in a hard-to-swallow pill. But you need to know that not all novelists are historical scholars. Look for two things:

(1) If the characters in a novel seem to think, talk, and act like twentieth-century characters, or (2) the obvious sole purpose of the book is the romantic plot, which could easily take place essentially unchanged in any time or place in history, then be aware that the history and/or the thought patterns of the characters may not be accurate. Do not rely on such books to give you a true picture of the history of the period, place, or movement you are studying.

If you are interested in more of an in-depth look at the specific events surrounding the lives of Pieter-Lucas and Aletta and their friends, go through the lists of resources I used and note those marked with an asterisk (*). These I would specifically recommend to you. Not all will be currently in print. Investigate your local church, public, college, or seminary libraries. When all else fails, request a book on an Inter-Library-Loan, usually available from your public library.

You might also contact the publishing house of your church's denomination or some other denomination you are wanting to study. They are usually excellent sources of books for your study. Denominational colleges and headquarters often have museums and/or archives packed with wonderful first-hand resources.

Remnants of the history of the Church are all around you. Just grab a shovel and start digging. I guarantee that, while you may get a bit dusty here and there, you will find some choice gems and just may become addicted.